BEST MAN RANCHER

MAISEY YATES

AN EX TO REMEMBER

JESSICA LEMMON

MILLS & BOON

First Published in Great Britain 2022
by Mills & Boon, an imprint of HarperCollins*Publishers* Ltd
1 London Bridge Street, London, SE1 9GF

www.harpercollins.co.uk

HarperCollins*Publishers*
1st Floor, Watermarque Building,
Ringsend Road, Dublin 4, Ireland

Best Man Rancher © 2022 Maisey Yates
An Ex to Remember © 2022 Harlequin Enterprises ULC

Special thanks and acknowledgement are given to Jessica Lemmon for her contribution to the *Texas Cattleman's Club: Ranchers and Rivals* series.

ISBN: 978-0-263-30387-2

0922

MIX
Paper | Supporting
responsible forestry
FSC™ C007454

This book is produced from independently certified FSC™ paper to ensure responsible forest management.

For more information visit: www.harpercollins.co.uk/green

Printed and Bound in Spain using 100% Renewable electricity at CPI Black Print, Barcelona

BEST MAN RANCHER

MAISEY YATES

One

"Six inches is too long!" Shelby Sohappy glared across the table, across all the flowers piled on the table, across the tulle and the candy strewn over the table, to her older sister.

But it wasn't Juniper's reaction to Shelby's words that caught her attention, and held her there.

She felt it before she saw it. His response. *His*, always his. The change crackled through the air. And she told herself not to look. She told herself to keep her focus on Juniper, the bride, her sister, her best friend, and direct all wedding preparation complaints to her.

But she turned her head anyway.

As if he'd put his finger beneath her chin and swiveled it toward him. That's how powerful the impulse to look was.

Kit Carson.

Damn Kit Carson.

Her eyes clashed with his, electric and upsetting. And his mouth curved—even more upsetting. "Six inches is too long? Maybe that's why I'm still single."

That earned a round of groans from the table—and Shelby should also groan. But instead she felt like her body had been lit up.

She had learned a lot since middle school.

That you didn't actually need algebra. That body glitter wasn't worth the hassle. That the girls who wouldn't let you sit with them would—in fact—peak once school ended and spend their adult years trying to reconnect with people they had once been mean to so that they could sell them lip gloss, leggings and the secrets of success and wealth and sisterhood, as long as you bought their weight loss shakes.

She'd learned that she was stronger than she'd imagined. That loss wouldn't kill you, even if you might wish it had.

But she hadn't learned how to control her physical response to Kit Carson, a man who was soon to be practically family, the best man to her maid of honor, her longtime, shame-fueled object of lust.

Yeah. She hadn't learned that.

"That's not why you're single, bro," said Chance, her sister's fiancé, and everyone laughed.

So Shelby laughed too. What choice did she have?

She felt like a foreign tourist pretending they understood what was happening around them. She was just lost. In ribbon curls and Kit Carson's excess of six inches.

How *many* inches more?

She didn't need to know the answer to that.

She didn't even need to *wonder* it.

Nope.

"Six inches," Juniper said, holding up a ribbon and a pair of scissors, and letting the edge glide effortlessly across it, resulting in a rather impressive curl, "is not too long at all."

Shelby ignored Chance and his brothers chuckling at that.

So did Juniper.

Shelby wondered, not for the first time, how the hell this had happened.

The Carsons and Sohappys had been enemies for generations. To the degree that the first time she'd spotted Kit Carson at a football game when she'd been in seventh grade and he'd been in tenth, she'd felt a deep, instinctive recoil in her soul.

At least, she liked to tell herself that's what it was.

Because it couldn't possibly have been anything else. She'd been dating Chuck already by then. Well, *dating* was a strong term. They'd been twelve, after all. They'd walked down to the diner in Lone Rock and had shared a milkshake with money Chuck had gotten collecting bottles and taking them to the can return.

They'd gone down to the river and skipped rocks.

They'd held hands. And he'd kissed her.

They'd started having sex when they were way too young, but hey, she'd been certain she'd marry him so the moral risk had seemed worth the reward.

And she'd been right.

She'd married Chuck pretty much as soon as high school had ended. She'd been so ready for that life. She'd loved him. Deep and uncomplicated.

And if she'd sometimes… If she'd been unable to keep herself from thinking of the man who'd first created a shiver of awareness inside her before she'd known what it was, she'd just blamed it on having been with only one man. Dismiss it as adventures she'd chosen not to have.

There had been moments in her marriage when she'd wondered if they'd done it too soon. If not dating other people had been a mistake.

When Chuck had died, she'd been so glad they'd had that life. That whole brilliant life.

From twelve to twenty-six. Thank God for all those years, because they hadn't gotten to grow old together. Just older.

She really didn't need to be thinking about any of this now.

But it was a wedding, so it was unavoidable.

And it was her sister's wedding, which made it more poignant.

Her sister's wedding to a Carson. That's what tipped it over into improbable.

"Who would have thought you'd be a bridezilla," Shelby groused.

Juniper was an EMT, and in general a very practical and nonsentimental soul. Before her engagement to Chance, anyway. Now suddenly it was all sentiment and fluffy dresses and ribbon curls.

"I haven't even begun to bridezilla," Juniper declared from her end of the table, which had all the Carson men looking worried.

The lone Carson girl—Callie, who had gotten married a while back and moved to Gold Valley, Oregon, a few hours away—was grinning. "I love this! I need more women in the family. To cause chaos and mayhem."

"You don't need any help with that, sis," Boone Carson said.

"I'm happy to contribute to family chaos!" Juniper said.

And Shelby couldn't help but feel just a little bit outside of all of this. It wasn't anyone's fault. Especially not Juniper's. Her sister deserved happiness. So much happiness. She had been there for Shelby in a profound way when Shelby had lost Chuck. And in all the time since. Juniper was her best friend.

But that didn't mean that Shelby couldn't find a way to have complicated feelings about this.

It made her think about her own wedding. And the terrible thing was… She didn't have a very clear memory of that day.

Which had seemed fine in the decade since it had occurred, when Chuck was still with her. She'd had the marriage. She hadn't needed more than good feelings and a few photos of the day.

She couldn't remember if they had sat around making wedding favors. She didn't think they had. Nobody should get married when they were eighteen. That was a whole fashion disaster. Shelby had worn a princess dress and a tiara. The entire thing had been a debacle. But of course, when you were eighteen, what you wanted out of the wedding was to be a princess. You thought a lot more about the wedding than you did the marriage. Not that her marriage hadn't been good. It had been. It had been great. Chuck had been her best friend, well, her other best friend, apart from her sister.

It was just, when you were eighteen you didn't really know what the rest of your life meant.

You still don't.

No. She didn't. Because her husband had gone and died and made her a widow in her midtwenties. But what the hell was she supposed to do with that?

Make ribbon curls, she supposed.

"We need to have all the wedding favors ready by tonight," Juniper said.

"Or heads will roll," said Chance, looking at Juniper as if seeking approval.

"That's right," Juniper said. "Heads will roll."

"Good luck with that," Shelby said.

"Yeah," Kit agreed, and she did her best to stop herself from looking at him, but much like her first best, this was not enough. Because she ended up looking at him. And he smiled. And she felt it. Hot and slow as it moved through her.

"If you make my bride upset," Chance said, looking right at his brother, "it'll be your head."

"If your bride can be upset about ribbon curl... I don't know, man."

"When was the last time you ever loved anything?" Chance said to his brother.

"I had a pretty damned good cheeseburger at about one o'clock today," Kit said. "I think I might've loved that."

She couldn't help it. She found herself laughing. And their eyes clashed again. This time, the electricity sent a shower of sparks through her, settling down between her thighs, and it made her twitchy.

This was the problem. When she had been in middle school, she had been able to write off the things that Kit Carson made her feel, but as she had hurtled toward adulthood, it had been impossible to pretend she didn't know.

But it was... It was wrong. It had been wrong because he was her enemy—by virtue of his family connection, nothing personal—and then it had been wrong—very wrong—because she was in love with another man.

Married to another man.

She gritted her teeth together. No. She wouldn't even think about it. She got up from the table, heading over to one of the coolers that were set around their little gathering. They had tables placed all around the yard, where different family members were helping with wedding favor assembly, and all around that were coolers with different beverages, and there was also a table full of snacks. She decided that it was definitely refreshment time.

She felt hot and unwieldy. Lost in the memories of the past, and the debate over ribbon curls, was the double entendre that had passed between herself and Kit. Well, not lost. It was just not the big thing that remained in the forefront. But the slow burn of it was left behind. She was uneasy, and she needed a moment with it.

She reached into the cooler and took out a bottle of beer. And then she heard footsteps, and straightened, looking across the cooler to see none other than Kit himself.

"Anything good in there?"

"They have the kind of beer that you would expect from a couple engaging in this level of wedding frippery. Does that answer your question?"

"Oddly, yes it does." He grinned, then reached down into the cooler, and took out the first beer his hand closed around.

She felt like saying something sharp. She felt like being mean and making him walk away from her. But the truth of the matter was, all of this stuff… This stuff was one-sided. He didn't know that she had a longstanding hated attraction for him. And yes, they had clashed on a few occasions. So there was… There was a thing.

Though, she denied it. And had denied it on multiple occasions. In fact, she could remember clearly one time when they had been down at the Thirsty Mule, and he had been goading her, while offering to buy her and her friends a round of drinks—it had been girls' night out. And Kit had kept on making comments about how Shelby and he *didn't normally get along.* There was *a whole situation with her,* and she *didn't like him.* On and on. Until she had screamed at him at the top of her lungs: *you and I do not have a situation.*

Of course, for the rest of forever, everyone in town had convinced themselves that there was a situation.

Chuck had just laughed about it. Thankfully. And he had written off her umbrage as the normal sort of umbrage that her family felt whenever the Carson name was mentioned. And she had never had to admit that it wasn't just Kit's name that made her feel all out of sorts. It was the man himself.

He grabbed one of the bottle openers from the top of the cooler and popped it easily. Then he reached out to grab her beer out of her hand. A few things happened simultaneously. The first was that his fingertips brushed hers. They were hot and rough, the way a man's hands were when he worked the land.

She didn't comprehend what was happening in the moment, and she did not release the hold on her beer.

Each of those realizations and moments occurred in one breath, and she found herself being dragged over the cooler into Kit.

"Easy," he said, taking hold of her arms. And she got an even more intense taste of the roughness of his hands. The heat there.

Oh, Lord. Oh, Lord, save her.

She was being tested, and she was failing. Here, at

the preparation for her sister's wedding, she was having a full-blown attack of lust for a man who was about to be family-by-marriage. The man whom she had spent all these years pretending she had no situation with.

It was a situation.

"What the hell were you doing?" she asked, still clinging to her beer, still being held on to by him.

"I was gonna open your beer, Shelby," he said, peeling the bottle from her hands, while he set her back onto her feet. "Just a beer. Not a situation."

That bastard.

He had gone over that same night. Those same words.

It did something to her.

Meant something to her.

She wished it didn't.

"I didn't say that I needed help with the beer," she said.

He moved the edge of the bottle opener beneath the perforated cap and flipped it up. "No, you didn't. But I'm nice like that. A real gentleman, some might say."

"Who? Who has ever said that?"

"Not entirely sure."

"No one has ever said it."

He shrugged. "Someone must have."

"Not me."

"You're the president of my fan club. At least I thought so. If not, this is awkward. Because I thought…"

"You did not."

And she felt herself getting red, because… Because, all this banter was just a little bit too close to reality.

"We're not enemies anymore, or did you miss the memo."

"I missed *zero* memos. Believe me. And I tried to talk my sister out of this whole thing. You know, back when she lied to your brother about being her ranch hand when he had amnesia. And then fell in love with him. Yeah. I tried to interfere with all that."

"When you put it like that, it sounds vaguely ridiculous."

"It does," she said.

But ridiculous or not, it had occurred. That could honestly be the subtitle of a movie about her life. *Ridiculous or not, it had occurred.*

He lifted the beer bottle to his lips, and she couldn't help but watch the movement of his mouth, his throat working up and down as he took a long pull off the bottle. Why was he so damned compelling. Why? He didn't have any right to be. He was just a cowboy. They were a dime a dozen around here. Hell, he was one of six boys. There really was no call for him to be all this compelling. She had been married to a rancher. This one shouldn't stir...

She didn't want to think about this. She didn't want to be anywhere near Kit Carson while she was dealing with marriage and wedding feelings. She didn't want to think of him in a game of compare and contrast with Chuck and what she had felt for him.

She had loved Chuck. The love of her life. That phrase couldn't be truer about anyone or anything than it was about Chuck. She had loved him from the time she was twelve years old. And was certain that she would marry him from that same time. She had loved the man until the day he had died, and in all the days since. Kit Carson wasn't owed the same mental airspace as Chuck.

"You got your speech all nailed down?" he asked.

"Yes," she lied. "It's going to be the best speech."

"And you're ready for the bachelorette party?"

"More than ready."

They would be hosting the bachelor and bachelorette parties at the wedding venue. Which was going to be at a ranch about an hour away, up in the mountains, Green Springs Ranch. They were all going to stay in the different buildings on the property, and the wedding would take place in one of the main barns. As maid of honor, it was up to her to plan the bachelorette party. As best man, it was up to Kit to do the bachelor party.

"How did you end up being the best man, anyway?" she asked.

"I drew the short straw."

"What?"

"It's true. We never really figured on any of us getting married. Not us boys. I mean, there's Callie, but… Well, we didn't really figure on her getting married either. But she did. But you know, as far as the best man thing goes, we drew for it. I drew the short straw."

"Doesn't that imply that it's a bad thing?"

"I'm paying for the bachelor party. I'd say that's the short straw."

Suddenly, she felt boxed in. Observed by too many people, or maybe it was just him. The way that he always looked at her. Like he knew. But nobody could know. Nobody could ever know.

"Better go," she said. "The ribbons aren't going to curl themselves."

"Nope."

She turned away from him, and she ignored the way she could feel his gaze resting between her shoulder blades. Like a touch. A caress. Yeah. She ignored that because to acknowledge it would mean acknowledging the spark between them. And she absolutely refused to do that.

Two

Kit Carson wasn't an idiot. Despite reports to the contrary. In fact, he had a pretty damned good head on his shoulders. He might make dumbass decisions out riding the rodeo, bold and rash and dangerous when he flung himself on the back of an angry bull, determined to see him in an early grave, but that recklessness had netted him a damn good portfolio, personal wealth and a hell of a lot of prestige in the rodeo community.

Not to mention the attention of a great many buckle bunnies. And so, it was to his great and eternal mystery that Shelby Sohappy got underneath his skin to quite this degree.

And it wasn't recent. The woman *always* had.

Dating someone else, engaged. *Married.* He had felt drawn to her like a moth to a flame. Like a deer in headlights. Like some other cliché he couldn't think of right now. All he knew was that he really wanted to see her naked.

He could have his pick of women. He had. But there was something about her. About the way they sparked heat off each other, the way that he flustered her, that made him interested. But she was off-limits. She'd been off-limits for a long time, but in all honesty, he figured another man's marriage was that man's responsibility. He had never made a move on Shelby, but he figured whether or not her marriage put her off-limits was up to her. Now that the Carsons and the Sohappys were no longer enemies, well, that changed things a fair bit. Now she was going to be essentially family. And that meant there could be absolutely no… Nothing. Anything.

Because that would make things difficult for Chance. And Kit didn't want to make things difficult for Chance. They had had a difficult enough life as it was.

Chance had found love, and good for him. Kit didn't have it in him.

Losing their sister Sophie when they were kids had just been too much for him. The loss, the feeling of failure when all the caregiving he did couldn't save her…

He'd been twelve and that weight had never shifted.

And more than that, the ongoing grief in the family.

He loved his mom, his dad, his brothers and his youngest sister, Callie, so damned much. And losing Sophie to a terminal illness had underlined how dangerous that love was.

Then there was Buck, his oldest brother, who'd been involved in a horrible car accident that had left him scarred, distant from everyone. They hadn't seen him in years and there was nothing Kit had been able to do to fix it.

There was just so much pain to manage in his family.

Lord.

He didn't want more of it. He never wanted a wife or kids. He didn't even want a dog. He didn't want to love any new thing.

That was the thing. He didn't love Shelby Sohappy. He wasn't even really sure if he liked her. He just wanted her. He was a man who knew that chemistry superseded common sense pretty much any day of the week. He had accepted that what they had was some kind of superior chemistry. The kind you couldn't manufacture even if you wanted to. And you wouldn't want to, but if you could, you would definitely direct it at somebody you'd never see again. Or someone who wouldn't get tangled up in your life. At least, that was what was ideal to *him*.

So yeah. Nothing much had changed. He couldn't have her back when she'd been married. He couldn't have her now. There had been a very small window where he might've been able to have her, but she'd been grieving. Fair enough.

He knew about grief. He knew how it changed you. How it fucked you up big-time. Changed the way that you saw the world. Broke down all the landscape inside you and didn't bother to rebuild the damn thing.

Yeah. He knew about grief. And it was knowing about that kind of grief that made him all the more determined to stay the hell away from this woman.

Too bad they were going to be in proximity for the planning of this wedding. They wouldn't be most of the time. He assumed that for holidays Chance and Juniper would go back and forth between the families, and Shelby didn't have anything to do with the Carsons specifically. But just for right now the woman was squaring his path.

He did his best not to think about how soft her golden

brown skin had been beneath his fingers when he held her there. Dammit she was beautiful. Her thick black hair was cut into a chin-length style that highlighted the heart shape of her face, her high cheekbones, her deep brown eyes. Her lips were full and dusky, a caramel color that he wanted to lick.

And he needed to not think of that. Not right now.

"There's dessert."

He looked across at the table where all the food was, and saw his mother setting three giant cheesecakes covered with caramel down onto the tabletops.

Dammit all. Caramel. That was really what he wanted to think about right now. In context.

Everybody made a grateful noise and he gathered around the table along with all of them, getting his piece and returning with it to the assembly point.

"The wedding is in just three days," Juniper said, as if they needed reminding. "And we need to get everything up to the venue and get it all set up."

"I don't know why the hell you didn't just get married at the Carson ranch," Kit said.

Juniper gave him a scathing look. "I'm not letting you win like that."

"Getting to host the wedding would be winning?"

Chance held up a hand. "Believe me. I have had that conversation. Back out now. You won't win."

"Now that's what I like," Juniper said. "A Carson admitting when he's beaten."

"It's just a Carson admitting he knows how to choose his battles," Chance said, grunting.

"Well, it's no problem," Kit said. "There's no shortage of pickup trucks between us. We can carry whatever the hell you need up that way."

"I got a pickup truck too," Shelby said. "And I'm the maid of honor."

"I don't think we need all the pickup trucks we have between us," Juniper said.

His eyes met Shelby's again, and she looked away, faint color on her cheekbones. She felt it too. He knew she did. He'd always known that. What he didn't know was what story exactly she told herself.

It didn't matter. He might want Shelby, but there was no way in hell he would ever do anything to make her his. She was the marriage-and-family type. She'd been in love, and she lost that love. He didn't want to step into that. Not even a little.

"I'll tell you what," Kit said. "You just give orders, and I will follow them."

"Speak for yourself," Shelby said.

"Would you rather take orders from me?"

She looked away from him quickly, and he realized that he...stepped into something. Because she didn't fire anything right back at him, and he almost felt guilty about that.

And then she looked up at him, dark fire banked in her eyes. "I'd like to see you try that."

He held back his answer. He held it back because everybody was here. He held it back because he didn't know how to make it not explicitly sexual.

He held it back, because the last thing in all the world he needed to do at this wedding preparation party was declare his sexual intent with a woman he was inextricably linked to through his brother's relationship with her sister.

Especially when he knew that he couldn't have any intentions toward her at all.

Shelby was exhausted, carrying all the baskets of various things into her cabin.

Juniper was helping, basket after basket of different wedding favors coming in after the other.

"You know," Shelby said, "I'm trying not to be nosy, or in your business, but aren't you marrying a super-rich cowboy?"

Juniper laughed. "What's your point?"

"My point is, you had to make all of this. The guy could *buy it*. Why are we doing favors for every table, and ribbon curls?"

Juniper looked at her, confusion etched into her features. "You really don't know?"

"I mean, your pride, I assume."

She shook her head. "I don't have any of that with Chance. We're getting married. We have a partnership. We don't divide things up, and we certainly don't keep score on what's his and what's mine or any of that. It isn't that. It's just I wanted to do this because this is what we did for your wedding."

Shelby blinked. "Is it? I was just trying to remember. And I couldn't. I just remembered the wedding dress. Which, by the way, you should've talked me out of."

"I loved it."

"Well. You were also a teenage girl. Neither of us were trustworthy."

"Do you really not remember? We wrapped all those different terra-cotta pots that we found for cheap down at the dollar store in pretty paper, made paper ribbons, and you had those potted plants up all around in the wedding venue."

She frowned, her forehead creasing. "Yeah. I do remember that. It's weird. I just don't… I don't think about it much."

"I'm sorry. I didn't mean to bring up a painful memory."

"I've been thinking about Chuck all day." Truth be

told, she thought about him most days. "It's unavoidable."

Juniper looked worried. "You didn't say anything about it."

"I don't want to make your wedding about my issues. It isn't about my issues. Your wedding is about you. And I'm so happy for you."

"You seem like you maybe aren't sometimes."

"It's not that. I think it's a little bit strange that you're marrying a Carson. All things considered. But I'm coming to terms of it."

"And it has nothing to do with Kit?"

She narrowed her eyes. "Don't push it." Juniper had never mentioned Kit, or Shelby's non-situation with Kit, until recently. Shelby didn't like the new development.

"Did something happen between you two?"

"No! When would anything have ever happened?"

"I don't know. I've never known. All I know is that when you see him…"

"Please don't finish that sentence, because my pride is hanging on by a thread, because I nearly fell down into the man tonight, and I don't need anything to compromise what remains of it. It is tenuous. At best."

"I don't think anyone else can tell," Juniper said quickly. "It's just that I know you. I know you really well."

"And you know me well enough to know that if I don't want to talk about it I'm not going to talk about it."

Juniper nodded. "You're right. I do know you well enough to know that. Sorry."

"It's fine. Like I said. I'm a little bit surprised, both because of his family, and the circumstances…"

"Oh, the thing that I did that you absolutely disapproved of because it was really messed up?"

"Yeah. That thing. Where you lied to the guy about who you were? And who he was?"

"It worked out," Juniper said. She winced. "Believe me. I have apologized many times over. And I do feel bad about it. Though, forgetting who he was... And me treating him like he was somebody different... It was the only way that we could really get to know each other. I know it sounds imbalanced. But... It's just how it works."

Shelby couldn't help it. Right in that moment, she sort of wished that she could have that. A moment to be somebody new. Maybe she needed to leave town. She had never really considered it before.

Losing Chuck had been destabilizing in every way. Leaving Lone Rock, leaving their land...leaving her parents, her grandparents—that was something that she couldn't even fathom. But it was hard to be here. Hard to be in a place where everybody knew who you were, where everybody knew your life story. So they looked at you like you were sad even when you had never exchanged three words with them, because they already knew through the grapevine exactly what you'd been through.

"I can see how that would work," she said, her voice feeling scratchy.

"It did work," Juniper said. "So are you going to head up to the venue early?"

Shelby looked around at all the things. "I don't see how it will work if I don't. I need to get everything set up for the bachelorette party, and I need to get all the party favors up there for that. Plus the wedding."

"He has six brothers. He will absolutely handle whatever needs handling."

"I'm your only sister," she said, fiercely. "And it

means more to me now than it ever has. Your… You and Mom and Dad and Grandma and Grandpa are all I have. I was supposed to make a family, an expanded family with Chuck. And I… I want to do everything for you. Just trust me."

Juniper looked at her, her dark eyes steady and level, and filled with compassion, and it put Shelby back to that night three years ago when Juniper had come over to tell her…

When Juniper'd had to be the one to tell her Chuck was in a car accident, and he hadn't made it.

Her sister was real. Genuine. When she said she wanted to be there for Shelby, it wasn't an empty gesture. She'd proved it that night. She hadn't passed the job off on someone else. She'd been the one to do it. She'd been the one to hold Shelby while she'd cried like she'd never stop.

"Oh, Shelby," Juniper said. "I'm so sorry that this is hard."

She loved that Juniper cared so much, but she really didn't want to take the focus off her either. This was her moment. Her love story.

Shelby was happy for her.

"I don't want this to be about me. I really don't. This is about you and your happiness. And I am thrilled for you. Yeah, weddings make me think about my own wedding. But don't think for one second that you're causing me any sadness. You couldn't. I live with the loss. Every day. He was part of my life for so long, and then just one day having him gone completely… It's awful. But it's different than it was right at first. And it isn't… I don't know how to explain this in a way that makes sense, but it isn't your wedding making me sad.

It's making me think about my wedding. But that isn't thinking about him more than usual."

"Thanks. I love you."

"I love you too."

They hugged, and Juniper left. Left Shelby with all these baskets.

Yeah. She was going to have to get them up to the venue, but actually, maybe that would be a good thing. It would give her a little bit of time to herself. A little bit of time to reflect.

The thing that made her feel guilty, really guilty, was that sometimes she was just tired of grieving. Just tired of… Of living with loss. She wanted to be done with it. But that was hardly fair. Chuck couldn't really stop being dead.

She laughed. She needed to move his things out of their bedroom. His clothes. She had gotten some out when Juniper had borrowed them for Chance. She hadn't taken them back. Hadn't put them back in the closet when they'd been returned to her. It had felt like a baby step. An important one.

But this house that she lived in alone still had the hallmarks of a home that was shared. And at some point she was going to have to change that.

There were other things that probably needed to change. She should make a crafting room out of that spare bedroom. Even though she didn't craft. She should make it a reading nook. Because it was never going to be what she had dreamed of it being. Even with Chuck, they hadn't been able to turn that spare room into a nursery.

There was no way that was going to change.

But letting go was just so hard. And sometimes…

Shelby didn't understand why she had to be the one to let go of so many things.

But her sister was getting married. And they were going to have a bachelorette party. One of epic proportions.

If Juniper wanted to hearken back to Shelby's wedding... Well, Shelby owed her a little bit of revenge, actually.

She smiled.

Oh yes. The bachelorette party was going to be an epic night to remember.

Three

Kit, Jace, Flint and Boone were all down at the Thirsty Mule getting drinks. The ramshackle old saloon had been the heart of Lone Rock since the late 1800s. It had the original saloon doors still swinging between the entryway and the bar. It was rumored the hole up at the top had come from a bullet that had shot the piano player stone-cold dead back in 1899.

Kit had it on good authority that it was actually from a jackass who put a pool cue through it in 1980.

Jace's best friend, Cara, was serving beers gamely from behind the bar, and Kit would be remiss if he passed up the chance to make a sly comment about his brother's friend in his presence. "Cara is looking pretty good."

Jace didn't look at him. "I will kill you. With my bare hands. And I'll enjoy it."

Jace insisted he was only friends with Cara. Kit believed him, mostly. Jace was also very protective of Cara, so whatever the reason, Kit's commenting on Cara's beauty often caused chaos. And Kit lived for it.

He grinned. "Why don't you just marry her already?"

"What are you, eight?" Jace asked.

"No. I am not eight. If I were eight I would be suggesting you marry the beer because you love it."

"I hate you."

"Hey," said Flint. "We are here to discuss our brother's bachelor party."

"Right, right. I'm the best man," said Kit, "so this is primarily my responsibility."

"Strippers," said Boone.

"Hell no," said Jace.

"I'm sorry, why are you opposed to exotic dancers?" Kit asked.

"Since this is the kind of event people are going to hear about." He tilted his head toward Cara.

"Again," Kit said, "if you are so beholden to Cara and what she thinks, you might as well marry her."

Cara began to walk toward them then, her blond hair pulled back in a ponytail, a short, spiked leather jacket making the point of her general demeanor for her. "What's that, Kit?"

"I said," Kit responded, grinning, "if Jace is going to be whipped by you, he might as well marry you."

"I won't marry him," said Cara. "I can't be tamed."

"I'd be happy to tame you for a while," Kit said, which earned him a glowing smile from Cara. All in with the intent of pissing Jace off.

"I will kill you," said Jace.

"Jace," said Cara. "Please. If anyone is going to kill Kit it'll be me. Or Shelby Sohappy."

The mention of Shelby's name was like a firecracker going off in his gut. "She doesn't have it in her."

"Yes, she does," said Boone. "She would kill you with a smile on her face. And she's got enough land that they'd never find your body."

Boone was a terminal smart-ass. He and his best friend in the rodeo, Daniel, had a reputation for being hell-raisers. Though Daniel was married and had settled in theory, rumor had it he hadn't changed at all.

He often wondered what Boone thought about his friend's behavior. It was tough to tell what Boone thought about anything.

Too much of a smart-ass, that was the thing.

"Well, good thing she has no reason for wanting to kill me."

"That's not really what I've observed," said Cara.

"Ah, right. I forgot. The all-seeing, all-knowing bartender," Kit said.

"You guys have a thing."

"We do not have a thing," Kit said. "In fact, she once told me that we have no situation at all."

"You don't say that to someone you don't have a thing with," Cara said. "If there's no situation, there's no need to remark upon the situation."

Kit shrugged. The fact was, they did have a thing, and he knew it. That *thing* was chemistry. But Kit liked his chemistry with women the way he liked his chemistry classes. Over quickly. Handled. Done. Graduated from. He was a satisfy-them—multiple times—and-leave-them type. He had done serious way early on in his life. He knew what it was like to have the burden of taking care of someone, and he never wanted it again. He had a huge family, and he loved them. All of them.

Even Buck, who was gone. It was exhausting. He didn't need to love anyone else. Not ever.

"Whatever you say, Kit. But anyway, why are you assuming that Jace is beholden to me? He can do whatever he wants."

"He wants to hire strippers for the bachelor party."

Cara looked at him, her eyes like daggers. "I'll never speak to you again, Jace Carson."

"Just a second," said Kit, peering behind Cara at some of the jars at the back shelf of the bar.

"What are you doing?"

"Checking to see if you have Jace's balls back there."

Cara was unmoved. She planted her hands squarely on the bar and leaned toward him, staring.

"And what are you doing, Cara?" he asked.

"Checking to see if you got any human decency in there. Because Jace has it. He is almost a gentleman."

Boone laughed so hard he nearly fell off the bar stool. "Jace Carson. A gentleman. That's because you only see him here in Lone Rock. And you never see him on the road. You've only seen a piece of him, sweetheart."

"Call me sweetheart one more time and you can find out whether or not the spikes on this jacket are a decoration or for practical purposes."

"That's my girl," said Jace.

She walked away from them, and Kit was just mad that she had managed to redirect his thoughts right back to Shelby.

Right. Like they were ever all that far from her to begin with.

That was the problem with Shelby. She was under his skin, and he couldn't even really say why. Just sex. That was the thing. He wanted her, and he had never been able to have her. Maybe he wanted her in part because she was so… So decidedly off-limits. Actually, it should be a little bit more resolvable these days. She was single, and the barrier had been broken between their families. Juniper and Chance were already getting married. There was nothing forbidden about an association between the two of them at all. That should make her less interesting. That should make him entirely less aroused by the thought of grabbing her and pulling her up against his body, lowering his head and tasting whether or not her lips were sugary, salty caramel like he imagined…

Dammit.

"So, what is the bachelor party plan, then?" Boone asked.

"Well, because I don't want our mother to kill us, I was never planning on hiring any strippers. However, I was thinking skeet shooting, some drinking. Darts. Pool. There's kind of a bachelor pad house up there, all outfitted for this kind of thing. And, we need to have a camping trip."

"A camping trip?" Boone questioned.

"Yeah. Like we did when we were kids."

They didn't talk about why. It was just one of those things. But the boys had gotten sent out of the house quite a bit when their sister Sophie had been sick and recovering from different treatments. Having the campout in the backyard was a way to get the house quiet for her.

It wasn't a bad memory. Not really. But that time would always be bittersweet.

It was something that they shared. All of them.

"All right."

"Yeah, I figured it would be good. Hell, we didn't get to send Callie out into the world with any warning. She just went and eloped."

"Yeah. With Jake Daniels. Of all the things."

"She seemed happy enough."

She was taken care of. And that was a big load off Kit's mind. When she had first come back to the ranch with him, Kit had been... Not very happy. He knew Jake from the rodeo circuit, and as far as he was concerned, Jake was a bad bet. He had been the kind of guy who was... Well, he was like all of them. He was a ho. A shameless, uninhibited man ho. And, the idea of him marrying Kit's sister had gone down like a lead balloon. But he had proved to Kit that he loved Callie. And more than that, he had proved that he was committed to Callie's safety. And that mattered. It mattered a whole hell of a lot. Because he had spent all of Callie's childhood worrying about her safety, and then she had gone and gotten the rodeo bug. And she couldn't do something sane like riding barrel horses. No. His sister had gone and gotten the bug to ride saddle bronc. And she had been insistent about it. Their dad had done basically everything in his power to block her from doing it, but she had gotten around that by marrying Jake and getting access to her trust fund.

But, the thing was, she was great at it.

She was great at riding saddle bronc. And she really brought something fresh and new to the event. She had invigorated rodeo-goers. And he had to be proud of her. From a feminist perspective even. But as an older brother, not so much. And there were just two different kinds of things that existed inside him. He was all for equality. But a lot less so when it came to the health and safety of his little sister. Let somebody else blaze trails. Blazing trails was dangerous, and he had a hard time admitting that it was all right for Callie to be out there doing it.

But Jake cared about her safety so much that it gave Kit some room to breathe.

"I'm planning to go up to the wedding ranch and check things out tomorrow," Kit said. "Get some supplies delivered, get the house opened up and set to go."

"I've got a date," said Boone. "So, I won't be up till a little later."

"You have a date," Kit said. "With who?"

"You know, I don't remember her name. But, she's one of the rodeo queens. She's coming through town, and I'm not gonna miss it."

"Great. Enjoy your booty call."

"I promised Cara I'd help her with a few things. But I'll be there the day before the wedding."

"You better the hell be. That's when the party's happening."

"Great. Well. We'll see you out there in a couple of days," said Flint.

"Yeah. Assholes. See you in a couple of days."

Shelby had somehow managed to get all the baskets of favors into the back of her truck, and all of the favors for the bachelorette party into the back seat. She was feeling pretty good about everything. She had some great favors for the bachelorette party, and she had been mean.

Because Juniper had been mean to her.

The problem with having your equally young and immature sister plan your bachelorette party when you were getting married at eighteen was that *everything* was immature.

Penis everything.

And so, Shelby had retaliated. Meanly. And with grown-ass adult money and the full power of the internet, that meant she'd been able to take what Juniper had accomplished and turn it up to the tenth power.

And she didn't care if her sister liked it or not.

Now, there would be real decorations too, but she'd had to get penis straws, a penis crown and, best of all, a very large vibrator to be the centerpiece of some flowers. She figured that Juniper and Chance might appreciate the gift.

They could take it on their honeymoon.

For just a moment, that stopped her short. She really didn't want to think about her sister hooking up and having sex. But the subject of honeymoons, and the thought of the vibrator, brought it all close to mind.

You don't need the guy. Just the vibrator.

And she had her own, thank you very much. She had invested in a pretty decent collection of them during this stretch of single time.

Eventually... Eventually there would have to be a guy. Wouldn't there? Eventually there would have to be one just so she didn't go crazy.

Except, she couldn't imagine it. Couldn't imagine being with anybody except for...

Unbidden, an image of Kit popped into her mind. No. She had spent way too many years being disciplined about him. She had never fantasized about him, no matter how it had hovered around the edges of her consciousness. Not while she was with Chuck, and not since. She was not going to undo all that good moral fiber in a moment of weird weakness.

So she shut that out of her mind. She was fine. And she wasn't envious. If she wanted to hook up, she could go hook up. It wasn't even flattering. Men were disgusting. They would literally hump a tree if given half the chance. It wasn't like she wouldn't be able to find somebody. There was nothing wrong with her.

She stood there in the driveway of the farmhouse where they would be having their girls' night. And she felt like that thought fell a little bit flat. It wasn't like there was anything wrong with her.

There was something sad in her.

Something a little bit dampened.

Broken.

Something that wondered if it would ever feel *alive* again.

Yeah, the thing about grief was, it changed. It didn't go away.

But there was a hole in your life where someone had once been, and the passage of time didn't make it stop being there. It didn't make that person not gone. For a while there, the grief had gotten worse.

Because it had been even longer since she'd seen Chuck. As silly as that sounded. For a few months it had been like... Maybe he was on a trip. Maybe he would come back. But at six months... She remembered very distinctly realizing she had not been away from Chuck for that long ever. Not since she had met him. It wasn't a vacation amount of time. It was significant. And it left her feeling raw and hollow.

That had gone away. That part of it. There were all those firsts she had to get through.

And there is a first you haven't gotten through yet.

She just didn't want to. Not yet.

She had kind of underestimated how her sister's being in a relationship would bring a bunch of stuff up to the surface for her, and she didn't want it to poison this experience. She wanted her sister to have this.

Wanted her sister to have a good time. Wanted it to be all about her. Wanted it to be special.

She did not want it to be about her pain. She just… She couldn't bear her own pain. She was sick of herself.

So she focused on her immaturity, her amusement at it all. And started taking trips from the house to the car.

The ranch was beautiful, set high atop a mountain overlooking the valley below. It had a gorgeous little farmhouse, a huge barn where they held all of the events, very rustic, and different from the one on Carson land, which was a bit too slick, according to Juniper.

There was another house spaced out in a different part of the property that Juniper had mentioned the men would be staying in.

The men.

Well, they weren't here right now. Shelby was by herself.

As if that's remarkably different from every other day?

No. She supposed it wasn't. But at least she wasn't alone in her house. It was a different kind of alone. It almost felt like a vacation.

She saved the load of penises for last. And she did laugh, when she pulled the big laundry basket that contained all those party favors out, and began to cart them toward the house.

"Well, fancy meeting you here."

She turned around, her eyes wide, and jostled the basket, one phallic straw springing out and down to the ground below.

Great.

Her basket of cocks overfloweth. In front of Kit.

"What are you doing here, Kit?"

"Same thing as you, I imagine." And then, he seemed

to realize what was in the basket she was holding. "Well, no. Not the same thing as you."

"Did you not have a basket of dick paraphernalia for the bachelor party?"

"Suddenly I feel remiss," he said.

She was doing her level best to cling to what little dignity she had and it was tough. It was real tough.

"It's not too late," she said.

"Do you have an extra?"

"Do I have an extra… Penis?"

A smile spread, slow and dirty over his face, and she wanted to… Punch him. She really wanted to punch him. "I just have the one, that's all."

She felt like she was going to choke. On horror, heat, arousal, or maybe all three. "Wow. Well, this has been delightful. How long are you up here for?"

"Until the wedding."

"You're not serious," she said.

"I am serious. I'm here to the wedding because there are some things to set up."

"No," she said. "No, because… I'm here until the wedding."

"Is that a problem?"

"No," she said.

"Good."

"Like I told you. We don't have…"

"We don't have a situation," he said, his eyes giving off way too much heat.

"Not even a little one. Not at all."

"Good to know. I'm glad. Because I want the wedding to be perfect. And I would hate for anything to interfere."

"Nothing will interfere."

"Good. In fact, we could probably be of some use to each other. What do you think?"

She blinked. And really, she had no reason to refuse him. If there were things that could be done, things that they could do collaboratively… It actually just made sense. Because the truth of the matter was, nothing had ever happened between them. Nothing beyond a few warmish exchanges that had left her feeling flustered. And that was all her. Kit was Kit, which meant that he was a flirt, because he didn't know another way to be. It was simply how he was, and that was the way of it. She knew that. There was no reason to go getting heated up.

So yeah. Why not. But not now. Because right now was awkward.

"Well. I'm just going to… Take my basket of penises and go."

"Okay."

"Maybe I'll have a bath."

"Okay."

And suddenly she felt overly hot, because it was like her mouth was just saying things, and she didn't have any control over it.

"I'm out of practice," she said. "With the talking to people. That I'm not related to. Sorry."

He nodded slowly, and right then, his expression did something sort of genuine. "I'm sorry," he said. "I'm sorry about your husband."

That he linked her lack of social skills with her loss was…weirdly touching. His awareness of it, of her as a person, was sort of unexpected. She didn't know what to do with it.

"Thank you."

She swallowed hard, and went into the house, and just as she did, she remembered what Juniper had told her about their family. That they'd had a sister. And she died when they were kids.

That was why he looked at her like that. That was why he said it with that kind of gravity. It was why he knew *I'm sorry* was enough. Because there were no platitudes that made it okay. There was no grand speech to give that was going to magically make it all less painful. It just… Was. It was lost. The loss was lost. You couldn't fix it. Couldn't go back. Couldn't change it. Couldn't hold on to him for five more minutes before he walked out the door to change the timing so that when the other pickup truck crossed the yellow line his car wasn't there. No. She couldn't go back. She couldn't fix it. She wasn't prescient. She hadn't been able to prevent it. She hadn't even had a bad feeling about the day.

No. She'd been over it a hundred times. Magical thinking didn't have any kind of place in the grief sphere.

And the way he'd said that. All practical. He knew. He knew. And she really appreciated that.

Who would've thought that she would appreciate an encounter with Kit. Well. And who would've thought that she would be standing in front of him with a basket full of phalli. But, it was that kind of day. It was just that kind of day.

And she really was going to take a long hot bath and put all of it out of her mind.

Four

The bachelor house was a big log cabin filled with animal heads and cowhide everywhere. He loved it. This was the kind of place where he would like to settle down. They all had cabins on their parents' property, and there really was no reason to buy up, especially when he was still traveling with the rodeo during the season. But the places at his parents' house were slick. They weren't this country. And he really liked things being this country.

He paused at the doorway and looked across the expanse of fields. It was dark now. But he could see a light on in the window of the farmhouse just across the way.

Shelby Sohappy.

They were on the same mountain. And there was nobody else around. That really was something. And he needed to stop thinking of her that way. It was difficult, considering she had been standing there with a whole barrel of sex toys.

He did not need to think about Shelby and sex toys. Not in the same sentence. Not in the same... Oh, the same fantasy. And it was getting there. It was getting there quick.

This was the problem with small towns. It was like they'd been engaging in foreplay for years on end. But he really was sorry about her husband. He tried to focus on that. He had liked Shelby's husband. He'd been a nice guy. He used to run into him out on occasion. He'd sometimes even sit with the Carsons and have a beer. He had just always told them never to tell his wife, considering the family had such a rivalry. But, being outside of the family, he hadn't internalized it to the degree that Shelby and Juniper did.

Yeah. He had been an easygoing guy. Short and stocky with dark hair and an easy smile. It really was a shame. A tragedy.

Too bad Kit had always wanted the guy's wife.

Didn't make it not a tragedy in the abstract, though.

It was one of the things that Kit would never understand about the world. The way that the good seemed to die young and terribly. And leave voids in the world that nobody could ever fix.

It was why he preferred to have as few connections as possible.

Well, *preferred* wasn't even a strong enough word. He lived his life by that code. By that creed. He hadn't fully appreciated the connections that would end up being built, though, when his siblings started to get married. He just had so many damn siblings. Callie had gotten married, and Jake Daniels had been brought into the fold. If they ever had kids, there would be nieces and nephews. And then there was Chance and Juniper. And the same went for them.

Babies.

Babies freaked him out.

They were so soft and vulnerable. When Callie had been little, he didn't think he'd ever gotten a wink of sleep. That was the problem with being a kid who'd watched his sister die.

You didn't trust anything. That was just it. He didn't trust anything, so it was better to just not love much.

He hadn't had any choice when it came to his family. They were big and boisterous. And he loved them with everything he had.

But he didn't have to add more people to the list.

While he was looking out across the way, the lights turned off. And he would've thought nothing of it, except there were lights on on multiple floors and in multiple windows, and they all went out simultaneously. So unless there was some kind of smart-switch situation happening—and out here he seriously doubted it—he had reason to feel a little bit concerned.

He hustled out the front door without thinking, and jogged across the field, heading toward the farmhouse. And just as he was about to knock on the door, it opened up.

"Oh," she said.

"Hey," he said. "What happened?"

"The lights went out," she said, her cheeks illuminated.

"Oh. Well. I can come in and take a look if you like. I got a flashlight out in the truck."

"Thanks, I…"

"Alternatively, you could come stay in the bachelor pad."

"Oh," she said. "No."

She didn't like this. His pushing her. But she needed help, and he didn't see why he shouldn't offer it. He didn't see why there needed to be such a big wall built between the two of them. Not now anyway.

"There's like ten rooms in there. And they're all vacant. And then, in the morning, we can sort out whatever the hell happened here. Seems better than stumbling around in the dark."

"Yeah, I guess so."

"Go get your suitcase."

"It's just an overnight bag."

She disappeared, then came back a moment later. She looked… She looked afraid. At least, as far as he could tell with only her cell phone flashlight lit up.

"You don't *have* to come with me. I can try to figure out why the lights went out here."

"No," she said. "No. You don't have to do that. It's fine. Let's just go. I'm starving. And with the lights out I can't cook any food and…"

"Do you have stuff in the fridge?" he asked.

"I have it in a cooler."

"I brought some steak. And I do have power. So I'm happy to grill for us both."

"I don't want to eat your steak," she said, wrinkling her nose.

"Hey. You offered to lend me a penis. So… I feel like it's a fair trade."

She choked, and tried to cover it with a cough. "Well, I didn't bring any of them with me."

"I'll take a rain check."

"That's very reasonable of you," she said, still wheezing.

"I'm very reasonable."

He reached out and took the overnight bag from her hands. But this time, he was careful not to touch her. When he had tried to help with the beer, he had touched her. And it had set off a whole thing.

He didn't need to go setting off whole things. Not again.

So they walked across the field together in relative silence, toward the bachelor pad.

And when they walked up the front porch and inside, she made a scoffing noise. "Well. I can see why they were putting you all up in here."

"Yeah. Who was all staying in your place?"

"Your sister. My mother. A couple of friends from high school. But this is going to be…"

"Oh yeah. There's a lot of us. And it's a lot of testosterone."

"Sounds great."

"I don't really think you mean that."

"Well, since you're offering to cook me steak, I'm actually not going to push you."

She hung back, though in the doorway, as he went inside.

He went into the kitchen, and got the steaks out of the fridge. They were sitting in a marinade, because he wasn't an animal. The thing about being a bachelor was if you were committed to that kind of lifestyle, then you needed to learn how to take care of yourself. And Kit liked good food.

He didn't see the point in living like a trash animal just because in many ways he philosophically was one.

"I'm grilling anyway," he said. "I had it preheating outside."

"Wow. I feel kind of honored."

A strange, haunted look crossed over her face. He

had a feeling she was thinking about another time. Another man.

And that is why you don't want to get involved.

"Yeah. You like… Grilling?"

"Obviously I don't," she said.

Dammit. He had been trying to ask an innocuous question, and he'd gone and stepped right into it.

"Yeah. No. I mean…"

"Yes. My husband used to grill."

He was still here, that guy, even though he wasn't here. Kit knew how that worked. He felt bad that he'd missed a connection here, with her. That he hadn't been more careful.

"Right. Sorry."

"You don't have to say *sorry*. It's… I mean, it's not as painful now. I just think about it all the time. You know, because you realize how absurd it is you can't turn and say something to someone who used to always be there. But they'll never be there again. It's ridiculous. So how can you… Not think about it?"

"Yeah. I know."

She nodded gravely. And he had a feeling she really did know that he knew. So that was good. He didn't have to explain it. He was not looking to have a heart-to-heart with her. Nothing that was personal. He wasn't looking to have a heart-to-heart with anybody.

"Grill's back here," he said, pushing open the double doors that led out to the grand outdoor kitchen area. It was a lot spiffier out there than it was inside.

"Wow," she said, looking up. It made him look up too. The stars above were a brilliant blanket of diamonds, and he really figured he didn't take enough time to appreciate that sort of thing. But he just didn't think much about it. Miracles and wonders and all that kind of stuff had been rendered pretty moot for him back when Sophie had died.

He had hoped.

That was the thing. Because he thought that the good guy won. And there was nobody better than his beautiful, tough little sister. And then it was like the safety net in everything had been pulled away. It hadn't made them afraid. Because Sophie hadn't done anything risky to get sick. He'd figured if death was out there... Well, then it would come for you when it felt like it. That was actually worse than becoming a shut-in or an agoraphobe. Just believing that no matter what, it might get you. So you might as well do whatever. He'd been hell on his parents during his teenage years.

And it had been hell on his soul.

Because it just... Everything felt tenuous. All the time.

But the stars were still there. He wasn't sure how many years it had been since he'd thought to look up at them before Shelby had just prompted him to.

It was a hell of a thing.

"I can see why they chose to get married up here. There's so little light pollution. I mean, I'm about to pollute it all with my flame in my grilling. But you know."

"The cost of progress," she said.

"True."

He put the steak on the hot grill, and watched as the flame rose up.

"Is there a salad or anything?"

"Of course. And baked potatoes. I did them before I came up. I'm not an animal."

"Well, that's kind of a revelation."

"There's one baked potato. We're going to have to split it."

"You brought up two steaks?"

"I don't take chances with steak," he said.

"Fair enough."

Silence lapsed between them. "This is very nice of you."

"Well," he said, shrugging as he looked down at the grill, "we are about to be family and all that."

"Not really. I mean *we're* not. It's not really like that."

"I guess not. But functionally it kinda feels that way."

She turned a small circle, then separated from him and went and sat down on the couch nearby. Her hands clasped in her lap.

"So," he said. "What is it you do exactly?"

She laughed. "What is it that I do?"

"Yeah. Your sister's an EMT, and you…"

"I make jewelry. I bead things. I sell a lot of it online. But… Yeah. You know. Things like that."

"Really?"

"Yeah. Do you not frequent the farmers markets around here?"

"No."

"Well. I'm very good. But mostly, I'm lucky to have family land, which I also work."

"Yeah. That is nice. I also benefit from that."

"And you're still riding…bulls?"

"I am indeed. Still riding bulls, and traveling around when I can."

"How long does a person do that? The bull riding thing."

He shrugged. "As long as your body can take it. Though, I admit it's not as easy as it used to be."

"What makes a person want to do that?" She was looking at him, something bright and mysterious burning in her eyes just then.

"Family business."

"And that's it? You do it because you saw the people before you do it?"

She looked a little bit disturbed by that fact. "Aren't we all doing that to some degree or another? I mean, it's easiest to take a path that you've seen forged, isn't it?"

"Maybe," she said.

"Why?"

"I don't know. I was feeling like maybe I'm not all that adventurous. But… You make bull riding sound the same as deciding to get married and have kids just because your parents did it."

"In a lot of ways, it's the same. You do this thing that seems like a legacy, I guess." But he felt a strange pang in his chest, and he didn't want to think too deeply about why.

"Except, you haven't done that part."

"No interest in it. So yeah, I guess it's not exactly the same. I knew how to get into the rodeo because it's the family business. But I don't have a whole lot of interest in the domesticity part. I have enough of it with the family I have."

"Makes sense."

"And you?"

"I think it's obvious what I wanted with my life, isn't it? I got married when I was eighteen. You don't do that if you don't want… That same thing. That thing your parents had. You don't do that if family isn't your dream. But I don't have it anymore. So… I guess maybe that's why I asked. How long you're going to do the bull riding. And when it ends, then what?"

"I don't know. And I'm not really sure I get how it connects."

"Because I'm living in this…*and then what* space.

The first thing I wanted is gone. So what do I do now? And I don't know the answer."

He didn't know why she'd chosen to ask him that. Maybe because they were relative strangers. Maybe because he was something entirely different to her, and to her family. Maybe just because the steak was good, or because the stars were bright.

Maybe to scare him off, because she felt the same heat burning between them that he did.

Whatever the reason, he found himself wanting to give her an answer. And he didn't have one. He wasn't deep. Not by any metric. But he wished that he had something to offer her.

"Maybe that's the secret," he said. "Maybe nobody knows what to do with that second choice. Because the fact of the matter is, we all end up living with the less-ideal scenario at some point. Whether it's work or family or... We all have to face it at some point. And maybe you never quite know what to do with that part of your life as clearly as you knew what to do with the first part."

That cut close to his bone. But it had nothing to do with bull riding.

"Eventually everybody loses someone. And the older we get the more someones we lose. And you're always living in that and after. Always." He shrugged. "It takes away little pieces of the life that you knew. Of the things that you imagined. And the more of those pieces you lose, the more you have to rebuild. I'm not sure that the answers ever get clearer or easier to see."

"So what then?"

He looked at her then, and he noticed a necklace around her neck. Made with fine little beads. "Did you make that?"

"Yes."

He did something he knew he might regret, and took a step toward her, reaching out and touching the center of the necklace. "And how do you make something like this?"

"With a thread, a needle and these little seed beads and…"

"Right. But do you throw them all on all at once and see the big picture?"

"No. You go one bead at a time. But you have some idea about where you're headed."

"Right. But maybe in life sometimes we just have the one bead. We don't know how it fits into the bigger picture. So we just have to keep going. One bead at a time. One step at a time."

"I didn't realize that you were a philosopher," she said, her breath quickening as she looked up at him.

"Neither did I. But you suddenly made me want to try it out."

She cleared her throat and turned away. "Don't overcook the steak. I like it medium."

He cursed and went over to the grill, poking one of the steaks with a fork and slicing it so that he could get a look at the color inside.

"Not overdone."

He stuck the meat on plates, and they went back in the house, where he added the baked potato and salad. "Want to eat outside?"

She nodded.

They went back outside and sat opposite each other on the patio furniture, the plates in their laps.

"I guess my worry is that maybe it's not making a picture. I haven't done much of anything for the last few years. Maybe I haven't added a bead at all. You know. So to speak."

"Well, grief is like that. And that's different. You need to give yourself time."

"Right."

"You know about my sister."

"Yes. I do. I'm sorry about that. It's hard. I can't imagine what it must be like when it's a child."

"Loss is loss. You don't need to go ranking it. But yeah. I… She wasn't well for a long time. And I took care of her. We all did but… I just wanted to make her comfortable. And sometimes that was impossible. But it obsessed me. Distracting her, trying to do things to make her happy… And when I lost that, I didn't really know what to do. For me, that looked like a lot of years of bordering on juvenile delinquency. But eventually I figured that wasn't a very good tribute to Sophie. And that was when I got serious about the rodeo. And it just gave me something to do that was… That was something. I'm not going to say I made anything for the greater good, but it brought me closer to my family again. Because that's what we do. So it seemed like a worthy enough pursuit. I guess bull riding is my 'and then.' There will be another one too. Because I can't do it forever."

"How many new lives are we supposed to live?"

"As many as we need to, I guess."

"I guess."

They ate in relative silence after that. He couldn't remember the last time he had a conversation that was so… It brushed up against all the difficult things he preferred not to think about. And yet, he wanted to talk to her because she was asking him those questions. Because it didn't come from a place of gawking at pain, but

of sharing it. Because she knew what loss was, and…
And that was the thing. If he could make the loss of his
sister mean something, he was always willing to take
that opportunity.

If it could be used to help her, well, that seemed like
a decent enough tribute. At least, the best he had.

When they finished up, they carried their plates inside and put them in the sink. It wasn't all that late, but
Shelby picked up her bag and began to sidle out of the
room. "So just… Any of the rooms upstairs that don't
already have your stuff in them?"

"Yep. I took the first one, because I'm lazy. So any
of the others…"

"Great." She walked slowly up the stairs. "Thank
you. For giving me a place to stay."

"Thank you for… Eating dinner with me."

"Yeah. See you tomorrow."

"See you tomorrow."

And then she disappeared down the hall, and he
couldn't help but feel that he had let an opportunity
slip by. But he couldn't quite say exactly what it was.

Five

When she woke up the next morning, she was breathing hard. Because the lingering effects of the dream that she'd had last night were still making themselves known in her body. She was tingling. All over. Because there had been a moment downstairs right before she had gone up to her room when she had imagined what it would be like if she crossed the space and kissed Kit Carson. She didn't let herself have those thoughts. She'd had them, yes, but she considered them to be intrusive thoughts. In the minute she was aware of them, she shut them down. But he was under her defenses, and he had been nice to talk to, which was maybe the most surprising thing. And that had opened up this floodgate. And her dream had been about a whole lot more than kissing. Her dream had been about scorching, hot, naked…

No. No. She wasn't doing that. She wasn't indulging it. Because she was going to have to go downstairs and head back over to the farmhouse, and she was probably going to see him. And she really didn't want to. She really did not want to have all this in her head when she did see him. That was going to make things impossible, and awful, and she really wanted to avoid impossible and awful.

So she got up, and got dressed, and shoved all of that out of her mind.

As she looked in the mirror, clipping a beaded barrette into her hair, she just stopped for a moment and stared at herself. Why had she shared all of those things with him?

It was being out of her house. Out of her empty house, and realizing that she hadn't done that in far too long. That her life was divided so firmly into this before and after that she had lost a lot of different pieces of herself. She didn't go out with her friends anymore. She'd done that when she was married. Had gone out sometimes with the girls, had dinner, had drinks. She had gone on weekends to vacation houses, and hung out and talked and laughed and ate food. She'd gone on dates with Chuck, and even though she wasn't… Even though she didn't have him, and even though she didn't really want to date, it just represented another thing that she had lost along with him. Because she had stripped herself down almost so she could focus on what she didn't have. Almost so she could hold the loss keenly against her chest and simply cling to it. Because who was she without it.

She hadn't known who she was without Chuck, and somehow that had morphed into her life being about the lack of him. And sitting in this completely different environment with Kit Carson, of all people, had spurred those questions. Maybe because she did know

he knew about loss. And he'd been so surprisingly giving with what he'd said.

Well, don't go romanticizing it.

*You think he's hot. You think he's hot, and that is a
little bit dangerous.*

She hoped that she would listen to her own scolding.

She shoved her pajamas into the duffel bag and went
downstairs. And she didn't get a chance to breathe,
didn't get a reprieve at all, because there was Kit, standing by the coffee maker, a mug in his hand.

"Good morning, sunshine."

"Good morning to you too."

"Busy day of wedding prep ahead," he said. "Though
I figure we ought to check and see what's up with the
power at your place."

"Yes. That would be good."

"Probably the fuse box."

"I wouldn't know where to find it or what to do." She
felt slightly embarrassed by that.

"I was married for a long time. My husband did all
of that. And now my dad does it because he feels sorry
for me and I lean into that."

He laughed. "I have to say, I kind of respect that."

"If you have to go through something terrible you
might as well take all the help that comes your way."

And she had shrunk her life so fiercely, down to
just her family, down to that house, that it seemed fair
enough to take all the sympathy that her parents were
willing to dole out.

The field was bright green in the daylight, the sun il-
luminating each blade of grass, fiery-gold-tipped green
all around them. There were purple flowers scattered
throughout, and she wondered why it suddenly felt like
she was waking up along with the world.

Like she hadn't really breathed or seen these things around her in the years since...

She looked over at Kit. And he was just as striking as all the natural beauty around them. He was wearing a black cowboy hat, a black T-shirt. It outlined his broad shoulders, his muscular chest and slim waist. He was tall. She was tiny next to him. Chuck had only been a couple of inches taller than her.

Kit Carson had always seemed like an entirely different species to her. The kind of man who could just as easily be on the silver screen, he was so much larger than life. He was not the kind of guy you could say vows to, live a life with in a modest home. Dream of warmth and comfort and children with.

He was a mountain. And she was not a mountain climber by nature.

But then, that was the before Shelby, she supposed. She had never needed to climb a mountain.

Why are you thinking about mountain climbing? It sounds sexual.

Yeah. It did. But there was a part of her that was still humming with feelings that were decidedly sexual. So why not?

They didn't speak as they crossed the field. And the only sound when they approached the house was their shoes on the porch steps.

It was a stark contrast to the bachelor den the guys were staying in. It was white and delicate, with a wraparound porch and lace curtains.

The kitchen was all done up in a cheerful yellow, and it made Shelby imagine what it would be like if she lived in a different house. If her view changed. Or her life changed.

There was nothing holding her here. Not really.

There was nothing holding her in place except herself. She could just start over. She could do whatever she wanted. She was still living like Chuck was in her life, but without any of the benefits. She had taken everything but grief from herself.

And it was just so… Starkly clear when she began to imagine what life might look like. She tried to take a breath, but it was hard. Her lungs felt too small. Or maybe it was her that was too small.

Her life.

And Kit Carson was large in the feminine space, and he seemed to fill up everything. Everything around her. Everything she was.

"I'm going to check the mudroom for the fuse box." He slid past her in the kitchen, and her breath caught when his warmth and scent tangled around her.

She didn't take a full breath again until he was out of the room. And then suddenly, all the lights came on. "There," he said, coming in. "That was easy. Just had to find the one that was tripped."

"You probably could've done that last night," she said.

"Yeah. I could have. But then you wouldn't have been able to have steak with me."

She felt herself smiling, felt her cheeks getting warm. Was he flirting with her? She wouldn't even know what to do with that. She never flirted. Not in her life.

Guilt hooked around her insides.

Because he was a forbidden object. She had made him a forbidden object all those years.

It was why she was so antagonistic to him usually.

Because what was wrong with her? She had the most wonderful man. He was everything. He gave her everything.

But Kit had always felt like sex and danger, and she hadn't trusted him.

Hadn't trusted him to care that she was married if they encountered each other in a bar.

And her deepest fear, her deepest unspoken fear, was that if he had ever drawn near to her… She would forget what mattered. She would forget that she had everything with the man at home. And throw it all out for this one burning, bright thing.

You wouldn't, though. Because you didn't. You never did. You never let him get close enough, it never happened. And it still hasn't. Not even after Chuck died.

So there. Her resistance of him, even now, was evidence of her purity. Of the fact that she wouldn't have done it. And it made her feel exponential relief. So there was that.

He might not be forbidden anymore, but her ability to resist him proved something. Something that mattered to her. Something valuable.

"I was going to go over to the barn today and start getting the favors in place and things like that." She looked down the hall toward where she had stashed all the baskets of things.

"I'm happy to help with that," he said.

"You don't have to."

"Yeah. I know. But you know what they say, many hands make light work and all of that."

And she really might as well say yes. Because truth be told, she enjoyed his company, and all of her issues that were swirling around inside her were her issues. So that was that. She didn't need to treat him like he was an enemy. Like she was afraid of him.

In fact… Why not be around him? Why not… Keep testing it?

"Great. I figured I would save some of the bachelor-ette party stuff, in part because I don't really want to live amongst the decorations."

"What?" he asked. "It's not your chosen decor motif?"

"I cannot say that it is. But, my house is more functional than decorative."

"I think I have the same straws at home."

"I don't think you do," she said.

He walked past her and into the hall, where some of the laundry baskets filled with favors were stacked. "Shall we carry these out to the truck?"

"I really should've left them. Instead of unloading them in the house."

"No big deal."

He grabbed them, in one stack, and stuck them in the bed of the pickup truck. Then they got inside the truck, and she felt a little bit less confident than she had before. In her decision-making.

Because suddenly being in such a tight space with him made her feel… Warm. And made her feel very tingly between her legs.

This was dangerous. He was dangerous.

She swallowed hard.

"Let's go."

She was trying to untangle her own motivations. What if she wanted to test herself and see if she was pure? Or did she want to fail the test?

None of it sat comfortably with her.

She felt scratchy.

Very, very scratchy.

She wasn't used to having to figure out her motivations. She was just used to existing. Get up, help her parents with chores around the ranch, work on her beading for a few hours, watch TV. Eat sometimes in between those things. Visit with Juniper maybe. Her life was simple. This wasn't simple. And she didn't know what to do with this more complicated calculation of behavior.

It was a short drive to the barn, and when they got there, they pushed the doors open and found it set for the ceremony. There were chairs, and in the back part of the barn there were tables for dinner.

"Wow. I really didn't think Juniper would ever get married. She was more of a love-them-and-leave-them kind of girl."

"Chance wasn't any different."

"I guess it makes sense that they'd end up together, then. Similar mindsets. And neither of them prepared for it."

He chuckled. "I suppose so."

She and Kit were different. Shelby was a lifer. That was the problem. She had wanted to be committed to one person forever. It was her ideal. It was what sounded like life.

She didn't want to go to bars and hook up. Didn't want to get to know anyone. The idea of having to fall in love all over again was… It actually just sounded exhausting. She had married a man who had known her since she was a child. He understood her. Melding their lives together had been easy. And now she was firmly set in her ways, and… The very idea of trying to figure out how to shape her life around somebody new made her want to lie down.

So maybe she wasn't a lifer anymore. She didn't want to date particularly, for all the afore considered reasons, but… She didn't really want love again either. She couldn't even imagine it.

"I'm glad they found each other. Either way. Expected or not," she said. "It's a… It's a good thing for them."

"Yeah," Kit agreed.

She cleared her throat and started to get all the little tulle-wrapped bubble bottles out of the laundry baskets. With their glorious ribbon curls trailing from them.

"There's supposed to be one for each seat at the table," she said. "Because everybody is supposed to blow bubbles when they walk through to go cut the cake."

"That seems very fluffy for Juniper."

"Yes. But apparently the wedding has made her fluffy. At least, she's fluffy in regard to the decorations. I don't think she would appreciate being called fluffy in general."

"No, of course not."

They got them positioned on the table, and then she looked down the aisle. "There should be everything to put the canopy together in the back of the truck."

"A canopy?"

"Yes. She's going to walk under a canopy to go down the aisle. We made a frame for it and got some tulle to wrap around it. I know how it's supposed to go together. She didn't say that we needed to get it set up, but I think we could."

"Sounds like a lot of work."

"Well. My sister is being high-maintenance, and I guess she's entitled to it. She was the bridesmaid at my wedding, and it was pretty damned high-maintenance."

"So this is payback?"

"I believe it is payback in part, yes."

They went out to the truck, and she found the metal poles in the bed, and then she took the carefully wrapped tulle out as well, and with Kit's help they took it into the barn. She directed him, telling him where to lay the poles out in the aisle, because she had seen Juniper's sketches of it all.

She had done some beading on the tulle, just to add some sparkle. To add a little bit of them.

She had done the same for Juniper's veil.

"Is there something to anchor these?"

"Oh, right. I forgot. There's a couple of cement forms in the bed of the truck."

"I will get them."

He left, and returned a few moments later, with big cement bricks in his hands. The poles were meant to sit down inside them, and they held them in place. They were really heavy, and he made lifting them look like it was a breeze.

And she couldn't help but watch. The play of his muscles. His forearms, his biceps. She watched as he made every trip, and she just stood and kind of stared. Openly.

He was… He was glorious. Kit Carson was the most beautiful man she had ever seen, and she felt it was a traitorous thought, one that made her feel as much guilt as it did excitement. And it brought her back to her dream. Because in her dream, she had crossed the kitchen last night instead of retiring to her room. In her dream, she had put her hand on his face and kissed his mouth, and then he had put his hands all over her body. He had taken her against the wall, his arousal hard and thick and devastating, and she had screamed her pleasure in a way that she had always thought was fake, and found nowhere this side of ridiculously overblown in movies and porn.

And hey, it probably wasn't to be found anywhere

outside of adult entertainment. Because she had dreamed it. It hadn't really happened.

She had certainly never experienced anything like that.

She shifted uncomfortably.

This was the problem. She didn't have experience in the sense that she had only been with one person. So her experience wasn't broad. But she'd had all kinds of sex. Years of it. Steady. Because she had been in a consistent relationship for so many years.

And when you were in a long-term relationship, you tried things. All the things.

It was such a scary line to walk. Because she had no idea what it would be like with someone else, but she also knew what was possible. And she really wanted to test the limits of what was possible with Kit. Or rather, her libido did. Or better, her more critically thinking self didn't want to do that. But sometimes when she looked at him, it felt like her critical self did not exist. It was just her replaced by a horny monster that she didn't recognize.

And again, she had to question what her motivation had been in doing this with him.

And why she was watching his muscles.

Did she want to resist? Or did she want to throw herself headfirst into something different?

Into something new.

"Can I help you with something?"

She blinked. And she realized she was standing there gaping.

"No. No. Sorry. I'm just… My sister is getting married. I'm just a little bit overcome. Emotions. I'm very sentimental."

She actually kind of was. She knew that most people wouldn't characterize her that way, but a woman who still had all of her late husband's belongings could hardly be considered anything but sentimental, she supposed. A woman who hand-beaded a bunch of details that no one would ever see, but she would know were there, could not be characterized as anything but sentimental.

"All right. Let's start getting this thing up." They started placing the poles, the supports and the different sections.

He found a ladder in the back of the barn, and they set it up, him working by stretching as tall as he could go and using the full length of his arms, and her needing the ladder every step of the way.

She showed him how the tulle was supposed to wrap around the frame, and she had to admit, he made a very skilled laborer.

"You would be handy to have around the house," she said, not thinking until the words escaped.

He looked at her, lifting a brow. "Would I?"

"To reach tall things. And open jars."

"I do know how to do both of those things."

"That's all I meant by it."

"I didn't think you meant anything else."

"Somehow I don't believe you."

"That is between you and your God. And not my concern."

"Everybody else is coming up today."

"Yep."

"I guess we better get that bachelor and bachelorette party thing ready."

"Definitely."

He took a step toward her, and she found herself scrambling back as if he had physically touched her.

He didn't react strongly, but it was the slight jolt in his frame that told her she had surprised him with her response.

"See you later, then. At the barbecue."

"Yeah. See you then."

And she had never needed to get away from another person so badly in her entire life. Especially not while feeling the intense desire to stay with him.

Six

Everybody gathered around the catered barbecue just outside the newly decorated barn. Family was here, and there were many friends thrown into the mix. The pre-wedding party was a big one, and he had a feeling tonight was going to be a pretty wild celebration.

But for now, the men and women were joined together having a potluck, and it was pretty damned good.

But he was still fixated on what had happened between him and Shelby earlier.

She had jumped away from him like his fingertips were on fire and he might burn her.

You know why.

Yeah. He could say that nothing had been happening. It hadn't been, strictly.

And yet, everything had been.

There was an undercurrent between the two of them that was difficult to ignore.

And need that was growing in his gut.

And it was complicated by the fact that their siblings were getting married, and she was vulnerable. He could see it. She was at a crossroads in her life, and she was looking for something, anything to hold on to.

And he was all right being a temporary mistake. Hell, maybe that was what she needed. But he couldn't be anything else for her.

So he needed to watch himself. And he wasn't all that good at watching himself. She was sitting with her sister, talking and laughing and eating, and he found himself a little bit overly fascinated by her.

"I can't believe how much you got done," Chance said. "You didn't have to do all the work. We were planning on getting some of it done tonight and tomorrow."

"Yeah. But I'm the best man. I wanted to do it for you."

"I have all these brothers. What good are they if they don't all help out?"

"Well, Shelby was in here doing it all, and I figured I shouldn't leave her to her own devices."

Chance looked at him, a little bit too sharp. "No. I suppose not. Awfully nice of you to assist."

He looked back over at his brother. "I think we both know that I'm not that nice."

"Yeah. So... Don't mess things up with my sister-in-law, please? She's been through enough."

Irritation stabbed at Kit. Primarily because his brother wasn't off base on things. But it was still offensive that he felt he had to tell him that.

"Yeah, I wasn't really planning on closing the loop in the family tree."

Chance chuckled. "Well. See that you don't. Honestly, the issue isn't... The issue is just that you and I both know that you don't want anything permanent. And she's been through a lot."

"Who hasn't?"

"Good point. Look, man, if the opportunity comes up for a little bit of fun, and that's what she wants, that's different."

"Are you warning me away from your sister-in-law, or are you giving me permission to have a one-night stand with her?"

"I'm actually not doing either one. You're both grown people. She gets a say in things. I am expressing my preference for you not making my life difficult."

"Got it. You don't want your wife to get mad at you."

"Correct. Or, my wife's grandfather, who scares the ever-loving shit out of me."

"Fair. Look, it's nothing I didn't think of already."

"How long have you two…?"

"Nothing's going on between us."

"No, I get that, but you're into her."

He shrugged. "I just think she's hot."

"Right. Well. Hey, whatever. Things are set up for camping tonight?"

"Hell yeah. Epic camping. It's going to be great."

"Good. After we play pool."

"Of course. We gotta make use of the house too. I just figured a little bit of sleeping in the woods was also in order."

"You thought of everything."

"I try to."

And he realized how true that was. He did try to think of everything. To the best of his ability. He tried to take care of everyone. Protect them.

He just knew how desperately short a person could

fall with those things. And it haunted him. He had a feeling it always would.

But tonight was about celebrating his brother. Sending him off into a new life.

Kit might never be able to see having a new life of his own, but he could definitely be happy that Chance would have one.

Definitely.

The party in the farmhouse was raucous. Luckily, their mother hadn't planned on staying in the farmhouse for this part, which was good, because if she had, they all would've died of embarrassment.

The alcohol was flowing freely, and Juniper, their friends from school and a couple of the EMTs whom Juniper worked with were all giddy and lessening their inhibitions. Shelby had opted for sobriety since she was running the whole show, and felt like she wouldn't be a great host if she let herself get too loose.

Are you just afraid of imbibing too much with Kit in the vicinity?

Well. It didn't matter if Kit was in the vicinity or not. He was out with his brothers, so it didn't matter. She was safe. They now had a buffer of all these people.

Still. Keeping her wits about her was probably the better part of valor.

But Juniper was living it up. She had her phallic crown placed on her head, and had a bright pink drink with a straw of the same color.

"This is immature," she said, lifting her glass to Shelby.

"I know," Shelby said. "That was the idea."

"Well, excellently done," Lydia, one of Juniper's friends, said, reclining back on the couch and laughing.

They had all put on club dresses, as if they were going out for a night on the town, and not just sitting in a farmhouse playing games with a group of women. But it was fun. Shelby hadn't done anything like this for a long time. It was fun to dress up just for herself. Just for a group of women. She had gone a little bit overboard. She was wearing a short emerald green minidress that had lived in the back of her closet for at least ten years. It did not fit the way that it once had, and her more generous curves made the hemline ride up higher, and it clung to her breasts and her stomach in a way that made her self-conscious now. Except… She looked at herself in the reflection of the window just quickly. If she saw it on another woman, she would think the woman looked great. So why she was being hard on herself she didn't know. Maybe it was just that harsh reminder of the passage of time. That she wasn't an effortlessly willowy teenager anymore, and that she didn't have a husband who just loved her through all the changes.

Love yourself, then.

That was the point of tonight. All the women were dressed up, just dressed up to please themselves in this group.

And yet, Kit was on her mind.

She really needed to get a grip.

This night reminded her a lot of her own bachelorette party, and she felt guilt at the way she seemed unable to separate Juniper's happiness from her own all those years ago. Maybe it was normal. Maybe it would've been like this no matter what. It was just that it should've felt happy, and not ominous.

Not strange and sad. This heavy reminder of the ways in which life can take unexpected turns.

She suddenly felt outside of the festivities. Being the sober one probably didn't help.

"Next game," she said.

She moved quickly into explaining the rules of the card game that had them matching up certain phrases with other phrases, creating the most outrageous combination that they could.

It quickly had everyone dissolving into fits of laughter, and she had beauty queen sashes with dubious honors printed on them to pass around to the women she deemed winners.

It was going on one in the morning, and they had music pumping, and everyone started dancing.

And Shelby couldn't escape that feeling that she was just... Standing outside, looking in. Participating, yes, but not really there also.

She could remember so keenly the night before her wedding.

Young and so filled with hope for the future.

And then... And then they'd been married. And it had been good. But there had been hardship. Figuring out how to pay bills in this small town, how to get enough work to cover it all, while knowing that they were lucky they had the house on her parents' property to fall back on.

The fact they hadn't been able to get pregnant, and didn't have health insurance so they hadn't had the luxury of going to a doctor and finding out why. They just kept hoping it would work.

It was supposed to. They were young, and they were healthy. And hell, they'd spent their teenage years trying desperately not to get pregnant, doubling up on all manner of contraception to make sure that it didn't happen before they were ready, and dammit, why couldn't it happen when they were?

They'd been happy still. It was just... She was ready. For that next part of her life.

They'd been saving. Saving enough money to go and get answers. To figure out what they needed to do. And then the accident had happened and...

She blinked, suddenly coming back to the moment.

It was like she had been watching a movie of her own life. From the night of that party to tonight. And it was... Jarring. To come back to this. Her sister was just starting down that road now. And Shelby had already walked on it.

She hoped it was better for Juniper in ten years. She really did.

But she suddenly just felt old, and like she really wasn't part of this for a reason.

There were no more structured games happening, people were just dancing, and she had a feeling they were all going to get sleepy soon.

She melted into the background of the room, and then slipped quietly out the back door. It was warm outside, not as hot and sticky as it had been inside, but pleasant, with a cool breeze blowing over the field.

She closed her eyes and let it wash over her as she walked off the porch down into the grass.

She felt tears slip down her face, and she didn't bother to wipe them away.

It was just a moment by herself. Just a moment to let all of this wash over her. Wash through her.

Just a moment.

And when she opened her eyes, she saw a figure, dark on the velvet blue horizon. And she knew immediately who it was, standing one hundred paces from her, with the bachelor pad to his back.

She didn't say anything. She just stood there, regarding him. He knew it was her. She didn't need to ask.

They had both left their respective parties.

She wondered why he had. Wondered why tonight was too much for him.

She took a step toward him, at the same time he took one toward her.

Until they had closed almost all the distance between them.

And she didn't know what she should do. If she should speak, or if they were past words.

They had talked last night when talking wasn't what either of them had wanted, and she'd known it. They had talked today, when all she had wanted to do was look at his fine form.

Sure, there was a lot of talking that could be done. A lot of concern about consequences and fallout. Disclaimers and things like that. But she had a feeling they both knew them. That they both lived in the pocket of the same sorts of concerns and there was no reason to put voice to them. No reason to break the spell of the moment with language that could never capture what was happening inside her anyway.

The truth of the matter was she wanted Kit Carson.

She had wanted him when she was a middle school girl and he was in high school, standing across the field from her looking like everything she had never thought she'd ever see in real life. She had wanted him as a grown woman, her heart firmly engaged in her marriage, her vows happily and meaningfully spoken. She had looked at him and seen the promise of desire fulfilled in a way she had never imagined. And she had turned away from it, because she had promised she would. Because love outweighed desire.

She had wanted him amid all the dark lonely days since, and hadn't even let herself fantasize about him because she was still testing herself. And why?

Suddenly, it was like she had let go of a burden that she'd been carrying all this time.

Why. Why was she still carrying it? What was she trying to prove? Why was she still trying to be… Strong? To be better? Why? What did it matter? What did it matter what she did? What did it matter whom she was with now? Her house was empty, her bed was empty. He was dead. Death had done them part. That was it, it was the end. And she wanted so badly in some ways for it to not be the end that she just couldn't…

But Kit was here. And she was so tired of being better than this fire that had ignited itself in her veins all those years ago.

She wasn't better than it. She was it. Entirely. Utterly. And tonight she wanted to burn.

She was the one who made the move. She knew that she would have to be. It was a fraction. A breath. But he saw it for what it was. And suddenly, she was in his arms. Strong and certain and hot. His chest was a wall of muscle, and she pressed her palms flat to it, felt his heartbeat raging there. He was tall, so tall, and she was disoriented by the height difference, but in the best way. She felt small and fragile, but it didn't undermine her. She was so used to being strong because she had to be. And right this moment, it didn't feel like she had to be. It didn't feel like it at all.

It felt like he was holding her up, it felt like he was holding her in place. It felt like he might be holding all the world on those broad shoulders, just for a moment, just for her.

She smoothed her palms up and down, feeling the hard delineation of his pectoral muscles and reveling in the answering kick of need between her legs.

Yes. She was a grown woman. And she knew what the hell she wanted.

She wanted Kit Carson.

No explanation. No apologies.

No disclaimers.

And he seemed to be of the same mind.

And just when she thought she might die of the frenzy that was whipping up inside her, he lowered his head. And finally, finally that hard, uncompromising mouth was softening over hers.

It was demanding, and he parted her lips roughly, sliding his tongue against hers as if he was voracious, hungry. Starving.

She whimpered, wrapping her arms around his neck and pressing her breasts flush against his chest.

And then she felt herself being lifted off the ground, like she weighed nothing, and she supposed to him maybe she did. And all of her insecurities from earlier tonight just melted away. Because her body fit against his. Because the years had changed her into the sort of woman who could withstand this. Because the years had brought her to this moment. Stripped away everything that had ever prevented it whether she wanted it to or not.

She was here. And she was the woman whom she was. The woman who could have it.

So she had to honor it. The changes. The aging. The weight. The loss. She had to honor it, because it was why she was here. And she couldn't hate herself, or second-guess, or warn herself off about consequences.

Because it was like this moment had been destined to unfold from the beginning.

And she refused to feel guilt over that thought either.

If the moment felt like fate, she was going to take that too. Because no one had asked her if this was what she wanted. If this was where she wanted to stand. If she had been able to pick her own life she would be back at home with her husband and the children they'd had years before, but she had been denied all of that, so she would have this. Unreservedly.

She would have it.

For the Shelby who stood here now. The Shelby with the thicker ass and thighs and rounded stomach. That Shelby. The Shelby who had loved and lost and felt so broken she didn't think she could ever stand again.

The Shelby who had always done the right thing in the face of temptation because doing right and being right and loving right had mattered.

But now only this mattered. Not tomorrow, and not yesterday. Only this.

And he was everything. Everything she had never allowed herself to fantasize about and more.

His lips were hot and all-consuming, and she felt his kiss burn through her like a wildfire. Burn through her without compromise.

She throbbed between her legs, excitement blooming in her midsection, her breasts growing heavy. Her nipples demanding his touch.

She had never kissed another man. And yet, it felt like because it was Kit it just fit.

And it was a good moment for it. For him. Because

she knew what she wanted. She knew what to demand of him. She knew where she wanted to be touched and how.

And suddenly, he moved his big hands down her back, down to cup her ass, and he squeezed her hard, commanding and possessive in a way she never experienced, and she realized that even if she might know what to demand, there were other things that he knew.

And suddenly, that feeling of inexperience, the lack of understanding of how he might touch her. Taste her. Of what he might choose, made her feel giddy with excitement and nervous like she was a virgin.

Because she knew where this was going. Wherever they had to go. Wherever they had to go to make it happen, she knew that this wasn't ending in the field. That it wasn't ending at a kiss.

With her legs wrapped firmly around his waist, he held her and began to walk back toward the bachelor house.

"You should put me down," she whispered, breaking the silence for the first time, and she regretted it. Because she had broken it with her uncertainty, and she didn't want to bring uncertainty into this.

But he did nothing but chuckle against her mouth, the way his breath filled her causing her to shiver.

"I'm good."

She realized that they were going into the house. "Everyone's camping," he said as he walked them up the porch, and she disentangled her legs from around his waist, feeling a little bit silly that he was carrying her like she was a koala bear.

But all he did was lift her up fully into his arms, opening the door and closing it behind them, before kissing her hard right there in the entry, deep and unending.

"This is what you wanted, right? You didn't want steak. You didn't want to banter with me about ribbon curls, or just stand there watching me drink a beer. Or even have me open yours. This is what you wanted."

She nodded slowly. "And it's what you wanted too."

"Back before we even had a situation," he said, the words rough and ground out.

And the explosion of desire that ignited in her was too all-consuming to deny. "Thank God," she said, and she grabbed his face and kissed him. With everything she had. With everything pent up and brilliant in her.

She kissed him. She kissed him because she didn't have another choice. She kissed him because he was everything. She kissed him because if she didn't she might die.

And then she realized they were moving again, that he was carrying her up the stairs.

"Good thing you chose the closest bedroom," she said.

He laughed, but it sounded strange. He pushed the door open, and then slammed it shut behind them, pushing the lock. "Just in case. You never know who's going to wimp out and try to use the indoor plumbing."

"Or notice that you're gone," she said softly.

"They are pretty wasted," he said. "And there are a lot of us."

"Yeah. My sister and her friends were pretty wasted too." She blinked. "You're not wasted." She just needed to check. Because if Kit Carson needed to be drawn to have sex with her, that was a little bit embarrassing.

"Haven't had a drop."

"Me neither."

And right then, as they stared at each other in the dimly lit room, she wondered if that was why neither of them had had any booze. Because if they were drunk, it would've dulled their senses for this. Would've created a gray area where one of them might have wanted to refuse because the other one was compromised. Or, they both could've been sloppy drunk, but then they wouldn't have remembered it. And there was one thing she knew for certain. This was her only shot. Because it was complicated, and neither of them wanted that.

This was just the fulfillment of a fantasy. And it was one she really needed. Because she was trying to find a way to move on. Trying to find a way to make a change, and this was it. It was what she needed. But it wasn't going to be a regular thing.

It was a singular gift that she was giving herself before she decided... If she was going to move. To change her scenery forever. To get herself out of the echoes of the life that she had before.

So yeah, she wanted to be present for it. And like he was reading her mind, he reached out and flicked the lights on. It was bright. Bracingly so, but she understood. He wanted to do this with everything lit up. With no mystery, with no fuzzy edges. And she found it was what she wanted too.

"Take your clothes off, Kit Carson," she said. "Because I have been wondering what was under them for far too long."

His mouth quirked up into a grin, and he set her down slowly on the edge of the bed. Her heart hammered at the base of her throat, throbbing insistently.

She shivered as he reached up and began to undo the buttons on his shirt. His chest was well muscled, covered with dark hair, and she squirmed in her seat, as her center throbbed, moisture flooding her, because she was just so damned hot for him.

Women weren't visual her ass. She could get off just looking at Kit Carson.

He shrugged the shirt off his broad shoulders, and her mouth went dry.

He was masculine perfection. His abs would have been highly regarded back when her family had first settled the area. They could've cleaned their clothes on them.

And he had those lines, narrowing down beneath his jeans, pointing down to that part of him that had hardened into an insistent bulge pushing at the front of his denim.

She moaned. She couldn't help it. And he laughed. But not her. He slowly undid the buckle on his belt, undid his jeans and kicked his shoes off as he shrugged his pants and underwear down. As he revealed the whole rest of his body to her, and damn. Just damn.

She had really never. Not even in her wildest fantasies. He was beautiful. Thick and long and just gorgeous. She had a healthy appreciation for the male form in general. She liked the look of a naked man.

But she liked the look of this naked man better than she had ever liked anything in all her life.

And then he did something wholly unexpected. He knelt down slowly on the floor in front of the bed, and looked up at her. The expression in his eyes was wicked, the curve of his lips a sin.

He smoothed his hands up along her thighs, beneath the hem of her dress. And he found her panties, grabbing them and dragging them slowly down, removing them, but leaving her shoes still. Then he moved his hands to the insides of her knees, parted her legs, and she felt her face ignite as he examined her, his expression one of filthy awe.

"Do you have any idea," he said, "how long I've wanted to taste you? You make me so hard. Do you know that? Do you know that I fantasized about you? I have a policy. I don't do the married-woman thing. Sorry. But it's been that long. And you tested me."

"Well, I didn't do the infidelity thing. So it's a good thing you didn't try."

"But now it's all good. And I have wanted you... I have wanted you."

He pushed her dress up, exposing her completely, and his gaze only seemed to get hungrier. Then he kissed the inner part of her thigh, and she started to shake.

She couldn't believe it was him. Kit Carson. Right there. Looking at her like that. Like he wanted to devour her.

And she knew he was going to. All of her nerve endings were at attention. Her whole body on high alert.

His mouth moved higher, pressing soft kisses on her thighs, and then, then, he put his mouth right over her, her center, and she let out a short, shocked sound, because even though she had known it was coming, the reality of it was just so much more. His mouth was hot and confident, and his tongue went deep inside her before he slid it over the most sensitive part of her, then sucked her deep into his mouth. He shoved his hands beneath her ass, and brought her hard against him, as uncompromising here as he was everywhere else.

And she lost herself. In the way his shoulders held her legs wide, and the rough feel of his fingers, digging into her flesh. And the white-hot pleasure that his mouth gave her. She lost herself utterly. Completely. She clung to him, and she felt her climax, quick and impossibly intense, building inside her, and she wanted to resist it. Wanted to stop it. Because once she had one, she wasn't going to have another, and she had really wanted it when he was in her.

But there was no fighting it. It was too good. Too enticing and tempting, so she let go. And she couldn't help it. She screamed. She rolled her hips in rhythm with the waves of pleasure that were moving through her. He rose up on his feet, growled and grabbed hold of her hips, lifting her back farther onto the bed as he covered her. He ripped her dress down, and then off completely, throwing it onto the floor. She was still wearing her shoes.

He kissed her. And she returned the kiss, wrapping her arms around his neck and giving him everything she had. He covered her, his chest hair rough against her breasts. And she moved her hands all over his body. His chest, his back, feeling all the muscles there, down to his ass. She parted her legs, encouraging him between them. And she could feel the hard press of his arousal against the entrance to her body. She moaned, rubbing against him, slippery with need, but he didn't give her what she wanted. Not quite yet. He lowered his head, and took her nipple into his mouth, sucking hard.

And she ignited.

He sucked her hard, and she wrapped her legs around his, arching against him, trying to assuage the ache between her legs. She was so close. Again. Already.

"Please," she whispered.

And then he thrust home.

She gasped. He was so big. And she hadn't been with anyone in a while. Years. So it was a little bit of a shock.

Sex toys were not Kit Carson. He was bigger and more. Hot and insistent. And he was in control.

He grabbed her hands and held them up over her

head as he began to establish a steady, hard rhythm that rocked her. Utterly. Mercilessly.

She looked up into his eyes, looked right at his face. The lights were on. And she wouldn't let herself forget. As if she could have.

She was with Kit. Kit.

And then, it was like everything around her was fire, and so was she.

Her climax ripped through her. Her need overcoming her as she cried out his name. As she felt wave after wave of desire pulsing through her.

And then he growled her name on his lips as he shuddered and shook. And if there was one thing that was better than finding her own release in Kit's arms, it was watching him find it in hers.

This man, the object of her darkest and most shameful fantasies, was surrendering to her.

To them. To this.

It was everything. He was everything.

And they were something else entirely.

And when it was over, she lay there, sweat-slicked, her heart pounding so hard she thought it was going to escape her chest.

"Oh, well," she said.

Because it was all she could say. They weren't wrong. They weren't exaggerating, those movies. You could lose yourself, lose your head. End up screaming and not care who heard you.

It was a revelation.

One she had always been a little bit afraid she could only ever have with him.

And there it was.

"Good for you?"

"Extremely," she said.

They lay there, and she looked at him, at his body.

And she was sad. Because she could've... Well, she could want this for a long time. She could want this forever.

That made something like an alarm bell go off inside her. She wasn't supposed to be thinking things like that. Wasn't supposed to be thinking in those terms. Because there was no point to it. None at all. They both knew what it was. "Thank you," she said. "But I really should get back. Because..."

"I know. Same reason I should."

"You know that this can't..."

"I think we both know exactly what this was. That's why we didn't talk about it beforehand, right?"

She nodded. "Yeah. So... I'll see you at the wedding tomorrow."

He nodded slowly. "Yeah. See you at the wedding."

Seven

It was tempting to be smug when he was the only one who woke up the next morning without a hangover. Except… He couldn't say with confidence that he didn't have a hangover of some variety. Of the Shelby Sohappy variety, in point of fact. Because that woman had turned him inside out. Had left him completely wrecked.

He had had a whole lot of sex in his life, but he never had anything quite like that.

He couldn't explain it. It was just her. The look of her, the feel of her, the taste of her.

"Hey, assholes," he shouted, experiencing a great amount of satisfaction when all of his brothers groaned. "Chance is getting married today, so you all better deal with the hangover situation."

"Do you think yelling at us is going to help?" Boone asked.

"I'm not trying to help."

"Why are you not hungover?" Chance asked.

"Superior genetics?"

"We have the same genetics."

It was his brother's day. He should be thinking of best-man things and being responsible, maybe even being happy perchance, but instead his mind was firmly fixed on the events of the night before. Of Shelby, and what it had felt like to finally touch her. To finally kiss her. To finally be with her. She had been everything, and they had been incendiary. It had been more than he had ever imagined being with her could be, and he had imagined quite a bit. She had been a revelation. There had been a connection between them for years. An ember that had burned bright, and last night it had exploded into a flame that had threatened to consume them both.

He knew that he was the first man she'd been with since her husband's death. He felt that. Like it was a weight to carry, a burden, and yet, he couldn't say he minded. Not really. If someone was going to be that man, it was better that it was him. Because he had wanted her for a hell of a long time, and there had been nothing he could do about it.

Well. Not again. And today they needed to focus on his brother and her sister. That's what it was all about.

So he rousted those idiots he called brothers, and got them fed, got everybody's suits ready to go.

Boone looked at him as he finished tying his tie. "Where were you last night?"

"What do you mean? I was with you."

"You see, I wasn't all that drunk. I noticed you leaving. And I noticed that you didn't come back for a couple of hours. So, where were you?"

"Maybe I was working on a surprise for Chance."

"Yeah. Maybe you were. Maybe you were working on a surprise for Chance, and that's all legit. But… I have my suspicions."

He narrowed his eyes. "Do you, now?"

"I do. I think that you found the maid of honor."

"And why do you think that?" he asked, his voice flat. Dangerous.

"Because you want her. Because you have wanted her for a record number of years. I think we all know that."

"That's interesting that *you* know that, Boone. Because *I* don't know that."

"Liar. Fucking liar. You want her. You know it. And I think something finally happened between the two of you."

"I think that I didn't ask for your opinion, Boone. That's what I think. So maybe you should take a little bow tie and get ready to go stand at the front of the church. Otherwise, we might recast you. You would make a charming flower girl."

"I would," Boone said. "I'm happy to tiptoe through the tulips anytime. But none of that deflects from the fact that I think you're a liar."

"Well. That is brotherly love, isn't it? You think that I'm a liar. What an asshole."

"Yeah. I'm an asshole. But hey, don't worry about it. I'm sure that Chance would be thrilled to know that you hooked up with his sister-in-law."

"Chance doesn't need to know. Does he?"

"Is that a confession?"

"You think what you think. What does it matter what I say or not?"

"Nothing. Just…"

"Yeah. I know. Be careful. Be careful with her because… All those reasons."

"Yes. All those reasons. Unless you're about to make like Chance and get everything together and make forever…"

"I get that you think she might want forever, but she doesn't. Not with me." He wasn't anything like her husband, and he didn't want to be. He wasn't ever going to be a forever guy, and if her past actions indicated anything… She was a forever type of woman. "That was just old business. Needed to be taken care of. It had been deferred way too long. Believe me. She doesn't want forever. She's had that. You know how it is. You lose someone… Nothing is ever the same again."

Boone got a faraway look in his eye. "Yeah. I know that." He cleared his throat. "I also know sometimes you…miss your chance with someone and regret it."

He didn't know what his brother was referencing, but it was clear something else was going on with Boone. And also that Boone didn't want to go into detail about it, or he would have.

"It wasn't about having a chance for me. It was just attraction."

"Whatever. I hope you had a good night."

"I fucking did."

"Good, then. As long as all involved were satisfied, I assume the day will go off without a hitch."

"It's not my day. It's Chance's."

"True. True."

And he kept that in mind as they assembled for the wedding. Kept it firmly in mind when the bridesmaids showed up. Kept it firmly in mind when Shelby, wearing a red dress that scooped low and showed off her stunning breasts, came to stand near him, because they would be walking down the aisle together.

"Hope you slept well," he said.

"Just fine."

"Did they notice you were gone?"

"When was I gone?" She looked at him with unfath-omable dark eyes.

"Guess you weren't."

That was how they were going to play it. Like it hadn't happened. Even though they both knew it had. Even though he had a feeling they were both replaying scenes of the night before as they stood there regarding each other.

"Yeah. I know."

They linked arms, and walked down the aisle, taking their place where the bride and groom would stand.

The wedding was beautiful. Went off without a hitch. And he was glad. He was glad for Chance. Because the man deserved some happiness.

And Boone was right. Unless Kit was willing to make changes—big changes—unless he was willing to abandon his entire life, he had to leave Shelby alone. He just did.

But it looked like Shelby was more than willing to leave him alone. At the reception she danced with just about everyone but him. A knot of jealousy formed in his stomach, but it should be gratitude. Gratitude for the fact that she knew what had happened between them was temporary.

He just wished it was more than once.

Maybe. But it wasn't.

And when they saw Chance and Juniper off, away from the barn, away on their honeymoon, he should have felt glad. Grateful.

Because their little dance together was done. Because the families could go back to being about as distant as they'd ever been. They would see each other occasionally. But not all that often.

Yeah. This was over. He had scratched the itch that was Shelby Sohappy.

And he should be glad that it had gone off without a hitch.

Shelby couldn't believe it. She really could not believe it. In a deep, profound way that had her ignoring the problem for four whole weeks. Until it happened again. She hadn't seen Kit Carson since the wedding. She had been telling herself that she was fine with that. But all the while, there was a growing unease, a growing sense of disbelief that had taken root inside her. She had a feeling it wasn't the only thing that had taken root. But it didn't seem possible. She had tried to get pregnant for years. Granted, she didn't really know what the source of her inability to conceive with Chuck had been. She had known that it could have been him, but she had just felt like the odds were with her. Women's bodies were tricky things. And it had seemed reasonable that the issue was her.

Yeah. It seemed completely reasonable, completely standard, really, that the issue would be her. They hadn't gotten to find out yet, though. And then in the end they hadn't. But this was two missed periods. Two. And that was two more than she had ever missed in her entire life.

She'd never been pregnant. Not once. She was as regular as cows that needed feeding, and there was no doubt in her mind that this missed period was not a coincidence. How could it be? How the hell could it be? And she knew that what she needed to do was talk to her sister. Confess everything. Figure out what the hell she was supposed to do. She wanted a baby. She had wanted a fresh start.

Those two things hadn't really gone together in her mind. Because, of course, she had wanted to be a mother in context with the marriage she had with Chuck. She hadn't really considered being a single mother. But here she was…

You don't know if you'll even be able to keep it. Eight weeks. It's not secure yet. You could just leave it. You could just keep ignoring it. You could not talk to anyone about it.

Except, she was already dialing her sister. Already time to find out where she was. As an EMT, Juniper was often on call, or in the far reaches of Lone Rock and the surrounding areas.

"Are you around?" she asked without introduction.

"Yeah. Pretty around. Are you at home?"

"Yes. I need to talk to you. I mean I really need to talk to you, and I need you to not tell Chance."

"Well, this is a little bit disconcerting. And I'm not sure what to do with it."

"Come over. Don't make any promises yet… Just come over."

Shelby started pacing. Pacing the halls of this house that still had her husband's clothes in it. It had been a whole thing coming back home after the wedding. Sleeping in the bed that she had shared with her husband, having gone to bed with someone else. And not just anyone else, Kit Carson, who had been a source of guilt and shame for her for all these years.

She had known that she needed to make a change, and she still hadn't done it. She had just sat in whatever all this was. Had just sat in her… Her fundamental misery, and she still hadn't made a move. Maybe this was her move. Maybe it was an answer to prayers that she hadn't had a voice for, hadn't had concrete words for.

"I'm here," she heard her sister call through the front door.

She scrambled back to the front of the house. "Thank God."

"What the hell is going on, Shelby?"

"I think I'm pregnant."

"Holy shit," Juniper said, staring at her.

"Yeah." She chewed the edge of her thumbnail. "I know."

"*How* pregnant?" Juniper asked, her eyes narrowed.

She felt heat creeping up the back of her neck. "Why is that the question?"

Juniper's expression went granite. "I think you know why."

Shelby coughed. "Well, that would be two months," she said.

"Coincides with my wedding date, doesn't it?"

"You can't tell Chance yet."

Juniper looked too all knowing, and it hurt. "Kit's the father?"

"You know he is," Shelby said, feeling defeated and seen and helpless. She knew that Juniper knew. That was the thing. Maybe that was why she wanted to talk to her sister more than anybody. Because she just already knew. And no matter how much Shelby had ever tried to deny it, Juniper had known that Shelby was attracted to Kit.

"You're pregnant though," Juniper said. "Really."

"I haven't taken a test. I've never missed a period. In all the time that I was married, and we tried. We were trying to have a baby, but I never got pregnant. Not one time. I was never late… Nothing."

"You didn't think about protection with Kit?"

"I didn't think about *anything*," she said, throwing her hands out wide. "If I had stopped to think about anything, I probably wouldn't have done it."

That was a lie. But it made her sound a little bit more thoughtful. A little bit more balanced and sane. So she was going to go ahead and go with that.

"Right. Well. You have to tell him."

"Why? He doesn't want… He doesn't want to have kids. He doesn't want to settle down."

"Neither did Chance."

"I don't think that I'm going to be able to contrive to give Kit amnesia so that he can forget all of his trauma and fall in love with me." Just saying that made her cringe.

"Anyway. I'm not in love with him. He's… He was this vaguely bad object that I had in my life and I… I don't know that I want to get married again. I don't know. I don't think that I love anyone else. I loved Chuck for all of my life. And it was special. I had this… This weird thing with Kit. And I hated it. I've never really known him, I've never especially liked him, and I just wanted to tear his clothes off. From the minute I first saw him. It's never been okay with me to feel that way. It's never been what I wanted. This thing with Kit has never been what I wanted. I do want a baby. I was even moving away, Juniper."

"You can't do that," Juniper said. "You can't give me a little niece or nephew and then move away."

She realized when she said that the moving thing wasn't feasible. Or fair. Moving away when she was having a baby. What would her parents think? Her grandparents? Well. What the hell were they going to think when they found out she was pregnant without a husband? That was the whole thing. It was a whole damn thing that she hadn't thought she would be dealing with when she was twenty-eight years old.

"Kit needs to know," Juniper said. "You need to give him a chance to do something."

"He's a Carson. He's an alpha male. What do you think he's going to do? He's going to storm in here and try to take over my life."

"So, tell him no. You're an alpha female, Shelby. And you know that. Why are you acting like he's going to run you over? He's not. You've got to handle this with honesty. You have to."

"Why?" Shelby said, knowing that she sounded petulant. "Why do we have to be grown-up about this?"

"Because you're going to have a baby. Maybe. The first thing you need to do is take a pregnancy test."

"Do you know if they expire?"

"I… I don't."

"Well, I have a few. In the bathroom. I was just avoiding them. I've been avoiding everything. I've been trying to pretend that it didn't happen. That all of it… Just didn't happen."

"Very healthy. But, it might be time to take a different approach. But I'm here. If you want someone here. I can also go if you don't want me here."

"I'm afraid to know," Shelby said.

"What exactly are you afraid of?"

"That it will be positive. That it will be negative." The idea made her want to burst into tears. Both of them. Seeing the results at all.

"Well, it's going to be one of those things. I'm sorry. That's just… A fact. But you want to know, right? So that you can start figuring out what you're going to do."

"I don't want to." She was about to say something

along the lines of she had been working way too hard to figure out what she was going to do for too long, since she had been thrust into a change she hadn't asked for. But she hadn't been. She had just been sitting. She hadn't chosen to lose Chuck. It wasn't the consequence of anything. It was an accident. A car accident that had changed her entire life in the blink of an eye.

But this… This was her fault.

This was the direct result of her actions. It was… She'd slept with Kit without a condom. And she had put herself in the situation, and just suddenly that felt a little bit powerful. She wasn't sure she would ever be able to explain that to her sister. Because it sounded a little bit unhinged. But… This was her life. It was a choice she made. To be with him, to not take precautions. So… Here she was. At least she was doing something. Even if it was just a reaction to something else she'd done. She had earned this.

This moment, positive or negative. It was something new. It was, in a very messed-up way, that step forward that she had been avoiding taking. And now here she was taking it.

"Okay. I guess I'll try one of the tests that I have."

"Okay. I'll wait for you."

With shaking hands, she went into the bathroom, and got one of the tests. She had taken so many pregnancy tests. In spite of the fact that she never had a late period. She had done it just because she had hoped. She had kept them on hand just in case. But they were good for three days before a missed period, and she had kept them and taken them three days before more than once. And now they had just been sitting there for a couple of years. No reason to be taken.

It was such a strange, familiar routine. But in the

past, she hadn't had a missed period. In the past, even though she had hoped, she had been certain of the outcome. She was not that certain here.

And when two pink lines came into view for the first time in her damned life, she could not believe it. She swallowed hard and exited the bathroom.

"It was positive," she said, standing there looking at Juniper, trying to gauge her expression.

"Oh, Shelby. You want this, though. I know you do. You want a baby."

Suddenly the intense misery that overwhelmed her was almost too much.

"I wanted my husband's baby," she said, her eyes filling with tears. "Why didn't we get to have that? All those years, and we didn't get pregnant. I didn't get to give this to him. He died and he never got to have it. And I'm... I'm going to do it without him. Because I had sex with someone else. Because I..."

"You're still alive, Shelby," Juniper said, crossing the space and taking her face in her hands. "You're alive. You're going to move on, you're going to do things that Chuck couldn't do. And I know it's not fair. I know. I loved him too. He was like a brother to me. Shelby, when I came upon the scene of his accident, when I had to tell you... It was the worst day of my life. It is still the worst day of my life. There is nothing that will ever match that. It was hell. We both went through hell. But you're alive. And he isn't. So yes. You're going to have sex with other people. You're going to smile again. You're going to be happy. You're going to feel good things and bad things. And if you want to, you get to be a mother."

"I could still lose this pregnancy."

"You could. But you could still be a mother if you

choose to be. You could still adopt, you could get fertility treatments until it happens. It's your life, Shelby. And nobody gets to tell you how to live it. And it doesn't have to stop. It doesn't have to stop just because you lost somebody. You don't owe him a half life."

"But it feels like I do."

"I know."

"And that it's Kit's makes it even worse."

"Why does it make it worse?"

She wanted to hide from that question. But she knew hiding was over. "Well, first of all, I can't keep it from him. And second of all... I feel guilty." She looked away, her throat aching. "Because it is wrong to be attracted to another person when you're married."

"No, Shelby. It's wrong to act on it. And you didn't. You never did. You can't help that you and Kit have physical chemistry. You could help what you did in response to it, and you did the right thing. You always did the right thing. You were good to Chuck. You were appropriate in your response to Kit. And you don't have anything to feel guilty for. You can't help your feelings. It's what you do with them."

"The sex was so good," Shelby said, breathing out hard. "I knew it would be. I knew it. I can't... I can't love him. I don't want..."

"Then don't. Don't. Like I said. It's your life. But if I'm going to strongly push you in any direction, it's to be honest with him. He is my brother-in-law. I cannot lie to Chance about this. I know who the father of the baby is, and I can't pretend that I don't. So... That just has to happen."

"I'll tell him," Shelby said. "It's another thing I don't really want to do. Or deal with. And that makes me a little bit tired."

"That's understandable. But you know, I did a pretty messed-up thing with Chance, and you called me out. I didn't let you in on my plans before I did it. If I had, I probably would've made a different decision because I would've seen the look on your face, and know that I couldn't lie to him like that. So let me be your conscience now. You've got to tell him as soon as possible."

"I need... I need a favor first."

"What is that?"

"Will you help me pack everything up here? I need to change the house. I need... I need new stuff. I need to get rid of the old stuff. Because it's been way too long, and it's starting to feel wrong. Really wrong. It's starting to feel creepy. I can't tell Kit that I'm pregnant with his baby with Chuck's clothes in my closet, okay?"

"Yeah. I can help you with that. I'll let Chance know I won't be home for a couple of hours."

"Don't tell him yet."

"I won't. I'll let you talk to Kit first. Just because I think that's the way it needs to go."

"Thank you," she said. "I really appreciate it."

And then, she and Juniper set about to make the clean slate that Shelby should've made for herself a long time ago. And it felt like more, like better than she could've imagined. Even though the sense of dread looming before her seemed nearly unmanageable. But all she could do was put one foot in front of the other, just slowly. One thing at a time. One piece of clothing at a time. One wedding photo at a time.

And she left one. Hanging on the wall, right in the center. Because there were fresh starts, and then there was ignoring the past in a way she simply couldn't. She would always be shaped by her marriage. By loving Chuck. She wasn't going to pretend otherwise. No matter what. And even though she felt steadfastly cowardly at the moment, that felt just a little bit brave. So she would take that. Cling to it. She didn't really have another choice.

Eight

It had been a fairly normal day. He had only thought about Shelby and what she looked like naked five times. Before coffee. So it was going well. He had thought about her maybe ten times more in the hours since. She had wrecked him. He hadn't been able to get excited about another woman since then. Hadn't even really bothered. He'd considered it one night at the Thirsty Mule when he had gone down to have a drink with Jace, but had abandoned it pretty quickly.

But hell, there was no reason to obsess about her.

What he needed to do was get back on the road. He had been flirting with the idea of retirement from the rodeo, and had been picking up more responsibility on the family ranch. He liked it. Liked the idea of being here with his brothers more. He had decided to take this season off. And yeah, he figured that was probably one foot in retirement. But he was in his thirties. He might be avoiding that "and then" stage of things, but he was definitely there.

He looked across the landscape from his vantage point on the back of his horse, flat and rocky, scrub brush as far as the eye could see. This place was home. And he tried to imagine it being home in a more permanent sense. He hadn't been settled ever. Even when he'd been a kid, they'd gone around the circuit along with their dad, staying in an RV when they could. They'd only ever had stability when Sophie had been ill. And even then, it hadn't been a real stable sort of stability. Having a sister in and out of the hospital wasn't stable. Having a sister die wasn't stable.

His phone buzzed in his pocket, and he reached into it. He had a text from Jace.

Shelby is here to see you.

And suddenly, his blood went molten. Maybe she had been thinking about him too. Maybe she was here to… Maybe it was just as bad for her. Maybe one time wasn't going to be enough. *What the hell is wrong with you?*

He didn't know. And he wasn't going to allow that question to land all that deep. Because he wanted what he wanted. He wanted her. And he was clear on that.

So he urged his horse into a flat-out run, the dust coming up high, rocks and clumps of mud all stirred up in his wake. And when he came up to the front of the barn, Jace was standing there, alongside Shelby, who did not look like she had come for afternoon delight. Or indeed, delight of any kind. Her expression was flat, something steely reflecting in her eyes. Her lips were turned down. It didn't make her any less sexy, not to him. She was still a pocket-size package of absolutely everything he wanted in a woman. But she didn't look like she was here for what he wanted.

"I need to talk to you," she said.

"Yeah. Sure."

Jace looked at him with cool speculation, and Kit curled his lip and lifted his hands, giving his brother an expression straight out of their childhood.

He could tell that Jace wasn't going to let him off all that easy. But for now, he was going to have a talk with Shelby.

"The barn?" she asked.

"Sure. If you want."

"We need to talk alone."

"It may have escaped your notice, but a lot of people live here. Alone is kind of a tall order."

"Then let's... Go for a drive."

"Okay."

He walked over to where his truck was parked, just in front of the barn. "Care to get in?"

"Sure."

His brother was handling his horse, and Kit started the engine of the truck, heading out toward the remote part of the ranch where he had just been. He drove over to the edge of a ravine, the view down below of mountains that looked like they might as well be made of moondust, red and yellow and black paintbrush strokes. It was beautiful. Still not as pretty as her. Even when she was... Well, she wasn't glaring. She was just not looking at him.

"What's going on? I've had a lot of strange interactions with you, but none of them have been silent."

"I have something I have to tell you. And I don't really know how to do that."

And just like that, the view in front of him seemed to

go sideways. Suddenly the mountains were to his right and the sky was to his left, and he didn't even know where his stomach was. Somewhere. Because there was only one reason for a woman you'd slept with to say words like that to you.

"Fuck."

"Oh, you guessed," she said.

"I need to hear you say it."

"I'm pregnant."

"Yeah. Well." There were spots in front of his eyes. A baby. A damned baby. And suddenly, all he could see was Sophie. Small and vulnerable and sick. Dying. And there was nothing he could do. The crushing weight that he felt every night when he went to bed. The need for her to be better. The knowledge that she wouldn't be.

And he just never... He never wanted to feel those things again. He never wanted to feel responsible for that sort of thing again.

He turned and looked at her. Hell. She was pregnant. Pregnancy was not an altogether safe condition. And so many things could go wrong. For her. For the baby.

"Have you been to the doctor?"

"No. I just took a test. I suspected... I suspected about a month ago. But I didn't want to jump to any conclusions. I've never been pregnant before. And I've tried. So... I didn't actually think that I could."

"Shit. I didn't even think about protection. I didn't even..."

"I didn't either," she said.

"It's not your fault. I mean, it's not your fault entirely. It's mine too," he said.

"Well, how generous of you to acknowledge your part in a process that I would be physically incapable of completing on my own."

"I'm not suggesting that I'm being heroic in taking responsibility. But you can't deny that some men don't or won't. And I'm not that guy. I'm not going to blame you or say that you should've said something or done something different."

But there was panic rolling through him. A sense of horror that he couldn't seem to shake, a sense of urgency. He needed to do something. He needed to take control of this somehow.

"I had to tell you, because I told my sister, and she can't not tell Chance. She told me there was a very tight clock ticking on that."

"Would you not have told me otherwise?"

She was silent for a long moment. That silence told him a hell of a lot.

"I don't know. Because I was thinking about moving away. And I feel like that offer still needs to be on the table. You don't have to be involved in this. I've wanted a baby for a long time. This isn't how I saw it happening. I told you. I didn't see it happening this way at all. I didn't think that I could. But I wanted a baby. I wanted to be a mother. You don't have to be involved. You can consider yourself an anonymous sperm donor."

"Like hell I will. Like hell I will. I'm not a sperm donor."

"What are you, then? We had a one-night stand, Kit. A one-night stand that might've been a long time coming, but you don't owe me anything. You and I do not owe each other anything. It was sex. Nothing more."

"I'm the father of the baby." And as soon as he said it he realized it was true. "The father, do you understand? Not a sperm donor."

"Do you want a child?"

"It's immaterial. I'm having one. That's how it is

for me. I can't have a child walking around on this earth and know about it and not claim him. Bottom line. That's just how it is. For me, that's how it is."

He hadn't wanted this. Hadn't wanted this worry, this burden or this responsibility. But it was here, it was happening, and he couldn't contort it into something else. There was no way. Absolutely no way at all. For him, it wasn't a matter of whether or not he decided to step up. He would.

"I could still lose it."

"But it's here now."

And suddenly, the silence seemed to swell between them. The enormity of that. The reality of it.

Even though it was barely the promise of a heartbeat right now, they had… Made something together. It couldn't be nothing. Not to him. It could not be nothing. "We should get married."

"No," she said, the denial abrupt and sharp.

"Why not?"

"Because it's not 1950, you dope. We don't need to get married. This is not a reason to get married."

"It's about the only reason I can think that I would ask a woman to marry me."

"Well, I'm flattered. How many women have you had to propose to?"

"None. You've never been pregnant before. I've never gotten anyone pregnant before. I don't generally…or ever, have sex without condoms. It was very important to me to avoid this. I didn't. In this case. So… I think marriage makes the most sense."

"I've been married, Kit," she said, her voice suddenly soft. "We didn't have a baby. And we were married. Husband and wife. Childless the whole time. Kids are not what marriage is. Marriage is about loving somebody. Being in a partnership. Marriage is about choosing *them*. Not… Some version of a family."

"I think marriage can be either thing. Sometimes people get married for that reason. Sometimes people get married for convenience. Sometimes people get married for kids."

"Not me. Not me. I will never get married for less than what I had before."

And he didn't know why, but that stuck in his chest. More than a little bit. But he couldn't argue with her. Not really.

"I'm moving in with you, then."

"No," she said. "There's no reason to do that. I could have a miscarriage. Something could go wrong. I don't even have the baby."

"So we can move in together after you have the baby."

"Or we share custody. Like grown-ups. Or we decide what it looks like then."

All these things were foreign to him. And none of it was making sense. None of it was clicking. He wanted her with him. All the time. He wanted to protect her. He wanted to keep an eye out for her. He wanted to keep surveillance on the baby in utero and out constantly. To make sure that everything was fine. To make sure they were safe. How could he keep her safe if he didn't have her with him?

"No. This is not going to work for me. You need to move in with me, or I need to move in with you. This has to… This has to be my choice."

"No," she said.

"I can't guarantee that I'm not going to fight you for full custody if you don't do this."

"Well, I will sic your brother on you. And I'm pretty

sure I'll win that fight. Because Juniper and Chance are going to side with me."

And there was the entanglement working against him in a way he hadn't quite envisioned. His brother was accountable to her sister. And he had a whole bunch of threats inside him all bottled up. A desperate bid to control the situation, and he couldn't do it. He couldn't do it, because she wasn't wrong. His brother would tear him a new one. Or just remove the part of his anatomy that had accomplished making the baby in the first place.

"Well, I'm going to be at your house. Every morning. On your damned doorstep. Making sure you're okay."

"Why are you being a nightmare? Why don't we get to know each other?"

"Because I don't want to get to know you. You're the mother of my child."

"It is a zygote, Kit. Calm down."

"No. I will not calm down. Because you can twist and spin situations in life all you want. And you can try to avoid thinking about the logical, reasonable outcomes of things, and you can try to live in denial, but it does not change anything. Believe me. I've done that. I tried it. I tried just…being positive and happy for my sister when she was dying and…trying to be optimistic. It doesn't change a damn thing. When shit comes for you, you have to deal with it. You have to be realistic."

"I'm realistic. Don't talk to me now like I've never lost anything. Don't talk to me like I don't understand that life is difficult. I do. I do. I know how hard things can be. You know I know it. You know I do."

"Shelby," he said, suddenly feeling like there was a boulder in his chest. "I don't see it working where the two of us are trading a kid back and forth on the weekend."

"It has to. Because that's the only thing that I can deal with. Kit, it's all there can ever be."

They sat in silence for a long time. "We'll see."

"This isn't a negotiation."

"And that's where you're wrong. Because it isn't just your life anymore. And it isn't just mine. We are going to have to figure out what's best for this kid. And I'm going to argue my position on that."

And he could see that he had stumped her there.

"So what now?" she asked.

"Let's schedule a doctor appointment."

"Okay."

"I'd like to be there."

"I can't argue with that."

"I think you could. I think for some reason, on this, you don't want to fight me."

He looked at her profile, and he saw tears welling up in her dark eyes. "Well, maybe I don't want to be alone."

"Good. I don't want to leave you alone. That's not how this should be. It's not what I want."

"I'll let you know when I schedule one."

"You going to talk to the rest of your family?"

"Yeah. I guess I have to."

"Would you like me to go with you?"

"Would you like to be a Kit-skin rug on my grand-father's floor?"

"Hey," he said. "I offered to marry you. You turned me down."

"Yes, but you did have sex with me outside the bonds of holy matrimony."

"And you had sex with me right back," he said.

"Point is, I think you should maybe not be there."

He did not like this. This woman's insistence on independence. And it wasn't because he didn't respect an independent woman. It was because it all felt… He wanted to pick her up and wrap her in a blanket and carry her around. He wanted to make sure that she was safe, that the baby was safe. It all suddenly felt so fraught and fragile he didn't know what to do.

And yeah, part of him thought… It would be easier if this wasn't happening. It would be easiest if something went wrong now.

But there was another part of him, a large part, the biggest part, in fact, that couldn't cope with the idea of something going wrong. It would be one loss too many. It would be unfair. Unendurable. He didn't want her to go through that pain. He didn't want to go through it again.

So you're gonna be a dad.

If he hadn't been sitting down, the idea would've brought him down to his knees. It was unfathomable. He had never thought about being a dad. He had shoved that thought way to the side if anything even remotely resembling it had come up. Yeah. It was not his ideal.

He didn't know what to make of it now.

"I actually need some time by myself," she said.

"Are you brushing me off?"

"Yes. I am. Because today has been a lot."

"I don't deny that. But don't you think that you and I should… Talk about this more?"

"I already told you, I don't feel secure enough in this even being a thing to worry about that just now. We don't need to be picking out preschools, or whatever you're thinking."

"I was not thinking that. But thanks."

"I assume you're going to tell your family?"

"I have to tell my family. Because of Chance."

"Fair point. I understand that."

"Right. Well. Since we're not doing it together, I expect I better drive you back to your car and let you get on with things, and then I'll get on with things." He didn't like it. He didn't like any of it. But he didn't really have a choice either.

He put the truck in Reverse, turned around and started to head back toward the barn. Started to head back toward where Shelby had left her car.

He wanted to do something. Wanted to kiss her. But they didn't do that. *You weren't going to be doing things like that. Yeah. And since when do you just take things lying down?*

He didn't. And he wouldn't. As she got into her car to drive away, he began to put a few very concrete directives in place. He was going to prove to her that it was better if they were together. That it was better if they made a family. He was never going to be her late husband. He was never going to mean that much to her. But they could have another version of a family. And he was going to prove that to her. Even if he had to seduce her around the idea.

Nine

"Well. He asked me to marry him."

"Good," Juniper said. "If he had done anything else I would've hung him out to dry and..."

"I said no."

"What?" Her sister's voice was a shriek in her ear.

"I said no, Juniper. I'm not going to marry him just because I'm pregnant."

"Okay. Forgive me. But I don't understand why not. Because you want a family, Shelby..."

"No. I wanted a family with the man I was married to. We were a family. I am not in love with Kit." The words stuck something tender and hollow at the center of her chest.

She wanted to cry all of a sudden. She had made it through that whole thing with him mostly without crying. Mostly. And she just couldn't...

She couldn't. This was too hard. It was scraping

against things she didn't want to examine. It was making her... Feel things.

She hadn't even been tempted to say yes to him for a second, though. Because the idea of Kit and marriage just didn't go together. The idea of taking the thing that they were, this wild, untamed thing, the sharp edges that made her feel exhilaration and shame all at once, and pushing them into the life that she'd had before... She just couldn't imagine that. Of course, she couldn't quite imagine him being a father.

The father of her child. She had spent a lot of time imagining herself being a mother, and in that picture, she was soft. Sitting in a rocking chair, holding a baby. She was a different sort of woman.

Definitely not the woman who had climbed all over Kit Carson and encouraged him to do dirty, incendiary things to her in that bedroom.

That was not the woman bursting with maternal instinct who wanted more than anything to nurture a child.

That woman had been a moment out of time. A moment of insanity. A moment to inhabit a different reality.

That woman could not be the one who took control now.

She looked around her house. Small and humble. She tried to imagine Kit filling the space.

She couldn't. But then, she had no idea what her life was now. She had no idea what she was doing.

And she had a feeling that she wasn't going to find answers anytime soon.

But the sad thing was, there was a timer ticking on her getting things sorted out now. A timer growing in her womb.

So sort things out she was going to have to do. Starting with her family. Kit Carson was a problem for another day.

All his brothers were assembled at the Thirsty Mule. Well. All except for Buck. But that was normal. Another shitty normal in the Carson family.

This was all of them now.

It had just so happened that they were all available. He hadn't actually purposefully put the whole squad together for this announcement. And really, he probably should've first told his mother, who was going to be so thrilled about having a grandchild she wasn't going to be able to deal, but that was part of the problem. She was going to want to see Shelby. She was going to want assurances that the kid was going to be around all the time. And frankly, he had no such assurances. So, his brothers were going first.

"Surprised the old ball and chain let you out of the house," Jace said, slapping Chance on the back.

"The old ball and chain is on call, and was also exhausted after a day working the ranch. She's got too much pride to let me pay for everything, so she's just still working her ass off. But you know, I like that about her."

"That she's stubborn?"

"Yeah. Believe me. It's one of her better attributes."

And unfortunately, Kit knew exactly what his brother was getting at, since he had tasted the steely determination that family had. And found that it was very good indeed. Though, it was also a source of irritation for him right now.

"It's good," Kit said, "that all of us are together. Because I have something that I need to tell you all. So it's probably best that I only have to do it once."

And it was probably good that Chance's wife had been working, or the whole story would've been blown already.

Jace looked at him with no small amount of suspicion on his face. But then, Jace had been there when Shelby had shown up today.

"Yeah. So. There's no easy way to say it. But... I'm..." He didn't really know how you were supposed to announce this. He was having a baby? He was going to be a dad? And so probably the worst iteration of that came out of his mouth. "Shelby is pregnant."

"Dammit, Kit," Chance shouted, practically crossing three bar stools to get near him. "You knocked up my sister-in-law?"

"Yeah. I did. So... There's that."

"Juniper is going to kill you. Hell. Does she know?"

"She does know. She just wasn't allowed to tell you until I knew, and it turns out she's been working since then, obviously, or you would know."

"When did you find out?" Chance asked.

"I know when he found out," Jace said. "That'd be about three hours ago."

"Yes it would. So it's not like it's a secret that's been being sat on for a hell of a long time. Except Shelby has known for about a month. But she didn't tell anybody. But she confirmed it today."

"Right," Chance bit out. "Because of course you fucked her at my wedding."

"She fucked me back. So, maybe dial your umbrage down a little bit."

"Are you going to marry her?"

"Well, Chance, I offered. I offered like the salt-of-the-earth, code-of-the-West motherfucker that I am. And she said no."

"Of course she did," Chance said, snorting.

And he was a little bit surprised to hear his brother ruefully accept that. Except… His brother got it. That was the thing.

"You know you can't tell them anything," Kit said, meaning the Sohappy sisters in general.

"Yeah. I do."

"And because of you, I can't go hard-line on it."

Chance nodded. "I can see that."

"So unless your wife can talk some sense into her…"

"My wife is better at inciting violence than talking sense, and again, I like that about her, but I just don't know that she's going to be the one for this."

"Damn," Jace said.

Boone shook his head.

"So what are you going to do?" asked Flint.

"Well, I'm going to go on the offensive. I'm going to prove to her that she can't do this without me."

"That's what you want," Jace said.

"I'm having a kid. I wasn't going to do this. It wasn't going to be my life. It wasn't going to be what I chose to do. But it's where I'm at. You know as well as I do that sometimes shit just happens."

"Though in this case," Flint said, "shit happened because you didn't wear a condom."

"Yeah. I am aware that I have responsibility in this."

"You know we are here for you," Chance said. "No matter what."

"Thanks. Now if you'll be there to be a buffer when we tell Mom…"

"She's going to be thrilled," Flint said.

"Yep," Jace agreed.

"The real buffer you're going to need," said Chance, "is when we tell Callie. Because she's going to read you the riot act."

"I can take it."

From his perspective, right now, he could take just about anything. Except having the situation left unresolved with Shelby. That he couldn't take.

But he was going to take charge of that. Immediately.

Ten

Shelby woke up, but she didn't get out of bed. She just lay there, the reality of her new life rolling over her.

She was pregnant. She was pregnant with Kit Carson's baby. There was no denying it.

And the sharp knock on her door seemed to underscore that.

Maybe it was her mom, coming to yell more.

There had been a lot of yelling last night.

It had all ended in tears. And everybody was fine now. She wasn't really surprised at the way that it had gone. They didn't want her to be a single mother. But they were reacting to stigma from a different time. And they were also acting like she was sixteen and not twenty-eight. She had the means to manage herself. She didn't care if anybody judged her. And anyway, they weren't going to. It just wasn't like that anymore. But they could not quite understand that. She understood. They were reacting not just because of the way the world was with women, but specifically because of the way the world was to Brown women. She got it. She had lived her whole life in her skin. But she was deciding to do this. And she was assured in that. She wasn't a kid. She wasn't doing this naively.

And she knew that her family would support her no matter what. They would rally around. It was just they had to air their opinions and grievances first.

And so sitting through the grievances had been a thing.

But she had endured it. And now… Someone was here for round two.

She was not quite ready for round two. Even if it involved smothering and apologies.

She rolled out of bed, and padded to the door. She pushed her hair out of her face and jerked the door open, and froze. Because there was Kit Carson. On her doorstep. Holding bags of groceries.

"What are you doing here?"

"I came to make you breakfast."

"I don't recall…" But he was sweeping past her, into the house, and she felt as if he had broken an invisible tape that had been stretched across the door. Like he had breached something. Changed it.

Because here was this man in her house. This man whom she had slept with. Who was not her husband.

And he was getting food out and setting it on the counter. And rummaging around for pots and pans.

"Coffee?"

"I'm not sure on the coffee rules with pregnancy. I think I can have one. But I might just do tea."

"Works for me. But I need some coffee. Will the smell bother you?"

"No," she said, watching, feeling dazed as he opened up a package of bacon and put a skillet on the stovetop. Her stomach growled.

He turned with his broad back to her, and she couldn't help but admire his form. His muscular shoulders, his narrow waist.

She really needed to get a grip.

But there was bacon. And Kit, and things felt very confused.

"I don't know if you like bacon. Or if you prefer sweet breakfast. But I figured I'd do up some pancakes also."

"I… I like food," she said.

And she felt grateful then that she didn't feel any sort of nausea. Because that, she was given to believe, was a hallmark of the early stages of pregnancy. And she really had felt… Mostly fine.

She had felt a grim sense of foreboding, but she hadn't been sick. Or even really fatigued.

Suddenly, she wondered if that was something she should be worried about.

Well, this was going to be a joy. Worrying about not feeling bad was certainly something she hadn't anticipated.

"What exactly are you doing, Kit?"

"I told you. I told you that I was going to try to bring you around to my way of thinking. I wasn't kidding. I also told you I was going to be involved."

"Well, I don't really think that I'm open to your way of thinking."

"I don't care. And I said this isn't going to be a one-way street. Sorry."

"I don't actually think you're sorry."

"Look," he said. "There's no point in us fighting."

The bacon began to sizzle in the pan, and her stomach growled.

"I don't know about that. Maybe there is a point to us fighting. We don't agree. So… It seems to me like there might be a reason for us to fight."

"There's not. We've got some time to sort this out. But I could be here. In the morning. I could take care of things. I can take care of you."

She looked at him, and there were sharp edges to the feeling that swelled within her. How was she supposed to agree to that? To the level of domesticity that he was proposing. How was she supposed to just… Believe that it would work?

It was like agreeing to let a tiger live in your house. Reasonable. Or indeed possible. That was the thing. She looked at Kit and she just didn't see how any of this was possible. Or how it could ever be.

"I've been taking care of myself for a long time."

"I get that," he said, taking a mixing bowl out of her cupboard—how was he finding things so unerringly? She could swear that he was better at maneuvering around her kitchen than she was. "But there's more to it now. There's a baby on the way. And you don't have to do this by yourself. You don't have to do this alone. So why should you?"

"Because, Kit. Because things change. And people die. And I don't even know how all this is going to work out. And jumping into it like this… I'm sorry. But it terrifies me." Admitting that made her feel small. Weak and pale, and she didn't want to feel like any of those things. She wanted to be a brave warrior woman. Somebody who had stared one of the worst things ever in the face and come out stronger.

Right now, she just didn't know how she was going

to cope with all of this. "We just… We just don't even know how all of this is going to pan out, and it scares me, frankly. It scares me. Okay? I just can't…"

"Yeah. It scares me too," he said, stopping and turning to face her. "I get it. I know how fragile things can feel."

Except she wanted to tell him it was different. It was all fine when they were talking about grief in vague terms together. He had lost his sister. She had lost her partner. The person whom she was building her whole life off of. It wasn't fair. But that was the thing about grief. It wasn't especially fair all the time. And sometimes she wanted to lash out at people when they told her they had also lost somebody. She wanted to say it wasn't the same. That they hadn't grown up with their husband. That they hadn't loved the way that she did.

Yeah. It wasn't fair. It wasn't fair at all. But sometimes she just… She just didn't want to be fair.

"Well. You're not carrying a baby. So I don't really know that you do know how fragile things can feel. Right now… It all feels precarious. It could go away. It could go away, it could just not actually be happening. And that… I can't make plans with you right now."

He turned away from her, and went back to the business of making pancakes. The bacon was still sizzling. The domesticity of it made her head hurt. Made her chest hurt.

Because this wasn't real. This was him trying to get his way. And it wasn't… It wasn't right either way.

"You're right. I'm not carrying the baby. I'm trying to help you carry a couple of things. I get it. I'm not even your plan B. I get that. But you know, I'm also not a total deadbeat. And I'm trying to prove that to you."

"I didn't say you were a deadbeat."

"I know you didn't. But I'm also not the person that you figured on doing this with. And I get the feeling that you're more comfortable with the idea of doing it by yourself because it affords you a certain level of denial."

"I did not ask for you to psychoanalyze me."

"No. It's freely offered. Lucky you."

"And what about you? Because I don't for one second think that you're doing anything in a way that isn't also just about protecting yourself. Because that's what we do. All of us people. All the time. We want to protect ourselves."

He paused again. And this time, when he turned to face her, his expression was improbably grim. "Yeah. You're not wrong about that. Here's the thing. I want to keep you safe. I want to keep the baby safe."

"You can't just do that."

"This makes me feel like I'm close to it. And I need that. Okay?"

"Do you actually…? Would it be easier for you if it all went away?"

"Maybe. Maybe, actually. But I don't want that either."

And neither did she. Because yeah. It would be easier if this particular baby went away, and if she wanted to have a baby she could just go do it with a turkey baster, and actually commit to the single-motherhood thing. But she didn't want that. Because in so many ways Kit Carson felt like her destiny, and while she couldn't explain it, standing there resisting it as hard as she was, this felt a little bit like destiny too. Or maybe she was just trying to find more excuses for the fact that he made her behave like a wanton. Either way, this was complex in a way she really didn't want. And yet, it was the reality.

"I don't either."

He nodded, his expression hard, and then he turned back to the pancakes. She was silent while he finished cooking breakfast. And she didn't have it in her to be stubborn enough to turn down the glory that was this home-cooked meal. Because it really did look good.

"So... Do I want to know why you know how to cook breakfast? Is it that guy thing? Where you have to know how to do it, because you have a lot of one-night stands?"

"No," he said, snorting. "My one-night stands never stay for breakfast, Shelby."

She scoffed. "But you do have them."

"I have, yes. And you haven't."

"Just you." Heat sizzled between them and she did her best to ignore it. "Here you are. At breakfast."

"Here you are. Having my baby."

"Here I thought I was having my baby," she said.

But the way that he looked at her, and the way that he'd said it, sent a shiver through her that had nothing to do with maternal instinct. It was that biological insanity that had brought them here in the first place.

"Mine too," he said.

"Right. Well. I guess so."

"If you enjoy the breakfast... There's plenty more where that came from."

She swallowed hard. "I think there needs to be some ground rules."

"Well. Let's go over the rules while we eat."

He dished up the breakfast for both of them, and she let him. Because it had been a long time since someone other than her mother had done anything like caring for her.

And she had to admit that she did enjoy it. A man

moving around her kitchen. In her house. In her life. But the more she was trying to turn her thoughts right side up, the more she had to really think about the implications of this. He needed to be in her child's life. In their child's life. It was what he wanted. It was important to him. And that meant that they were going to have to be civil. More than civil, they were going to have to deal with each other. The passage of time. The way their lives might change. Proposing that they stay separate was safe in a lot of ways. Things would never be worse between them than they were now. They wouldn't allow for it to get sticky and toxic.

Sure, there was the unknown. Whether or not he would marry someone else.

She didn't think that she would.

But…

She ignored the cramping in her stomach that came as a direct result of that thought.

He wasn't really the marrying type. And anyway, if he ever became the marrying type, that was his business. She just felt possessive about it right now because… Well, she was pregnant with his child. That gave her the right to be possessive, didn't it?

It was just a temporary state of being. While she housed part of his genetic material. So there. That seemed like a logical place to put it.

He set the plates on the table, her mug of tea. And she sat in front of the plate, across from him, her heart thundering harder than she would like.

"We have to keep this like this," she said emphatically.

"Excuse me?"

"We're almost friends. And I think that's probably the best place for our relationship."

"We're almost friends?"

"Yes," she said. "We had that really good conversation the night before the bachelorette party…"

"And then we had sex the night after. So why is one of those things a bigger deal than the other? Because it seems to me, the sex is actually why we're here."

"It seems to me that that is an instructive lesson in the nature of sex, and what it can do to a relationship. So I'm thinking that we don't do that again. That's what I'm thinking. I'm thinking, no sex. Because sex caused a whole lot of problems." She felt herself getting warmer and warmer each time she said the word *sex*, and she would really like to be done with that. But she had to act like it didn't matter, because she had to act like maybe they could be friends, because she needed that to be true and real and what was going to happen, because she had to get some control in the situation. She didn't have any, that was for sure.

And she needed it. That was one thing about grief. It had kept her isolated. But it was her grief to deal with and nobody else's, so while people were occasionally on hand to try and be there for her, it was essentially an all-by-yourself sort of thing.

And… She preferred that. This was joint. A partnership. With a man whom she didn't actually have a relationship with. Yes, she had long-standing avoidance of him because of her desire to see him naked, and then they'd talked, and she found that she quite liked him. And then they'd had sex, and she had found out she quite liked his body. But this was different. They had to be different. She clung to that image in her mind. The soft, sweet maternal life. Where she sat in a rocking chair and held the baby, and felt complete. Yeah. She tried to sit with that. For as long as possible.

"We're going to share custody of the child. And have to see each other. And right now, this feels good. It feels companionable."

"Companionable?" The way he asked that, low and flat and gravelly so that it echoed between her thighs, made a liar out of her, but she couldn't afford to let him know that.

"Yes," she said. "Pleasant, even. Why shouldn't we be able to share breakfast with each other? We should, right? This would be ideal. You could come over, we can have a meal. We get a family dinner sometimes. We could share custody, but also share a life."

"There's a thing for that. It's called marriage."

"No. That's disastrous. If we get married we're going to need very specific things from each other. It's going to be about us. This needs to be about our child. And so… No arguing. No sex. None of that."

"No sex."

"No."

"You're cool if I go have sex with other people?"

She ground her back molars together. "Totally fine. I have no claim on you. We are going to be a *Modern Family*."

"What if I told you that I'm not predisposed to very modern ways of thinking?"

"Then I will tell you to go find some enlightenment. Climb to the top of the mountain or something. Commune with nature. Eat a Twinkie. Do something to reach an elevated state of being."

"What if I told you this doesn't work for me?"

"I don't want to fight with you," she said, feeling like she was tearing strips off herself even while she talked, showing the ugly wounds she carried, showing her deepest self. She hated it. "I desperately don't

want to fight with you. Because my life has been a series of fights with everything that has happened to me,
with everything that is going on in the world, with…
My whole soul for two years now, and I am tired. I am
just tired of the relentlessness of it. And I need this to
not be hard."

"I hate to break it to you, sweetheart, but I think having a kid is hard. I think change on this level is hard."

"I don't want it to be," she said, the words coming
out choked. She just wanted something nice. Something
good. She just really wanted to be happy. "I don't want
it to be. I think you're a good guy. I do."

"Why? You found me irritating all the times before,
and we had one conversation and I gave you a couple of
orgasms and now suddenly I'm a good guy?"

"You also cook me bacon," she said, her voice small.

"You don't really know me."

And how did she tell him that she did? She knew the
particular way the sun illuminated his hair and revealed
wheat and gold and glory every time it did. How did she
tell him that she knew the way that his eyes lit up when
he saw a woman he wanted to take home, because she'd
seen that happen more than once at a bar, and she had
always been held captive by the dance between him and
the woman that would never be her. How did she tell
him that he had caused her pain on deep, deep levels?
Shame. That he had made her question whether or not
she was a good person. And yet she had still found a
way to live her life and stay away from him, and some
of that was because… She had admiration for him.

Some of it was because of him. Just like the other
feelings were about him.

How did she tell him any of that?

She didn't even like going over it to herself. Because the

more she sat with it, the more she dwelled on it—which she had never done when she was married—the more she had to acknowledge that he had been a thing always.

"I've seen you around. For a lot of years. I just think that you are a decent guy. If I didn't think that I would've handled all of this very differently. That's the truth of it. But I think that we can do this, and I think that we can be happy and... I just really want that."

She was begging him now. Pleading with him. "I really need to be happy."

"Then I'm going to do what I can to make you happy."

"Oh, don't get mixed up in that. You can't make me happy. But you can contribute to my happiness, or make things more difficult. I would like it if you were trying to contribute good things."

"What's the difference?"

"There's too many things that have happened to me that you didn't have anything to do with that have made things hard. So it can't be up to you to fix them."

"Yeah. Again, I don't see why."

"Because it isn't like that. Okay?"

He shrugged. And she had the feeling that wasn't an agreement. She had a feeling she hadn't one. She had a feeling that he was going to be a lot more difficult than she anticipated.

But if he would just shrug and make pancakes, then that was fine.

"Do you want to know the first time I thought you were beautiful?"

She lifted her face, her eyes clashing with his, horror hitting her square in the stomach. "I'm not sure that I do."

But part of her, this desperate, fluttering part of her, did want to know. Why wasn't that part of her dead? Why had not that part of her died with Chuck? This part of her that acted like a teenage girl, and wanted… To have her crush tell her that she was pretty. That's what he was. Her crush.

Her crush she was having a baby with. Her crush she'd slept with. But a crush nonetheless.

"Yeah. Well. Let's just get it out in the open. You think that the way that we are is the way that it's going to be. So I think that we need to get some stuff out there. Don't you?"

"I don't know."

"Yeah. Well. I'm a decisive kind of guy. It's a risky proposition though it may be… I remember seeing you when you first got engaged to him. And you were hanging out down in front of the bar. I think you and your friends were angling to get some beers bought for you. But you were too young. And you were laughing. And I remember the way the sun kind of hit you from behind. And you were just lit up. And it wasn't just the sun. It was your joy. And I just remember your hair was so shiny and perfect, and your skin was brown all lit up in gold. And I wanted to touch you. And there was a ring shining on your finger, and I knew that I never would. And it's a funny thing. Because I have a level of deep acceptance about that which I can't change or have in this life. Which I'm not in charge of. That comes from loss. Maybe *acceptance* is a strong word, I don't know. But I get it. I'm not in charge of everything. But it just felt… It really felt like a kick in the face. In that moment. That I could want you like I did, but never have you."

The words took the breath out of her lungs, and like all other beautiful things in her life… They were a complication. She wanted to feel flattered, but that wasn't enough. It was too easy of a response. Too shallow.

"I didn't know," she whispered.

"Why should you? It wasn't a thing that could happen. It wasn't a thing."

Did she tell him? It felt risky. It felt like standing on the edge of a cliff. But if this really was about honesty… Could she actually let the unspoken hang between them? Or did she need to say something?

"The first time I noticed you I was in middle school. You were playing football. And I thought that you were… Like a movie star."

"Is that so?"

"Yeah. Unfortunately."

"So we just kept missing each other."

"Yeah. We just kept missing each other."

"Well, we managed to make it stick when we didn't miss, didn't we?"

"I am deeply uncomfortable with all of this," she said, putting her face in her hands.

"Life's uncomfortable."

"So are you… You're going to stay here? You're not going to go back out to the circuit?"

"Yeah. I expect that's what I'll do. I was looking for confirmation. On what I should do. And this pretty much decides it for me. I have something to stay for."

"Yeah."

And there was something about that that settled her. He had something to stay for. And she had something new to live for. This child.

And she was filled with terror about it all going away, but this felt good. It felt right.

They could do this. They could do this and it would be okay. It had to be.

"Shared custody." He was mumbling and muttering while he used a pickax to get granite up out of the

ground to clear out the field, and finally, Jace acknowl-
edged the muttering.

"What's going on?"

"She thinks that we're going to have a platonic relationship wherein we share custody of the child."

"Sounds mature," Jace said.

He looked at Jace. Hard. "And you would be fine
with that?"

"I didn't say I would be *fine* with that. I said it
sounded mature."

"Well. I'm not fine. And maybe I'm not mature."

"And what are you going to do about it?"

"I brought her breakfast this morning. And I aim to
keep doing that."

"Keep bringing her breakfast?"

"Yeah. And dinner. I want her to see that she can't do
this without me. Hell, I want to make it so she doesn't
want to do this without me."

"And what do you want exactly?"

He thought of the way they'd been this morning,
sitting at the kitchen table, that low-level hum of need
between them.

"I want her," he said. And suddenly, it was like the
sky had broken open and rained down to hallelujah.
Like God had slapped him across the face and said: finally, dumbass.

"I want her," he said again. Emphatically. "I don't
want to be friends. I don't want to share custody. If we
are going to have a baby, we need to be a family. And
hell, how else am I supposed to keep her safe?"

"Fine. But what does that have to do with her?"

And he realized that was the thing. She had said
that this needed to be about the baby. But for him it
would never just be about the baby. He had wanted

her, and they'd slept together because of that long-held desire between them. Longer than he'd ever even realized. At least on her end. And he couldn't separate the things. The pregnancy was a direct result of that desire. It wasn't on its own. It wasn't he could never be neutral about her. He never had been. He wanted her. In his bed every night and damn everything else. He wanted to keep her safe. And that meant keeping her with him. He wanted… He wanted to take care of her.

"Are you in love with her?"

Everything in him shied away from that. That felt like a bridge too far. That felt like the kind of wound you didn't come back from. And anyway, she might be attracted to him, but she was in love with a dead man.

"I want her. Functionally, for me, it's all the same."

"Well. Let's hope your plan to bait her with food works."

"I have some other things to fall back on if it doesn't."

"And that is?"

"She didn't get pregnant for just playing checkers."

"Yes. I guess not."

"How about you?" he asked. "You ever…"

He shot Kit a look. "Don't go there."

"I haven't gone anywhere. You don't even know what I was about to ask you."

"Was it about Cara?"

"Actually no. But way to go. You just shone a big ole spotlight on yourself."

"Well, no. Generically and to Cara. Cara needs to be protected at all costs. She's been through enough. She's a strong woman, and I care about her. But it isn't like that. Protecting her means… Never… Ever."

"What's so wrong with you?"

"I could ask you the same question, Kit."

"It's not about me," Kit said. "About love in general. It's a lot of work. I love you. I love everyone in this family. I'm going to have a kid. I… I don't need more. I don't need heavier. I know that Shelby feels the same way. Life has taken it out on her pretty hard too."

"Well, Godspeed. Make sure you include dessert with dinner."

"Good idea," he said.

He wasn't happy with any of this, but he had a plan. And that was the kind of man Kit was. If it was broken, he'd do his best to fix it. He may not have wanted to take on something like this, but he was now. And he would do the absolute best with it that anybody ever could.

Eleven

He went to her house every day for the next couple of weeks. He made breakfast, and three times a week, he made dinner.

They sat together and they ate it. And they talked about their childhoods—it was interesting to hear her side of the family dispute, which, of course, involved his ancestor cheating in a poker game and stealing the land from her family, and though he had already accepted that version of events after Chance and Juniper had gotten together, it was important that he heard it from Shelby herself—but they also found out they weren't all that different. They had been raised on the backs of horses. Raised to love this place. Generations of blood were soaked into the dirt. And they could respect that in each other.

He loved hearing about how her grandmother had taught her to be. How she'd learn to cook traditional recipes, and how her family tried to hang on to their traditions, their ways, as much as they could, while her parents also worked to give them all the advantages of the current culture right along with it. As someone who hadn't grown up with cultural tension, it was interesting to hear about it. And he found it meant something that she trusted him with the stories. They didn't talk about her marriage. They didn't talk about grief again. And they didn't really talk about the future.

But knowing about Shelby's foundation mattered.

He was supposed to be making her realize that she needed him. But all this was growing an attachment that he hadn't quite counted on. One that he hadn't anticipated.

But he had to wonder if Shelby just felt like they were growing that friendship she wanted. For him, it was something more. Something deeper.

He had her doctor appointment marked on his calendar, and when the day arrived, he got up early to make her breakfast like he always did, then he went to the bathroom and threw up. Though he didn't let her know about the throwing up.

He realized that he was… He was not handling this well. Because he knew as well as anyone that life just didn't always hand you good things. What if they went and there was no baby? What if all of this was gone before they got to have it? He wasn't sure that he could handle that. He wasn't sure… Yes. He wasn't sure about any of it. He knocked on the door, and she answered, looking tired. And maybe a little bit sick herself.

"You okay?"

"Yeah," she said. Then she groaned. "No. I'm nervous. Because if not for the positive pregnancy test, and the missed periods, I don't know that I would even know I was pregnant. And I did some online research…"

"Damnation, woman. Don't you know better than that?"

"It can indicate that you have a low level of hCG. Which could mean that something is wrong."

"Well, that's a fucked-up mess. Feeling worse when you're pregnant is better?"

"It's just what I read. I don't know… I don't know. I'm almost twelve weeks. So it's like… If everything is okay today, then maybe everything is okay. But what if it's not okay? What if we just spent all this time… For nothing?"

"Let me make you some breakfast."

"I don't think I can eat."

"Well, let's do our best."

He didn't tell her that he'd thrown his guts up forty-five minutes earlier. Because what was the point in letting her know that he wasn't any better off than she was? He wanted to spare her that. He didn't want to validate any of her worries.

He made a scaled-back breakfast, and they both did the best they could to eat. Maybe she was trying to be brave for him too. The thought made him smile a little bit.

"Let me drive," he said, opening up the passenger-side door of his truck and guiding her into it.

"Thank you," she said. "For being with me. It actually does mean a lot, and you know that I hate to admit that."

"I do know that, Shelby. I know you don't like to admit to needing anyone."

"I don't need you," she said, in defiance, and it made him laugh. In spite of it.

"Of course not," he said.

"I don't," she said. "I can't afford to need anybody. Not ever again. Needing people just… It just hurts in the end. It just hurts and hurts, and what's the point? You can't control whether or not you get to keep a person, so you can't really ever let yourself need someone."

"You know, I get that." Except he hadn't needed his sister. It wasn't that. But he understood how fragile everything was. "But I'm not sure that cutting yourself off from those kinds of connections is a good thing either."

"I didn't ask."

"I guess you didn't."

The little clinic that they went to just outside town was old and quaint and had definitely seen better days. And he didn't know what to expect from any of it. He'd never done anything like this before. Never been to a place like this.

"I come here for my yearly," she said. "So. You didn't need to know that." She was scribbling on paperwork and sitting deeply in one of the vinyl chairs.

"Why don't I need to know that?"

"It's not the kind of thing that we really need to share."

"I'm about to go into a doctor appointment with you. I can certainly handle mentions of your yearly."

And yet, it was notable in difference, because he had certainly never been in a relationship with a woman that was this intimate. And they'd only slept together one time. It was weird as hell.

But it also didn't feel… Bad. Not at all.

They got called into the room, and she sent him out while she got dressed in a hospital gown. He thought it was a little bit silly, all things considered. But when he came back in, she was lying on the table, covered by a blanket.

"So what exactly are they going to do?"

"I think they... Check for a heartbeat? And maybe do an ultrasound. To check how far along and all that."

"Well. We already know that," he said.

"True. I guess a lot of people can't be sure. But we're sure."

"Yeah. Pretty damn sure."

The door opened and an older, short man came in, and began to speak in a soothing voice, explaining exactly what he was going to do. Which was essentially what Shelby had said she thought would happen.

There was a small portable ultrasound machine and the doctor brought it up to the side of the bed. Kit suddenly felt frozen. He hadn't been prepared for this. He didn't know what the hell he'd been prepared for. But not this. Not the knowledge that they were going to see the child now. She looked similarly distressed, and reached out and took hold of his hand. He squeezed it tightly.

The doctor lifted up her gown and pushed the sheet low, before squirting a gel over Shelby's stomach, and putting the wand there. The sound was instantaneous. A strange pumping, whooshing sound that filled up the room. And then they saw movement. "Holy shit," he said, leaning into the screen. "Is that it?"

The doctor looked at him in a vaguely scolding manner, but Kit didn't care. "Yes. That's the baby." He wiggled the wand, and then moved it down lower. "And feet."

"And the heartbeat?" Kit asked.

The doctor moved the wand again, and he could see

a fluttering gray thing, surrounded by black. "There it is. I'm just going to take some measurements."

Shelby squeezed his hand, and when he looked at her, he saw that her lips were pale. "Are you okay?"

She nodded, but didn't say anything.

"Based on what I'm seeing here, and on the dates you gave me… I'm going to put the date at March 1."

It seemed like both an eternity and a blink away. And he couldn't quite process the entire situation.

"Everything looks normal?" Shelby asked.

"Everything looks on track," the doctor said. "Exactly what I would expect to see."

"So I just… What do I do?"

"You come back in a month," the doctor said. "We should be able to do an ultrasound to establish the gender then if you'd like."

"Yeah," Shelby said, her eyes suddenly bright. "Okay."

The doctor left them, and Kit prepared to go too.

"It's okay," she said. "You can stay."

Without being asked, he turned to face the wall as she got up. He listened to the sound of her putting her clothes on. Fabric against skin.

Normally, he would be turning this into something a little bit more sensual. But for now… All he could think about was what he had just seen on the screen. All he could think about was the reality crashing in on him.

It looked so small and helpless. It was contained inside her body. There was nothing he could do. Nothing he could do to make sure that this went well. For him or for her.

"Are you okay?" he asked.

"Yeah," she said. "You can turn around now."

She was dressed again. And she looked so vulnerable. He wanted…

He wanted to protect her from everything. And what an uncomfortable feeling that was.

Because he knew that he couldn't. Because he knew that the world was cruel. Because he…

"Why don't we go home," he said. "You can take a rest. I'll be back by tonight for dinner."

And he realized that he'd said *home*, like it was theirs. But she didn't correct him, so he didn't bother to walk it back.

He didn't want to. And when he dropped her back at her house and said goodbye to her, he marveled at the fact that his relationships usually centered on sex. This one… Well, sex had certainly played a part in it, but there was all this other stuff, and it made it so singular. Different. Unlike anything he had ever even imagined.

In that sense, he was almost glad that she put a moratorium on the physical. Because it had forced them to get to know one another. It had forced them to build this other thing.

And he wanted to keep on building it.

He didn't know what that meant, or where it was headed.

But there was something about his plan that seemed unfocused now. It wasn't about him anymore. It was about her.

And that was the strangest realization of all.

Twelve

She woke up crying. She was glad she had the nap after the doctor appointment, but she had a dream... This dream where Kit was sitting in a rocking chair, shirtless, holding a tiny baby, somehow the epitome of her fantasies, both sexual and domestic all at once, and seeing him there with that familiar wood paneling behind him, seeing him enmeshed in her life, had made her cry in that dream. And when she'd woken up, the crying hadn't been only in the dream.

She tried to get herself together. She went to sit and work on a bracelet that she'd been beading for a few days now, but she couldn't focus.

She was pregnant. Really pregnant, and there was nothing wrong.

Kit had been there for her exhaustively... And she was... She was having a really hard time. With everything. She didn't understand how her life had gone from stagnant and stuck to this. She had wanted something different, but this was decidedly more different than she had been anticipating.

He was coming for dinner. He was cooking for her again. He did it for her all the time, and she just...

She was beginning to feel helpless. Like all these changes were spinning out of her control. It certainly wasn't the sweet, easier life that she had planned for.

That she had thought she would maybe begin to pursue.

Maybe the problem is you don't know what you want.

She did. She wanted the baby. She wanted everything to go smoothly with Kit.

She was not ready for him to show up, and when he did, she felt pretty raw still from everything.

"How are you?" And it was the concern that got her. The concern that made her want to run and hide from this. From him. But she didn't have the luxury of doing that. It was all supposed to be easy, right? Because they were friends?

Except when he breezed past her and went into her kitchen, grocery bags in hand, she had the sudden realization of why it wasn't easy.

They were having a marriage. All this intimacy, emotional and deep. Sex had at least been a distraction after their conversation about grief at the ranch, but... This was just all the emotional stuff. Nothing else.

He threw a dish towel over his broad shoulder and started to take ingredients out of the bag in front of him. She didn't know that was such a sexy thing to do, but it was. That sort of determined and focused competence. More than competence. The thing about Kit was that he was great at everything he did.

Get it together.

He got out a cutting board, and some vegetables, and began to slice through them with ruthless efficiency. And she was enthralled.

Trying to wrap her head around this moment. This life. And suddenly, it was like all the feelings were just too big for her. All of this. Because how was he here in her kitchen. And how was she here, pregnant with his baby? And what was her life? Was she still herself even?

It had seemed simpler when it was sex.

Because the sex wasn't like anything else. It was like a fantasy. It wasn't like her marriage. It wasn't like building a life. It was like burning everything to the ground. In an incendiary flame. It wasn't thinking or talking. It let her make him into something less complicated. Muscle and rough hands and a hard body.

That's what it let her have. And so she did what her body was begging her to do. What her senses demanded. She moved up behind him, and pressed her breasts to his back. She felt him go still. Completely and utterly still. He set the knife down flat on the counter, and then he growled, turning around and cupping her face, her chin held tightly in his palm. "What exactly are you offering me?"

And suddenly, this was dangerous Kit. The one who had put everything she knew in jeopardy every time she saw his face. The one who made her question everything.

It was that Kit. Yeah. That one.

"I would think that was pretty obvious," she said, sucking a sharp breath as she moved her hands to the front of his jeans. Her knees buckled. But thankfully, he was holding so tightly to her that she didn't fall. Because there he was. Hard and rigid already beneath her hand. Big and heavy and she could remember what it had been like to have him inside her.

Yeah. She could well remember.

Her breath hissed through her teeth as she let her fingers skim his hardened length. "I want you," she said.

"Do you?"

"Yes," she said. "I want you, now. In me."

"Me? Or are you thinking about someone else?"

"I have never thought about someone else when I wanted you."

And that was when he growled, feral and rough, and walked her back so that she was pressed flat against the kitchen wall. Her shirt was tugged up violently over her head, cast onto the floor. Her bra followed, and he kissed his way down her neck, her collarbone, took one of her sensitive nipples between his lips and sucked.

"Shit," he breathed. "You're more beautiful than I remembered."

He moved his hand with carnal reverence over her breasts, down her stomach, where he flicked open the button on her jeans and lowered the zipper.

Then he pushed his hand down beneath the waistband of her underwear, and found her wet with need for him. Because it only took a second.

She gasped, her head falling back against the wall as he began to stroke her. This was… This was that wild sex. That wild desire. Wild desire that she thought wasn't real.

It was so starkly different from what she'd had before. What she had before had been nice. What she had before had been manageable. And there was nothing manageable about Kit. He was too big. Too wild. Too much. He was something she couldn't control, and she'd been foolish just now thinking that she could.

That this was her game. That she could take him and make him into something that she could dominate. It wasn't possible.

Because here in her house where she had built a life before, he was breaking her into small little pieces. Something she was afraid she would never be able to put back together. But her life was broken, so why shouldn't she be?

Is it broken, or are you just afraid of what's been built?

She shoved that thought aside, because she didn't want to think. She wanted pleasure. She wanted sex. She wanted Kit and his cock and nothing else. She didn't want anything more than this gloried, heady desire that was unlike anything she had ever experienced. And before she knew it, she was naked, with him fully clothed before her. He knelt down, lifted her leg up over his shoulder and parted her wide as his mouth made contact with the heart of her, already slick with her need as he began to lick her, deeper and deeper until she was shaking. Until she was clinging to his shoulders and crying out with unfulfilled desire.

Damn him. It was a blessing. A curse. Everything, all rolled into one.

It was light and shadow and impossibly out of reach.

And yet there she was, clinging to him for all she was worth, her fingers speared into his hair as she held his head right there. Just there. She rocked her hips, lost in the pagan rhythm that he set with his wicked tongue. And then she burst. Broke open. Shattered. Gasping and crying out his name.

And she knew that this was just another game that she had lost.

But before she could protest, he straightened, lifted

her up, flipped that dish towel off his shoulder, set it on the counter and then set her bare ass right on top of that. "Didn't want you to be cold," he said against her mouth.

"Oh," she said, her brain a fog.

Then he stripped his shirt off and her mouth went dry. And her brain went blank.

He was the most beautiful man she'd ever seen.

And her need was a desperate thing. Clawing at her. And there was no biological excuse for it. She was already pregnant. She was already pregnant, and so there was nothing to hide behind. This was just need. Pure, filthy need. She'd already had an orgasm, but it wasn't enough. Because she wanted to feel his possession. She wanted his cock buried deep inside her. When she cried out his name.

She wanted him. All of him. She wanted to lose herself and find herself all at once. And she knew that the only way to do that was...

He undid the buckle on his jeans and tugged the zipper down roughly. She pushed his jeans down his lean hips, and he freed his arousal, drawing her close to him as he pressed slowly into her heat.

"Kit," she shouted, almost embarrassed by the intensity of the demand wound around his name.

She couldn't. She could not. And yet she was. They were. Because it was all the things and everything, and it was him and her together. Like nothing and no one had ever been.

Did everybody feel like this? Except, dimly, she knew that not everybody had this. So no. Not everybody felt like this. Because she'd never felt like this before. Like sex was a wonderful mystery that they alone had unlocked. That only they could ever figure the combination that would make this particular pleasure click.

He was so big and hard inside her, like he was made to fit her. Just a bit too much, but in the very best way.

She didn't want her sex comfortable. She didn't want it easy. She wanted hard and rough with a slight bite of pain. And he delivered. Cupping her ass as he pulled her against him, thrusting hard inside her and leaving her breathless each and every time.

His strokes were deep, and she lost herself in it. In this. In him.

She looked into his eyes, and she felt what burned there resonated in her soul.

And it terrified her. Made her tremble. Made her want to look away. Made her want to escape, but he held her face still as he drove into her again, and again. As her own desire wound around her like a golden thread, making her shiver.

Making her come apart at the seams.

And then she broke. Crying out his name just a moment before he shouted hers, spilling deep inside her, his hardness pulsing deep within her.

"Kit," she whispered. And he kissed her. Her mouth, her forehead, her cheeks. He kissed her and kissed her like there was nothing else he wanted to do in the whole world.

Like he was shocked and unmade by this thing she was.

In her house. In her little house that she had shared with Chuck for all those years.

And suddenly, she couldn't picture Chuck in it. And sadness closed her throat. Made her gasp. Made it hard to breathe.

"We'll have dinner later," he said, scooping her up and carrying her from the kitchen into the bathroom. As if he had been here a hundred times. As if he lived here.

He turned the water on, and she waited, shivering as he undressed all the way. And when the water was warm, he put her in the shower and moved his hands over her body, gently, with great care. The warm water washed over her. And it did something to her. She didn't know if it was healing or hurting. She honestly couldn't tell.

"I…"

"Hey," he said. "You are okay. You're okay."

And she didn't know how he could say that. Because he didn't know. He didn't know. He wrapped his arms around her and pulled her naked body flush against his. He moved his hands over her curves, and he kissed her. Kissed her until she couldn't think.

Then he turned the shower off, dried her off and carried her to the bed, where he left her for a full forty-five minutes. And she just lay there. Feeling shell-shocked. Afraid that he would join her. Afraid that he wouldn't. And then he appeared wearing only a pair of jeans, holding two plates of food. He handed her one, and she took it, curled up beneath the blankets still. Then he got into the space beside her, on top of the blankets, his own plate on his lap. "How you doing?"

"Hungry," she said, drawing the plate up to her face.

"Good. Eat."

But how did she tell him? How did she explain the strange, fractured feeling blooming in her chest? Like a chip had been put into a windowpane long ago, and now the pressure, the cold, the heat, something, was making that crack expand. Spider outward.

"I think we should get married, don't you?"

And she didn't know how to say no. Not this time. Because what leg did she have to stand on? It had made sense to kiss him an hour ago. It had seemed like the best idea in the world. Like it would wrench some control back. Like finding that sexual connection again would somehow erase the tenderness that they'd found. But it hadn't. Here he was, in bed with her, eating dinner.

"I don't… I don't…"

"I want to take care of you," he said, and she was so grateful he'd said that. Because that wasn't marriage as she knew it. And somehow, that made it feel safer. "When my sister was sick, my brother and I made her a little wagon. And we decorated it. I spent hours taking her around in that thing. Like she was a little princess. And I loved it. I think I believed in things still. Different than I do now. Like I believed that there was some kind of healing power in love. I couldn't fix her. And if love could've healed her, then she would've been here. Believe me."

And oh, she knew that. She felt it. Deep in her soul, and it just hurt. It hurt so much to hear him say this, she wanted him to stop. It wrapped itself around her own grief and regret and pain. Around the futility of loss, and the merciless movement of the world as it kept on spinning even after your heart had been crushed.

She knew what it was like to wish love could save someone.

To be devastated that it couldn't.

Even as his words hurt, she felt closer to him. Felt like she understood him.

"And I'm… I spent a lot of years afraid," he said. "Afraid that I'd lose her. And then I did. And then I was afraid when my mom got pregnant with Callie. That something would happen to her. That something would happen to the baby. And it's like I've spent my whole life on this hypervigilant watch. Thinking that somehow… My love was gonna stop something from happening. My… My will for everything to be okay was going to fix something, and I always thought that caring was just so exhausting I never wanted to care for another person as long as I lived. Not an extra one. But I care for you. I'll even give you a ride in a wagon if you want."

And her heart just felt like it cracked in two. Because she was tired. She was tired and he wanted to carry this. She was tired and he wanted to carry her. In a wagon. It wasn't some empty gesture from some guy who didn't know the weight of loss. He knew. And he still wanted this. And she could have it. Because it was different. Because… Because she was just so damned tired of being by herself. Because she wanted him to touch her every night. Because she wanted her baby to have a father. And maybe because she was scared and didn't want stigma.

"I'll marry you," she said. "I'll… Yeah."

"We don't have to have a wedding."

She nodded, tears filling her eyes. "Good. Good. I don't want to have another one."

"We just need to go sign the paperwork and do the thing. You don't even have to really formalize all that. We can have a court witness if you want."

"I would like that. Thank you. We can just tell everybody that we eloped. I think that would be for the best."

"Do you want me to move in with you or do you want to move in with me?"

And she realized she hadn't even been to his house. And she was torn. So torn, because having him here in this place, in her bed was… Unfathomable. But she had imagined raising the baby here.

"I don't know yet," she said.

"That's okay. We don't even have to move in together right away. We've got time."

"I hear a *but*."

"Yeah. But, I think we should get married. As quickly as possible."

"Are you afraid I'll change my mind?"

"Yes," he said. And she had to laugh. Because she sort of was too. And she couldn't really put her finger on why. No. She really couldn't.

"You want to go get a marriage license tomorrow?"

"Sure," she said.

"Do you want me to leave you alone tonight?"

She shoveled in the last bite of her dinner. "I don't know."

"I tell you what. I'm gonna stay."

And he stayed on top of the covers, with her naked beneath them, and pulled her to him, holding her close. And that was how they stayed all night.

Thirteen

Kit felt like he should feel a little more about getting Shelby to agree to marry him. Like he should feel triumphant or something. But he didn't. Instead, he felt a vague sense of disquiet that he couldn't quite put his finger on. Because he didn't feel… Like you did when you accomplished something. At least, not what he really wanted. But he couldn't quite figure out what he wanted. He couldn't really say either what had possessed him to tell her the story about Sophie. But nonetheless, the next day, they went to town with the appropriate documentation and went to the courthouse to file for a marriage license.

"Getting married again," the older woman in the register's office said, smiling at Shelby. "I'm so happy for you, honey."

"Thank you," Shelby said, her cheeks going dark pink.

"We'll want to come back and do the thing in three days," Kit said.

"Not a problem," the woman said. "There are plenty of spots available. Just call ahead, and Sherm will be happy to do the ceremony."

"Great," he said.

"Boy, your families really did get rid of that feud, didn't they?"

"Yeah," Shelby said. "I guess you could say we did, Rose. Thank you."

When they walked back out of the courthouse, onto the main street of Lone Rock, which didn't hold a whole lot, Shelby looked tired. "I need to make a stop by Carefree Buffalo. They have some money for me. Because they sold a few of my pieces."

"Yeah," he said.

He walked down the street with her, and into a little shop that sold handmade knives, jewelry and leather goods.

There was a little corner with a variety of beaded items. Bracelets, earrings, barrettes.

"You did all these?" he asked, pointing to the display.

"Yeah," she said, looking embarrassed.

The owner of the store came out, and Shelby greeted him, and what they were saying kind of faded into the background.

He watched her, and he watched her in a different way than he ever had. He knew her now. The rhythm of her. The way that she smiled, the way she laughed. The way she breathed. He had shared a bed with her last night, and he had never shared a bed with a woman all night. They hadn't had sex in that bed, and it had felt as astonishingly intimate as what had taken place in the kitchen. If not more so. He just... When she turned to look at him, a lingering smile from her conversation with the shopkeeper on her face, his heart stopped. Everything stopped. He was in love with her. He was in love with her, and that was why he wanted to marry her. He'd never been in love. He'd never wanted to be. He thought it sounded like work, and heavy work at that. But it didn't seem heavy, loving her. It was all in the showing up, every day. And it wasn't carrying the weight of the world on his shoulders. It was… Feeling like the weight of her and all her concerns wasn't all that heavy. And like maybe his life wouldn't matter if he was walking around carefree, with empty arms.

Maybe that was it. He just… He just wanted her. Her. And all of the baggage that came with it. And he didn't think she loved him. She loved Chuck. And that was fair. Maybe he was way too tied up in some things that made her feel guilty for her to ever have feelings for him. Or maybe she would just never be in love again. But that didn't change the way he felt. It didn't mean he didn't want her. Because he did. Dammit all, he did. But he knew he couldn't tell her. Not now. Because she just agreed to marry him, and he didn't want to rock that boat. So Kit Carson kept the truth of it to himself.

And it struck him, when he dropped her back off at her house, that he had probably loved her for a long time. And it had all just been about waiting for the right time. So he was still waiting for the right time. That was all.

Shelby didn't tell anyone in her family that she was getting married today. They had taken the first available spot with the judge that morning.

Kit had not spent the night. He hadn't the last two nights. They'd had dinner. They'd had sex. Because she couldn't keep her hands off him. And there was a wild determination in her need for him. But now that she'd given in to it, she didn't want to control herself at all. Was angry that she ever had. Now that she had given in, she wanted to do it over and over again. Because somehow it made… Somehow it made the fact that she was marrying him seem more distant.

But then he picked her up, and he was wearing a black button-down shirt, a black hat and a pair of dark jeans. And he was holding a beautiful bouquet of flowers, and suddenly everything seemed just a little bit too real.

"Hi," she said.

"You look beautiful."

But she'd worn jeans. And a tank top. And she suddenly felt like there was something wrong with her. But he said she was beautiful, and it made everything inside her hurt.

She didn't wear her wedding ring anymore. But suddenly the idea of wearing a different one…

But maybe he didn't have one. They hadn't talked about rings. But he had brought flowers.

They got into the truck, and he put it in Reverse. "Did you get rings?"

"I did," he said.

"Could we… Could we put them on now? Or after? But not during?"

"Whatever you need," he said.

"We can just put them on now," she said, starting to rummage through the bags that were in the truck.

And suddenly, he pulled over to the side of the dirt road they were still on, and took out the boxes with the rings. Then he took her left hand in his, and opened up the velvet box. Inside was the most stunning diamond she'd ever seen. "Kit…"

"I hope you like it. I got a carefree buffalo."

"It's beautiful."

His eyes met hers, there in the truck. And suddenly… Her stomach dropped. Because she thought that maybe if they put them on now it wouldn't feel the same. It wouldn't feel like marriage. It wouldn't feel like a promise. But as he slipped that band on her finger, she knew that she was an idiot. Because this felt so real. She had gotten a marriage license, and he was putting a ring on her finger, and it was real. "Shelby…" She went to pull away, but he put his hand on her cheek and held her fast, and then he was kissing her. Deep and hard.

"Kit…"

And then she couldn't speak, because it was them. Him. And she just always wanted him. No matter what.

And when they parted, he was breathing heavily. Then he opened up the next box. And inside it was a gold band. For him.

And she looked up at him, fear and regret coiling through her. "I can't."

And there was a grim sort of determined look on his face. "Well, I won't wear it until you can."

Then he steered the truck back onto the road, and they kept on going into town. It was a pretty short drive, and they got there and were able to park out front.

They went inside, and waited to be called into the judge's chambers.

"Good to see you," the judge said to Shelby.

"You too," she said.

Rose was their witness. And Shelby held the bouquet that Kit had brought in sweaty hands.

"None of your family come?" Rose asked.

"Well, I… No," Shelby said. "We didn't exactly tell them."

"You're eloping," said Rose. "So romantic."

Her hands trembled as Kit took them in his.

"We won't be exchanging rings," Kit said.

"All right," the judge said, clearly not put off by it at all. But she imagined that in the world of courthouse weddings, that wasn't all that uncommon. But then it came to vows. And she could feel tears pushing against her eyes. Feel herself breathing far too hard. "Do you, Shelby Sohappy, take this man to be your lawfully wedded husband? In sickness and in health, for richer or poorer, as long as you both shall live?"

As long as they lived. That was it. As long as you lived. That was all.

It ended after that. Her first marriage had ended. And here she was, on the verge of another life.

She was terrified.

"I do," she said before she could lose her nerve.

"And do you, Kittredge Carson, take this woman to be your lawfully wedded wife? To have and to hold, in sickness and in health, as long as you both shall live?"

And it was like the world stopped. The whole world. "I do," said Kit.

"And now, by the authority given to me by the state of Oregon, I pronounce you husband and wife."

And without being told that they could kiss, Kit pulled her into his arms, and kissed her. And she clung to him, kissing him back, because he was the lifeline in the moment, even as he was the thing that made her tremble.

And when they parted, it was over. She had a husband. Another husband. But Kit wasn't another of anything. He was… Somehow she had married Kit Carson.

And she didn't know how she was ever going to get her head around that. She expected him to drive her back home. But he didn't.

"Kit…"

"I decided we ought to have a honeymoon."

"A honeymoon?"

"Yeah. Just…figured we'd stay at a nice place on the Deschutes River. Enjoy the view. Some good food."

And she found that she didn't have words. She didn't even know what to think. He turned on the radio, and there was a Jimmie Allen song on, and she tried to focus on the lyrics, and not on her confusion as they drove on the highway, headed north.

"Where exactly are we going?"

"Bend," he said.

"Oh. I didn't know you were wanting to go into the city."

He chuckled. "I just thought it might be nice to go somewhere a little… You know. Nice."

It took two hours to get there. They pulled into a hotel that she'd never been to before. Right there on the Deschutes River.

"I packed an overnight bag for us," he said as he reached into the back of the truck and produced it, before getting out and heading into the lobby.

And she just sat there. Feeling stupid.

Then she got it together, unbuckling and scrambling out behind him, walking into what was a beautiful, woodsy room with high ceilings and metal art all over the place. Fish and elk wrought from iron standing proud over stone tiles.

"This is beautiful," she said.

"I just wanted… I wanted something to mark the day."

And suddenly, she just wanted him. She wanted him,

because it might do something to blot out the feelings that were rioting through her. The things that felt sharp and jagged and a little bit broken.

It took a moment for them to get all checked in, and then they went upstairs, to the suite down at the end of the hall.

"Kit," she breathed. "This is too much."

And she hadn't fully appreciated until just then that she had married a man with money. She just hadn't thought about it at all. Well. That was… Handy. She supposed. Except she didn't really want for much of anything in her life. Except she…

And then she couldn't think, because Kit was kissing her.

And at least when Kit was kissing her, she could blot out all her doubts and just feel.

Fourteen

He kissed her like he was starving, because he was. Like he was gasping for air and she was the only source.

He should've told her his plans. He could see that she was a little bit shell-shocked. The rings, the vows, everything, that it had all been a little bit much for her. And it was tearing him apart. Breaking him open. Because he needed her. He needed this. He wanted... He wanted her to feel like his wife. Because she damn well felt like it to him. He wanted this to matter. He wanted it to be everything.

Maybe he wanted too much.

But life had knocked him down and kneed him in the groin enough times for him to know that things weren't magic. For him to know that this might be hard. For him to know that he might always be competing with a love that had been thwarted before its time had come to an end. And maybe there was no competing with that. Not ever. But he didn't want to compete anyway. Not really. He wanted to be different. He wanted to be singular. He wanted to be new. He wanted to be Shelby and Kit, nothing that had come before. And nothing that could ever come after. He wanted to be everything.

And so he kissed her, walking her back to the bed as he stripped the tank top, the jeans, the determined non-wedding outfit from her body. Whatever she needed to do. But he wanted her to be his.

If this was the only way to do it, if this was the only way to reach her, then he damn well would. So he stripped her naked, the sight of her bronze curves filling him with awe, filling him with need. He wanted this woman. He wanted her more than he wanted his next breath.

"Lie down," he ordered. "I want to look at you."

"Kit…"

"You're my wife," he said. "You're mine."

And suddenly, a deep feeling of possession burst inside him. He could scarcely breathe around it. Couldn't think. All he could do was feel.

"Damn, you're so pretty. So damned pretty."

The words came out rough, almost violent. But it was a violence in him. Tearing through him, rioting through his chest, making him feel like a stranger to himself.

And there was a glint of something, something like fear in her dark eyes, and he wanted to make it go away. But he also wanted to push. To push past it.

Because every time they came to this point, and it felt like an important thing, they didn't get further. Something stopped them. There was a barrier that went up, and he didn't know what that was. Didn't know how to fight it. And he wanted to. Because he wanted… He wanted everything.

He stood at the foot of the bed and began to take his clothes off slowly.

He looked at her, and he knew that she wanted him. He knew that she wanted this, this thing that burned between them hotter and brighter than anything.

He slowly undid the buckle on his jeans, undressed and moved to the edge of the bed. "Get on your knees," he commanded. She obeyed, and it was a strange and beautiful thing to see her, still filled with fire, but not fighting against him at all.

"Take me in your mouth, Shelby."

And he made sure to keep his gaze locked with hers, to hold her captive with his eyes as she moved forward, curling her fingers around his aching cock as she lowered her head to take him into her mouth.

The soft sound she made vibrated through his body, and he thought his soul had exited the building.

Kit was pretty sure he was deceased. A ghost. Just from that soft, slick contact from her lips. Her tongue. She lowered her head and took him in deep, pulling back slightly when it was clear it was a little too much for her. And there was something about it that thrilled him. Something about it that made him feel like a god. And maybe that was wrong. Maybe it was messed up. But he didn't care. Because… How could it be? How could it be when he just loved her? When he wanted to possess her in every way. That was the thing. When he wanted all of it, every last thing. Her and nothing more. And he wanted… He wanted her to prove to him right now, beyond a shadow of a doubt, that it was more than just desire. Because while it was desire on a level he had never known, it was something more.

She'd been under his skin for a long damned time. And he knew what it was now. That thing that he was so afraid of. That thing he could never name. And why would he? She'd been off-limits to him. In love with someone else. And it was entirely possible she still was. Entirely possible that he was competing against her love for a dead man. And he was alive. So he would make mistakes. He would frustrate her. They were going to have a child together. They were going to be under different stress. And she hadn't chosen him. Maybe it would be easy for her to resent him. Maybe he would never be able to live up to all that. But they had this. They had this, and she was sucking him like he was her favorite damn thing. And that was real.

Maybe for her it wasn't love. But he would take emphatic, absolute need. He would take desire that was undeniable. Desire that transcended common sense. Desire that was more, shot higher, farther into the stratosphere than anything else either of them had ever experienced. And for him, it would be love. Always.

And it was like some truths broke open inside him. All around him. All that stress, all that care. It was love. Always. And the grief that he felt over the loss of his sister was all that love with no one left to care for. But it was still there. Love was something that couldn't be taken away. And somehow, during a blow job, he was having the single greatest moment of clarity in his life. Maybe because he had never loved anyone or anything more than Shelby. Maybe because he loved the vision of the life they could have. Enough to risk everything. But even if that vision didn't come out perfect. Even if it was never everything, he would love her. Because love was a sacred space, one he could choose to dedicate his whole soul to. One that could live on, no matter what was given in return. No matter what.

He felt himself reaching the end of his control, and

he gripped her hair tight, guiding her head back up. "I want to be inside you."

Her lips curved up into a coy smile. "I mean. Technically you were."

"You know what I mean."

"Yeah," she said, but the word was heavy, and it was like she knew. Heavy with need. Heavy with the intensity of all that they were. And he was on fire with it.

On fire with all of it.

He kissed her. Drowning in her. If he never had anything but her, it would be okay. He wasn't marrying her for the baby. He'd married her for her. And she was his wife.

His wife.

His knees nearly buckled with the wonder of it. He kissed her, laying her flat on the bed, her legs parting for him. And he entered her in one smooth thrust. The feeling of her body holding him like this, of being in her, overwhelmed him, no matter how many times it happened.

He knew she'd only had one lover other than him. And he had a fair few. But none of it mattered. Not now. Because this wasn't like anything. She wasn't like anything. They were altogether new and glorious. They were the stars.

He could remember well that night, before the first time he'd ever touched her, when he looked up at the sky and noticed those stars.

Like he was seeing them for the first time. She made him see things. She made him feel things. She took him from the gray haze of grief, and she painted his world all different colors.

And he never wanted to go back. And he didn't have to. He lost himself in her. Over and over again. And when she trembled beneath him, crying out his name, he released hold on all of his control. All of it. He kissed her, his mouth against hers as he said the only thing that existed inside him. The only truth. The only thing that mattered. "I love you."

She was lying there, awash in sensation and pleasure after the intensity of their coming together, and his words were rolling over her like a tsunami. And she couldn't find anything to grab on to. She didn't know what to do. She was drowning. In sorrow, and guilt. And regret. He loved her? He loved her.

That wasn't possible. Not Kit Carson. Kit Carson, that object of her desire. Whom she had considered dangerous and something else altogether. Because he had been part of the Carson family.

Because she was supposed to love someone else. She did love someone else. She did.

She did.

And she couldn't betray him. Not like this. Not like that. When she had… She had wanted Kit. She had wanted Kit while she was married, and if she loved him now too, and she was having a baby with him, then what had she kept for the man she'd made vows to?

You made vows to Kit too.

She couldn't breathe. She was panicking.

"You don't need to say anything," he said. "But I wanted you to know. I didn't marry you because of the baby. I married you because I wanted to be your husband. Because I fell in love with you, Shelby. I don't know when. It seems silly to say years ago, but maybe it was then. But for sure in these last weeks. It was like all that electricity between us came together and started to make sense. Maybe it was just waiting for the right time. Hell, I don't know. But I love you. I love talking to you. I love being with you. I love being in you. And I don't ever want to be with anyone else. Not ever again. I just… I just love you. And when I say that, it's from a position of having worked really hard to climb that mountain. But I realized something. I love my sister, even though she's gone. But I love her still. I don't know. I guess I felt like I lost that. But I didn't. I still get to have it. I still get to have love. It's a miracle."

He was being so raw. So honest.

It was Kit and she couldn't handle it.

It was so deep and she didn't want to go that far.

She couldn't.

"I don't feel that way," she said. "Because it isn't the same. I had a husband. And I loved him."

She felt sick. She felt like she was going to throw up. Or maybe die.

"I had a husband and I loved him. And I can't…"

"What?"

"I just feel so guilty. I feel like I'm betraying him. And myself. I feel like… I don't want this. I don't want to love you. I can't love you."

"Shelby. I'll wait. I don't need you to do a damn thing. We can go on like we have. Like we always have. We can go on like this."

"Maybe you can," she said. "But I can't. I just don't think I can. I think… I think it was a mistake."

"It wasn't a mistake."

"All of it was," she said. "How can I… How can I think that this would work? I just… It isn't going to. It can't."

"Shelby, my love isn't dependent on you giving it back. All I know is that the first time I noticed you, it changed something for me. And it took all these years for it to lead here. I can wait more years. I can wait more."

And she didn't know why that infuriated her. Why he was acting like this was okay. Like maybe it was a good thing. When that word, when the idea of him…

"This isn't love. Not as I understand it. This… This is something else. It's chemistry. It's desire. I want you. I want to be with you. I like you to do things to me that I've never liked before. I like doing things to you that I've never liked before. I always knew I wanted your body, Kit. But that's the kind of man you are. You're a really great body."

Guilt lashed at her.

"Is that all?"

"It's all you can be for me."

"Well, I'm the body that married you. I'm the body that helped to make this baby. I'm the body that loves you. But I'm gonna prove to you that there's not a time frame on this. I want you to take my truck, and go home. Take all the time you need."

"This is our honeymoon."

"You just said you didn't want all that."

She felt like her pain was pushing her into the ground. Like she was being driven farther and farther into a hole.

"I just want to leave you with one thing."

"What's that?"

He turned around and took something out of his overnight bag. The box that had his ring in it.

"Now what I want you to do is keep this. And when you're ready, you put it on my finger."

"I won't… I can't…"

"Then you give it back to me."

She couldn't, though. She couldn't make her hand

release it. She wanted to be able to have him in her life. She wanted to keep sleeping with him. She wanted him to be a father to her child. She wanted… She wanted all of that without any risk. And it was a misery. Standing there frozen. Not being able to take either thing that she wanted. Not being able to be… As strong as she wanted to be. As good as she wanted to be. As brave.

"That's what I thought. Hang on to it."

"How are you going to get home?" she said.

"Don't worry about me, Shelby. I'll figure it out. I've got family. I've got time."

She took the truck keys, and she took the ring. And she started to collect her clothes. Then she walked out of her honeymoon suite like she hadn't just entered an hour before. She walked out with her heart on the ground, or maybe it was just back in the room with him. All she knew was that she needed to protect something. Except right now… She felt like she didn't have anything.

You have his truck keys, and his wedding ring.

Yeah. She had those two things. And what the hell was she supposed to do with them?

Fifteen

Well. That had not gone well. He sat down, bare-ass naked on the end of the bed in his honeymoon suite. And he did something he really didn't want to do. He called his brother.

"Hey, Chance," he said. "You up for driving to Bend?"

"When?"

"You know. Now, maybe?"

"Why?"

"Well, I'm in Bend. Because I got married and my wife just left me and took my truck."

"What the fuck did you do?" asked Chance.

"I didn't do anything, actually. But thank you. I just told her that I loved her."

"Oh. Well. I'll be there in a minute."

It didn't feel like a minute. And really, it wasn't. It was a hell of a long time before his brother managed to get there, and by the time he did, Kit was a little bit drunk.

"Oh, boy," said Chance. "So she rejected your ass?"

"Yeah. I… I'm in love with her, Chance. I'm in love with her… And… She's not in love with me."

"I think that's bullshit. I think you know that too."

"Do I?"

"Yeah. I think so. I think she's scared."

"Yeah. I get that."

"And why exactly aren't you scared anymore?" Chance asked.

"I don't know. The same reason you aren't. Love is just more important."

"It is."

"I'll wait for her."

"That's how you know it's real. It feels urgent. But if you can be patient… If you could be patient, then… It's the real thing."

"I've been patient."

"Yeah, I know."

"It's all right with me if she still loves him. Maybe for her, that's how it will always be. But for me… It's fate. There's nobody else but her."

"I don't see why you can't be her fate too."

"Well, I respect what she had."

"You're here. And you're together. I suspect that her real problem is that she's a little bit afraid that you and her might have been inevitable."

Well. That made sense. But it was a damned optimistic view.

"And how is it that you have so much faith in that?"

"Because it took amnesia, a very strange lie and a whole lot of letting go for me to find love, but I did it anyway. I believe you'll have the same. So… That's it. I just believe in it."

He was going to cling to that. And he did. The whole ride back to Lone Rock. That was what he clung to.

Sixteen

She should go talk to Juniper. She should go talk to somebody. Anybody. But instead she found herself driving to the graveyard. It made her feel grim and sad, and she didn't go there all that often, because there was something so definitive about it that she just hated.

But that plot had been meant for the both of them. And there was just something… There was just something… She parked in the cemetery parking lot and lowered her head over the steering wheel and started to cry. Deep, wrenching sobs. And somehow, she couldn't make herself get out.

Finally, she did. Finally, she caught her breath enough to do that.

She got out of the truck and walked down the familiar path to where Chuck's gravestone was.

"This is weird," she said. "I'm not given to talking

to you. I guess you know that. Or you don't. I... I don't know how I feel about it."

But the stone was unresponsive. And the ring was heavy in her pocket.

Real.

The weight of it was real.

Present.

Here.

Now.

And suddenly, she felt so stark and clear what Juniper had said to her when she'd first confessed that she was pregnant, and the guilt that she felt. That Chuck would never be a father, that he would never have had that dream, but she was moving on and living. Because she was alive.

She didn't know if she believed in the idea that a person had a set number of days. In the idea that when it was your time it was your time. In fact, she had resisted that hard, because it had felt like in no way could it be her twenty-six-year-old husband's time.

But she supposed in the end it didn't matter. He had the years and the life he'd been given. And they'd been happy.

Her heart had been his, because she'd given it to him, and even with her attraction to Kit, she had devoted her love and her body to the man she'd made her vows to.

Till death do us part.

And it had parted them. So much earlier than she'd anticipated. But it had.

And she was holding herself back. Holding herself back with a foot in her old life. No. Worse. With her heart in her old life.

What if she let go? What if she listened to Kit?

Listened to what he'd said. That love wouldn't go

away. It wasn't gone. It was different. But it lived in her. What if she trusted that? And what if she quit feeling so damned guilty that she had fantasies about Kit?

She wanted to cry. Wanted to weep at the injustice of everything.

But not at the life she was living now. For the first time in a very long time. She was angry that the world was cruel and Chuck had died too young. But she wasn't angry that she was here with Kit. She wasn't angry that she was having his baby.

"I'm happy."

And she had to put her hand over her mouth to stifle a sob.

She was happy. She loved Kit.

And the sound that tore from her body was half exultation, half despair.

She loved Kit Carson. And it wasn't like anything else. They were everything. They were obsession and heat and fire and love. They were a previously undiscovered passion that she hadn't known existed. They were connected. And they always had been. And if fate was real, then maybe she had to accept that she'd been walking toward him all this time.

Maybe she had to accept that she had been Chuck's fate. And they'd had love. And it had been real. But where his road ended, hers kept going. He had been love. And it had been real. But her fate went on. It went forward.

She felt…giddy and guilty and afraid, because how could it be this easy? How could it be this clear? Was it okay that Kit felt like fate? Was it okay if he might be the love of her life?

And on the heels of that came desperation. Fear. And it all became clear. It wasn't the guilt. It was that what she felt for Kit was so big... That if she loved again, and she lost again... She had survived Chuck. But she couldn't survive losing Kit.

She couldn't survive it.

She loved him. In a deep, all-consuming way. As a woman who had known loss. As a woman who had known risk. As a woman who had been married before, and knew what things she would do differently now. Yeah. Because she knew a good marriage. But she also just knew marriage. And the truth was, if she could start from scratch... Kit would be whom she chose. Because they had something more complete. They had a chemistry that you couldn't deny.

And that didn't mean she regretted what she had before. She didn't. It didn't mean it didn't matter. But she was older, and had more perspective. And she knew... She knew the hardship that life could bring your way. She knew the cost of love.

But oh, admitting that Kit was more... That was... She felt like her soul had been bruised. There was the pain of what was behind her, and the fear of what was before her, and she just... She didn't know quite how she was going to go on. Except she could. Because she was here. And it was a gift.

And she remembered the wonder on Kit's face when he'd said that he loved her. When he'd shared with her his realization about love.

There was still more to learn. For him. For her. They were having a baby. And they were married.

She knew why she was here. She had to leave the idea of no one but Chuck as her husband behind her. She had to put away the visions of the life she thought she would have. Because when she put Kit's ring on his finger, he was the one and only. He was the love of her life. Because her life stretched out before her. Her fate, because how could he be anything else?

"You were a good husband," she said. "And I loved our life. It ended too soon. And now I have to keep living. Now I get to keep living." And it was like a weight had been lifted from her shoulders. This revelation that made her feel bruised also made her lit up.

Because she could be happy. There was no limit to that happiness. There was no limit to the love. If only she was willing to stop standing in the past. She had already experienced the loss. And no amount of clinging to it would change it.

No amount of clinging to it would keep her safe.

It would just keep her living a half life, and she needed to want better for herself. She really and truly did.

She walked back to the car, tears still on her cheeks. And she took her phone out of her pocket and dialed her sister. "Juniper… Do you by any chance know where Kit is?"

"As a matter fact I do. But… After you find him… You and I need to talk. Just about everything that's happened."

"Yeah. We do. But after I find Kit."

Kit was sitting at his house, on the front porch. And he knew that waiting out here today was probably pretty foolish. But… He couldn't bring himself to stop waiting. Couldn't bring himself to stop looking.

And then, his own truck came driving up the road. It was his wife.

His heart leaped up into his throat.

She parked in front of the porch, and got out, scrambling toward him, and his initial response was to feel worried. Seeing those tears on her face.

"Are you okay?"

She started to cry. Deep, wrenching sobs that shook her shoulders. "How can you ask that? After what I did to you. How can you still care?" she sobbed. "How can that be the first thing that you ask?"

"Because I love you. Because I've decided to care no matter what."

"I'm okay," she said. "I'm just… I love you," she said.

And he knew they needed to talk. He knew they did. But right now all he wanted to do was kiss her. Kiss those words right from her lips. "I love you," he growled, and he carried her up the steps into the house. They were a fever. She tore his clothes from his body, and he tore hers from hers. This was theirs. It had been theirs for all these years, and they hadn't been able to do anything about it, and now they could do whatever they wanted.

So he stripped her bare, and laid her down on the floor, made her cry out her love for him at least ten more times before he satisfied them both, shaking as he found his pleasure inside her.

"I love you."

And then he picked her up, ready to carry her to the bed.

"Wait," she said.

"What?"

"I just have to get…" She scrambled down from his arms, and grabbed her pants, then she took the ring box out of the pocket.

"I have this for you."

"Damn, sweetie."

They were naked, in his living room, and she was standing in front of him like she had at their wedding.

"I just wanted… I just needed… I want to make vows just for you. For us. Vows that are like the stars we looked at together. Because I thought a lot about what I want. I thought a lot about marriage. About what it is. And about what I want us to have." She brushed a tear away from her face. And he knew right then that no bride could ever have been more beautiful than his. Naked in front of him. Honest and open and not hiding at all.

"Kit Carson," she said, "I think you might be my fate." He'd never cared much for that word. Because he hadn't had a lot of good things in life that could be attributed to fate. But he wanted to believe she was fate. That they were.

So he chose to believe it.

She drew in a jagged breath. "And I have spent a long time trying to avoid that thought. I felt guilty that I was attracted to you. It felt like a sin. And I wanted to make it something less than it was. But my road was always going to lead to you, whether I knew it or not. I can tell you honestly that I made vows to another man, and I kept them. But he's not my husband anymore. I just say that, because I want you to know that these vows that I'm making to you I'm going to keep. I'm gonna keep them with everything I am."

A tear trailed down her cheek and he reached up and wiped it away. He wanted to make all of her pain easier. Always. He knew too much about life to think he could keep her from it entirely, but he could carry some of it.

"I'm not married to you because of the baby," she said. "I know that marriage is more than that. Deeper than that. I love you, and I want to share a life with you. House with you. A bed with you. I love you because you make me feel things I didn't know were possible. I love you, because… Even just talking to you… It made me feel like I could shake myself out of this hole that I was standing in. That place where I was stuck. You made me feel that way. And I really wanted that. But then we… We became more. We became what I think we were meant to be."

"Shelby… I love you. And I know for a fact that I was meant to be with you. And there were all these things, all these terrible things that made me feel like I couldn't be with anyone, but when I sat back, and I honored what I lost instead of just being angry about it… That was when it made sense. That was when I could love you. And I really do love you."

"I love you too," she said. "So much. I love you so much and it was all just fear. I'm not gonna say I don't… That I don't feel any now. I do. It's scary. Feeling all of this. It's terrifying. Because, Kit… You're everything in a way no one else has ever been. The way that we talk. The way that we are. And I resisted… The image of you in my house, the image of you in my life, because… It's just so much. It's everything. I was never afraid that I couldn't care about you enough. I was always afraid that if I admitted it, it would be too much. And I promise you… If it ever feels like too much, I'm not going to pull away again. I'm going to lean right in."

And then she took the ring out of the box, and took his hand in hers. And she slipped that band onto his finger. "For better or worse. In sickness and in health. Till forever."

"Till forever," he agreed.

"Also…six inches is patently not enough."

He chuckled. "Glad you came around to seeing things that way.

"I love you."

"It was always you," she said. "It's always you."

Epilogue

Their daughter might not be able to walk yet, but she made a beautiful flower girl.

And when Shelby Carson married her husband for the second time, with a wedding dress and both families in attendance, and no tiara, it was one of the happiest days of her life. She had wanted to have a wedding, a real one, because she wanted everybody to share this with them. But the happiest day of her life was the day she had chosen him for real. For always.

She looked at the head of the aisle, and she saw him standing there. Her gaze had always found him. Always, for all these years.

And she knew that it always would.

* * * * *

AN EX TO REMEMBER

JESSICA LEMMON

One

At the bar of the Silver Saddle, Vic Grandin tipped a fresh bottle of ice-cold beer to his lips and let out a sigh. Tonight at the family ranch he'd gotten into it with his oldest sister, Chelsea, over—what else—who was going to be in charge of the place once Dad retired.

Butting heads with Chelsea over him being the "chosen one" was nothing new. She and Vic were oil and water and had been since the day he'd been born. His four-years-older sister was a force to be reckoned with, and it just so happened he was the reckoning who'd come to set her straight.

Dad had chosen to put Vic in charge. It'd been decreed from the day Victor Jr. and Bethany Grandin learned they were having a baby boy. Their *only* boy, as it turned out. Vic had three other siblings—all sisters—but none of them had given him the hell Chelsea had.

He pinched the bridge of his nose, figuring he wasn't

going to come to a solution tonight any more than he'd skip the TCC charity pool party tomorrow. He hadn't been in a partying mood lately, but he was resigned to going. Attending the Texas Cattleman's Club parties was tradition in Royal, Texas. In other words: *mandatory for all members.*

Maybe it wouldn't be so bad. He could try his luck tomorrow and talk a curvy, bikini-clad woman into warming his sheets for the night. He'd been no stranger to strangers in his bed for the last decade or so. Why change now?

But a quiet voice inside warned that a hookup would be less satisfying than it sounded. He'd been on a sort of sexual hiatus for just that reason. Lately the company of a good woman—even for a night—had made him feel empty. A tough sell for a man who'd been seeking the rest of himself for as long as he could remember.

Before he could remind himself to snap out of his shitty mood, a musical voice wafted along the shining bar top, over his left shoulder, and dripped like honey into his ear canal. Beer bottle hovering in midair, he paused, allowing the sound to coat his body in a familiar, aching warmth. He knew that voice. The soft, kind quality of it when she was being polite, or the tremor of hurt it held whenever she was angry.

Aubrey Collins had never truly been capable of meanness. During their long-deceased relationship, meanness had been reserved for him.

He turned his head after bracing himself for seeing her, but the sight of her still sent him into a spiraling, sputtering tailspin. Her profile—the cute nose, full pouty lips and long, carelessly styled auburn hair— served as reminders of all he'd lost. Those features were virtually the same as the day she'd thrown his engagement ring at him and told him under no uncertain terms to go fuck himself.

"Evening, Ms. Collins," he drawled, unwilling to let her flee the premises without first acknowledging his presence. He guessed their interaction wouldn't end well, and he'd likely feel like shit on the drive home as he remembered the hand he'd had in turning his starry-eyed good girl into a jaded, bitter woman.

Since Vic was no stranger to bad ideas with worse consequences, he wouldn't let her leave without talking to him. She'd either ignored him or avoided him over the years, but there'd been no missing hearing her ask for her take-out order a moment ago. He figured he had a few minutes, tops, to converse with his ex.

She faced him, smooth, fiery red hair sliding over one delicate shoulder. A shoulder covered with the capped sleeve of a floral dress. She looked every ounce the girl next door, but he knew beneath that tasteful frock lay a seductress who'd let loose with him more times than he could count. Now she was closer in proximity to him than she'd been in years, her green eyes flashing a warning not unlike the shake of a rattlesnake's tail. He wasn't scared. She couldn't hurt him any more after rejecting him so thoroughly years ago.

"Mr. Grandin." A regal eyebrow arched over grass-green eyes. They weren't piercing or sharp, but gentle. It was a dichotomy he hadn't expected when they'd met as teenagers, much like her red hair didn't equal a hot temper. Though with him, she had managed to argue damn well. And hold a damn good grudge.

He spun the beer bottle in his hand and tried for small talk. "What brings you out tonight?"

"Takeout. I had a craving for dessert, and no one does cannoli better than Bo."

Cannoli. She loved the dessert, with its cinnamony shell and sweet ricotta filling. Bo went the extra mile and topped it with fresh whipped cream, house-made chocolate sauce and a cherry, which was likely why Aubrey had come here to buy the confection. Or it could be that it was nearing nine at night and the bakeries around town were closed.

"I hear you're announcing the chili cook-off winners tomorrow," he said, opting to stick to what little they had in common. Sadly, their attendance at the event was about all they had left.

She turned her body toward him, curves subtle but visible in the simple dress. Short cowboy boots were on her feet, which made him remember how they used to ride together on his horse whenever she visited the ranch. The wind would blow her hair, and his senses would be filled with the soft fragrance of wildflowers and Aubrey. She was standing two seats down from him, but the electricity that had always zapped between them hummed in the air all the same. He'd felt that way the first day he'd laid eyes on her. She'd been a high school freshman and he was a sophomore with no idea how fucking lucky he was about to be. His luck would eventually run out, and faster than he would have liked.

"Announcing the winner is an honor bestowed upon teacher of the year, you know." She feigned vanity as she flipped her hair. Hair that had tickled his cheek when he'd first kissed her, and later, his chest—and lower—when he'd talked her into doing a host of bad-girl things with him. She'd turned him into a shuddering, brainless mess back in the day. He'd bet she still could.

Damn memories. What he wouldn't give to lose every last one of them where she was concerned. The great ones only reminded him of worse ones. What was the point?

"I heard. Congratulations." He hated the bend of their bland conversation, but he was out of time. Her name had been called by a hostess, who came from the direction of the kitchen carrying Aubrey's to-go order.

"Thank you. It included an honorary TCC membership for the remainder of the year, so looks like we'll be seeing each other around."

He ignored the skipped beat of his heart. Would she show up with a date to future TCC engagements? He didn't know if he could tolerate seeing her with another man.

Her smile for the hostess was genial as she took the paper bag by the handles. She offered him the same smile and paired it with a generic "Good to see you." Like she was talking to a mailman or a clerk rather than the man she used to love with her entire being. He refused to let this opportunity pass without doing something. *Anything*.

"Why don't you let me buy you a drink? You can eat your cannoli here." He had no idea where that ill-fated suggestion had come from, but he doubled down, pulling out the high-backed stool next to his at the bar. "I promise I'll be nice."

Fingers looped around the paper bag's handles, she let out a disbelieving laugh. "*Nice* is not a description of Vic Grandin one hears very often."

"No, I s'pose not. Come on." He slapped the seat for emphasis. "One drink."

She was thinking about it. He could tell by the way she tipped her head and pursed those luscious lips. Lips he suddenly needed on his more than another sip of beer. If he could talk her into staying for a drink, maybe he could talk her into more. What'd be the harm in one kiss?

She glanced at the exit, as if calculating how long it'd take for her to sprint to her vehicle, before looking back at him. She shook her head, and that's when he knew he'd convinced her. She held up her index finger. *"One."*

His heart leaped like he'd scored the winning touchdown in the big game. He couldn't stop his grin as he ordered her a chardonnay from the bartender.

"Actually, I'll have a martini. On the rocks, extra dry. Two olives." She turned keen eyes on his as she pulled a plastic container from the bag. "Seems you don't know me as well as you think you do."

"Seems so." Vic blew a laugh from his lips and watched the bartender make a drink he'd never in his life seen Aubrey order. When she pried off the lid to her dessert, he leaned close, catching a whiff of her clean-cotton scent. "Are you gonna share that with me or what?"

"Or what," she replied, her smile painted on. At least that's what her smile felt like. Like she'd slapped on a faux joker's grin from cheek to cheek. She'd had a long week, and all she'd wanted tonight was to sit down with a bottle of wine and her favorite movie. First, she'd eaten dinner—a salmon Caesar salad she'd made herself—but by the time she'd reached for the wine, the idea of a cannoli from the Silver Saddle had introduced itself into her mind and refused to leave.

Now she was here, a martini she didn't want in front of her, and she was eating dessert with a man she didn't particularly like. She used to love him, but that'd been a long time ago.

She sipped the bitter drink and licked her lips, vow-ing to choke it down for the sake of her pride. Vic wasn't allowed to presume what she needed or wanted out of life. Not anymore. She was no longer the innocent six-teen-year-old who'd been enamored with him, or the eighteen-and-a-half-year-old who'd practically begged him to take her virginity. Hell, she wasn't even the twenty-year-old who'd bounced her engagement ring off his chest after a horrible argument.

She was thirty now, an adult. Teacher of the year. Honorary TCC member. Single, sure, but no longer ignorant of the ways of the world. And she had a PhD in Vic Grandin. She knew beneath that charm there was a man who relished having control. A man who believed he was God's gift to everyone.

But. She'd grown up and understood that punishing him with the cold-shoulder treatment wasn't helping her evolve as a person. She saw him around Royal often—how could she not when the Grandin family roots ran four generations deep into their ranch land? She'd see him at the TCC pool party tomorrow, and again next month at the Halloween masquerade, and, oh, don't forget the Christmas festivities. Perhaps she should have refused the offer of membership…

As unpalatable as the idea of forced conversations with him was, she was done keeping to herself. She had a life, too. Accepting the offer to announce the chili cook-off winners was only the beginning of her being out and about more. She and Vic might as well call a truce. She took another drink of her disgusting martini, narrowly avoiding a shudder.

"Since when do you drink martinis?" he asked, sounding unsure.

"A while now," she lied. "I see you haven't veered

from the same red-labeled beer you were drinking when you were underage."

"Don't fix what's not broken." He sucked on the beer bottle, his throat moving as he swallowed. She took a good look at him up close. From dark wavy hair she knew was soft to the touch to espresso-brown eyes she'd sworn she'd glimpsed her future in. His solid build had filled out some, but his jeans and flannel shirt and the boots hooked on the rung of the chair hadn't changed a bit. She shouldn't admire him but couldn't help herself. This was Royal. She could throw a rock and hit a guy wearing a flannel and boots, but Vic looked better than any Texan had a right to. Especially given how well she knew him.

They drank and chatted about his parents and hers, his family's ranch and what it was like for her to teach high schoolers. Maybe it was the martini loosening her limbs, but she found herself relaxing into the conversation. Leaning on one elbow, she finally surrendered the dessert container to him.

"Really?" His smile was one of delight, sending a strange jolt of awareness through her. From her chest to her belly to parts too long neglected to acknowledge.

While she hadn't been much of a partygoer over the years, she had kept busy with work. Her passion for teaching followed her home like a stray puppy, one she welcomed and nurtured. That meant a lot of nights spent planning and grading, but her students were worth it. They, and her career, had become Aubrey's whole life. Which meant dating had taken a back seat. She'd made some effort to date over the last ten years she and Vic had been apart, but not as much as he had. *Nowhere* near as much as he had.

"Hurry before I change my mind." She offered him her spoon.

"I haven't eaten one of these in ages."

He polished off the remaining cannoli in two bites, licking a dollop of whipped cream from the spoon. Watching his tongue swipe the sweet cream from his upper lip shook her good sense from her head like a cup full of dice. She remembered how he'd lain waste to her with that tantalizing mouth…when he hadn't been bossing her around with it.

He plucked the cherry from the container, still dripping with chocolate sauce, ate it, and then dangled the empty stem between them. Narrowing one eye, he asked, "Think I can still do it?"

"With the practice you've had over the last ten years?" She folded her arms and tried to appear not to care that he'd been with other women since her. She *shouldn't* care. "I bet you can do it with your eyes closed."

"I'll take that bet." He closed his eyes, dark lashes casting shadows on his cheeks, and popped the stem into his mouth. As he worked his jaw, she took advantage of the moment and soaked him in. His handsome face, the bad-boy scruff that had been absent when he'd dated her and the divot in his chin she'd always found unforgivably sexy.

He opened his eyes and caught her staring, his schoolboy grin as mischievous as the day he'd asked her out after class that first time. Then he produced the cherry stem between his teeth. He'd tied it in a knot with his tongue, which ushered in more memories of how good he'd been with that part of his anatomy when they'd been together.

He held the knotted stem between his index finger

and thumb and fixed his gaze on hers. "Wanna do something crazy?"

Too late.

"Like what?" she heard herself ask. There was a rogue part of her chanting, "Do it, do it!" Entertaining that voice was as ill-advised as having a drink with Vic in the first place. *That's it. No more martinis.*

"Like relive our past. The good part. The best part."

She was already shaking her head.

"Hear me out, Aubrey with the auburn hair." He grinned. She couldn't help smiling at the nickname he'd sung loudly and obnoxiously whenever he'd passed her in the hallway on her way to Advanced English. His voice low and husky, he rumbled, "Spend the night with me. No talk about the past or the future. We'll do what we're best at doing, feel that sweet, sweet release we're both aching for, and in the morning you can pretend it never happened. What d'ya say?"

"I say you're crazy," she breathed while a visual of him kissing her deeply, his hand beneath her bra, danced merrily in her brain. The worst part was that she wasn't half as offended as she should be.

"Yeah, I am. But who cares?"

Why, oh, why was she considering his offer? She'd be insane to hop into bed with him again—certifiable. He somehow read her expression—or maybe her thoughts—and gave her the nudge that would seal her fate. After checking if anyone in the mostly empty bar was listening—they weren't—he leaned close and dipped his voice into seductive territory.

"Remember how good we were together, Aub? I'll deliver, mark my words. I'll make it *so* good, you'll forget your own name."

She had to chuckle at his audacity, even as desire slid

honey-smooth through her veins. It'd been a long time since anyone had delivered on half that promise. She knew from experience Vic's suggestive tone wasn't for show. Ten years hadn't dulled the white-hot memories from when they were naked together.

"And then we go back to normal like nothing happened?" She put her hand to her throat and toyed with her necklace, hardly able to believe her own ears.

"Hand to God." He raised a palm. "We'll never speak of it again."

Two

Two days later

Aubrey blinked her eyes open and instantly wanted to shut them again. Her head ached, but it wasn't a normal ache. It wasn't like when she slept on her neck wrong or spent too much time looking down at her laptop. It was a full skull ache, with battering rams and spikes that'd been driven in by sledgehammers. She reached up to touch her temple, and that's when she encountered the bandage. Not a huge white gauze wrapped Van Gogh style, but a decent-size patch covering some sort of injury.

Also, she was not in her bedroom at home, recovering from too many Vic-induced orgasms. She was...in a hospital room?

Her mother leaned over Aubrey's supine form, worry

lines bisecting her fair strawberry-blond eyebrows. "How did you sleep?"

"Um." Aubrey looked around at the muted tan walls, the uninspired abstract floral paintings, and finally down at the scratchy white sheets and avocado-green throw covering her lower half. Even in a suite, with no need for a privacy curtain, there was no missing that she was in a hospital bed. Aubrey shut her eyes and tried to think back on what could have landed her in here, but her mind was a literal blank. "What happened?"

Her mother's gaze slid to the side, where Aubrey's father, Eddie, stood, his smile broadcasting as much worry as Mary's frown. He was a gentle man, and Aubrey had always been Daddy's girl, but the tenderness with which he looked at her was scaring her a little.

"You took a spill, gingerbread," he said, using her nickname from when she was a small girl. "Just a light knock on the head. But we couldn't be too careful."

"Oh." She didn't have any memory of the "spill" she'd taken. Patchy memories would be concerning, but she didn't even have those. "Where was I when it happened?"

"It doesn't matter, dear," her mother said, which was a weird response.

"Of course it matters." Aubrey pushed her hands into the mattress and sat straighter, earning a spike of pain down the back of her skull for her trouble. She held her head in her hands and breathed deeply, her eyes settling on the blanket and the matching avocado-green gown she was wearing. "I can't remember what happened. That's a problem."

"It's not as bad as you might think." A throaty female voice entered the room ahead of the woman who owned it. The doctor had a full, friendly face and sleek black hair, and she was at least an inch taller than Aubrey's father. She carried an iPad in one hand, which she glanced down at as she introduced herself. "I'm Dr. Mitchell. How are you feeling?"

"I— My head hurts. And I can't remember falling. Is anything broken?"

"No broken bones. The cut on your head was minor. You can probably lose that bandage in a few days." Dr. Mitchell hummed as she scrolled through her tablet. "I see you fell during the chili cook-off at a pool party of some kind."

"The TCC charity pool party," Aubrey said automatically, but she didn't recall being there, only that she'd had it on her schedule. "I was announcing the winners, right?"

"The stage collapsed while you were at the podium," the doctor answered calmly. "You were knocked unconscious, which can be very serious. Overall, your scans looked good, and there is no swelling in the brain. It's normal to have gaps in your memory in the meantime. They should return little by little."

"Gaps? How many gaps?" Aubrey's heart raced as she absorbed the news. She fell and knocked herself unconscious? Her memory *should* return? None of it sounded like good news to her. Her parents were wearing twin expressions of worry, and the doctor was talking to Aubrey like she was younger than the sixteen-year-old students she taught. A wave of relief covered her as she realized she remembered that, at least. She was a teacher, high school. Advanced Writing 101. "I was voted teacher of the year."

"Well, that is some accomplishment. Congratulations." The doctor offered a pretty smile that reached her eyes. Aubrey wanted to trust her, but she was having trouble not fleeing from the room in a panic. "It's important for you to rest. Take it easy."

"The school year just started," Aubrey huffed. "I have lesson plans. I have students counting on me to—"

"You have to rest, honey," her mother said. "Doctor's orders."

Aubrey turned to Dr. Mitchell and pleaded with her eyes.

"I can't allow you to return to school until I'm satisfied you've recovered. I suggest you stay with your parents for the foreseeable future. They told me they have plenty of space."

"I repainted the guest room," Mary Collins chirped.

"No, Mom. I… I'll stay in my apartment." Wherever that was, she thought as another dart of panic embedded itself in her chest.

"I'm sorry, Aubrey. You can't be alone right now," the doctor said.

"Well, then I'll stay with Vic." That made the most sense. She wasn't moving home like some prepubescent child. "Where is he, by the way?"

Her mother's jaw dropped while her father's mouth pulled into a tight line of disapproval.

"Vic's not welcome here," her father growled. She knew Vic wasn't her father's favorite person, but it was about time he got over it. They'd been dating for nearly fifteen years at this point.

"You have no right to keep him from me. He's my boyfriend. I love him. I need him, especially since I can't remember anything." She squeezed her eyes shut and pounded her balled fist on her leg. Her eyes sprang open, her heart thrashing as a memory descended. "We were eating cannoli together the night before the pool party."

"Vic?" her mother asked.

"Yes, Vic!" Aubrey laughed, thrilled to have uncovered a recent memory. "Then we..."

One look around the room reminded her she shouldn't share what happened after. The moment he'd taken her hand and led her from the Silver Saddle. They'd driven separately, for reasons she couldn't recall, so he'd followed her to her apartment. He'd kissed her the second she let them inside, his hands sliding around her waist. He'd tasted like vanilla whipped cream and heaven. She remembered the rest of the night in vivid Technicolor. The way he'd taken off her clothes slowly, kissing every revealed patch of skin. How he'd murmured compliments and encouragement into her ear while he made love to her in her bed. He'd stayed over but left early the next morning, kissing her goodbye and leaving a mug of coffee on the nightstand as she lay blissfully sated and hugging her pillow.

"We...hung out," she finished lamely. "Anyway, I need to see him."

"I think that would be a splendid idea." The doctor's eyes twinkled before she turned to Aubrey's parents. "Can you give Vic a call? Tell him to swing by, that Aubrey is well enough to see him and is asking for him."

"He's probably worried sick." Aubrey figured that must be true. After the night they'd shared, how could he not be here? "I don't understand why he's not by my side. That's not like him."

She shook her head, trying to will forth more memories, but there was a significant gap where Vic was concerned. While she recalled the sensual night they spent together with pulse-racing clarity, the last memory of him before that one was when they'd been in high school together. Although, that sort of made sense.

They'd fallen in love during those tender early years, so those memories were embedded in her brain deeper than most. But she couldn't shake the idea that there should be more mundane memories. Of dinners out and coffees at his ranch. Of I-love-you phone calls or text messages while she was at school.

"I'm scared," she said to her shaking hands. "I can't seem to remember much at all. What if my memory never comes back? What kind of life can I lead living in the dark?"

"Try not to worry." The doctor placed a hand over both of Aubrey's. "Remember what I said. Don't try too hard and they will come. I've worked with many patients who have suffered head trauma. This isn't as uncommon as you might think."

"It's not?"

"Nope. Your brilliant brain knows what it's doing. In the meantime, we're going to call Vic. Get him right over here."

Aubrey nodded. Panic wasn't going to help her heal any sooner, but she couldn't stop the anxiety from descending. Her parents exchanged concerned glances, and she shook her head, not understanding why they were trying to keep Vic away from her.

"He probably had an emergency at the ranch. He's got a lot on his plate." She had no specific recollection as evidence that was true, but it felt true. She was going to have to trust the rest of her senses in the absence of memories.

"I'll prescribe meds for the headache," the doctor told her as she tapped her iPad. Then she turned to Aubrey's parents. "If you have a moment, I can explain Aubrey's medicine and a few guidelines she needs to follow."

"Sure," Mary answered, Eddie by her side.

"Mind if I borrow your parents and send in a nurse to treat your headache, Aubrey?"

"That's fine. As long as you come right back with Vic." She aimed that command at her father, who gave her a solemn nod.

"All right, gingerbread."

Vic had given up pacing in the waiting room an hour ago. Now he sat on the uncomfortable chair and bobbed one knee up and down while he checked his email on his phone. Trying to work remotely was a waste of time, but he needed to occupy his mind while he waited to see Aubrey. Without the distraction of social media or work, all he'd done was worry himself sick. He wasn't leaving this hospital until he saw she was okay with his own two eyes.

At the chili cook-off, she had taken the stage, looking more gorgeous than the night before, when he'd slipped into bed with her at her apartment. He'd promised they'd never speak of it again, but the moment her bright green eyes landed on his, he'd decided to hell with his promise. He'd planned on waiting until she announced the winners and scooping her into his arms. He didn't give a shit who saw—his best friend, Jayden, his sisters or Aubrey's parents. But his plans hadn't worked out.

Just as she'd begun her speech, the stage crashed down on one side, sending Aubrey flying off it. Vic had pushed his way through the crowd that had been closing in collectively to help. By the time he reached Aubrey, her mother was on the phone with 911 and Eddie Collins was telling him to "stay the hell away from my daughter."

Vic had been on the brink of telling her father that his daughter had been sleeping in his arms not twenty-four hours ago, but Jayden had rushed in and restrained him. Good thing, too, or who knew what sort of scene Vic would have made.

Instead, he'd fallen back, waiting as Aubrey was checked by paramedics and then following the ambulance to the hospital. Jayden had insisted on going with him, but Vic refused. The accident had shifted the vibe of the evening from best friends each looking for a woman to share the night with to one of concern and worry.

What Vic hadn't told his best bud was that he *hadn't* been looking for a woman to share the night with. Not after spending the previous night with Aubrey. Feeling her beneath him for the first time in ten years had been nothing short of a miracle, and miracles didn't occur often in his life. Holding her in his arms, her breaths tickling his neck as she slept soundly, he'd decided his life had been shitty for far too long. As grateful as he was for his wealth, his community status and his family, a piece was missing. Could Aubrey be that piece?

When Vic had rushed to the hospital behind the ambulance, he'd been told to sit in the waiting room. He'd pushed his luck, approaching anyone wearing scrubs, telling everyone who would listen that he needed to see his fiancée. A white lie, but one he'd hoped would gain him access faster.

Finally a thin, angular blonde nurse had come out to assure him that Aubrey was fine, but her doctor was limiting her visitors. Vic hit the roof. He'd used plenty of swear words to communicate how dissatisfied he was with that answer. That's when Eddie had emerged from a long hallway and threatened to call the cops.

Vic had laughed as he'd explained to Eddie that the cops in Royal wouldn't touch him. Everyone knew Victor Jr. would have their asses if they laid a hand on his only son. If pressed, Vic could make one phone call and have complete access to Aubrey's room—hell, this entire hospital. Then Aubrey's mother, Mary, had stationed herself between them. In a calm, motherly tone, she'd explained that the doctor's advice was designed to protect Aubrey. Mary had placed a hand on his arm and had said, "If you care about her, you'll cooperate."

It was a low blow, but she'd forced his hand. Vic promised to behave, adding the caveat that he wouldn't leave the waiting room until he was allowed to see her.

Now, after having spent several restless hours alternating between sitting on an uncomfortable chair or wearing the carpet to threads with his frantic pacing, Vic wasn't sure if he could keep the first half of his promise. He couldn't sit here another second without an update.

When he was halfway to the nurses' station, the nurse readied her frown for him as Mary and Eddie materialized from the corridor. He rerouted and raced to them, trying to read their expressions and failing. Was it worry he saw on Mary's face, or fatigue? Was Eddie angry simply because he'd been angry at Vic for the last decade, or had something awful—*more awful*— happened to Aubrey?

"What's wrong? What's going on?" Acid hit the back of Vic's throat thanks to too many cups of stale hospital coffee.

"She's awake, and she's asking for you." Eddie didn't sound happy about the fact. The man had his reasons, but Vic wasn't letting that stop him.

"Good. Let's go."

"Before you go in, we have to talk," came the calm

cadence of the doc who appeared at Mary's side. She extended an arm. "I'm Dr. Mitchell."

He shook the older woman's hand and listened while she explained Aubrey's state. Memory loss, at least partial, was described in medical terminology that didn't make Vic feel any better.

"Like brain damage?" he clarified, wondering if he might puke on the nice doctor's shoes.

"Her scans don't show any permanent damage, but the brain is tricky. Memories return in a trickle or a flood, but it's best that Aubrey remembers at her own pace, without anyone overwhelming her with facts in an effort to jog her memory."

"But she's asking for me, so she must remember me." Vic glanced at Mary.

"She remembers you." Mary smiled. Aubrey's mother had always liked him more than Eddie had. "And us. And that she's a high school teacher. She doesn't remember the fall…and a few other things."

Like the night we slept together?

"Aubrey believes you are a couple," the doctor interjected. "Her parents tell me you haven't been together for a long while."

"Ten years," Eddie put in.

"That's…not entirely true," Vic mumbled. Eddie's face hardened.

"Well, it's important to do what's best for Aubrey." Dr. Mitchell made deliberate eye contact with Aubrey's parents and then with Vic. "It's my recommendation to let her come to her memories on her own, but in the meantime, you should go along with what she believes is true."

"Seriously?" Vic asked, trying to wrap his head around this new twist.

"As long as it's not harming her in any way." Dr. Mitchell smiled.

"You don't know him." Aubrey's father glared at Vic.

"Eddie!" Mary admonished her husband. Then to Vic explained, "Too many facts too fast could overwhelm her and cause a setback, or worse."

"What could be worse?" Vic asked, his voice cracking.

"Right now she remembers quite a bit," the doctor continued. "Her vocation, the people around her. She mentioned her lesson plans and how she needs to return to work. There's no way I can clear her yet, but if she makes substantial progress, soon. Rest and consistency are the two most important aspects of her healing. She can take part in other activities, though I'd like her to avoid spending too much time with electronics—no binge-watching television shows or scrolling through social media on her cell phone."

"She's staying with us until she's better," Mary told Vic. He nearly laughed. Aubrey loved her parents, but when she left for college, she'd shared with him how she was glad to finally have her independence.

"I understand you have a ranch, Vic," said Dr. Mitchell.

"Yes."

"No horseback riding until I say."

He opened his mouth to agree when Eddie growled, "She's not going to be spending time with him."

"She can do whatever she damn well pleases," Vic growled back.

"Listen." The doctor held up both hands. "I'll reiterate, this is not about you or what you want for Aubrey. This is about what's best for *her*. So while your manly show of territorialism is very impressive, you are going to have to take a step back and allow Aubrey to be in the lead. She's a capable, intelligent woman who has suffered a hiccup in her memory. If you behave yourselves, she'll have a better chance of fully recovering that memory. Which is what we all want, right?"

"Right." Eddie answered first and spoke to Vic next. "And when her memory returns, she'll recall the hell you put her through. Then she won't want anything to do with you. The doc's right. My daughter's smart. She knows what's best for her. She knew ten years ago, too, and it wasn't you."

Vic stepped into Aubrey's hospital room alone, thank God. He hadn't been sure what to expect, though he wasn't surprised by her washed-out skin and limp hair, red-rimmed eyes and hospital gown. What did surprise him was her reaction when she saw him. She immediately started to cry.

He rushed to her side, and she grabbed his hand, kissing and nuzzling his knuckles. She told him how scared she was and asked why he hadn't been here earlier. She mentioned she'd been afraid he'd forgotten about her.

"I was here. I was in the waiting room. They wouldn't let me in." He sat on the edge of her bed. Leaning over her came naturally, as did the temptation to kiss her. He resisted. Her gaze was locked on his, her eyes open and vulnerable. That was a recent development. Even after they'd slept together two nights ago, she hadn't looked at him with this sort of raw trust in her eyes. She'd had her guard way up. Hell, they both had. The release and afterglow of sex had been worth any discomfort that followed, but they had each been careful not to reveal too many of their secrets that night.

This tenderer version of Aubrey had been missing for

a decade. She seemed genuinely relieved to see him, her hand stroking his forearm the way she used to whenever she was anxious.

"I can't believe my dad kept you from seeing me. He's ridiculous."

Rather than agree, which Vic did, he said, "I'm here now."

"Good." She sniffled and smiled. "Bust me out of here, will you?"

"As soon as I can," he promised. She wouldn't do well confined to this room, that was for sure. "Your doctor's a smart lady. She knows what's best for you."

"She said it'll take a while to regain my memory." Aubrey shook her head and looked out the window. "Amnesia, Vic. Like a damn Lifetime movie."

He had to chuckle. She was sure acting like herself—her wry sense of humor in place, her vulnerability, her pinpoint honesty. She was going to be fine. He'd make sure of it. If he had to scour the entire state of Texas—or the world—for a medical team who could help her recover, he would.

Though her father's promise that she would hate Vic once she regained her memory gave him pause. Vic wasn't so stupid to think she'd live and let live once she remembered the way they'd broken up back in the day. It was probably best to trust Dr. Mitchell, and in the meantime, Vic would provide what Aubrey wanted whenever she wanted it. Right now, miraculously, she wanted him.

He'd take that second chance, short-lived though it might be. He'd take that all the way to the bank.

Three

"I wish you'd let me help," Aubrey complained from her parents' wide front porch. She held the front screen door open for her father, who wrestled the remainder of her luggage into the house.

Her mother bustled in after him, arms loaded up with a vase of fresh, colorful flowers, a teddy bear with a ribbon around its neck, and several novels. All gifts from Vic, as he'd visited her routinely while she'd been forced to stay in the hospital for observation. The longest week of her life. Especially without the distraction of television or her cell phone. She hadn't been able to read much, either, thanks to her head hurting if she concentrated for longer than fifteen minutes.

"You're not allowed to help." Her mother winked as she issued the warning for the second time. "Stop being so stubborn."

"I'm not." Aubrey followed them inside with a shake

of her head. She hadn't magically regained her memory during that week of abject boredom, but the nurses and her doctor assured her that patience was key.

She trailed behind her parents as they dropped off her things in her old bedroom, now a guest room. The days of posters taped to the wall and rows of journals and stationery on the desk were long gone. Her mother had chosen a sophisticated color palette for the room. Muted blue-gray tone for the duvet as well as one accent wall. The other walls were painted eggshell white, including an upcycled dresser and the nightstands on either side of the double bed.

"It's like a hotel." Aubrey poked her head into the recently painted bathroom. "You said you were remodeling, but I had no idea it would look this different. Unless I'm forgetting?"

"No, no." Her mother waved her off. "You haven't seen it yet. I just did it!"

"Well, I like it." It would have to do, since Aubrey wasn't able to return to her apartment yet. Her apartment, which was decorated in the colors… She paused, her hand frozen on the bathroom light switch as she tried to picture her apartment.

Nothing.

"You all right, dear?" Mary asked.

"Yes. Totally fine." But Aubrey wasn't fine at all. She'd called up a blank rather than being able to picture her own bedroom. The way she'd called up blanks in many areas of her life. Some moments were crystal clear and bright. Others were lost in a black, cavernous void.

"I'll start dinner. Come on, Eddie. I need you to fire up the flattop grill for the steaks."

Her parents wandered down the hallway chatting as Aubrey knelt to unzip one of the suitcases her mother had packed for her. As she unearthed her clothes, she instantly felt better. The patterns and styles were familiar, and she recognized a college sweatshirt as one of her favorite go-to garments. She found lots of sleeveless shirts, her preference, as they showed off arms she worked out regularly at her apartment's fitness center. Her mother had also packed several dresses, floral patterned and solids alike. Aubrey usually paired her floral dresses with cowboy boots—check—or with her favorite brown sandals. She lifted a jacket and found them, the same pair she'd envisioned, at the bottom of the suitcase. Hugging the shoes to her chest, she shut her eyes and tried to picture walking into her closet.

Again, nothing.

She blew out a sigh and reminded herself not to rush. Dr. Mitchell had discouraged her from trying too hard, which had caused several headaches already. Aubrey had hoped she'd be able to picture something as mundane as a closet, though. Maybe if she instead thought of being in her bedroom… Eyes still closed, she pictured Vic setting a mug of coffee on the nightstand right before he kissed her goodbye. The memory bloomed to life on the backs of her eyelids.

"I'm taking off. I made you coffee." His voice was low and rocky. His sexy morning voice. It seemed like eons since she'd heard it.

"Okay." She opened her eyes to take one last look at him. He was wearing last night's jeans and flannel. He needed to shave, but then again, no, he didn't. She preferred a bit of growth on that firm jaw of his. As long as he didn't grow it out too long to completely hide the divot in his chin, she wouldn't complain. Not to mention how talented he was with the mouth surrounded

by that scruff. She could still feel it grazing the insides of her thighs...

"Mmm." She opened her eyes and smiled as the puzzle pieces slid together. Vic had walked out of her bedroom while she'd hugged her pillow and watched his very fine ass retreat down the hallway. She could picture the decor of her bedroom clearly now: crisp, clean navy blue and white, with framed black-and-white photographs hanging on the wall. One of a mountaintop, one of a steer peeking through a wire fence.

She *remembered*.

She'd sat up in bed and sipped her coffee, several naughty and delicious details of that night dancing in her head. Sex with Vic had been exquisite. From the moment he'd peeled off his shirt and revealed a tanned, thick chest. So familiar and yet so different from when they'd first been together. To the moment he'd slipped her out of her clothes and laid his lips on her collarbone. Her skin had sizzled the moment his mouth touched her bare flesh, and when he'd pulled one of her nipples onto his tongue, she'd nearly burst into flames.

She remembered their night together, all right. None before it, which was odd, unless she counted her early college years. There seemed to be an awfully wide gap in her recollection...

"Progress is progress," she said aloud, pushing out the threat of panic. Dr. Mitchell had told Aubrey to expect her memory to come back gradually. She'd take the small progress she'd made today as a win. She wasn't going to beat herself up for not remembering everything all at once.

She stored her clothes in the dresser and hung her dresses in the closet. At least she'd remembered her evening with Vic—an entirely lovely memory.

Downstairs, she found her mother chopping vegetables for a salad. Aubrey nudged her out of the way and began slicing cucumbers into neat rounds, unreasonably satisfied when the slices were even. She hadn't lost her ability to cut veggies, or walk, or chew. She had so much to be grateful for.

"What time's dinner?" she asked her mom.

"Forty minutes or so. I have mac and cheese in the oven. That'll take the longest."

"I love your mac and cheese. I'll let Vic know."

Knife poised over a tomato, Mary regarded her daughter with raised eyebrows. "I'm not sure that's a good idea."

"Dad is going to have to learn to live with disappointment. Me being here is an adjustment for all of us, but I'm not changing my day-to-day lifestyle just because I'm under your roof. I'm thirty years old, and if I didn't have to be here, I wouldn't."

"Aubrey—"

"You can't keep me from seeing Vic because I'm living here. This is a wild—and extenuating—circumstance."

It was ridiculous enough not to be allowed to go back to her apartment. Aubrey had argued about that, too, but had come to understand the doctor's reasoning. Dr. Mitchell had warned Aubrey that she could have a dizzy spell and fall in the shower or wake disoriented, having no idea what'd happened to her or where she was. The doctor had added that a familiar environment could overwhelm Aubrey with too much input, worsening her headaches or causing the memories she did have to retreat.

Losing more of her memory was unacceptable, so Aubrey agreed to bind and gag her independent nature for the sake of her healing. Anyway, her mom and dad were both retired teachers who were home most of the time, save for a few speaking engagements here or there. Staying with them would give Aubrey time with them, as well as someone looking over her who wasn't a nurse. It was the best solution. Well, not the *best*.

Aubrey had considered asking Vic if he had room at his place, but instinct warned her against mentioning it to him. They didn't live together, and there must be a reason. Plus, he was busy with the ranch most days. She refused to rattle around in his house—whatever that looked like—waiting for him to come home from work.

She was certain he'd invite her over soon enough, and then she could close another gap in her memory. They could make new memories of being in bed together while they were at it. A grin pulled at her lips.

"Just like when you lived here." Her mother clucked her tongue. "You were over the moon for that boy then, and your father couldn't tell you otherwise."

"Why are they so angry with each other?" Aubrey frowned, unable to recall a plausible reason. "I know Dad's protective, but I'm not an innocent virgin any longer. Vic took that from me a long time ago."

"Aubrey!"

She laughed at her mother's cartoon expression of shock, bugged-out eyes and everything. "Come on, Mom. Don't act like you don't know Vic and I have—"

Aubrey's cell phone rang, saving her poor mother from further trauma. She reached into her shorts pocket and pulled out her phone, excited to see Vic's name on the screen.

"Hi, babe" came out of her mouth feeling both familiar and foreign at the same time. What an odd sensation.

"Hey, uh, Aub," he responded with the slightest hesitation. "Do you need anything, or do your parents have you settled?"

"I'm settled." She walked out the front door and stood on the porch, soaking in the eighty-five-degree weather. September in Texas was still summer, and felt like it. She loved the heat. The sun warmed her skin and reminded her she was alive, the day holding a million possibilities. "Would you like to come for dinner? Mom's making mac and cheese."

"I love your mom's mac and cheese," he answered, his voice low and sexy.

"After dinner you can take me out."

"Take you out?"

"Yes. *Out*. I've been wearing a hospital gown for a week, and I can't spend another minute with my doting parents. I am willing to be polite through dinner, but then you have to steal me away."

His rich laughter sent shivers to the surface of her skin in spite of the hot evening. "You sure you want me to do that?"

"Who else would I want to rescue me?" She paced around the outside of the house, admiring the thick bushes and colorful flowers surrounding her parents' pristine covered porch. Through a window she saw her mother bustling in the kitchen. "You could bring me to your place tonight. For some alone time."

There was a lengthy pause before he said, "I'm not sure you want to come to the ranch just yet."

She frowned. He still lived at the ranch? Granted, his family's home was massive. She remembered the stats—it was hard to forget a number like *sixteen thousand square feet*. The Grandin family home could easily house the entire family and more. With private entrances dotted throughout, she'd rarely stepped through the front door.

"Fine. I'll have to settle for you coming for dinner. We can drink iced tea on the porch, or you can take me out for ice cream after. I miss you."

He cleared his throat. "You do?"

"Yeah." Why wouldn't she?

"Ah, let me finish up and I'll be over. Can I bring anything?"

"Just your sexy self, in a perfectly tight pair of blue jeans. How'd that be?"

She heard the grin in his voice when he said, "Sounds good to me, sugar."

Vic ended the call with Aubrey and stared at the cell phone in his hand in wonder. He hadn't fully wrapped his head around what had transpired during the last week. Namely, that his ex missed him and wanted to spend the night with him.

"What was that about?" His sister Morgan echoed his thoughts as she stepped into his office. Two years younger than him, she was the sister who was almost always on his side. Likely because she didn't give a hoot or a holler—her words—about inheriting the ranch. She owned a fashion boutique called, aptly, The Rancher's Daughter. She knew what she wanted out of life, and it had nothing to do with raising cattle.

"Aubrey invited me to dinner at her parents' house."

"First you two hook up before the cook-off and now you're reconciling?"

Vic hadn't exactly shared that he and Aubrey had hooked up, but Morgan had questioned why he'd been at the hospital guarding Aubrey like a sentinel. He'd answered that they'd had dessert together before the cook-off, and then Morgan had rightly concluded, "Oh my God, you're sleeping together!"

He stood from his chair and grabbed his Stetson from the hook on the wall. He didn't always wear it, but today felt like a good day to start. He could hide his lying eyes beneath the brim. "She doesn't remember we're not a couple, Morgan. She's suffered a serious accident and is asking for my support. What the hell am I supposed to do?"

Morgan twisted her lips to one side. "It feels wrong."

It did. And yet completely right. There'd been a time when he'd have done almost anything for Aubrey. Showing up for her in her time of need felt as natural as breathing to him. "Don't worry. I won't take advantage of her."

Or take her to his bedroom in the private wing of the house, strip her naked and make love to her again. That sounded way too good to his own ears, especially since the memory of doing just that burned hot. But he refused to sleep with her when she had no idea they weren't a couple. The night after the Silver Saddle last week had been different—she'd known what she was getting into. And, damn, had they gotten into it.

Morgan's eyebrows bent as she twirled a lock of long red hair around a manicured fingertip. Unlike Aubrey's auburn locks, his sister's hair was pale red, her skin fairer. "I don't like lying to her."

"We're not lying to her," he said for his sister's benefit. "We're giving her room to remember on her own. Doctor's orders." He placed the hat on his head and sidled past her. "And for the record, I don't like it, either."

He left his office, shutting the door behind him and Morgan, and met his oldest sister, Chelsea, in the hallway, her folded arms and firm line for a mouth what he'd grown accustomed to.

"Say it quick," he warned. "I'm late for dinner with Aubrey's family."

"You're using her."

"I'm not," he said through clenched teeth.

"She hasn't given you the time of day for ten years, and you're waltzing into her life like you never left it."

"It hasn't been ten years. They were together recently," Morgan said in his defense.

"I have this, Morgan," he told his well-meaning but meddling sister. To Chelsea, he said, "Aubrey feels safe when she's with me. I'm doing what her parents and her doctor asked me to do."

"Safe? With you?" Chelsea laughed. "After you tried clipping her wings and making her the pretty little housewife of your dreams? If I recall, she dumped you for it."

"Well, Chels, I don't particularly care for your opinion on the matter."

"I didn't want your opinion on Nolan, either, baby brother."

He gritted his teeth. He'd done his fair share of poking his nose where it didn't belong in Chelsea's budding relationship with Nolan Thurston, but that was different. He'd been looking out for the family ranch, his legacy. "I have a second chance with her, and I'm taking it."

"You won't win her back." Chelsea raised an eyebrow.

"I'm not trying to win her back." He'd settle for her no longer hating him. More than that would be a stone-cold miracle, but her not hating him would be a solid start. Since he'd taken her to bed last week, he'd realized not having Aubrey in his life had reduced him to a primitive version of himself. He'd been growling at his family, lashing out in his own defense and metaphorically pissing on what he'd perceived as his territory.

He wasn't so arrogant as to think Aubrey would take him back, but if they could be cordial, and she could allow him to be in her life at some capacity, well, he thought he might be able to evolve into a halfway decent human being.

"I think it's sweet," Morgan said.

"Sweet!" Chelsea emitted another humorless laugh. "Vic, you are the most arrogant, self-centered man I've ever met, outside of Daddy. You are in this for *you* and no other reason."

His temper warmed his cheeks and caused his fists to curl into tight balls. He reminded himself that Chelsea had never understood him. She had long accused him of resting on his laurels while she did the heavy lifting at the ranch. For years she'd seen only what she wanted to see: that she was losing the ranch to her selfish brother. The truth was he did more than she'd bothered to give him credit for, but he also wasn't blameless. That was too big a discussion for the small amount of time allotted them in this moment.

"I gave up on trying to win your favor a long time ago, Chels." He wearily pushed past her and walked toward the exit. To Morgan, he said, "Don't wait up."

Four

Vic drove to Aubrey's parents' house, a doorstep he'd sworn never to darken again. He knew Chelsea was upset for reasons other than him lying to Aubrey, but he couldn't help feeling a tug of guilt at her accusation.

Chels never had approved of his confidence and didn't hesitate to remind him of his "cocky" nature. He'd be the first to admit his bullheadedness was a character flaw, but he'd come by it honestly. He'd inherited the art of stubbornness from his namesakes, his grandfather and his father. The third Victor in line, Vic had been entrusted to run one of the largest ranches in Royal, Texas, a job description that called for leadership.

Decisiveness and boldness were two qualities required for the ranch to stay profitable for generations to come. What Chelsea perceived as arrogance was Vic doing what their father had charged him to do. Taking over meant *taking over*, and that's exactly what Vic intended to do. If his sisters had been paying attention, they would've noticed that shit ran uphill, not down, when things went wrong. Being in charge was an enormous responsibility.

Not that it mattered at the moment. The family ranch wasn't stable. The question of whether or not there was oil beneath both the Grandin land and neighboring Lattimore property remained unanswered. Ever since a claim on the estate had been made by Heath Thurston, the land Vic called home had been threatened. If Heath seized the land, there'd be no family ranch for Vic, Chelsea and Layla to work.

A terrifying prospect.

He parked in the Collinses' driveway and shut off the truck. Leaning back in his seat, he considered how most people would not agree to play house with their ex. Vic wasn't like most people. The night they'd shared recently had been memorable enough that he'd show up wherever Aubrey asked him to. He wasn't a weak man, but when it came to his high school love, he didn't possess the strength to tell her no. Not when, in her fragile state, she looked at him like he'd hung the moon.

Nothing was better than when she smiled at him, as wide-eyed as when he'd first turned her head. Her admiration when they'd been teenagers had been infinitely better than the acrimony that'd followed years later.

During the long months following their split, he'd given up on winning her back. Eventually he'd reentered the dating world, but it hadn't taken long to realize that he wasn't going to find Aubrey's equal anywhere in this town—or the state. Hell, probably the whole damn solar system. So, fuck scruples. He was taking this opportunity to be in her circle for as long as she'd allow. He knew he still didn't deserve her, but it'd be nice to feel good for a while. It beat stressing out over the ranch while simultaneously handling the pressure of being the Grandin golden child.

At Eddie and Mary Collins's front door, Vic raised a fist to knock. He hid the bouquet of daisies behind his back, pleased when Aubrey opened the door instead of either of her parents. Her eyes were wide and excited before she saw the flowers, and then when she did, she melted like he'd brought her a dozen gold bars instead.

"They're for your mom. I hope you're not disappointed," he told her.

"I live here, too, so we'll both enjoy them." She grinned. It'd been her vibrant, sunshiny smile that had first hooked his heart. He hadn't seen it aimed at him for far too many years.

She clutched his wrist and dragged him into the house he hadn't seen since Aubrey left for college. No, he took that back. He'd come here once after they'd broken up. Vic had literally told Eddie he'd come to "talk some sense into her" for dumping him on his ass. Eddie hadn't let him inside, and Vic figured that'd been for the best. Any other attempts to reach her had been ignored or thwarted by her parents, and the rest was ancient history.

History Aubrey had *forgotten*.

"Mom, Vic's here. He brought you flowers." Aubrey released his arm and bustled around the kitchen filling a vase with water and unwrapping the daisies to arrange them on the dining room table. The same dining room table where he'd shared countless dinners with the Collinses when things had been good. The same sunken living room where they'd played Pictionary on a few innocent nights. The same plaid sofa where Vic and Aubrey had spent a not-so-innocent night while her parents had been away on vacation.

"Thank you, Vic. That's very thoughtful." Mary's mouth was a neutral line. She'd never been as angry at him as Eddie, but who had been? Even Aubrey hadn't matched her father's ire after she'd given the engagement ring back.

"Do you want a beer, babe?" It took Vic a second to realize Aubrey was addressing him.

"Sure."

She cracked the top off a red label and handed him the bottle. Then she pushed an empty platter into his other hand and shoved him toward the back deck. "Take this to Dad, will you? He'll need it for the steaks. Dinner's almost ready."

He couldn't say no to her sweet, sweet smile, despite her sending him into the lion's den.

Outside, Vic offered the platter. Eddie narrowed his eyes but accepted it. Aubrey's father drank from his own beer bottle as he and Vic regarded the smoking grill in silence.

"Thanks for having me," Vic tried.

Eddie, his eyes on the steaks sizzling away on the flattop grill, squared his jaw. "We both know she deserves better than you."

That hadn't taken long.

"But you're who she needs right now. You, for some reason—" he waved the spatula in Vic's general direction "—bring her *joy*."

Vic, on the cusp of defending himself for doing exactly what Eddie—at the suggestion of the doctor—had asked Vic to do, was unexpectedly mollified by those words. Aubrey had forgotten their troubles and their shared pasts. Vic had been charged with standing in as her boyfriend to help her avoid further trauma. But joy? Joy was a tall order. When was the last time he'd brought a woman *joy*? The idea of it was a treasure he hadn't expected to find.

"I'd never lie to her if I could help it." Eddie flipped the steaks over to finish cooking. "Just so happens I can't help it. I love her more than anything on this earth."

"I understand, sir." And he did. At one point Vic had loved Aubrey more than anything on this earth, too. Before he'd screwed up and made her hate him. He was ashamed to admit that a fair amount of the bitterness between them had fueled some of his bad behavior in the past. That wasn't her fault, but at the time he'd laid some of the blame on her. And since he had yet to forgive himself for his repugnant behavior, the least he could do was be here to support her. Maybe he could make up for at least part of the pain he'd inadvertently caused her over the years.

"If for one moment I believe your presence is making her life harder—" Eddie began.

"Got it," Vic interrupted, cutting off whatever idle threat Eddie might make. Back when Vic and Aubrey were kids, Eddie's words had held less weight. Vic had believed he was above reproach with everyone. Now that he was older, and hopefully wiser, he understood her father's concerns.

What Eddie didn't know was that Vic intended to do whatever was best for Aubrey, and damn the consequences. If that meant going against Eddie's wishes, so be it.

"Have they killed each other yet?" Mary set the piping-hot casserole dish on a hot pad on the dining room table.

"Not yet." Aubrey backed away from the window before one or both men spotted her. So far she'd witnessed puffed chests and the swigging of beers. They weren't making eye contact. Dad was staring down at the smoking steaks like if he didn't watch the grill they might up and run for the Texas hills. Meanwhile, Vic was studying the sunset like it was his last before he went to live in an underground bunker.

"Dad sure can hold a grudge," she murmured as she joined her mother in the dining room.

"Your father has his reasons." Mary gave her daughter a pointed look as she fished silverware from the china hutch drawer.

Aubrey guessed her father's reasons were ones she should know, but there was a big empty space whenever she tried to remember why he didn't approve of Vic. Aubrey was his little girl, and he was as protective as usual, but her father's glower seemed to go beyond that reason.

"Steaks." Vic swaggered by and delivered the platter to the table. Aubrey's mouth watered, but it wasn't the steaks causing her to drool. It was *him*. The solid, sturdy build, the thick dark hair she'd recently run her fingers through. A flash of the sexy night they'd spent together fired every last one of her cylinders. Him sliding deep inside her, those dark eyes fastened on hers… "Hungry?"

She blinked him into focus and lifted one eyebrow. "Starving." She didn't mean for dinner and held his gaze long enough to communicate as much. Vic offered a sideways smirk, but it died the second Eddie stepped into the house.

"Let's eat," Eddie said.

Dinner was blessedly uneventful, with small talk

about anything and everything *not* having to do with Vic or Aubrey. Dad talked about sports and Mom about her book club. When the topic of the Texas Cattleman's Club pool party came up, her father quickly changed the subject. Aubrey didn't have the foggiest memory of the chili cook-off.

"Was the winner announced or did I ruin the contest?" she'd asked. The table had fallen silent, the scraping of knives and forks on plates halting at her question. "Who has the best chili in Royal, Texas, anyway?" She'd taken a bite of her steak and chewed, preferring to treat this odd circumstance as run-of-the-mill, but she hadn't received an answer.

"This is very frustrating," she told Vic now. They'd finished their dinners, and her mother had refused her offer to help with the dishes.

Aubrey and Vic walked down the long, winding driveway side by side, the crunching of gravel underfoot interspersed with crickets sawing away in the tall grass. "I don't see why no one can give me a summary of events."

"Are you a doctor now?" Vic came to a halt and faced her, his silhouette grainy in the dark and backlit by the moon. Even in low light, he was the most handsome man she'd ever laid eyes on. "Patience used to be a strong suit of yours, Aub."

"I want to remember. I *need* to remember."

"You will," he said with enough authority that she believed him. As if her amnesia was nothing more than a blip on the radar of an otherwise normal life. That soon she'd be driving, playing brightly colored games on her cell phone and returning to work. She missed her normal life. She loved teaching more than anything, and not having the comfort of her routine—even one she couldn't remember every detail of—was difficult.

He started walking again, bypassing his truck rather than climbing into it. She was fine with prolonging the evening, though she wished they had more privacy. Dad was probably peeking out the window at them right now.

Vic clasped her hand, and she wove her fingers with his, the warmth of his touch going a long way to making her feel better. "Enjoy the moment. That's all you have to do. Live your life until your memory returns."

"I have one *very* vivid memory of us from the other night." She squeezed his hand.

"Oh yeah?"

"Mmm-hmm. The night before my accident. My bedroom. You taking my clothes off and running your tongue over every part of my body. You were starved for me, Vic, like it was the last time we'd be together. It was hot."

She didn't miss when his arm stiffened against hers.

"Don't worry, we're far enough from the house they can't hear. I don't understand why we couldn't lie and say we're going out for ice cream and then sneak into my apartment for a quickie, do you?" She certainly wasn't incapable of physical affection. She could walk, talk, recite her favorite Walt Whitman poem. She was missing a few measly pieces from her past, that was all.

"Sex is, not, um…" Vic swiped his brow, looking uncharacteristically nervous. He wasn't shy. Not at all. He knew what she liked and delivered each and every time. Well, the times she could remember. "Your health is more important."

"Sex is very healthy." She leaned against his arm, relieved to hear his soft laugh in the dark.

"I know, honey. It does us a world of good. But I

beg of you, stop reminding me what I'm missing out on when I'm trying to be noble."

"Nobility from Vic Grandin." She sighed, defeated. "I don't like it."

His grin literally weakened her knees. She clutched his hand tighter. What she wouldn't give to have him naked and next to her tonight. "Can I at least have a kiss?"

"When did you turn into a siren?"

"I don't recall you complaining in the past."

"Ain't that the problem?" Proud of his quip, he winked. She balled her fist and socked his shoulder.

"All right, all right." He tipped his head to the side. "One kiss, but then you have to let me go home. Your daddy's watching."

She wanted to say she didn't care if God himself was watching, but she decided not to press her luck. She wasn't as fragile as everyone thought she was, but she could also admit that she didn't know what she didn't know. Hell, for what little she remembered, she could be a Russian spy with a death toll that rivaled that of a seasoned hit man instead of a hometown teacher.

"I'm not a Russian spy, am I?"

"What?" He laughed the word, his breath coasting over her lips. She tipped her chin in anticipation.

"Nothing." She was going to have to trust the people who loved her for a while. She could live with that.

He closed the gap and touched his lips to hers. They hovered there, mouths moving, arms touching, fingers intertwined. He cradled her head and deepened the kiss, a gentle slide of his tongue on hers, polite but completely mind-altering. The slower he went, the more he savored the kiss, the more she wanted him. Impatient, she speared her tongue into his mouth, yanking the front of his shirt in an effort to get closer to him. Their bodies bumped, her belly encountering hardness behind the fly of his jeans. *Yes, yes, yes.* This was what she wanted. To feel what he felt for her. To have him again and feel a modicum of normalcy in a completely abnormal situation.

He sucked in a sharp inhale. She lost his lips, and the rest of him, her breasts brushing his chest as he pulled away. His expression was playful but scolding when he took a literal step away from her and shoved his hands deep in his pockets. With a shake of his head, he said, "You always knew how to make me forget my place, Ms. Collins."

"I guess we have that in common, Mr. Grandin."

She spun on her heel to head back to the house, along the way trying to decide if she was more disappointed or flattered by his words.

Five

Vic arrived at his office in the Grandin family home the next morning and was immediately surrounded by his two older sisters. Chelsea and Layla were standing, arms folded, foreheads creased.

"What'd I do now?" He moved to the coffee cart on the back wall, relieved someone had been saintly enough to brew a pot before he'd arrived. He'd had a virtually sleepless night after the kiss Aubrey had given him in her parents' driveway.

The old Vic would have thrown her into his truck and left a cloud of dust in his wake as he raced her to his bedroom. Once there, he would have finished what she'd so brazenly started. But since the night he'd recently spent with her, he'd realized he'd been a selfish ass for way too long. Add to that her compromised memory and his starring role as her white knight and there was no way he could act on his impulses. If not for a sudden attack of conscience, he could've spent last night making love to her on every sturdy surface in his room instead of lying on his back, wide-awake, with a hard-on that wouldn't quit.

Being mature sucked.

"You didn't *do* anything." Layla sounded sincere. Her wavy blond hair was down, her mouth set in a determined line. The look was uncommon given she'd been happier lately. Ever since she'd fallen in love with and married Josh.

"We're here for the quarterly meeting, as per Daddy's request," Chelsea said.

Shit. He'd totally forgotten. His head had been elsewhere last night. On the faint freckles dotting the bridge of Aubrey's nose, and the feel of her tight little fist clutching his shirt. She'd wanted him, and he'd refused her. God, he was a jackass.

"Well, where is he?" Vic sipped his coffee as he glanced out of the office window at the stables. No sign of his father anywhere.

"We thought you would know, you two being so close and all," Chelsea answered with a smirk. Vic refused to take the bait. He didn't have the energy to argue with her today.

"I'll saddle up Titan and find him." Cell reception was spotty in many areas of their expansive ranch.

On the back of his gray roan Percheron, Vic rode the perimeter of the ranch in search of Victor Jr. No sign of his father's horse, or his wide black cowboy hat, but he did spot a woman at the edge of the Grandin property, right where it butted up against Lattimore land.

"Help you?" he called out as he approached the stranger. Her hand rested on the hilt of a measuring wheel. "You're a surveyor."

"How'd you know?" A quick lift of her eyebrows told him she was surprised to see him, but she hid it with a smile. "Was it the measuring device or my bright orange safety vest that tipped you off?"

The woman was both tall and slender, wearing a flannel beneath that safety vest paired with jeans and boots. The way she looked him dead in the eye suggested she wasn't the least bit intimidated.

"This is private property."

"No worries. I'm done here," she answered.

"What *were* you doing here?" He didn't expect an answer, but once again she addressed him directly.

"I was hired."

"By who?"

"By whom, you mean, and the answer is Heath Thurston."

Heath. Of course. That bastard was getting bolder by the minute. The reminder that Thurston was still trying to wrap his grubby paws around the deeds to the Grandin and Lattimore ranches made Vic see red.

"Have a good day now. That's a beautiful horse." With a flip of her blond hair, the slight woman made her way to the road with her equipment in tow. Vic made sure she was gone before heading back to the house himself.

On his way he encountered Layla, who was riding a fairly cooperative mustang today. She trained horses, so she knew what she was doing, which was why she'd soon be opening her own ranch with Josh. Vic felt the odd pinch of loss that she'd be here at the family ranch less and less…so long as they could hold on to it.

The mustang grumbled his complaint but came into line as Layla walked him next to Vic and Titan on the way to the house.

"Who was that?" she asked.

"A surveyor hired by Heath Thurston."

"Damn," his sister said under her breath.

"Yeah, I know."

"How do you know she was sent by Heath?"

"She told me. Apparently no one is being shy about the land they want to take from us and the Lattimores."

"We have what everyone wants, Vic. Look around."

He took in the blue skies and the ranch land dotted with cows of all colors. Utopia. A utopia they could lose if Heath Thurston continued to press the issue of oil rights. The other man saw it as his way of righting the scales. His deceased mother and half sister weren't here to fight for the land they were presumably promised, so Heath was doing it for them. Heath's twin brother, Chelsea's fiancé, Nolan, had decided to remain neutral.

Vic didn't buy it.

He'd never admit to his sisters how much the threat scared him, or how close this litigation was coming to causing a serious kink in his family's and the Lattimores' lives. Vic cared about this ranch, beyond running it for his pride's sake. This was his family home. He refused to lose it.

"The Grandins and the Lattimores have been neighbors for as long as anyone can remember." He squinted up at the bright blue sky covering their lands and beyond. "Can you imagine if—"

"No," Layla interrupted. "I'm not going to imagine what if." Her eyes were as hard as steel, but he saw fear behind them. He'd do anything to protect his sisters from what was going on right under their noses. He felt so damned helpless in this situation. "I might be building a life of my own, but the Grandin ranch will always be home."

They dismounted at the barn, leaving their horses

to be cared for by the stable hands, before they walked back toward the house.

"I'm heading back to my ranch to see how the construction is going. If you spot Daddy, send my regrets on missing the meeting." Layla slapped Vic's shoulder and wandered off in the direction of her car.

Some days the idea of everything resting on his shoulders wasn't as romantic a notion as it had been when he was younger. He'd imagined wielding both power and control like his father, with a fair hand. Vic had prided himself on being firm and decisive, but now that he was older, he saw how many situations were not simply black and white. There were as many shades of gray as on his horse Titan, and those shades often bled together, making for a muddy canvas. Individual colors were impossible to distinguish.

That made him think of Aubrey. There was no black-and-white way of thinking with her, and she'd muddied his mind more than anything. When he'd gone to dinner last night, he'd resolved not to kiss her. He'd changed his mind the moment she'd followed him outside. One look into her jade-green eyes and he hadn't been able to tell her no. Not when she'd looked at him like she still loved him. Which, he supposed, she thought she still did.

He scrubbed his forehead and sighed, the day feeling long already, and it'd only just begun. When he stepped back into his office, his coffee had gone cold and his father was sitting at Vic's desk.

"You're late. Layla and Chelsea have gone."

"You're the one taking over, son." His father shrugged.

Hell, here they went again.

By the time the sun was setting, Vic was well and truly beat. He needed sleep, or at least to destress. Typically he'd call Jayden so they could go out, but the question was *go out and do what?*

Drink beer? Flirt with women? Not only did Vic not want to flirt with other women, but he was practically betrothed now that he was pretending to Aubrey they'd never split. He didn't mind as much as he thought he would have. For the last ten years, he'd been judicious about the women he dated, so he hadn't made any future plans. A future with a woman was something he'd only imagined with Aubrey, back when she'd worn the engagement ring he'd put on her finger.

He'd slipped right back into that mode of thinking. It was like they'd stepped into a time machine and had traveled back to high school. The hand-holding, the kisses in her parents' driveway, denying each other the sex they so desperately wanted... He'd held out for a little over two years before he and Aubrey slept together. Her first time. His first time. He wasn't typically sentimental, but thinking back on those days caused his chest to constrict. They'd lost so much, which made for an odd parallel to potentially losing the family ranch.

Without overthinking it, he picked up the phone and called her. When her sweet voice answered, he said, "About that ice cream you wanted..."

Thirty minutes later he and Aubrey were sitting outside Dairy Prairie, a new ice-cream shop in Royal. He'd gone with a scoop of rocky road on a waffle cone, while Aubrey had opted for double-chocolate macadamia nut on a wafer cone. Having licked her way down to the base of the cone, she took her first bite. At least the torture part of the evening was over for him. Watching her pink tongue lap away at the sweet cream had sent his brain free-falling into the gutter.

"Doesn't that taste like Styrofoam?" he asked before

taking a bite of his waffle cone. Crisp, sugary delicious-ness. "Wafer cones are tragic."

"I like wafer cones." She shoved him, rolling her eyes playfully. He soaked up the moment. He'd learned the hard way to treasure her not looking at him like he was a horrible person. "How was your day at the ranch?"

The stress he'd been successfully avoiding rolled back in like the tide. "Peachy."

"And your sisters?"

"Oh, you know. Chelsea is engaged to Nolan Thur-ston. Layla is married to Joshua Banks. Morgan is single and maintaining her role as everyone's favorite Gran-din." Just the facts. He didn't know how much Aubrey knew, or what she remembered.

"Married, wow. Did I forget the wedding?" Her lips pulled into a small frown.

"No. We didn't go. They were married in Vegas."

She took a moment to digest that news, then tilted her head. "Is this where you wait for me to argue that *you're* my favorite Grandin?"

"Definitely not," he answered honestly. "Morgan's my favorite, so if you chose her, I'd understand."

"I know you and Chelsea have always been at odds, but at her core she wants what's best for the family."

Like for him to stay away from Aubrey? He wouldn't tell her about Chels's miniature tirade yesterday. It'd hurt Aubrey's feelings. Plus, Chelsea was wrong. He wasn't causing any harm sitting on a bench outside an ice-cream shop and talking with Aubrey. Hell, he was *helping*. Being with her was as good a destressor as any. No, the best. Which was likely why he let his guard down and bitched about his day rather than carefully tiptoeing around what was happening with his family. He'd never held back with Aubrey and didn't much care for it now.

As they finished eating their ice-cream cones, he shared about coming across the surveyor, who he'd learned from his father was named Ruby Rose Bennett. She'd been hired to poke around on the Grandin and Lattimore land in search of actual oil beneath it. "Heath is trying to carve out a piece for his family, but what he doesn't realize is there are other families he could destroy in the process."

Aubrey slipped her palm into his and wove their fingers together. The weight of her hand in his and the other resting on his biceps took his anxiety down a few more notches. "It's awful someone's threatening your ranch. I can't imagine the tension it's causing both your family and the Lattimores."

Always thinking of everyone else, that was his Aubrey. She wasn't *his*, per se, but they were overlooking that inconvenient fact for the moment.

"Chelsea and I have always butted heads, you're right about that. But not on this topic. She and Nolan have agreed to be neutral parties and let the legal battle play out without a fight."

"Wow."

"Yeah." Vic's laugh was dark. "Don't be fooled. She has plenty of fight left in her."

"You mean over who inherits the ranch," Aubrey said, proving she'd retained quite a bit of memories from when they were younger.

"Chels has always believed she should be in charge because she's firstborn."

Aubrey hummed in thought.

"What?" he asked, unable to stand the suspense.

"Do you think it's fair?"

"That Chelsea gives me hell when it wasn't my decision to run the ranch in the first place? No, I don't."

"No. Do you think it's fair that Chelsea was passed over simply because you're a man?"

He opened his mouth to argue, but rather than trot out a defense about how it was not only fair, but also deserved since he'd worked damn hard at the ranch, he paused. The fact was Chelsea worked damn hard, too. She always had. Vic hadn't seen the ranch issue from Chelsea's point of view very often over the years, if at all. He'd been too busy smugly declaring how he'd been handpicked by his father and grandfather to be in charge.

Damn. That'd been the same guy who had pushed Aubrey away. Was it any wonder she left and never turned back?

"What if you and your sisters ran the ranch together?"

"Ha!" His grin faded fast when Aubrey regarded him sincerely.

"Sharing responsibilities is a plausible compromise, Vic. The three of you are smart and care deeply about the family ranch. No one would work harder to keep it running for generations to come."

"If we can't stop these interlopers, there won't be a ranch to fight over, Aub. If there's oil on the land, they'll destroy every inch of it searching for black gold."

"All the more reason for the Grandin siblings to work together."

He'd always loved her sweetness, but he hadn't always appreciated her pragmatism. He placed his free hand over hers in a show of appreciation. The idea of a compromise with his sisters, especially Chelsea, used to seem like defeat to him. Young Vic would have sooner died than admit his oldest, bossiest sister was right. Admittedly, there was a version of him that still didn't want to cede control over what was destined to be his. Then again, hadn't he been thinking earlier today how stressful it was to handle everything on his own? Losing the ranch was too steep a price to pay to preserve his pride.

"You're right," he said.

Aubrey gasped, clutching her chest as if she were having a heart attack. "Did Vic Grandin admit that I was *right*?"

"Stop it," he told her when she drew the attention of surrounding patrons with the mini scene she was making.

"Look forward to an end to this heat wave, folks," she announced to no one in particular. "Hell has frozen over!"

She opened her mouth—to say what else, he had no idea—so he leaned in and stamped a hard kiss onto her parted lips. She softened beneath him, and a hum worked its way up her throat, where it reverberated against his lips.

It was heaven.

Kiss complete, she folded her arms and did her best to look inconvenienced. "You win this round, Vic."

But she wasn't inconvenienced. He could see how much she'd enjoyed that kiss by the blush staining her cheeks.

Six

"I'm not sure this is a good idea," Aubrey's mother said for the eighteenth time, or was it for the *eightieth* time?

"Yes, you've made that clear." Aubrey swiped shiny lip gloss onto her mouth and, satisfied with her reflection, turned to her mother and held out both arms. "What do you think?"

"You're so beautiful it's hard to believe you came from me."

"You're still a fox from head to toe, Mary Collins. Never let anyone tell you differently." Aubrey fiddled with her naked fingers. "Did you pack any of my jewelry when you went to my apartment? I'd love a ring or a necklace." All she had with her were the diamond stud earrings she'd been wearing the night of the cook-off.

"I didn't think to grab any, but I do have a Christmas gift socked away for you."

Aubrey pressed her palms together. She loved nothing more than Christmas, unless it was early Christmas presents. "I beg of you. I'll never ask for another thing again if you give it to me today."

"Some things never change." In her bedroom, Mary pulled open a drawer in her jewelry chest and plucked out a blue Tiffany & Co. box.

"Mom." Aubrey stared, overwhelmed. Her mother had bought her nice gifts before, but a piece of jewelry from Tiffany was far from the norm. "This feels special. Unless I'm forgetting a few years' worth of extravagant gifts?"

"No," her mother said. "You are not forgetting. Your father and I had a very good year with our investments, and we're treating our daughter."

Aubrey opened the box top to reveal a delicate gold chain with a key pendant. In the center of the key was a diamond. "It's...wow, so beautiful."

"You'll always have a home with us, no matter where life takes you. I bought it before your accident, but the sentiment is more apt now. Since you've been temporarily displaced." Her mother hooked the necklace around Aubrey's neck and turned her to face the full-length mirror.

Last night, Vic had called her and asked if she wanted to go out to a nice dinner. Aubrey had nearly leaped for joy. Dinner at her parents' house and a trip to an ice-cream shop were nice, but she wanted to have a *real* date with him. Preferably one that ended in his bedroom, which she fully intended to talk him into as soon as possible.

That morning, in preparation, she'd taken a Lyft to Saint Tropez Salon for a trim. With her auburn hair styled in luscious waves, she'd then popped into the Rancher's Daughter for something to wear tonight. Morgan had been behind the counter and had helped Aubrey pick out a stunning siren-red A-line dress. The skirt was knee-length and swishy, the sleeves missing, perfect to display her toned arms. At Morgan's further insistence, Aubrey had also purchased a sexy, strappy pair of shoes—with low heels, since spindly ones weren't a challenge she needed. The necklace from her mother pulled the entire look together.

"It's perfect. Thank you, Mom." She hugged her mother tight. When she let go, she noticed the worry lines etched into Mary's brow anew. "Don't start. He's taking me dancing, not stock-car racing."

"At least you took a car into town rather than drive yourself."

"See? I listen sometimes." Aubrey smiled.

"When you fell, you weren't doing anything remotely dangerous. How can I be sure you're safe out there?"

"I'll be on level ground, and I'll be with Vic. I'm in the best, most capable hands."

Twenty minutes later, Aubrey opened her mother's front door to find Vic beneath the covered porch. He wore a dark pair of jeans and boots, a collared shirt and a sport jacket. His shirt beneath was open at the collar, giving her a peek at the tanned column of his throat. And the way the jacket showcased his broad shoulders was nearly too much to process.

"Aubrey. God, you look beautiful." His awestruck expression sent droves of goose bumps down her arms.

"Do you like it?" She held out the skirt and did a quarter turn. "Morgan helped me pick it out."

"Hell yeah, I like it." His cunning smile appeared, making her wish they could skip dinner and go straight to him taking this dress off her.

"What time are you coming home, gingerbread?"

her father interrupted—on purpose—from his recliner in the living room.

"I don't know," she called back, unable to mask her frustration. To Vic, she said, "They treat me like I'm a teenager."

"We do not," Mary chimed in, sneaking up on her. "We are treating you like you have an injury. You shouldn't press your luck."

"I won't let her out of my sight," Vic vowed, but his eyes never left Aubrey's.

The short drive landed them at the valet station of Sheen, a restaurant constructed almost entirely of glass. She'd wanted to try it the moment she'd heard about it. When Vic had mentioned the restaurant, she'd carefully asked if he'd ever taken her there and he'd said no. "It'll be the first time for both of us."

He offered his arm and walked them inside. The hostess swiftly seated them at the rear of the dining room, where a candlelit table for two was shrouded in shadows. Aubrey gawped at the kitchen, in full view in the center of the restaurant. What a unique and modern atmosphere.

He pulled out her chair for her and ordered a bottle of something she'd never heard of before. "What was that?"

"Chardonnay. Unless you'd like a martini?"

She cringed. "No. I won't be having another of those."

"I thought martinis were your thing?"

"I don't know what made me order one at the Silver Saddle, but I distinctly remember not liking it."

He seemed contemplative about her admission but said no more about it.

She lifted the heavy, leather-bound menu, taking her

time reading each mouthwatering description. "What do I choose?"

"Anything you like," he responded easily. "We're celebrating."

"What are we celebrating?"

"You. Me. Isn't that enough?"

"You mentioned dancing?" She swept her eyes over the dining room. There was no dance floor, unless he intended to hop onto the tabletop.

"Not here. Across the street at the botanical gardens. They have an outdoor tent, and afterward, we can visit the butterfly garden."

"I love that garden." She knew that on an intuitive level, at least. She could call up a picture of the lush green setting and multicolored wings fluttering around her. "You must have taken me before."

His smile faltered. "Not me. You went with friends, I think."

"Oh. Right." It was so odd not being able to place him in the memories she did have. It was like he'd been erased from some of them.

"Are you feeling okay?"

"I guess so. It's odd how I recall some things but others are blank. I can't explain it. Why can't I remember you? You're the most important person in my life. You should be there." Her heart burned with unspent emotions—frustration, worry, fear.

He reached over the table to take her hand, giving her fingers a squeeze. "None of that matters tonight, Aub. We'll make as many new memories as we can until the old ones return."

She swallowed back the tears that threatened. "If they return."

"When they return," he corrected.

"I miss my apartment," she admitted with a weak smile. "How do you live in your family's home without losing your mind?"

"We're not exactly on top of each other at the ranch. Morg and I practically have our own wings. Layla and Josh are living in a hotel while their ranch house is being built. Chels is staying with her fiancé. The house is emptier than it's ever been."

"Intriguing." She hoisted a teasing eyebrow.

His eyes darkened with intent, but he didn't speak.

The sommelier delivered their wine, allowing her to taste first. It was buttery and smooth, the perfect chardonnay. When they were alone again, Vic raised his wineglass in a toast.

"To new and lasting memories."

She'd drink to that.

Vic sipped his wine and watched the beautiful woman across from him at the table. She was exquisite and, for tonight, his. He was playing with fire by bringing her out for a romantic date, but a plan had hatched and hadn't let go of him yet.

If he could make enough good memories with Aubrey during his time with her, then when her memory fully returned, the good would far outweigh the bad.

In theory.

He wasn't sure of that, or really anything anymore. His foundation was less bedrock than shifting sands in an hourglass. His recent crisis of character had cropped up when he'd stepped in to play the role of Aubrey's boyfriend. Admitting to her that he'd been shortsighted when it'd come to him inheriting the ranch had shaken him further.

In the past, plenty of people had written him off as

arrogant and entitled. A role he'd played to perfection. Growing up, his father and grandfather had never given Vic any reason to believe he wasn't 100 percent worthy of the good things in life coming his way. Which was probably why he'd behaved like a self-consumed prick. He'd taken Aubrey for granted back then. In his mind, there was simply no way she would walk away from him. He'd seen himself as the ultimate catch. Husband material, through and through.

With ten years of dirty water under the bridge between them, it would take a lot to convince her he'd changed for the better. Ironically, if it wasn't for her accident, he could kiss the idea of this reunion goodbye. He might have been able to talk her back into bed with him, but her guard had been up that night after the Silver Saddle. Chances were good she'd never have considered him as anything more than a bed buddy.

Back when they'd split up, he'd been shocked when she'd thrown the engagement ring at him. He'd been an arrogant teen who'd grown into an arrogant twenty-one-year-old. Things always went his way—and if they didn't, he got off with a warning. Speeding tickets, a brush with the law for underage drinking at a party, sneaking into his neighbor's backyard and using the pool... Vic had been let off the hook more times than he could count. His family name afforded him privilege, but Aubrey was a privilege he didn't appreciate until she was long gone.

Their final argument as an engaged couple had been venomous and heated, the venom coming mostly, if not completely, from his side. The conversation had started off innocently, with her mentioning grad school. When she'd skipped off to college, he hadn't seen enough of her. He couldn't wrap his head around *more* years without her. Her priority had become studying and not him, and he hadn't liked it one bit. When she'd mentioned wanting to continue her education, he'd been completely ungracious.

"Graduate school? What the hell for? You'll be my wife, Aub. A pampered woman, a mother to my children. What more could you want?"

He flinched now as he thought back to what a selfish asshole he'd been. In his desperation to keep her close, he'd done the complete opposite. He'd pushed her so far away, she'd seen no other option than to leave him permanently. He guzzled down the rest of his glass of wine before refilling it from the bottle on the table.

"More stress at the ranch?" Aubrey asked. Their shrimp bruschetta arrived, and he lifted a strip of candied bacon off the top and gnawed on it. He figured it wasn't a lie to say yes.

"Yes, but nothing I can't handle."

"I'm not surprised. You've always excelled at your job."

Humbled by the compliment, he redirected to her. "You're one to talk, teacher of the year. I'm proud of you."

"Thank you." The wistfulness in her smile was genuine, but her smile faded when she added, "I miss work. I was just getting to know my students. When I sent my lesson plans to the substitute taking my place, it was like handing someone my firstborn. I'm itching to go back and do it myself. Immediately after typing up that email, though, I had a headache behind my eyes. I'm beginning to worry I'll never be normal."

He reached across the table and took her hand again, regretting that he wasn't on the same side of the table so he could hug her close while he reassured her. He realized it wasn't his place, but he couldn't help standing up for the woman she was—the woman she would be again. "Listen to me, Aubrey. You will recover and be more of a force to reckon with than you were before. You always knew what you wanted, and you were strong enough to say it."

"Well, guess what, Vic? I want more than to be your little wife and pop out your babies. I have dreams, too. I want to achieve things in my life that have nothing to do with you. I know that's hard to believe, seeing as how your future's been preplanned from birth, but the ranch is not my dream. The world doesn't stop and start on your command, and neither will I."

"Is it any wonder why I love you?" Her current wide-eyed admiration was at odds with the fiery speech she'd given him before she'd ended them forever.

He knew she meant the *I love you*—at least, some part of her did—but he couldn't reconcile that love with their tumultuous breakup. It was embedded so deeply in his hippocampus, he doubted even a knock to the head would erase it completely.

Seven

The Royal Discovery Botanical Gardens were made up of, according to the welcome sign, "8 Acres of Land Serving as a Texas Oasis."

There was a massive white tent furnished with outdoor air conditioners. On their way to the tent, they approached a round decorative fountain. Aubrey, her hand in Vic's, stared down into the splashing water where pennies to buy wishes had been tossed, and she wondered what they represented. Love? Money? Memory recovery?

"Penny for your thoughts?" Vic waggled her hand when she didn't answer right away.

"I have an embarrassing question," she finally mustered the courage to say. She looked up at his handsome, questioning face. "Why don't we live together? I'm sure there's a plausible reason, but I can't remember it."

Them living apart made no sense. They'd been dating since high school and were in love with each other, and yet he lived on the ranch with his family and she had her own place. Funds weren't a problem for Vic, and she had a healthy bank account as well. Why hadn't they purchased a slice of land to call their own by now? The answer seemed just out of reach.

"Aubrey…"

Frustrated by his tone, which hinted he might blow her off instead of give her an answer, she held up a palm. "Please don't tell me you're trying to protect me by not telling me why."

"Okay." He inhaled deeply, pausing to glance over his shoulder at the tent where ticketed couples were entering. He was probably wishing he'd taken her inside to dance rather than lingering at the Contemplate Your Life fountain. Finally, he turned back to her. "You were prioritizing graduate school when we were trying to decide on a future. We haven't spoken about it since."

"At all?"

"Not a word." He held her gaze steadily. He wasn't lying. She could tell.

Graduate school. The mere mention of those two words sparked…well, not a memory, but a feeling. She'd passionately pursued school and had made education her priority. Had she prioritized her career over Vic? It didn't paint a pretty picture of her former self.

"It was the right thing to do," he said. "My future was laid out for me, so at the time I didn't understand your drive to go to school and have a career separate from what I could provide. I was wrong, which you told me. Then you proved it to me. You achieved exactly what you set out to do, Ms. Collins."

"And it ultimately didn't hurt our relationship." Her hand in his, she noted the stiffness in his fingers as well as his answering silence. No matter what arguments must have ensued around that very topic, they were here, together. She hadn't blown him off to date a frat boy or given up on them. She'd instinctively known Vic was the best man for her.

"Would you like to go inside?" he invited.

"I didn't wear my dancing shoes for nothing."

"Slow songs only. Doctor's orders."

Lights were strung and a twinkling chandelier hung from the center of the tent. A four-piece band on a stage played sophisticated, smooth jazz. Perfect for slow dancing.

Couples of all ages were either sitting at the sparse round tables enjoying sparkling cocktails or swaying to the music on a parquet dance floor atop the manicured lawn. Potted plants, in a variety of sizes from tall to stout, were arranged in the corners, small engraved signs announcing the genus and species jabbed into the soil.

"Not only an entertaining evening, but an educational one as well," she said as she stroked a particularly broad Monstera leaf.

"I thought you'd appreciate that. Do you want a drink?"

She shook her head.

"How about a dance?"

"That I'll take."

Nothing felt more right than joining Vic on the dance floor. They fell into sync with each other as they moved to the music, her hand in his as he held her close. Dancing with him while wearing a beautiful dress sparked a memory from their past—more clear and crisp than any she'd had since the accident. She laughed aloud, so thrilled to have it shining bright for her to observe.

He smiled with her. "What is it?"

"A memory. It came out of nowhere and now here it is, crystal clear. Prom. My senior prom." She arched an eyebrow. "I wore red."

"Everywhere," he growled against the tender shell of her ear. "From a lacy bra and panty set to the dress with no sleeves. Not a single spaghetti strap to save me."

"Nope. Nothing but cleavage for days, and I wore a push-up bra. I was on a mission." She'd planned the perfect night—she'd vowed to lose her virginity to Vic on prom night. He'd been patient. She'd been patient, though they'd had plenty of make-out nights at his family's house or hers that had nearly trampled over that line drawn in the sand. If she was anything, it was decisive. She'd known what she wanted and had refused to let anyone talk her into—or out of—sleeping with him.

"We couldn't be stopped," she whispered, butterflies of excitement fluttering in her stomach. "And now here we are, roadblocks everywhere."

"Tell me more about prom. Since you so keenly recall the circumstances of the evening."

"You mean you don't?"

"Oh, I remember." His lips hovered over hers, his breath warm against her mouth. "I remember every last hitched breath and honey-sweet taste." He backed away, taking some of her focus off the past and placing it squarely in the present. "I want your take on it."

"It was a lot like tonight." She rested her other hand on his shoulder and squeezed. "You kept promising to treat me well after we left the dance. I was nervous, and you were totally collected."

"I was not." He chuckled, his grin both boyish and charming. "I was scared to death I'd screw up and you'd hate it and never touch me again."

"You were?" How had she not known? "Confident, capable Vic Grandin?"

"I didn't want to disappoint you."

His sincerity was an arrow to her heart. She wrapped both arms around his neck and held him close. "You didn't disappoint me."

"No, I didn't. But there was a power shift that night." He led her into a smooth turn. She followed, finding it easy to trust him. "You could get me to do that anytime you wanted."

"What about now? You don't seem as easily convinced."

He kept his smile, and he didn't tell her no. Maybe she was getting somewhere.

"We've been seeing each other, but we haven't seen *enough* of each other, if you catch my meaning."

He angled his head, those dark eyes sparkling with thoughts he wasn't sharing. He'd caught her meaning, all right. She toyed with his hair, scraping her fingernails upward. A slight shake spanned the width of his shoulders. Yes, she was far from powerless when it came to Vic. He was as weak for her as she was for him.

"It's been a couple weeks since we rolled around in bed together. We're due. Don't tell me you don't want me, too. I can see it."

"You can feel it, too." He grabbed her hips and bumped his pelvis against her. A hard, unyielding part of him had definitely received the sex memo and was on board.

His gaze slid to the side, presumably to check if anyone was watching them—they weren't. "You have talked me right into trouble. I hope you're proud of yourself."

She beamed up at him. She was, actually.

"Stay here with me for a song or two so I can calm down, and, I beg of you, talk about *anything* else."

"Anything?"

"Anything not sexy." He raised an eyebrow.

"You're no fun in your old age. I recall you eagerly sliding the hotel key card into the door and tearing my prom dress in your haste to have me naked."

"Yeah, well, what you don't know is how hard it was for me to last longer than getting you naked took," he said, and she had to laugh.

It wasn't like him to be self-deprecating. He wore it well, though the expression of chagrin faded into one of complete and utter confidence in a blink. That long-ago night, he had lasted a lot longer than he'd jokingly stated. She'd been ready to go again shortly after, and so they had. The lie she'd told her parents about them going to a friend's party after the dance was easy to justify. She was in love. Vic was the only one for her. What better way to spend her prom night than in his arms?

She'd been an hour and a half late for her 2:00 a.m. curfew, but her mother hadn't been upset. Dad had been another story, but her mom refused to let him stay angry. "We were young once, too, Eddie," Mary had reminded him.

"Those were the good ole days," Vic said, sounding oddly solemn. "We didn't know it back then."

"*Hello.* We're not dead yet. We have plenty of good days left. If you'd let yourself have a little fun." She poked him in the center of the chest and waited for him to laugh and agree. He didn't.

"There are times you're not remembering, Aubrey." Pain bloomed in his brown eyes. "All couples argue. You don't remember the bad times."

"I don't remember many times, bad or good," she

amended. "But I know what feels right. This feels right. Being apart, even for a few days, feels wrong. I understand why we chose to live separately initially, but it doesn't make sense to me now. No matter what memories return about us arguing over where to eat for dinner or who should drive to the restaurant, I can't imagine not wanting you." His heart pounded, strong and sure, against her palm. "I'm not as fragile as my doctor and my parents believe. I'm here, Vic. All of me. That fall didn't change the core of who I am."

He stopped moving, standing still in the middle of the dance floor, his eyes drilling into hers as other couples swished around them in a blur.

"I hope with everything I am, Aubrey Collins," he said, his lips hovering over hers, "that you're right."

"I'm right," she promised, leaning up for a kiss he returned. As his mouth moved over hers, she lost herself in the moment. A beautiful moment she promised to remember until her dying day.

Eight

"We're cooking tonight," Layla announced as she strolled through the open doors of the barn. "Josh and I. We'd like you to bring Aubrey to dinner with you."

Vic had come in here to think, and he did his best thinking while riding Titan. Now saddled up, the gray speckled horse was itching to go out and run, and so was Vic.

"You're cooking?"

"Yes. Here at the house, obviously, since Josh and I don't have one yet. The staff has the night off, so the timing is perfect."

Like he'd told Aubrey, Layla and Josh had been living at the hotel until their new house was built. They didn't exactly relish the idea of living here as newly-weds, which he understood. But dinner? That was new.

"Why?"

"Why?" She blinked at him, waited and then filled

the gap when she determined he had no more to say. "I'd like to use the gourmet kitchen at the house to practice. We won't have a cook like Mom and Dad do, at least not right away. And you eat too many cheeseburgers."

"Do not," he argued, but she wasn't wrong. He led Titan from the barn into the sunshine-filled day. "Bringing Aubrey to dinner isn't a good idea, Lay."

"Why not?" His sister followed him outside. "Afraid she'll remember what actually happened between you two?"

After the kiss they'd shared, and Aubrey practically begging him to take her to bed, yeah, one could say he wasn't eager for the bad memories to come flooding back.

"I ran into her at Morgan's shop in town the other day," Layla said. "She mentioned we don't see enough of each other. What was I supposed to do? Blow her off?"

"Yes." Titan snuffled his agreement. "You could have blown her off. Or you could've invited her to coffee that day. Not invite her here, to ground zero."

He gestured to their family home, the massive Western-style structure a hulking behemoth against azure skies. Aubrey had thrown the engagement ring at him in this very driveway.

"You can't keep her from remembering," Layla said gently. "It's the best thing for her."

"I know." But was it so wrong to want this part to last awhile longer? He wasn't ready to let go of the Aubrey who beamed up at him while reminding him how they'd lost their virginity to each other long ago. It was hard not to delay the inevitable. "It's just you and Josh?"

"And Chelsea." Layla wouldn't meet his eyes when she added, "And Nolan."

"Nolan?"

"His twin brother isn't anyone's favorite person, but Nolan is not Heath. Nolan is also with Chelsea, so you'd better get used to it."

"At least tell me Morgan is coming."

"Nope. She's doing inventory tonight, and Mom, Dad and Grandma are eating at the Lattimores'. Barbara is showcasing her recipes from her upcoming cookbook."

"A family dinner wasn't the circumstance under which I pictured bringing Aubrey back to the ranch for the first time in years," he grumbled.

"Come on, baby brother. Aubrey loves us." Layla swatted his hat off his head. He caught it before it hit the dirt—barely.

He hated when his older sister talked to him like he was a kid, especially when she followed it up with the hat thing she'd done way too often when they *were* kids.

"You can't say anything to Aubrey to jog her memory. She believes we're together, and her doctor thinks it's best if she comes to any other conclusions on her own."

"No one will blow your cover. Chels and I would never do anything to disrupt her healing. Tell me you know that."

He knew that, but he didn't answer. Worry was writhing in his stomach at the idea of Aubrey being here. In this house. Would she remember their horrible fight from years ago?

"She's not allowed to work right now, which means she's not seeing her friends. She has her parents and she has you. She needs a bigger support system than that. We all do."

Dammit. He didn't like when Layla was right—when either of his older sisters were right. Not to mention a family dinner, with Aubrey and his sisters' significant others present, would be a good time to talk to them about the future of the ranch after Dad retired. Better still was the fact Mom, Dad and Grandma weren't going to be there.

He frowned as he recalled the conversations he'd had with Dad over the years. Victor Grandin Jr. was a good man, a strong man. He cared for his family and his children. But he wasn't what anyone would consider progressive. Like the Cattleman's Club had once been a boys' club with the archaic mantra of "No Girls Allowed," so had their father come up to believe the only person capable of running the ranch would be a son, not a daughter.

Layla was the best horse trainer Vic had ever seen, and Chelsea was dedicated to being hands-on at the ranch. She kept a close eye on their stock, which had a direct effect on the bottom line. Vic, though he could repair a fence, rope a lost calf and shoot a rogue coyote from an impressive distance, was better utilized behind the scenes. He'd been taught to view the overall workings of the ranch as one big piece, with each person in his or her sweet spot. His sisters thought he merely delegated, but there was nothing mere about running this place. It took more than a little know-how to delegate properly, which was the part they didn't see.

Regardless of what they believed he did or didn't do, his sisters' hard work and passion had been essential to the ranch. When it came to the herd or the horses, he didn't have his sisters' expertise, which was why he trusted them implicitly. It was past time he told them as much. As Aubrey had reminded him the other night, a threat to their home was the best reason for the Grandin sibs to work together.

Titan blew out a frustrated snort, stomping one foot to the ground to further voice his impatience.

"What time's dinner?" Vic asked.

Layla grinned. "Seven sharp. I hope you like Italian food."

"Everyone likes Italian food." He made a show of rolling his eyes. "I don't have to eat burgers every day, you know."

"Thanks, Vic." Her sincerity threw him a little.

"You're welcome. Hey, before you go—" He climbed on Titan's back. "Why don't you throw a saddle on one of your pet projects and come out with me? I'll race you to the east fence."

Her eyes flared with excitement. "Give me five minutes!"

She jogged to the barn as Vic broke the bad news to Titan. "We have to wait on Layla, buddy." Meanwhile, he trotted the horse in circles around the paddock to warm up. Not five minutes later, Layla came out riding a black gelding, neither of them able to contain their excitement.

"On your mark," he called out.

"Go!" Layla blazed past him.

"Shit," Vic muttered. Titan picked up on the urgency, double-timing it to catch up with Layla and her gelding.

Vic helped Aubrey out of his truck, keeping hold of her hand as they approached his family home. She expected a jolt of familiarity at the sight of the massive, elegant house. While there was a tingle of "been here before," her memories were sparse. It was almost like she hadn't been here in years. She tried to envision his bedroom but called up an image that could've been

Vic's room—or a photo she saw in an issue of one of her mother's home-decorating magazines.

"Everything all right?" He stopped short of the wide front steps that led to a sprawling porch to study her in the waning light, concern etched into his forehead. He'd been checking on her a lot lately. It must be hard for him to see her like this, to worry about her recovery at a time when the family ranch should be his sole concern.

"Of course." She slapped on a smile. She wasn't going to ruin Layla's dinner tonight over nothing. When she'd bumped into Vic's sister, Aubrey had been thrilled to recognize the other woman on sight. She would have known Layla's blue eyes anywhere. The rush of certainty had propelled her over to say hello. Layla, gracious as well as poised, had greeted Aubrey with a hug. After a short chat, Aubrey had mentioned how isolated she'd been for the last few weeks, and that's when Layla had invited her over for dinner sometime. Aubrey had accepted, and Layla promised to give Vic the details. And, apparently, the blonde middle Grandin sister had whipped together a dinner party in record time.

"What's Chelsea's fiancé's name again?" Aubrey asked as Vic opened the front door.

"Nolan Thurston, twin brother to the asshole trying to find oil on our land."

"You're not going to be like this all night, are you?" Layla was standing in the foyer, arms folded, forehead creased. "They haven't arrived yet, so you're safe."

"I don't care if they overhear," he said. Hopefully the evening went smoothly. Aubrey prickled at the idea of everyone squabbling tonight.

"So good to see you again, Aubrey. Come meet my husband, Josh." Layla led Aubrey away from Vic, who followed behind them as they stepped into the large, state-of-the-art kitchen. Josh stood at the stovetop sautéing something green. He had a muscular build, dirty-blond hair and oh—look at that—blue eyes like Layla's. They were a match made in Barbie dream heaven, an absolutely stunning couple.

Once pleasantries were exchanged and Aubrey was equipped with a glass of wine, Chelsea and Nolan let themselves in. Chelsea announced herself with a "We're here. Hold your applause!"

Nolan was tall and well-built, his features unlike Josh's in nearly every way. His hair and eyes were dark rather than light, his thick eyebrows expressive and possibly visible from space. He had a sensual smile, which was decorated with a dense five-o'clock shadow. He made a nice match for dark-haired Chelsea, whose willowy frame was draped in a fancy cocktail dress.

"What's the occasion? I've never seen you look better," Vic said, sweeping in to kiss his oldest sister's cheek.

"I know a backhanded compliment when I hear one," she returned. Before Aubrey could be properly intimidated, Chelsea turned her wide, toothy smile on her. "Aubrey Collins. How are you?"

"Good, thank you," she answered, thrown by the formality. Instinctively, she gave Chelsea a quick hug. "It's good to see you. Congratulations on your engagement."

Nolan's arm wrapped around his fiancée's waist, and Chelsea blushed prettily—a sight Aubrey had rarely, if ever, seen.

"Everyone sit! It's done!" Layla rushed by with a piping-hot dish of cheese-covered pasta. Josh followed, a platter in each hand, steam billowing in his wake.

Dinner was delicious—fettucine alfredo with slices of grilled chicken, a dish of garlicky broccolini and

Texas toast slathered with butter and freshly grated Parmesan cheese.

Aubrey had eaten her fill two bites ago but couldn't help polishing off the remainder of her bread. She reclaimed her forgotten wineglass and took a sip as the vibe around the table took a turn from casual to serious.

"Since Mom and Dad are next door," Vic started, "tonight would be a good night for us to talk about the future of this ranch and what we're going to do about it."

"Which we've decided to leave to the authorities," Nolan said.

"And by *we*, I am referring to the Grandins who own this ranch, not the twin brother of the man trying to wreck it." Vic's tone was lethal.

"You're not over this yet?" Nolan tossed his napkin onto his empty plate.

"Heath trying to steal our birthrights out from under us? No, Nolan, I'm not over it."

Aubrey touched Vic's leg beneath the table. He gave her a subtle nod that said *I've got this*.

"In case you haven't noticed, Victor," Josh interjected, "we're in your sisters' lives for the long haul. Might as well accept that."

"It's Vic, and my sisters can speak for themselves. They were doing it long before either of you entered the picture." A truncated silence descended, the room buzzing with tension. Aubrey wasn't sure if the other men were being polite or if Vic's air of authority had silenced them both. Vic eased back in the formal dining chair like a cat lounging on a sun-drenched windowsill. "As I was saying, the future of this ranch has always been clear. Our grandfather and our father decided when I was born that their namesake would be the one to run it."

"Oh, here we go." Chelsea held up her wineglass. "Someone top me off."

Nolan poured more red wine into her glass. Aubrey was surprised when Vic smiled.

"We know what you're going to say," Layla said. "No need to ruin everyone's evening while you restake your claim."

Vic winked at Aubrey before linking their fingers and resting their joined hands on the table. What was he up to?

"I was telling Aub about the surveyor and the problems we're having." He sent a glance to Nolan, who narrowed his gaze in response. "And she brought up a valid point. Chelsea has long believed she deserved the top spot at this ranch."

"Hello? Firstborn," Chelsea said before taking a swig from her refilled wineglass.

"You're right," Vic said.

The entire table fell silent, most notably Chelsea, who was frozen into a solid block of *Did I just hear that?* She snapped her jaw shut and shook her mane of dark brown hair. "What did you say?"

"You are a force to be reckoned with, Chels. I've always believed as much. No one works harder than you on this ranch—" he nodded at his other sister "—unless it's Layla. Believe it or not, what I do is more complicated than it looks. Logistics isn't easy with the many moving parts on this ranch. You two are amazing out there in the mix, but I was taught to run the show from a different vantage point."

"Lording over your sisters isn't a vantage point," Josh snapped.

"I wasn't lording," Vic said. "I was ensuring we turned a mean profit, a lot of which is thanks to my sisters. I could show you the financials, though I suspect my sisters have taken their fair share of peeks at them when they thought no one was looking." His pointed gaze at Chelsea and Layla drew smug smiles from both women. "I could detail the long and tiring list of blowhards I have to talk to on a routine basis to keep our prices top dollar and our reputation squeaky-clean in this industry. I suspect your talents are better utilized in your own specialties. To quote Samwise from *Lord of the Rings*, what we need to do is *share the load*. Neither of you wants to deal with the bullshit I do each day, and I don't have the skill set to do what you do."

"Did Aubrey put you up to this?" Chelsea squinted one eye in suspicion.

Aubrey didn't confirm or deny with her answer. "Sharing the responsibilities gives everyone what they want. Layla, you'll have more time with Josh on your own ranch. Chelsea, you and Nolan will have more time together as well. It will also free up Vic's time, so he can spend more of it with me." She drew their joined hands to her chest and hugged his arm. "It's win-win-win."

Vic cleared his throat, shifting slightly in his seat. Aubrey didn't mind sticking up for him. While he'd been bullheaded in the past about who should be in charge and why, he also worked very hard on this ranch.

"Thanks, Aub," came his gentle reply.

"You're welcome, Vic."

He lifted his wineglass in a toast. "From here on out, the Grandin siblings aren't going to allow Dad to have the final say in our future. We're going to choose our own path—the same path. There's no sense in us veering off in three different directions when we want the same thing. Even if you two—" he nodded at Chelsea and then Layla "—take some distance from the family ranch, I will still need your input. I trust you two more than anyone. We're stronger together."

Layla was the first to raise her glass. "Agree. Even though you cheated when we raced to the east fence, you're right about the ranch."

"I didn't cheat." Vic's hoisted eyebrow backed his claim. "*You* cheated. You raced that gelding out of the stable and took both Titan and me by surprise."

"The gelding's name is Lester. And I'm faster than you and you know it." Layla smirked.

Chelsea raised her glass as well. "I admit, brother. I don't want any part of what you do. Dealing with the Texas elite and their brethren requires a degree in bullshit. Which we all know you have."

"Thank you, sis." Vic's sincere acceptance of the insult set off a ripple of laughter around the table. Whatever tension had snapped in the air before had been defused. Nolan and Josh and Aubrey raised their glasses, and everyone drank to the Grandin family truce.

Nine

"I'm impressed," Aubrey said as they walked outside after dinner.

Vic hadn't said what he'd said at dinner to impress her, but her approval bolstered his pride.

Night had fallen, the glow of a fat full moon cloaking the field. They passed the paddock, casting long, eerie shadows across the path where they walked.

"So, about the race to the fence. *Did* you cheat?" she asked.

"Hell no!" he answered with a laugh. "Layla raced that black beauty straight out of the stable and rode him like the hounds of hell were on her tail. Titan hates to lose almost as much as I do, though, so we nearly killed ourselves to catch up. Layla knows I won. She stopped arguing, didn't she?"

"Yeah, I guess she did. I love your sisters. They're so strong. It's enviable."

He stopped short of the stable to turn to her. "Why is it enviable? You're as strong if not stronger than either of them."

"I don't feel strong. I feel like the ghost of someone who *used* to be strong."

"Take it from me, Aub. You speak your mind, and you prioritize what matters. You don't let anyone bully you into what you don't want. Much to my chagrin, at times."

She smiled. "Because I'm not the agreeable housewife you always dreamed of?"

The comment was so close to what she'd said when they'd broken up ten years ago, his heart began galloping. If she remembered that argument, it could be the crack in the door she needed to recover the rest of her memory. He wasn't ready to let her go yet. Not when he'd just begun winning her back.

He had the acute sense he was running out of time. He knew it, even if Aubrey didn't. Her memory would surface sooner or later. He was betting on sooner, which didn't give him much time to impress upon her how much she still meant to him.

"Can I see Titan?"

"Of course."

His stallion's regal gray head was poking out of his stall when Vic and Aubrey approached. The horse blinked wide, knowing eyes when Aubrey smiled up at him.

Vic loved his horse. All horses. He was amazed by their ability to tune in to the emotions of others—horse or human. Titan held Aubrey's gaze steadily before nudging her shoulder, his way of asking for scratches.

"The noses are the best," she murmured, stroking the baby-soft skin of the horse's muzzle. Titan closed his eyes and enjoyed Aubrey's attention. Vic knew just how Titan felt.

"He likes you."

"He probably likes everyone. Don't you, boy?"

Titan blew out a snort in response, and Aubrey laughed. Then her laugh faded as she stroked the horse's forehead. "What if I don't recover my memory?"

"You will."

"But what if I *don't*?" Her green eyes were filled with fear and curiosity in equal measures. She was asking him for honesty, something he'd been half-assing since he agreed to step back into her life. So, he told her the truth.

"If you don't, you don't." He shrugged. "Your doc won't keep you from work forever. And after you're cleared, you won't have to live with your parents like I do."

"In such squalor." She gestured in the direction of the house.

It was good to see her smile. He wished she'd keep smiling. He could only imagine how frustrating it was not to be able to fill in the gaps of her memory. Which was partially why he tipped his head and asked, "Want to see the loft?"

She screwed her lips to one side. "Should I be suspicious of your motives?"

"No. Well. Maybe." He claimed her hand and led her away. Titan complained about the loss of attention, but Vic mentally promised to give the horse extra scratches for his gentlemanly behavior. He released Aubrey's hand and nodded to the set of stairs leading to the top of the stable. They were new, unstained and smelled of fresh pine.

"These weren't always here," she said. "There was a ladder, right?"

"See? Your memory's returning already. Go on. I'll follow you up." He grabbed a clean blanket from the stack on the shelf, figuring the horses wouldn't mind if he borrowed one.

She walked up the stairs, and he followed close behind in case she lost her balance. He was playing with fire bringing her up here, but she would only have good memories of him if she had any at all. He certainly hadn't forgotten the nights they'd spent up here after dark, the moonlight slatting through the open window while they lay naked on a bed of fresh straw.

"Haven't done this in a while," he confessed as she wandered around the spacious loft. He hadn't ever brought another woman here, and he hadn't brought Aubrey since they were young. It was sacred, this space. And like he'd time traveled back to those days, he had the sudden urge to take off her clothes. To make love to her while confessing how she still tied him up in knots.

"What's wrong?" she asked, picking up on his silence.

Too many things to mention. He shook his head and confessed, "Maybe this is a bad idea."

Fingertips stroking a hay bale, she turned to face him. His anguished expression said what he wouldn't.

He was worried about her. He'd shadowed her every footfall as she'd climbed the stairs, his arms open to catch her. Her knight in a black Stetson. He hadn't worn the hat tonight, which gave her an unobstructed view of the concern etched across his forehead. Moonlight caught the angles of his hard jaw as well as the feisty bad-boy glint in his eyes that'd been there before he'd reconsidered his intentions.

She took the blanket from his hands. "I know what you're worried about."

"You do?" His Adam's apple bobbed as he folded his arms over his chest.

"Yes." She wasn't going to let him ruin this evening, not when they both wanted the same thing. She untucked her plaid shirt from her jeans. "You're trying to take it easy on me because I'm injured. You're worried that you'll cause a setback for me, and then you'll never forgive yourself for it." She unbuttoned the bottom two buttons of her shirt. He watched as she slipped each pearlescent button through the fabric. "You have to trust that I know what's best for me."

She finished unbuttoning the shirt, noting the exact moment the worry left Vic's expression and dark hunger overtook it. She tossed the shirt aside. He took another step closer to her, his hands going to her waist.

The only sounds around them were the occasional whinny from downstairs and the tight, anticipatory breaths she was taking. She turned her attention to the buttons on his shirt next. "I remember."

His voice was a dry husk when he asked, "What do you remember?"

"Stargazing on horseback." She plucked at another button. "Whispering as we checked the stable to see if your daddy or any ranch hands were in here. Climbing up into this loft with a blanket and a stolen bottle of whiskey from your parents' liquor cabinet."

He grinned. "Our getaway."

"As if your enormous family home hadn't offered enough privacy."

"You liked it outside better," he said.

"I liked it with you any way I could get it, Vic Grandin." She opened his unbuttoned shirt and smoothed her hands over his heated skin. Firm pecs, the perfect sprinkle of chest hair and a taut belly. He was a beautiful specimen of a man. And he was all man. Not the skinnier version of the boy she'd fallen in love with, though he was there, too. She could see the nervous twitch of that boy's smile. She placed a kiss on his chest, closing her lips over his bare skin as she inhaled. His cedar-and-citrus scent mingled with the fragrance of hay, taking her back in time ten years.

He tipped her chin as she was about to kiss his chest again. "Aubrey, before you—"

"I trust you. More than anyone. Now you have to trust me. You're right. I'm strong. I know what I can handle and what I can't." She pulled his belt free, snaking the thick leather through his belt loops and tossing it to the floor. "I can handle you."

"That a fact?" His smile returned, the lust in his eyes crowding out his earlier concern.

"Why don't you try me and find out, cowboy?" She cupped where his jeans tented, finding him primed and hard for her. He held himself in check, but only barely. His nostrils flared. His gaze rerouted to the overflowing cups of her bra.

He tugged her close, dipping his face until his lips hovered a hairsbreadth above hers. "Last chance."

She pushed to her toes and crushed her lips to his, hugging his neck and pressing her breasts against his chest. He bent and lifted her, cradling her ass in his wide hands as she wrapped her legs around his body. Then he moved to a hay bale and plopped her onto it, where they made out long and slow.

His mouth slanted over hers, hungry and impatient, the pace intentional. Every part of her body responded, from her tightening nipples to the liquid heat pooling in her belly. She wiggled and squirmed as he stroked her tongue with his, seeking relief where she needed it most.

He'd always been good at this. She had been kissing Vic for years and had never once been disappointed. He poured his entire self into a kiss. Everything he wanted to say but didn't. Whenever they were physically together, nothing else mattered. Not time or place or any argument they'd had about their combined futures.

Eyes shut, she pulled her lips from his. That thought tried to unlock the door to another, but the key wouldn't quite turn.

Vic kissed the side of her throat once, twice, while she waited for clarity to come. It vanished before a memory could form. When his lips hit the tender skin behind her ear, she stopped her mental struggle. Time was the key to her healing. Time, and really delicious sex with her boyfriend.

She unbuttoned his jeans and unzipped his fly, wedging her hand behind the stiff denim. What she encountered was smooth, thick and long, and guaranteed to make her smile. The last time they'd slept together had been the night before her accident, which was way too long ago for her taste.

Vic, no longer arguing about her health, kicked off his boots and shucked his clothes. He helped her off the bale and out of her clothes next, resting his lips over hers as he laid her out on the blanket.

He worked his way down her throat, then glided his tongue along her collarbone. By the time he set his mouth to her nipple, he'd reduced her to a pleading, panting woman with only one thing on her mind.

"Please, what?" He smiled against her breast, his inhalation leaving goose bumps on her skin.

"Don't tease me," she warned, but she barely meant

it. She couldn't remember feeling this carefree before. Had she?

"Yes, ma'am." He kissed his way down her stomach and to her hip bones before settling between her legs. Once there, he knew how to please her—slow, then fast, before slowing down again. She clutched his hair in one fist, arched her neck and gave in. He was in control of her pleasure, leaving her free to float untethered, no worries clogging her mind.

Moments later, she gave in to pleasure so acute she almost couldn't bear it. She muffled her cries with one hand until Vic surfaced and replaced that hand with his mouth. And while she was kissing him, she felt a single tear leak from each eye that she didn't bother hiding.

Ten

On the night they'd spent together after he'd sworn they'd never sleep together again, caution had closely followed their orgasms. Now there were no roped-off areas, no caution lingering in her eyes, no awkward covering of her naked body. She was the picture of bliss. Her eyes were drawn, her smile adorably goofy, and she was laid out nude like she was as unashamed as she'd ever been with him.

It was hell leaving her to dispose of the condom, but he did, taking care to tug on his jeans before jogging down the stairs. He returned to the loft to find her sitting on the center of the blanket, wearing naught but his plaid shirt.

He'd thought he preferred her naked to clothed, until she was covered in his navy-and-green flannel. *Because she belongs with you.*

Guilt spiked in the center of his chest, but he told it

to go to hell. She'd assured him that she trusted him. She'd reminded him that she knew what she wanted. He couldn't regret what had just happened if he tried.

Nothing had felt more right than sliding into her, watching her eyes sink shut and her mouth drop open. Unless it was the moment she'd wrapped her legs around his back and scratched her fingernails across his shoulders. That'd felt pretty damn right, too.

"I thought I was too full for that sort of acrobatic workout." She emitted a throaty laugh. "Guess not."

He crossed to where she sat and folded her against him, moving the collar of the shirt to the side to place a kiss on her neck. "Were you cold?"

"I was, but with you here I'm not. If we were in your room or my apartment, I'd still be naked. Is that incentive enough for you to take me indoors?"

As if he needed more incentive than her cries coating his ear canal as she came. Although, his bedroom held memories that could thwart his plan to win her back. He frowned, considering. She'd seen the ranch, been inside the house, chatted with his sisters. And then there was the loft. Aubrey hadn't had a memory that would endanger this version of them...*yet*.

She leaned back against his chest and let out a sigh. He knew her sounds—even after not being with her for years, he still knew them.

"Something on your mind other than round two?" He hugged her waist, and she held his hands, toying with his fingers in silence before she finally answered him.

"Are you planning on getting married?"

His nose in her hair, he inhaled, unsure how to respond.

"We've had to have talked about it. Humor me, and remind me why we've been dating since the age of sixteen and haven't progressed past sex in the loft." She twisted her neck to look over her shoulder at him. "That wasn't a complaint, by the way."

He could lie and say they'd been too busy to talk about it, or he could tell her the truth, which was that they'd been engaged once, but she'd changed her mind. Vic had promised to do what was best for her in this situation, and in no way was reminding her of a tumultuous time ten years ago helpful to her recovery. When he answered, he let his reply hover in between truth and fiction.

"We've talked about marriage. Like moving in together, the timing wasn't right for us." He didn't think he'd ever spoken truer words about his and Aubrey's relationship.

After they'd broken up, he'd been angry. He couldn't fathom why she'd throw away everything they'd built. He'd known in his gut she'd never find someone better than him. When he'd returned to the world of dating, he'd had a similar epiphany—he'd never found anyone like Aubrey.

The women he'd dated had been beautiful, intelligent, self-starters. Sleeping with them had rewarded him with physical relief, but he'd never found the connection he'd had with Aubrey. Over the years, it'd become painfully clear he'd never find the solace he'd found in her. Aubrey was his own personal Halley's Comet. Once in a lifetime, and he'd never believed he'd be lucky enough to have her come around again.

When he'd propositioned her at the Silver Saddle, the ache in his chest had been unbearable. The morning after their incredible night together, he'd walked away, reminding himself of his promise to her. He'd told her it'd be like the sex had never happened. He'd meant it at the time. Having her back in his life and knowing there'd be no happy ending for them would be sheer torture.

Now he was in some sort of bizarre limbo. She hadn't forgotten the night they spent together, but her mind had altered the circumstances surrounding it. She didn't remember their agreement. She'd woven their steamy night between the sheets with the people they'd been prebreakup. Back when she'd been his world, and he'd been hers.

Until she'd gone to college.

He used to tell himself she'd changed when she went to school, but now he understood that she'd become more of who she already was. She cared about others, revered education and was warm and patient with everyone she encountered. He'd admired her abilities and her intelligence, but he'd also been blind.

He'd been solely focused on himself—on his legacy. His father was the king, the ranch his castle. Victor Jr. saw Vic as the prince who'd be crowned after he retired. Vic had been raised to believe that he knew better than anyone—his mother and grandmother, his sisters and Aubrey included—what was best for the Grandin family. He'd never stopped to question if that was true or not.

To him, Aubrey's interest in graduate school hadn't been about her pursuing her dreams, it'd been about delaying each rite of passage on the way to his ultimate goal: inheriting the ranch. When she'd told him she wasn't ready to be a mother, he'd had a vision of his future kingdom crumbling. He didn't have a backup plan. His father hadn't asked his opinion about the ranch or his future but had simply told Vic what was expected of him. And Vic, in his attempt to appease his father and step up and be the man he'd been tasked with becoming, had argued with Aubrey and had ultimately lost her.

He'd failed at strong-arming her into doing what he wanted. Was it any wonder she'd decided not to marry him? Had their roles been reversed, he never would have stayed with her. He wouldn't have changed his lifelong goals for anyone.

He'd been so shortsighted.

Thankfully, Vic wasn't a cocky twenty-one-year-old anymore. He was a grown man navigating the choppy waters of real life. With the threat of losing the ranch his family treasured, and possibly losing Aubrey for a second time.

She impatiently tapped her fingers on his hand before unhooking his arms from her waist and moving away from him. She stood and pulled on her jeans, her movements jerky.

"Where are you going?"

"Just say it, Vic. You're not interested in marrying me. I don't need my memory back to know that. Your stony silence says everything you're not." She pulled off his shirt and tossed it at his face, redressing quickly, her back to him. "I don't believe you're being careful because of my injury. You're like this all the time, aren't you?"

"Like what?"

"Distant."

He bit his tongue to keep from explaining how she had no idea how *distant* he'd been during their decade-long separation. Though that might have been a better option than what he said next. "I've always wanted to marry you, Aubrey."

Her green eyes widened. He stood and yanked on his shirt. "Come on."

She eyed his outstretched hand nervously.

"I'm not going to let you stand here and say things that aren't true. You said you could handle me, right?"

She blinked at his palm one final time before sliding her hand into his. He led her from the loft, along the gravel path and up the stairs to his private entrance.

She'd said he didn't want to marry her, but nothing could have been further from the truth. Hell, if he'd known then what he knew now, he would've fought harder for them, and damn his stupid pride.

Vic opened the private entryway to his suite, ushering Aubrey through the doorway ahead of him. She navigated a short hallway that opened to a small kitchenette on the left. His bedroom was on the right, if it could even be called that. The massive space held a wide bed with rich mahogany-colored leather head-and footboards. A matching leather sofa and recliner faced a large-screen TV, and in the corner of the room was a desk and a tall shelf lined with books. It was like his own apartment nestled inside the house. A corridor past the kitchen opened to a sizable bathroom with one other doorway bisecting that hallway.

When she faced Vic, she found him watching her carefully. He was standing at his dresser, top drawer pulled open. He motioned for her to come to him, and she did, each footfall leaden with inexplicable dread.

No memories came, only a strange, disembodied sensation. He plucked a pale gray velvet box from the drawer and then opened it to reveal a platinum wedding band set. A chunky diamond surrounded by other smaller diamonds winked in the bedroom's ambient light, and her breath grew stale in her lungs.

"I've had this ring in my drawer for ten years. We

disagreed about the future—you wanted a different life than I wanted. It's not that I didn't want to marry you, Aub. Like I told you, the timing was wrong."

The ring was beautiful. She didn't know much about jewelry. She didn't know the name of this particular shape of diamond. She didn't need to know anything except what it represented: a future—their future. One that Vic had planned for with her in mind. Standing here, the ring in its box mere inches away, she suddenly wanted the future it promised more than anything.

With a shaking hand, she plucked the ring from its velvet bed. "I can't believe it."

"I don't know how else to prove it to you."

She peered up at him, the diamond band between them. "You've had this for ten years?"

He nodded. "Every last one of them."

"You didn't give up."

"No. I guess I didn't." He gently took the ring from her grasp and tucked it back into the box, shutting the lid. It was like watching her future recede into the distance. She'd already lost a chunk of her past. Losing her future as well was unacceptable.

"You wanted to marry me, but you never asked."

He placed the box back in the dresser drawer but said nothing.

"And now? Are you waiting until I regain my memory? Are you worried if I don't, you won't be interested in spending a lifetime with me?" She could almost understand that way of thinking. What if she backslid? Or had health problems that affected her for years to come? How could she expect him to stay by her side and care for her when he could live an unburdened life without her?

"No." He gripped her upper arms and bent to look

into her eyes. "Listen to me carefully, Aubrey Leann Collins. Me wanting to marry you has nothing to do with your memory or lack thereof. But…"

"But?"

"*You* wanting to marry *me* has everything to do with it."

She shook her head, the riddle making no sense to her. He spoke before she could argue.

"Trust me, beautiful. If I thought it was fair to you, I'd move heaven and earth to marry you as soon as possible. You deserve a big proposal and a bigger wedding. You also deserve to know—to remember—the facts before you agree to spend a lifetime with me."

"Why wouldn't I want to marry you?" She wrapped her arms around his neck and met his honest, espresso-brown eyes. "I love you. I've always loved you."

He looked lost for a moment, his eyebrows bent, his mouth pulling down at the corners.

"Vic. I love—"

He smothered the sentiment with a kiss. A long, lovely kiss she found it so easy to lose herself in. His arms embraced her, hugging her close as he drank her in for a leisurely minute. When his lips left hers, she hummed in her throat.

"Fair warning," she whispered. "When you ask, I'll say yes. We'll move into our own home and have a few Grandin babies. A whole new generation will inherit your family's ranch. How's that sound?"

His expression of disbelief faded into one hot enough to burn down the entire house. She'd settle for igniting the sheets.

"Let's try out your bed."

"Good idea," he growled and then, once again, stripped off her clothes.

Eleven

Aubrey twisted her hands as Dr. Mitchell thumbed through a stack of papers. She'd spent most of a day last week at the doctor's office, undergoing a battery of tests to determine if there'd been any improvement. The other woman hummed, then nodded, then hummed again.

"I'm pleasantly surprised." Dr. Mitchell's kind smile made the good news better.

Aubrey let out a nervous laugh, notably relieved. "I was worried you'd tell me something I didn't want to hear."

"I might. But overall, I'm pleased with your progress."

Aubrey wasn't. Over the last month, she'd been the opposite of barraged with memories of her life. The recollections came more as a trickle, and even then they weren't complete. Though she'd recalled many bits and pieces of her life, a significant chunk of her memory was AWOL.

"You have had many memories, and better yet, you haven't forgotten anything from the last few days." Dr. Mitchell set the paperwork aside. "According to Vic, anyway. You two have been spending a lot of time together."

"Yes." She'd filled out the questionnaire and then had asked him to corroborate her memories. As the doctor had mentioned when Aubrey had picked up the forms, "There's no other way for me to know if the new memories you're creating are sticking."

Aubrey had joked to Vic about leaving out her *stickiest* memories of the loft and the time spent in his bedroom. He had given her a wicked grin and said, "I'll spare your doctor the filthy, fantastic facts, but you should feel free to share them with me in as much detail as possible. And if you'd like a reenactment, just yell."

She'd been understandably nervous about the assessment. Would Dr. Mitchell tell Aubrey that she was healing too slowly? Would any of her answers trigger a warning?

"Does this mean I can return to work?" Aubrey asked.

"You're close, but not yet. I'd like to see a bit more progress before you take on the stressors of returning to the workforce."

"But I—"

"You love your job. I understand, Ms. Collins, but good stress is still stress. I would also prefer you didn't drive yet, as an extra precaution."

Aubrey let out a frustrated sigh and then blurted, "What about riding a horse?" She'd wanted to climb onto Titan the moment she'd laid eyes on him.

"This is a common question among you Texans," Dr. Mitchell said with a chuckle. She stacked the paperwork and tucked it into the file by her elbow. "I moved here from Chicago, and after nearly eight years, I still can't wrap my head around those animals."

Just when Aubrey thought her request would be denied, the doctor continued, "No *bronco* riding, but if you want to go for a steady trot, I don't see the harm. Navigating an open pasture is different from changing lanes in thick freeway traffic. Give me the benefit of not worrying about you behind the wheel yet. Okay?"

"Okay." Aubrey would take the win. A tepid trot on horseback was at least some forward progress. She exited the doctor's office and found her mother in the waiting room. Aubrey quickly relayed the state of her health as they walked out of the hospital and to her mother's car.

"Will you drop me off at the Grandin ranch? I want to surprise Vic."

"I don't care what your doctor says, I'm not comfortable with you riding a horse." Mary's mouth pulled into a frown as she steered out of the parking lot.

"It's not like I'm in a rodeo. I miss riding. I feel like it's been forever."

"Ever since you and Vic—" Her mother shook her head as she drove.

"Ever since me and Vic what?"

"You stopped riding ten years ago."

Funny how that timeline seemed to coincide with not only her memories of him, but also the engagement ring hiding in his drawer. "Why?"

"You were focused on college."

Again with the college excuse? Hadn't she known that it was possible to be, do and have more than life as a college student? She understood pursuing her beloved profession had taken dedicated attention, but what about the years after she'd earned her degree? Why hadn't she returned to doing what she'd loved before? Like riding horses, or marrying her freaking boyfriend?

"I'm not allowed to go back to work yet, so this is the first good news I've had in a while. I'd appreciate if you didn't ruin it for me," Aubrey clipped. Her frustration was aimed at the wrong person, but she couldn't help herself. "I will call a car service from your house if you refuse to take me to see him."

"All right, all right. Goodness, you're spirited today." Mary sounded reluctant when she admitted, "I've missed this side of you. Maybe this incident is a blessing in disguise."

Aubrey liked the sound of that, especially since she had been enjoying her life lately. She had no way of knowing if she was behaving differently than normal—but she had zero complaints.

As her mother pulled into the Grandin ranch and parked next to the stable, she warned Aubrey for the fifteenth time to be safe. Aubrey promised she would and then practically ran from the car in pursuit of her newfound freedom.

An absolutely gorgeous redhead was angling for the front door of the ranch house, wearing a sexy floral dress and a pair of cowboy boots. Vic barely suppressed a smile as he cupped his palms around his mouth and shouted Aubrey's name.

She turned and started his way, her soft auburn waves lifting on the breeze. He loved when she wore her hair down. And when she flashed him a dazzling grin, he felt Cupid's arrow slide into his chest for the felling blow.

It was official. Vic was a goner for Aubrey Collins once again.

She broke into a run toward him, which caused another arrhythmic pattern in his heart. He caught her, hugging her close and inhaling the clean sunshine scent of her hair.

"The doctor cleared me to ride," she said as he set her feet back onto the ground. "Let's throw a saddle on Titan and take him out!"

Her eyes twinkled as she turned her head to look toward the stable where he'd just been. When she looked back at him and took in the state of his dust-covered attire, she frowned. "You're a mess."

"Thanks." He swiped hay off his sleeves. "I was helping the stable hands feed the horses. I've been enjoying being out here in the elements lately. A good leader should know what the hell's going on with his ranch."

She propped her hand on her hip. "And this has nothing to do with proving to your sisters that you're more than a delegator?"

"That's…secondary." He palmed the back of his neck, uncharacteristically sheepish. "Are you sure you want to take Titan out now?"

"Yes! I'm like a jack-in-the-box that's been wound too tight. I have so much pent-up energy I feel like I'm going to explode. I want you to ride with me. Keep me safe."

He found it particularly hard to say no to her when she appealed to his protective side. If he was sure of one capability in his arsenal, it was that he could keep Aubrey safe—especially from the vantage point of atop a horse.

"I have a confession first," she said.

His heart sputtered to a halt as his mind introduced any number of memories she might confess. Had she remembered one of their arguments? *The* argument? "Oh yeah?"

"I don't remember Titan, and I don't know why."

Well, *he* knew why she didn't know Titan. Aubrey had been long gone from Vic's life when he'd bought the horse five years ago. With no easy way to explain that, he said, "Titan responds to the genuineness of a person. And you, Aubrey," he said, taking her hand and leading her to the stable, "are as genuine as they come."

He made short work of saddling up the horse. Titan was a gentle giant and had never been interested in tossing anyone off his back. Seeing Aubrey topple off that stage the night of the pool party had shaved years off Vic's life. If the unthinkable happened and she fell off his horse, he'd throw himself off with her if he had a shot at preventing her from injury.

He helped her into the saddle and then joined her. Titan seemed to intuitively know he was carrying precious cargo. The horse took them the easy way, his gait rhythmic as he followed the fence line. It felt right to have Aubrey's hair tickling Vic's cheeks, her back leaning against his front as they rode.

They used to ride together, around the ranch. She always wanted to pet the cows, and he'd gotten the biggest kick out of that. Back then, while he'd respected and cared for the animals, he'd looked at them more like a commodity than living beings. Aubrey had opened his eyes to the kindness in theirs, to the literal sacrifice they were making so that Vic and his family could live a good life. He'd gained a lot of respect for the living, breathing creatures that were a part of this ranch. Aubrey had changed him for the better in that way—and countless others.

The midday sun played in her hair, which glimmered like spun, copper-colored silk. Having her around this last month was the ultimate second chance. Like in the movie *It's a Wonderful Life*, Vic was destined to wake out of the alternate reality to find everything as it had been. And when she remembered everything and resented him for playing her, he'd already decided what to do.

He was going to fight for her until his dying breath.

He hadn't fought for her when she left the first time. That was a mistake he refused to repeat.

"I remember this," she gasped. She snapped her head around to look up at him. "Vic, I *remember* riding with you. I'm sorry I stopped. I was so focused on school."

He didn't correct her, though he knew the real reason why she'd quit riding. It was because she'd never come to see him after the breakup. That night had been so final, so ruinous, they hadn't even managed to salvage a friendship.

"God. It's like it happened yesterday," she continued. "Isn't time weird?"

"The weirdest." He'd been having major flashbacks himself.

"I just… I wish I could remember more. Dr. Mitchell told me not to worry, but how am I supposed to do that?"

"You never liked being out of control."

"You're one to talk."

"We had that in common. Which is probably why…" *We argued so much about our future.* "Why, uh, we've butted heads on occasion."

"How else could we be so skilled at the making-up part?" She rested her head against his shoulder. When he thought of the years they could have spent fighting and making up, his heart crushed like an empty soda can.

"If you want to pick a fight with me, Aubrey Collins, knock yourself out. Not literally, though." He tightened his hold on her, and she freed an elbow and shot it into his ribs.

"That was bad."

"How bad?"

"*Bad* bad."

This was the Aubrey he remembered. Paired with a kinder, tenderer version of himself that he remembered. He hadn't always been a stubborn ass who wanted to corral her. In the beginning, he'd liked the way she challenged him. Once the power she'd managed to wield effortlessly had overtaken him, though, he'd been scared down to his spurs.

His grandfather and father ran the literal roost, and Vic had mistakenly believed, as the only Grandin son, that would also be his job. He'd been inexperienced both in relationships and in managing a ranch this size. He'd feared that taking an ounce of attention off his work would cause the entire outfit to collapse.

When Aubrey had insisted on continuing on to graduate school, he'd seen no pros, only cons. The idea of her stressed about earning a decent salary, or her fate being chosen by faceless city board members, drove him crazy. It was Vic's job to take care of her. She was his princess, and he'd wanted to build a carefree life for her. And he could admit to the sliver of doubt that'd crept in when her drive and ambition had made it seem like he hadn't offered her enough.

He'd been immature and shortsighted, and they'd lost years together because of it. Well, this time he wouldn't go down without a fight. She belonged with him.

She always had.

Twelve

"What is that?" A reddish-brown lump in the golden brush stirred and then stilled just as quickly. The small, round, fur-covered animal was breathing. She could see its back lifting and dropping.

"A calf slipped through the fence. He's hiding," Vic answered.

A mournful wail came from the calf's mother, a brown-and-white cow, mooing her warning to Vic—or maybe encouragement to her little one. The calf didn't move a muscle.

"Is he hurt?" she asked as Titan's head came up, the muscles on his flanks tightening beneath her legs.

Vic leaned forward and whispered one word. "Coyote."

Her eyes followed his pointing finger to the thin dog lurking beyond the brush. If it cared that they were there, it didn't show. Its predatory gaze was locked on the calf.

"Where there's one, there's more," Vic murmured.

"That's not very reassuring."

"No. It's not."

He dismounted, skirted the calf's hiding place and began whistling and clapping at the coyote and its unseen pack. Only then she did see them—and hear them—as they yipped and ran off into the trees beyond the field.

The mother cow mooed her concern. Vic reassured her with, "I'll get your baby. Don't worry."

From his belt, he unclipped a rope and fashioned a lasso. His second toss landed around the calf's neck. Only then did the calf burst to life, struggling to escape while its mother wailed in protest. Aubrey's heart lurched. She had a soft spot for animals, and clearly neither of them understood that Vic was trying to help.

Thankfully, he returned the calf to the safety of the other side of the fence mere moments later. Once the baby was reunited with its mother, the larger cow licked and doted.

Aubrey smiled at the sweet interaction. "She's a good mama."

"She is." He watched the scene for a moment before he looked up at her, eyes squinting against the sun in spite of the Stetson on his head. "You were the one who taught me that, you know. You were always pointing out the beauty in these beasts. I never noticed before I met you."

He climbed back into Titan's saddle and wrapped his arms around her waist. Together they watched as the lost duo rejoined the herd on the hill.

Once they were out of sight, she rested her hand on his and said, "You'll make a good daddy."

The rigid set of his arms around her communicated that the compliment might have fallen short. Had the topic of children been hallowed ground? Something they'd spoken of in the past or, possibly, *argued* about? She had a funny feeling they had alternate viewpoints on the topic.

"I always thought so."

She didn't miss the note of wonder in his voice. "And I didn't?"

He guided Titan back to the trail. "It was less about me, more about you."

She was a teacher. She loved children. It would make sense if she'd been eager to have a family of her own. Had she postponed one love for the other? The more she learned about her past, the less she wanted to remember.

They rode silently for a few minutes before she spoke again. "Thanks for bringing me out. If you're too busy to give me a ride home, I can call a car."

He surprised her by saying, "Or you can stay with me."

"Really?"

"Yes, really," he answered with a soft chuckle. "Call your parents and let them know I'll bring you by in the morning. In the meantime, I have a shower with our names on it."

She warmed at the idea that she hadn't spoiled the mood tonight by reminding him how difficult she'd been about their future. "A shower sounds lovely."

"Wait'll you see what I do to you in that shower," he said against her ear. "I'm going to make sure you never forget how good you had it with me."

"What do you mean, *had*?" She twisted her neck to look up at him. "Are you going somewhere?"

"Not by choice, Aubrey with the auburn hair. Not by choice."

Titan trotted, steady and slow, as Vic guided him up onto a small hill. The sun was dipping low in the sky, the trees along the horizon black silhouettes. She sat, Vic's arms wrapped around her waist, his cheek against hers, while they watched until the last dab of light slipped behind the mountains.

So, her life hadn't been perfect. And there were parts she couldn't remember, for reasons she couldn't comprehend. What had happened in the past no longer mattered, not when everything felt so right in the moment.

When she was with Vic, she knew all she needed to know. She knew she loved him and he loved her—the fact he hadn't said it yet hadn't escaped her attention, and there was an engagement ring in his dresser drawer meant for her. She'd been trying not to think too hard about what he said about her changing her mind after her memory returned. Everything about him screamed that he was a man who'd never abandon or betray her. What more was there to know?

She reached behind her and wrapped one arm around his neck. He kissed her cheek as the breeze blew, bringing with it the sweet smells of wildflowers and grass.

She had tied herself to this man fourteen years ago. She trusted her decisions. She knew what was best for her.

"Vic?"

"Yeah, honey."

"About that shower..."

His low chuckle vibrated along her back. "You got

it," he said before clucking his tongue at Titan. They silently trotted back to the stable.

With Aubrey in the privacy of his suite, Vic kicked off his boots and reached for the stud on his jeans. Aubrey, a playful glint in her eyes, lifted the skirt of her floral dress to show her thighs, and then her panties, before dropping it to hide them from view. She repeated the dance while he wrestled with his jeans, too engrossed by the show to pay a damn bit of attention to what he was doing.

When she whipped the dress off and threw it at his chest, he nearly tripped over the stray leg of his jeans on his way to her. He caught her at the dresser, backing her against it to give her a thorough kiss.

Then his mind strayed to the box in the top drawer.

To the very engagement ring Aubrey had returned to him with no intention of taking it back. The same Aubrey who had just assured him he'd make a good father, and who continually asked about their future. A future that, until very recently, had been a pipe dream.

"Are you okay?" she breathed. Her lips were swollen from his kisses, her chest flushed pink and her nipples pressing the thin fabric of her bra.

"Yeah." He dived back into the sanctuary of her mouth, unbuttoning his shirt and tossing it behind him. "We have to take a shower first." He gave her one more fast kiss. "I smell like cow."

"You smell like *you*." Her eyes flashed, an undeniable heat communicating how much she wanted him. That look poured itself into the center of his chest, where a groove of longing had been carved over the long and lonely decade he'd spent missing her.

She pulled down the cups of her pale yellow lace bra

to flash him. Just as quickly, she covered herself, her hands going to her matching panties next. Her panties had *always* matched her bras. God, he loved this woman.

The thought stopped him cold. Of course he knew that—he'd known that. He'd refrained from telling her because it wouldn't be fair to her. When she remembered everything, he needed her to understand he hadn't been simply toying with her heart this second time around. He was here for the long haul—if she'd have him.

Big if.

"Don't you like yellow?" She arched her back, and he closed his larger hands over the most exquisite breasts he'd ever seen, felt or tasted.

"Hate it," he lied. "I'd better take this off." He unhooked her bra, and it followed the same path to the floor his shirt had. Her breasts were a perfect handful. The first time he'd seen those pale peach nipples, he'd been a slack-jawed seventeen-year-old with the most painful erection of his life to date. He felt a similar way seeing them now. Even after he'd had them on his tongue countless times. Even after he'd plucked them to eager peaks while making love to her the other night.

He rolled his boxer briefs off his legs, his erection springing free. Aubrey lost the panties, throwing them at his face. He caught them midair, his reflexes every bit what they used to be, and chased her across the bedroom to the shower. She didn't resist him long. He pressed every naked inch of her against every naked inch of him as he blindly felt for the shower door. He tested the water, determined it was the ideal temperature and shoved them both inside.

"I miss this." She sighed against his lips as rivulets of water rolled off her chin.

"Me, too." He blinked, the shower spray bouncing off his cheeks. He didn't know if she meant that she'd remembered the times they'd showered together or if she was being hyperbolic, but he sure as hell meant it. He missed this. He missed *her*. He missed every second of holding her close and kissing her. Of seeing her matching panties and bras. He'd lost years thanks to his own stubbornness. He refused to rush tonight.

Lowering his face, he kissed her slower this time, pushing his tongue past her lips to savor her heady flavor. When she moaned into his mouth, he coasted one palm along her ribs and cupped one of her breasts in his hand. He took one succulent peach nipple between his thumb and forefinger, then flattened her back against the tile wall.

His eyes drilling into hers, he ran his other hand down her torso until he reached her center. She widened her stance in silent permission, giving him ample room to play. The trust between them was a major turn-on. Her auburn curls tickled his fingers and then he slid home, pushing into her wetness with two fingers as his thumb played her clit.

"You're smoking hot, Aubrey Collins." He nibbled her bottom lip, watching as her green irises were swallowed by black pupils. "Do you like this?"

"Yes." She shuddered as steam rose around them.

"No one can turn you on the way I do. No one can make you feel as good as I make you feel." He had the urgent need to claim her. To remind her, so that when she did remember, she would search as fruitlessly as he had for a replacement, and, like him, she would fail to find one. He didn't doubt that she'd experienced someone else in their time apart, but he wanted her to know she wouldn't have to stoop ever again. He'd be here—he'd always be here.

"Yes." Her eyes rolled back into her head as he continued touching her and turning her on. She'd only be satisfied by him from here on out.

"Say it."

"Just you, Vic. Only you."

He hadn't fully earned this woman, but pride laced through him all the same. He ended the kiss when her breathing increased, her tiny mewls prefacing her inevitable climax. Because he could take her there. No one else.

Not ever again.

"There, *there*." She gripped his wrist, and he zeroed in on her clitoris. Stroking her diligently, he kept his gaze locked onto her beautiful face while he worked. There was nothing better in this life than watching her come. From the heated flush that worked its way from her chest to her cheeks, to the way she squeezed her eyes closed, to the moan escaping her lush mouth.

Awestruck, he witnessed all three, wrapping his free arm around her to keep her from sliding down the shower wall.

He wanted nothing but to line up to her entrance and slide home. To feel her clutch around him and hear her breathy pants in his ear. To pound them into a merciful oblivion until they were so weak from the effort, they'd be forced to sleep on a pile of towels on the bathroom floor.

Her eyes opened lazily, a wonky smile following.

"We need a condom," he huffed, the words ragged. He dropped his forehead to hers in defeat.

"But I like it in here." She pushed her bottom lip out into a pout.

"You'll like it out there, too, where I can maneuver." He cupped each side of her face and kissed her, then made the epically difficult decision to stop. "What was I saying?"

"You were talking about maneuvering." She spun off the shower knob. "I can't wait to see what comes next."

"*You* come next." He dragged her from the shower, leaving a river of water from their dripping bodies as he angled for the bed. "Then it's my turn."

Thirteen

"These sheets are soaked," Aubrey complained as she sat up, her bare back chilly and damp.

"You're welcome." Vic was lying on top of his bedding next to her, wearing nothing but a smug and wholly sexy smirk. Her eyes lingered on the valleys and grooves of his abs and pectoral muscles. The broad shoulders. The penis that was no less impressive at half-mast and resting on one thigh. She'd always loved the shape of him. Even the hair under his arms and on his chest and legs turned her on.

"Soaked from the shower water." She threw a pillow at him.

He pulled the pillow away from his stupidly handsome face to reveal he was grinning, too. How could either of them do anything short of grinning like fools after what they'd done? First off, it was fun. Secondly, it was *damn fun*.

"What were we thinking, not drying off first?"

He looped an arm around her waist and tugged. She yelped as she landed ungracefully on top of him. Once there, she decided to stay, her nude body stuck to his. This was easily the most confusing time of her life, and yet she had no problem finding an immense amount of joy.

"We've perfected sex," she told him.

His grin broadened. "You think so?"

"I think so. Don't you?"

"I *know* so. Everyone else in the world believes they're having amazing sex. They have no idea we're the ones having the best sex possible."

She kissed him lightly. "Poor souls."

"I won't tell if you don't," he whispered against her mouth. Something about his smile reminded her of the tender way they'd fallen for each other when they were teenagers. Vic Grandin was, like his name, *grand*. He'd walked around their high school like he'd owned the place. And when her mother overheard her saying so, Mary Collins had concluded, "He probably does. Do you know who his father is?"

Aubrey had been accepted by the Grandins from the moment Vic introduced her to his family. Layla and Chelsea and even protective, younger Morgan had liked her instantly. Aubrey's parents were more involved with their daughter's dating life than Vic's were with his. He seemed to have no curfews and was able to do what he wanted when he wanted. Which reminded her...

"I should tell my parents I'm not coming home before it gets any later." She leaned off the bed and made a fruitless swipe for her dress. Her cell phone should be in the pocket. She was unsurprised to feel Vic's hands palm her butt while she reached.

"You have the best ass," came his compliment.

"You say that like you're not tired of seeing it yet."
Got it! Her hand around the dress, she pulled it into her
lap. Vic was lying on his belly, head propped on one
fist. She gave his bare butt a light slap. "I like yours,
too. Now be quiet so I can tell my parents I've decided
to stay."

She pressed a button and commanded, "Call Mom."
It rang once, twice, then three times, and she gave up.
"They must be at dinner. I'll send a text instead." She
kept it simple, typing, Staying with Vic tonight. He'll
bring me home in the morning. Good night.

She wrinkled her nose when she tossed her phone
onto the bed.

"What is it?" Vic asked.

She folded her legs beneath her. "Why do I feel as if
I'm doing something I shouldn't?"

"Because for years you were." He kissed her knee.
"You were lying about staying at your friends' houses
and I was sneaking you into my room at night."

"It's hard to sneak into a private entrance. Besides,
Victor Jr. and Bethany let you do whatever you wanted.
I was jealous. My parents are like a pair of hawks. Take
this situation, for example. I'm living with them." Which
honestly hadn't been *that* bad, but she was tired of rotat-
ing the same fifteen articles of clothing. She didn't care
what people who favored a capsule wardrobe said, she
needed more options. She had a closet full of clothes at
home she'd like to utilize. "Maybe you could run me by
my apartment before you drop me off in the morning."

"Why?"

"I need a fresh outfit for dinner tomorrow night. I'm
tired of wearing the same clothes." She finger-combed
her damp hair. "My friends from school invited me to

a Tex-Mex taco bar for margaritas. It was Primrose's idea."

Boy, had Aubrey been relieved to know exactly who Primrose was when she'd called. And when the older blonde mentioned that Elise, Hailee, Brooke and Brandie would be joining them, Aubrey had been further relieved to remember each of her coworkers with stark clarity. She called up a mental picture of them easily and remembered what classes they taught without having to think about it.

"How are you getting there? Is your mom going?"

"*No.* I do not need a chaperone."

"What about a driver? I'll take you. I'll sit at the bar and mind my own business."

"Actually, Prim mentioned that Brandie was bringing her new boyfriend, and Brooke was bringing her husband, Kal, so maybe you will have a few dudes to hang out with. If you're sure you're not going to be put out driving me there and back."

"How can I convince you that you're not an inconvenience to me, Aubrey?" He rested his hand on her leg. She had to admit that was nice to hear. She'd felt like an inconvenience since her accident. She'd been the very definition of someone to fret over since she'd been discharged from the hospital.

She squeezed his hand. "I can't tell you how much your support has meant while I'm going through this. Not being able to work has made my days really long. I understand why I never used social media before, but it sure would come in handy when I run out of chores to do with my mother. I swear, that woman never stops cleaning the house. I nearly opened an account out of desperation, but the liability risk is too high. I'd rather not give any of my students' overly involved parents an excuse to complain."

"Impossible. You were teacher of the year. Parents trust you with their trust-fund kids implicitly. And you don't have to stay with your parents indefinitely. You're always welcome here."

"Oh, no, I wouldn't want to be in the way."

"It'd solve your clothing problem, though."

"How?"

"You wouldn't have to wear any if you stayed with me." He flattened her on the bed, rolling onto her and trapping her there with his weight. She closed her eyes and savored everywhere his lips touched, grateful to have him in her life and to be in his.

Vic had never been to Clara's Cantina. He wasn't sure how he'd missed this one—he loved Tex-Mex food. The restaurant was shack-like by design, with cowboy hats hanging from the walls and strings of lights shaped like chili peppers draped across the bar. The vibe was loud and raucous inside, but a bit less so on the open-air veranda where he and Aubrey were headed.

"I can't believe you've never been here," she said as she wove around packed tables, each adorned with baskets of chips and dishes of salsa.

Offering to drive her hadn't been completely altruistic on his part. Her memory loss was still very much a factor, and he couldn't be sure what her friends would say when she brought up her "boyfriend," Vic. She'd mentioned at least one name he recognized from their years in high school together. One friend who would undoubtedly remember when Vic and Aubrey dated, and probably knew they'd broken up as well. Elise and Aubrey had been close back then.

He'd been reminding himself all day that he was simply looking out for Aubrey's health, but if he dug deep, he could admit he was also running interference. He'd made a pretty good case for them living happily ever after, but he wasn't ready for her to learn the whole truth yet—or at least he wanted to be there when she found out.

The five women at the table stood when they spotted Aubrey, clapping their hands and whooping. Diners at surrounding tables glanced over long enough to confirm a celebrity wasn't in their midst, and then returned to their conversations. Then he saw her.

Elise Baxter.

Aubrey was pulled into hug after hug, her friends complimenting her on her outfit or her hair. Elise made a beeline straight for him.

Shorter than Aubrey, Elise stood at a petite five feet tall, her dark chin-length hair shorter than it had been when they were in high school. Her round, dark brown eyes were narrowed on him, broadcasting her disproval. She'd never liked Vic. He used to believe it was because she was jealous of Aubrey and wanted to date him herself, because of course he had. From the vantage point of a grown man, he recognized his own embarrassing teenage bravado. More likely Elise didn't like him because she'd seen what he hadn't: Aubrey had been too good for him back then.

"What the hell are you doing here?" she snapped.

"Keep your voice down." He smiled for show. Aubrey was chatting with the other ladies, not looking in his direction. "Aub doesn't remember everything about our past. In her mind, we're together."

"In her mind? It looks like you're together in body as well."

"When her memory returns, I will tell her the truth. The doctor doesn't want any sudden memories to ruin the progress she's made."

Elise's eyebrows bent in sympathy. He knew she cared about Aubrey. They all did.

"I'm here because she wants me here," he said. "I'm doing this for her, which is what I'm asking you to do as well." When Elise's features hardened again, he added, "Please?"

She folded her arms over her chest and lifted her chin. "Fine. But if you hurt her again, Grandin, you'll have to deal with me."

"You'll have to stand in line behind her father." He raked a hand through his hair. He was irritated that everyone thought the worst of him, but at the same time he understood why. "For her sake, if you could cover for me if this conversation dips into our relationship, I'd be grateful."

"This is wrong." Elise shook her head but agreed with him when she said, "I'll do it for her."

"Thank you."

She speared him with one final glare before going to give Aubrey a hug and a sunny smile. He did his best to relax, introducing himself to both Brooke's husband, Kal, and Brandie's boyfriend, Roger. Rather than sit next to the two other men, Vic sat next to Aubrey. Something else Elise didn't appear to like.

"Introduce your handsome corn cake, sweetheart," the woman introduced to him as Primrose said in a thick Texas accent. She was broad and blonde, the permanent dimple denting her left cheek making her appear as if she never stopped smiling.

"I've never introduced you to Vic?" Aubrey's eyebrows centered over her nose.

"Of course she has!" Elise interrupted. She turned to Primrose and nodded while she explained, "Remember at the teacher of the year ceremony? We met him that night, some of us for the first time."

"Not Elise." Aubrey shot a thumb over to Vic. "The poor dear had to endure this one in high school."

"Well, you were the poor dear who had to date him." Elise's smile was stiff before she turned back to her friends. "Vic was seated with the principal and his assistant and their spouses. Remember?"

"Oh, of course." Brooke was the first to catch on to what Elise was trying to do. She jabbed Brandie with an elbow. "We saw so many people that night. Sorry, Vic."

"No big deal."

"How have you been feeling lately?" The woman introduced to him as Hailee directed the question at Aubrey. Her build and clothing style reminded him a bit of Caitlyn Lattimore, his best friend Jayden's sister.

"Better each day," Aubrey answered as she poured herself a margarita from the pitcher at the center of the table. "I still have gaps in my memory, but the doctor is confident they'll return."

"Quite a few gaps," Elise muttered. Vic shot her a warning look.

"Yes, that's true." Aubrey sipped her drink. "This is delicious. Anyway, I've been leaning fairly hard on Vic." She grabbed his hand on the table and squeezed his fingers, looking up at him with trusting eyes. His stomach sank. "He doesn't mind, though."

"I'd do anything for you." He meant it down to his bone marrow. When her memories of the past came back, he'd be there for her. He'd dry her tears or allow her to yell at him. He'd take her fists if she pummeled his chest and declared she hated him for lying to her.

He'd defend her parents if needed. He'd drive her to the doctor's office or to dinner with friends or to work and home again once she went back to teaching—anything to prove to her how much he cared.

He'd given up on Aubrey once in his life. He wouldn't do it again.

Fourteen

The next morning, Aubrey and her mother sat on the wide front porch, rocking away on a pair of rockers stationed to the left of the door. Thick green grass stretched alongside the dusty driveway beneath a clear blue sky. It was a perfect day in Royal…almost.

Last night had been fun, more fun than Aubrey had had in a while. She hadn't seen her friends since before the accident, so time with the girls had been good for her heart. After the initial "how are you feeling" questions, everyone had gabbed about work. Having the spotlight off herself and onto what she loved—her job—had been a relief, even if it did make her miss work tenfold. She'd realized then just how exhausting it'd been to solely focus on her injury and healing from it.

Vic had been comfortable and conversational, the perfect foil for her that evening. She didn't feel the need to watch over him or check on him. He'd chatted with the ladies and guys alike. Football or footwear, he'd commented on both topics. More than a few times he'd sent the entire table into fits of laughter. Even Elise had laughed along, and she'd seemed disapproving about him at first. The food had been delicious, authentic Tex-Mex like Aubrey had been raised on, and the margaritas were cool and refreshing.

When Vic had dropped her off at her parents' house after dinner, her face had hurt from smiling. He'd kissed her in his truck and then had kept on kissing her…up until her father turned on the porch light as a nonverbal warning. Vic had commented that he felt like a teenager again, and she'd admitted to feeling the same before climbing out of his truck and going inside.

So, why, after an idyllic evening filled with friends, food, drink and kissing Vic, had Aubrey woken this morning with a tight ball of dread in her stomach? She couldn't understand it.

She'd lain in bed an hour ago, the clean scent of fresh sheets surrounding her, staring at the ceiling. Memories of last night popped into her head one by one, like when Primrose mentioned she hadn't remembered meeting Vic before. Or Elise's insistence that they'd all met him at the awards dinner. And there'd been something about the way her friends had laughed. A little too loud and often, sometimes exchanging glances with each other Aubrey hadn't understood the meaning behind.

She'd ignored the blip of concern in the moment, blaming her lack of social interaction or her uncooperative brain, but by this morning the events of last night had felt…well, *forced*. As if her friends had been performing. She'd told herself she was overreacting, but at the same time, she thought the observation significant.

"Did you and Vic have a nice dinner?" Her mother,

a notoriously slow riser, finally spoke, jarring Aubrey out of her hectic thoughts.

"I thought you'd fallen asleep over there."

"Darn near. I had to down half of my coffee before I could form words. How'd I rise and shine back when I taught school? The mind boggles." Her mother shook her head as if amused by her own thoughts. "I miss work sometimes. Gave me something to do with myself."

Mary was a retired English teacher. Aubrey had followed in her mother's footsteps after watching her mother grade papers and read essays by the light of the evening news. Her job had always looked fun to Aubrey.

"We had a nice time. I feel a little off, though. Talking about school and students with my coworkers made me realize how much I miss work." Maybe that's what this bizarre feeling was—her mourning her former routine. Aubrey loved interacting with her students, assigning papers and then reading and grading them. She found ways to encourage and praise every student, no matter what.

When she was younger, she'd pestered her mother with a zillion questions about teaching. She'd shadowed her mother at work for a high school paper. Aubrey had a deep love of learning, so choosing to go to college had been a no-brainer.

She hadn't been ready to marry and start a family at such a young age—not with her entire future up for grabs. No wonder it'd pissed her off when Vic suggested she stay home and have his babies rather than pursue graduate school.

"…you have years and years to teach. Don't worry, you'll be back soon enough," her mother was saying. But Aubrey hadn't been listening for the last several seconds. They'd audibly ticked by alongside each of her heartbeats, which were currently reverberating like a gong in her ears.

What was that thought about Vic and him wanting her to...*have babies instead of going to graduate school?*

She blinked, more confused than when she'd woken up this morning. She couldn't call up a time or place or any snippet of the conversation in her head, but it *felt* real. As real as the rocking chair under her butt and the mug of coffee warming her hands. The feeling of dread returned tenfold. That thought didn't feel like a thought at all. It felt like a *memory*.

"Honey, are you all right?" her mother asked.

"Yes. Yeah." She rubbed her temple where the start of a headache was brewing. "I'm, uh, trying to decide what to do with myself today."

"Lucky for you, I need help reorganizing the bookshelves. You can help me."

"Yes, *so* lucky." Aubrey forced a smile, cupping her mug with both hands to hide the shake in her arms.

She was still wrestling with the off feeling as she finished her coffee and then followed her mother inside. Thirty minutes later, the contents of the massive bookshelf in her mother's office were stacked on the floor and across two desks. Her mother swiped the dust from the top of the shelf and declared it was as clean as it would become. "How about a BLT for lunch? With avocado."

"Sold." Aubrey was hungry after having only coffee for breakfast. "Do you need help?"

"Sure do. Put all of this back for me, will you?" Mary waved in the general direction of the stacks of books, plants and the occasional figurine. Then she walked out, leaving Aubrey to handle the task.

She put away the large books first, mostly hardback coffee-table books about photography and travel. She came across one she recognized, a book about the solar system she'd referenced for her science fair project in her junior year in high school. She'd built a model of the planets, and a darn good one at that. She cracked the spine and found her second-place ribbon wedged between the pages. Gold, not blue like the first-place ribbon had been, but she'd been proud of the win. Vic had told anyone who'd listen that Aubrey should have won, and that Timothy Leighton, who'd won first place, had only claimed first place because he was a kiss-ass.

She smiled at the memory as she continued flipping through the book's pages. Then she came across a long, slender sheet of paper. No, not paper. A strip of photographs. The pictures were of her and Vic at the science fair, from one of those box-shaped, curtain-covered photo booths. In the photos she and Vic were smiling, kissing or pretending to sleep. The bottom one was her favorite. She'd been making a goofy face at the camera, but his eyes had been on her. His expression was raw and beautiful. She could see the love he'd had for her captured in this photo. It radiated even now, as real and alive as it'd ever been.

Or maybe as it used to be.

With a frown, she carefully folded the photo strip in half and tucked it into her back pocket. Her headache had arrived, either from not eating or the bout of over-thinking she'd suffered since opening her eyes today. She made quick work of filing the rest of her mother's books and mementos onto the gleaming wood shelves, and then went to join her for lunch.

Vic and Jayden were perched on the fence surrounding the Grandin property, boots hooked on the bottom plank, watching the sun go down on a long day.

Jayden had been Vic's best friend for as long as either of them could remember. Hell, probably since birth. The second-born of the Lattimores, Jayden was wealthy, handsome and Vic's age. Once Vic had been single again, and it'd been clear that Aubrey wasn't changing her mind and coming back to him, Jayden had been there for him. He'd acted as Vic's wingman whenever they'd gone out, and vice versa.

Jayden didn't take life too seriously, which, at the time, had been exactly what Vic had prioritized. Considering a future with anyone other than Aubrey had been too painful—it still was. But what Jayden *did* and had always taken seriously was his family's ranch.

"Alexa is checking in with the PI again," Jayden said, circling back to the topic they always seemed to be talking about lately. The fate of the ranches was still up in the air, and it'd been impossible not to bring it up whenever they were hanging out. Alexa was Jayden's younger sister, and also the family attorney. She had been in direct contact with private investigator Jonas Shaw, who was looking into the issues on the ranch. "Whenever she finds out more, I'll send her over to update you and your family. We're in this together."

"Appreciate it." Vic tipped his can of beer to his lips.

"Hey, what are better-looking best friends for?" Jayden grinned. The asshole. "*Now* are you going to tell me why you're messing with Aubrey Collins, or are we going to pretend that isn't going on?"

"I'm not *messing* with her." Vic heard the defense in his own voice.

"Okay. So you're *not* sleeping with your ex-girl-friend, who doesn't know she's your ex-girlfriend, thanks to a knock on the head?"

"Don't tell me I have to convince you that my motives are pure, too."

"Are they?" Jayden hopped off the fence railing and landed in the grass, then he reclaimed his own beer can that had been resting on the fence post. "What're your plans with her, anyway?"

Vic hopped down as well, one hand in his pocket as he finished off his beer. Jayden didn't want to hear this, but he'd asked, so here went nothing. "I'm winning her back."

His best friend's dark eyebrows shot up. "And when she remembers she hates you, then what?"

"She's changed. *I've* changed. Back when we were arguing over graduate school and whether or not she was ready to be a mother, we were kids ourselves. I know I was an arrogant asshole—"

"Was?" Jayden laughed, then held up a hand. "Last one."

"Yeah, sure." Vic balanced his empty can on the fence post. "Are you honestly telling me you're happy bedding women who don't stick around?"

"Yes." Jayden didn't flinch. "Are you sure you're ready to trade your single status for a woman you haven't been with for a decade? She has a life you know nothing about, Vic. You don't know *each other*. You only know who you used to be. When she remembers she threw the engagement ring at you, she is not going to be happy you have been lying to her this entire time."

"I'm not lying!" Vic shouted. He couldn't frame it

that way or he'd lose his mind. "Not really. I'm just... not filling in the gaps. Which her doctor asked me to do, by the way."

"I sincerely doubt her doctor's orders had anything to do with you taking her to bed, or tricking her into falling in love with you before she remembers why she doesn't."

"Dammit, Jayden." Vic didn't know what else to say—probably because what his best friend had said sounded true. And worse, it felt true.

"Look, I'm all for you reconciling with Aubrey. She's great, and she makes you better. You two used to be inseparable. I remember what a miserable jerk you were after she left."

"Thanks a lot," Vic grumbled.

"*But,*" Jayden continued, "this needs to be done under honest pretenses. Tell her the truth. She's strong. She can handle it. The question is, can you?"

"I can handle it," Vic said automatically, though he wondered if he could. Telling her the truth might break her heart and simultaneously land him back in the miserable-jerk stage Jayden had described. "I've given her nothing but solid reasons why we belong together. She'll understand my motives."

"And if she doesn't?"

"I'll convince her. I'm not going to let her walk away this time without her knowing how I feel about her. Life isn't going to work out if we try to find someone else to fall in love with. I've been out there and tried, and I assume she has, too."

"She doesn't remember that, either, I'm guessing. The trying-with-other-people part."

Vic shook his head. "She thinks we've been together nonstop for fourteen years."

It sounded bad when he said it aloud. Like he was trying to manipulate her into being with him. Except for one thing—

"She loves me." Vic watched Jayden's face fall. "She tells me over and over. I want to tell her not to, that she doesn't have to, but…" He rubbed a spot in the center of his chest, the one that had been aching with longing for weeks now. "It feels good, man. It feels really, really good to hear her say that to me again."

Jayden palmed Vic's shoulder in support, his expression broadcasting both sympathy and warning. The man was as close to a brother as Vic had ever had, which was why he would listen to whatever Jayden said next—even if it hurt. By the look on his face, it damn well might.

"It should feel really, really *wrong*. What you and Aubrey have currently has an expiration date. You love her, you want to marry her and walk into forever together, that's fine. I'll be the first in line at the funeral for your single-guy status. But you have to level with her. She deserves not to be the last one to know, Vic. If you love and respect her, *tell her*. Otherwise this ticking time bomb is going to reach zero and then…" Jayden spread his hands and made an exploding sound.

His best friend had put into words everything Vic knew in his heart to be true. His excuses were good ones, arguably honorable. He'd come back into her life—again—for her. To help her through her healing. With a practically clean bill of health, she'd soon be returning to work. He couldn't follow her everywhere she went in case someone told her the truth—he couldn't delay the inevitable. Someone would let slip that Aubrey and Vic hadn't been together for a decade, and then she'd never forgive him.

It was time she learned the truth about what had happened. Even if it meant he would be fighting harder for her than he'd fought before, he would tell her the real reason why her engagement ring was in his dresser drawer.

He'd proposed years ago. She'd chosen not to marry him in the end.

Fifteen

Vic hadn't been this nervous since he'd planned to take Aubrey's virginity—and give up his own—the night of her senior prom. He'd booked a room at a fancy hotel in Dallas and had arranged for strawberries and champagne to be sent to the room. The butterflies in his gut were more like flying dragons when he'd picked her up at her parents' house. He'd been positive Eddie and Mary Collins had seen the sweat on his brow for what it was—not a reaction to the Texas heat, but guilt seeping out of his every pore.

His nerves had given way the moment he and Aubrey had walked into that luxury hotel room. He'd been positive forever was in their future. He'd already purchased an engagement ring with the intention of proposing on her graduation day, which he'd ended up doing. Marriage was inevitable for them, so he saw no reason to wait another minute to actually be with her. She was his destiny, and he'd promised her an evening she'd never forget. Except she *had* forgotten.

Two years after that, he'd made another significant purchase and had planned another surprise for his fiancée. As fate had it, the night he'd tucked a gold key with a red ribbon into his pocket was the same night they'd argued about their future for the final time.

"I'm so tired of your mood swings, Vic Grandin!" Aubrey shouted.

"Keep your voice down."

"Why? Who cares if your sisters overhear? Or your parents. Or everyone in the entire state of Texas!"

"Me!" he shouted back. *"I care. And that ring on your finger should make you care. My sisters and parents are about to be your sisters and parents, too."*

The argument had been devolving since they'd started. It'd picked up speed since its downhill trajectory, and he'd be damned if he knew how to stop it. Making matters worse, he circled back to the comment that had started this ill-fated conversation.

"Ever since you went off to college you think you're too good to live a lowly life as a Grandin. I could buy you anything you want, and you don't give me credit for that, Aubrey."

"Did it occur to you, golden boy, *that I don't require a pampered life? I have wanted to be a teacher since I was a little girl. I want to earn my own money, not have it handed to me."*

He ignored the insinuation that he didn't work for his and instead focused on what was really bothering him.

"Becoming a teacher requires the initial bachelor's degree you're in the middle of attaining. Why graduate school? Why extend your college sentence another two or three years? Is the idea of marrying me and starting

*a family that repulsive?" He was lashing out, and he
didn't fully understand why. All he knew was that he'd
been ready to marry Aubrey Collins since he'd kissed
her for the first time. He'd assumed they'd be married
immediately. She'd wanted to wait a few years, and he'd
agreed to wait. He'd been patient, and now she wanted
to put off the wedding again?*

Looking back from an adult standpoint, he understood why he'd lashed out. He'd been hurt. If he'd had
a brain cell in his head at the time, he'd have seen that
his anger was masking inadequacy he hadn't come to
terms with. Instead, he'd yelled and defended himself.
Not his finest moment.

*"News flash," Aubrey continued. "My going to grad-
uate school has nothing to do with you and everything
to do with me and what I want out of life. You're not the
only one with aspirations, Victor Grandin the Third."*

*He hated when she called him that. She added "the
third" whenever she was upset with him, knowing it
upset him. He wasn't a carbon copy of his grandfather
and his father. He was the sole male heir in a new generation. He planned on taking the Grandin family ranch
to its pinnacle. He'd make his family* billions. *History
books would rave about how he'd exceeded everyone's
expectations. His sisters would finally have to admit he
was capable and talented.*

*Aubrey folded her arms and pressed her lips to-
gether. Her chin quivered and her eyelashes fluttered.
He didn't recall having seen her angrier. "Admit it, Vic,
we've grown apart."*

*The accusation hit him like a sucker punch. He
blinked away the red in his vision.*

*"You met someone, didn't you?" he said between
clenched teeth. It was the only logical explanation for*

her not wanting to marry him. "You met an educated guy who wants to be a professor when he grows up, and you believe common interests far outweigh the life a glorified ranch hand could give you. Admit it."

Her mouth fell open. "You have a lot of growing up to do. And yes, that is my college experience talking. If you truly believe I've met someone else while still seeing you, then marrying you is the worst idea I've ever entertained."

Her comment was a dagger straight to his gut. His next words weren't thought out, and they sure as hell weren't kind. "If that's the way you feel, then you shouldn't marry me. You can strut your college-educated ass off my property, but fair warning—if you walk away now, you'll be begging to come back."

She flinched, hurt radiating through her beautiful features, but she shored herself up a second later, tore the engagement ring from her finger and threw it at him. "Fuck you, Vic."

He'd never once heard her drop an F-bomb, so in a way it had been a bomb. The mushroom cloud had hovered over his head as she stomped to her car. He'd followed her, shouting as she drove off that she'd come crawling back to him. He'd promised her he'd be counting down the hours until she returned.

Shame coated him as he remembered that night in graphic detail. It was like it'd been tattooed onto his skin. He'd been an entitled, arrogant asshole at the end. Was it any wonder why she'd never spoken to him again? It'd been a miracle she'd agreed to go to bed with him the night he'd bought her a drink at the Silver Saddle. It'd taken some balls to ask her for more after having been so shallow.

Hands gripping the steering wheel of his truck, he

surfaced from the bad memories and focused on the road. His Aubrey with the auburn hair sat next to him, singing the words to a song on the radio. How did she remember lyrics but not one of the most significant memories from her past? In a way, it would have been easier if she'd remembered on her own—preferably during one of the nights she'd spent at his house. Then he could've held her close and explained how this was their second chance. He'd remind her that she'd been the one who asked for him after the accident—didn't that count for something?

She shut off the radio when the song ended. "How much longer?"

Excitement danced in her eyes. He'd wanted to kiss her since he'd picked her up but had resisted. He had no right to take anything more from her. Not until she knew the whole truth.

Permission had come via her parents, who had spoken to Aubrey's doctor. He'd confessed to Mary and Eddie that he couldn't spend another moment keeping Aubrey in the dark. He loved her but couldn't tell her. Not when she didn't fully understand the circumstance. He'd expected a fight, but her parents had agreed. Her doctor gave the green light. Aubrey was ready.

Vic sure as hell wasn't.

During their drive, she'd mentioned that she'd been feeling unsettled lately. He pressed gently, asking her why. She'd shared that she'd felt confused, and he'd promised she wouldn't be confused after today. And then he told her he had a surprise for her.

"It's just up the road," he answered as he drove closer to their destination.

"Are you sharing what it is, or do I have to wait?"

She loved surprises. She loved him. After she learned the truth, would she still?

He held her hand while navigating through a posh neighborhood lined with large houses. "Does any of this look familiar?"

Outside her window was a landscape of lush green lawns, blooming flowers and fall decorations on porches.

"Yes." She gasped. "This *is* familiar. We've driven through this neighborhood before, haven't we? It feels like it's been a while."

"It's been a long while. Over a decade." His spine stiffened as he slowed down. They were close. "We used to pretend we were shopping for our dream home. You picked your favorite, I picked mine."

"And they were the same one!" She laughed. "Oh my God, I remember! It was a transitional style, brick and stone. Two-car garage. Do you have any idea how good it feels to remember? So good."

He hoped her excitement held through what he'd brought her here to tell her.

He presented his ID at the gate separating a ritzier part of the neighborhood from the one behind them and then drove the short distance to the house she'd described.

"Vic? What is this?" she asked when he pulled into the driveway. He'd had the interlocked paver-stone driveway laid two years ago.

"I bought the house. I never told you." When she gawped at him, he gave her a tentative smile. "Surprise."

The tears came as another laugh stuttered from her lips. "You're serious."

"Yep. Hop out and I'll show you the inside."

As he slipped the key into the dead bolt, she hugged him from the side. He turned to embrace her, holding her tight and never wanting to let her go. Would she be this happy a few minutes from now? He doubted it.

He unlocked the door and ushered her in ahead of him. They stood at the base of a long foyer, which led to the rest of an unfurnished home. To their right was a living room with built-in bookshelves, ideal for housing Aubrey's massive book collection. To their left, a dining room large enough to host both his family and hers for Thanksgiving or Christmas dinners. He took her hand and led her through the arched foyer to the stairway leading upstairs.

There wasn't a speck of dust in the place, thanks to the cleaning crew he'd hired. During the anger stage of their breakup, he'd been convinced he'd move into this house one day, and then she'd regret leaving him when she saw what she'd missed out on. When he'd hit the grieving stage, he'd kept the house up in case a miracle occurred and she came back to him. After that, well, he hadn't needed a reason. Maintaining the house had become habit, and the idea of letting it go felt like a death. He'd revisited the notion of moving in here himself but ultimately hadn't been able to stomach it. Even though she'd never stepped foot inside, he saw Aubrey in every corner and crevice.

"This is incredible. I can't believe you did this! How soon can we move in?" Her hopeful expression was too much to take. What he wouldn't give for them to be this way forever. Excitedly building a life together, piece by piece, no gap in her memories of them being together to worry about. From the start, he'd known it would be a bad idea to lie to her. He'd vowed to do what was best for her, but somehow that had become lost in what was best for him. He prayed she could forgive him—and find enough good reasons to stay with him after he told her the truth.

"How many bedrooms?" Her voice bounced off the walls and ceiling as she craned her head to look up at the second floor.

"Four bedrooms. Three and a half bathrooms." He'd figured they'd have at least three children, so the house would hold them for a while. "Before we talk about, ah, moving in, I have something to tell you. Would you like to sit down?"

Her excitement morphed into worry as she chewed on the inside of her lip. "Is it bad?"

"Not…exactly."

"If it's bad news, and it feels like it might be, say it fast."

He'd had an idea of what he wanted to say since the night he'd talked to Jayden, but he hadn't decided in what order to say it.

"Oh my God." She put her hand over her heart. "You're breaking up with me, aren't you?"

"What? No. Aub, that's the last thing I want. I— Listen. Can you not talk until I'm finished? I have a lot to say."

She nodded and then walked up a few stairs. Lowering onto the third step, she rested her elbows on her knees and pressed her folded hands to her mouth. Then, she waited.

Fuck. He didn't want to do this. He didn't want to look into the eyes of the woman he loved and tell her he'd kept a very big, very important secret from her. But he owed her the truth.

No matter how badly she took it.

Sixteen

Vic paced the floor in front of her for the count of ten. He stopped in front of her, put his hands on his hips and looked her dead in the eye. Then he said the last thing in the world she expected him to say.

"We haven't been a couple for ten years."

She opened her mouth to ask what the hell he was talking about, but he lifted his hand to stay her interruption.

"In fact, we've barely spoken during the last ten years." He pushed a hand through his hair and watched her carefully.

What followed were a number of things that sounded foreign but *felt* true. He mentioned proposing to her at her graduation party in front of her family. She immediately called up the exact spot in her parents' house where she'd been standing. He brought up the time they'd argued about her going to graduate school, which matched the random memory she'd had the other morning. And, finally, he slid together the pieces of the night they'd shared before her accident.

"At the bar, I asked you to come home with me for old times' sake. I promised to make you forget your name. I swore you'd never have to see me again after if you said yes to one last time." He swallowed thickly, the picture of remorse, while her blood pressure rose higher and higher. "You forgot that part, believing instead that us sleeping together was evidence that I was currently in your life. But I wasn't, Aubrey. Not before that night."

"We shared cannoli," she said, the words sounding like they were coming from someone else. She pictured him that night, smug and grinning, offering her a cherry stem he'd tied into a knot with his tongue. The edges of that memory were sharp and clear, in full focus for the first time since her accident. He'd promised her a wicked, delicious time in the sack. She'd forgotten that part until now. She'd forgotten how he'd charmed his way into her pants.

Anger pushed her to her feet like a shot. She was surprised she didn't go rocketing straight through the roof.

"You fell the next day," he continued, hands out as if begging her to hear him out. "Your parents tried to keep me away, but I was at the hospital, in the waiting room, the entire time. I swore not to leave until they let me see you. Your doctor agreed it was a good idea to bring me back into your life. At least until your memory returned."

She let out a humorless laugh. "You all lied to me."

"Your doctor was worried that if your memory returned too fast, you'd suffer a setback. None of us wanted that. We could have lost you once, and we weren't willing to risk it again."

His tender tone wasn't comforting her, it was *infuriating* her.

"I stopped by your parents' house a few days ago, when you went shopping with Elise. I told them I couldn't keep this from you any longer. Your mom called your doctor and explained the situation. Everyone agreed it was the right time for you to know the truth."

"Everyone except for me. Also, I'm questioning the validity of my doctor's medical degree right about now."

"I never meant to hurt you, Aub. I was trying to help."

"You strung me along. You treated me to dinners and dates. You took me to bed." Her voice shook in a way that scared her. Had she ever been this angry in her life? But then she recalled, vividly, the moment she'd unceremoniously returned Vic's engagement ring and decided that yes, once before, she'd been this goddamn angry. "You let me believe in a future for us when you had no intention…" Her voice trailed off as she backed away from him, thoroughly disgusted.

"I didn't intend for it to go this far, I swear. I thought—"

"I told you I loved you." She swept her hair behind her ears while staring at him in disbelief. Could she have been stupider? "You let me believe we were in love this entire time."

"We were. We *are*." He took a step closer to her, but she lifted an arm, warning him not to come closer. "I told your parents how much I love you. I still love you, Aub. I never stopped. If it hadn't been for your accident, we might never have had a second chance."

"A second chance?" Memories flooded over her like

a bucket of ice water. She remembered. She remembered *everything*. The proposal. Showing off the ring to friends and family. Her decision to attend graduate school and the argument that followed.

"You told me I'd come crawling back."

"Aubrey—"

"Was this a twisted revenge plot? Were you retaliating because I broke your precious pride? Did you buy this house out of spite? Did you bring me here to show me what I could have if I allow you back into my life?"

He opened his mouth to respond, but she kept right on talking.

"You accused me of cheating on you with a faceless, nameless college guy."

"I asked. I didn't accuse."

"Same thing."

"Can you— For just a second, can you imagine what it was like for me back then? How hurt I was hearing you didn't want to marry me?"

"Oh, are you the victim here? I'm sorry. Here I thought I was the one with a traumatic brain injury causing me to forget *the most important part of my life*!" She was yelling now, and forced to grip her head as pain shot through both temples. There was too much to process. Too many old memories to reconcile with the new.

They came in tsunami form, laying waste to everything she thought she knew to be true. The idea of marrying Vic, destroyed. Her steadfast trust in him, demolished. The love she'd felt for him, washed away.

"Please, Aubrey."

"No. You have one final task on your Aubrey to-do list, and that's to drive me to my parents' house. On the way, I don't want to hear anything you have to say. You owe me at least that."

He watched her for the count of five before agreeing with a nod. He gestured to the front door. She kept her eyes on the exit rather than admiring the house as she left it—a house she'd never live in. She kept her head down when she walked past the freshly mown lawn. A lawn her future children would never play on.

She'd lost her future with Vic in one fell swoop, and he had been the one who'd taken it from her. The worst part about it was knowing he'd betrayed her not once, but *twice*.

There wouldn't be a third.

Vic didn't speak during the drive back to her parents' house. Not until he parked in the driveway. "Can I—"

"No. No to whatever it is you're going to ask." A tremor of regret slipped down her spine at his sincere expression. She shook it off. He'd lied to her for too long. She wasn't going to give him the chance to explain his way out of it—or *buy* his way out of it by offering her a dream home. "No to living with you. No to marrying you. No to you ever touching me again. In fact, I don't want to speak to you again. We have nothing left to say to each other."

She hopped out and slammed the truck door, the aggressive action renewing her strength. He sat in his truck in the driveway, engine idling. He could sit there until the cows literally came home. She meant every word of what she'd said.

"Mom! Dad!" She threw open the door and tossed her purse onto the kitchen counter.

Her parents were in the living room, books open on their laps. Her father blinked as if he'd just woken from a nap. He slid his glasses onto his nose.

"How could you betray me like that?" she asked

them both. "How could you let me believe that Vic was a part of my life?"

"Now, honey, calm down." Her father set his book aside.

"Not going to happen." She turned to her mother. "You had plenty of opportunities to tell me the truth. I thought we were growing closer. And you—" she pointed at her father "—you have always protected me. Did you decide there was a time limit on safeguarding your daughter?"

"We were following your doctor's—" he started.

"Orders. I've heard, I've heard. I'm going to pay her a visit next. I'm going to drive myself there. She was worried about me driving, but tumbling into bed with my ex-boyfriend was well within the confines of her Hippocratic oath."

"Dr. Mitchell explained her concerns in detail. The human brain is a complicated web of—"

"Daddy! Seriously. Stop."

He did, his shoulders sagging under the weight of what Aubrey could only guess was guilt. "I'm sorry. We're both so damn sorry. We made a mistake because we were trying to protect you. We love you so much."

"You should have seen Vic when he was here," her mother interjected. "He was truly agonized. Practically in tears when he confessed he was in love with you. He said he wanted more than anything to win you back. He begged us to let him tell you the truth himself. He's taken on the blame, but it's not his fault. We had hoped him being back in your life would give you a safe place to land while your memory returned. You were so happy whenever he was around."

She tried not to let the words penetrate, but picturing Vic here, his heart on his sleeve, cut her to the core. The man she had spent the last month believing she loved was a different version than the man she'd driven away from ten years ago. That night she'd broken his heart and hers. She'd cried and cried, stubborn tears she'd believed might never dry.

But they had.

They had dried, and then she'd made the epically stupid decision to go to bed with Vic because he'd been charming and offered her a knotted cherry stem. But she'd made a life for herself without him. It was a good life. One without regrets. It could have stayed that way, too, if he hadn't come along and shown her a glimpse of the life she'd lost out on. Including the dream home they'd imagined moving into when they were younger.

That bastard. He'd used the best part of her—her trusting heart—against her. She'd never forgive him.

"Vic and I have issues that are our own and none of your damn business."

"Like it or not," her mother replied, "you were happier before you knew the truth."

"Ignorance is bliss, Mom? Really? Any happiness you thought you saw was a fabrication. It was based on the fairy tale you were allowing me to believe."

"Darling, we love you," her mother continued.

"I know you do." Her voice wobbled with unspent emotion. Anger and sadness, regret and heartbreak warred for first place. "I suspect Vic believes he means it when he says it, too. That's not what's up for debate. The question is how will I choose to move forward now that I have the complete information. Only I can make that decision. And I have." She swung to face her father, adding, "I've decided to move out immediately. I'm going to return to my apartment, and I'll let you know when *or if* you're allowed to see me again. You're both going to respect my privacy. Like I told Vic, it's the least you can do."

Her piece said, she stormed to her borrowed bedroom and slammed the door. She flipped the lock, yanked her suitcases out of the closet and began packing her clothes. While she did, she cried.

She cried out of grief at Vic's and her parents' betrayal. She cried out of joy for her regained memory. And she cried out of sadness, because the ugly truth was that she *did* love Vic.

She loved him more than she should, especially knowing that he'd kept her in the dark about their past. A tiny voice in the back of her mind asked what else he'd been lying to her about.

Could she trust the man she'd spent the last several weeks with? Or had he been charming her for his own gain, much like he had the night at the Silver Saddle?

Seventeen

Vic had stuck around the Collins house after Aubrey slammed his truck's door. He'd sat in their driveway, debating whether or not to knock on the door and then further debating how long to give Aubrey to tell her parents off before he knocked on the door.

He'd settled on twenty minutes. It'd been Eddie who'd answered. Mary had been at the kitchen table, wadded tissues in her hands, eyes red.

"Hey, Vic," Eddie had said mildly. Which had been ever so slightly alarming, as Eddie rarely greeted Vic with anything less than disdain. "Come on in."

"Is she all right?" Vic stepped inside, surprised when Mary came to him for a quick hug. When she'd patted him on the back in a motherly fashion, a torrent of emotion hammered him. Once upon a time, these people had been his future in-laws.

"It's not your fault," she'd assured him. "It's ours. She's upset. She'll be all right."

Mary hadn't looked as if she believed herself, but Vic could tell she was trying to be strong for him, the man who'd let this mess go on far longer than he should have.

Eddie had told him that Aubrey was packing and that he planned on taking her back to her apartment. "I know my daughter. She needs time to process. She needs to be alone for a while."

"I'd offer to help, but…" Vic had shrugged, feeling useless. Eddie had shaken his head, silently confirming it'd be a bad idea to offer.

That was five days ago.

Five days was as long as Vic was willing to wait before he went to see Aubrey. His texts had gone unanswered. He didn't bother calling her in case she was pissed off enough to block his number. He'd sent flowers, but anonymously. Who knew what she'd done with them. No doubt she'd figured out they were from him.

At her apartment door, he steeled himself for rejection, no matter what form it took. Whether she screamed at him or slapped him, he'd weather her storm. He'd do it for her—because he loved her.

He rolled his shoulders, looked up and down the quiet hallway and then knocked lightly. He wished he knew where her head was at. It'd help to know if she was crying or—

The door swung aside, and she stood there, jaw squared, head cocked as if daring him to speak. She wore flat white tennis shoes and a floral dress that hugged her subtle curves. She was at once the sexy, strong-willed woman who'd talked him into sleeping with her and the vulnerable woman he hadn't meant to take advantage of.

She wasn't smiling. He wondered if she'd ever smile at him again.

"Yes?" she clipped.

"Five minutes." She began closing the door. He stopped it with his hand and sought her emerald eyes for any sign that the Aubrey who loved him was still in there. "Two minutes?"

Her features softened briefly before she opened the door and invited him in. She shut it with a snap.

"You kept them." A vase of wildflowers stood in the center of her kitchen table. His heart buoyed. Maybe she didn't hate him.

"It would've been wasteful to throw them out. Even if they are from the man I never want to speak to again."

"You're speaking to me now."

"What are you doing here?"

Right to the point. Still, he couldn't help delaying the inevitable.

"You have a nice apartment." He wandered from the kitchen, painted sunny yellow, to the vibrant turquoise-and-white living room. Red throw pillows decorated a futon, and a bookshelf in one corner was overflowing with books. He thought of the bookshelves in their dream home. Of how living there with her seemed even further away than it had the first time she'd left him. "The last time I was here, I didn't really look around."

"You have one minute left," she reminded him tersely.

"Letting you go was the biggest mistake I ever made," he blurted. He was out of time and out of excuses. She needed to hear the raw truth, and if she was granting him a minute to say it, he was going to use every second. "The day we fought over you continuing college, and delaying the wedding... I have no excuse for my behavior except that I was an entitled twenty-one-year-old jackass."

She inclined her chin in agreement.

"I was angry with you at first. I kept telling myself I deserved better. That if you loved me, you'd marry me right away, school or no school. But hear me, Aub. I was the one who pushed you away. A few years later, I accepted that I'd blown it. I wanted to call and check on you, but I didn't. At one point, I bumped into your dad at an event in town. He told me you had a boyfriend. Hearing that wrecked me. Just split me in two. I decided I was going to get over you, finally, and rid myself of the pain. Then the grief came. It stayed a hell of a lot longer than the anger."

Her eyebrows bowed in sympathy, but her body language was closed. Feet together. Arms crossed. Lips pressed into a flat line. He'd known this wasn't going to be easy. Hell, he didn't deserve for her to make it easy on him. Years ago, he'd stubbornly believed that if he told her to leave, she'd come back. Instead, he'd altered the course of both their lives.

"When I heard your voice over my shoulder that night at the Silver Saddle, I would have done anything to convince you to have a drink with me. It was my last shot, or so I thought. A Hail Mary that never should have worked. But then you said yes. It was a miracle."

"It was a weak moment."

"It was a weak moment for me, too. Believe me." If he'd have let her walk out of the tapas bar—if she'd never spotted him sitting there—he could have spared his heart shattering all over again. "I never dreamed we'd have a second chance. One night, sure, but I knew the morning I walked out of your bedroom that was it. Then, after your fall, you were asking for me and—"

"All your dreams came true?"

He blew out a breath. He understood why she was upset. But she was still listening, so he tried again.

"Since that night we slept together—the night you had your memory," he added, watching as her cheeks tinged pink with either embarrassment or anger, "I knew I couldn't leave you alone like I promised. I didn't have a plan, but I figured we'd run into each other here and there at the club. I'd hoped I could build on that great night, and you could learn to trust me again. The accident was as unexpected as you asking for me when you woke up. I didn't want to lie to you, but you were just so…" He lifted a hand and dropped it "…*you*. And you were looking at me like you used to and…" He blew out a breath. "God, I couldn't say no to you. I've never been so undeserving. I know that. But I decided to show you how I'd changed. I decided to prove to you how much you mean to me. I'd hoped, once your memory returned, that you could find it in your heart to forgive me. I'm still hoping that. I swear, Aub, I'll never lie to you again."

"Damn straight you won't," she said, but her voice had gone quiet and her arms had loosened from their position over her chest.

Had she forgiven him? If he took a step toward her, would she accept him in her arms?

"I never stopped loving you." His words laid him bare, and for the first time he related to the vulnerability Aubrey had been feeling lately. "Through the angry times and the grieving times, and the apathy that ate up most of my twenties. I know what I did was unfair to you. But you have to believe me when I tell you it came from a genuinely good place. I wasn't exacting revenge when I took you up to that loft, or watched the sunset with you, or showed you our dream home. I was falling in love with you. Again."

He pulled the velvet box holding her engagement ring from his jeans pocket and set it on her kitchen counter. Her eyes widened, her head already shaking back and forth.

"Don't say anything yet. Please. I want you to know I'd marry you in a heartbeat if you'd take me back. If you don't…" His heart splintered at the possibility. "If you don't, you should keep the ring. Like my heart, it was always yours."

She didn't cry or shout. She didn't accuse him of playing her or open her arms for a hug. She stood stock-still, her face blank, unreadable. When she opened her mouth, he had no idea what she'd say.

"Time's up."

…but it sure as fuck wasn't that.

Aubrey pulled open her apartment door, the action echoing her sincerity. She wanted him to leave. He would leave.

In the hallway, however, he couldn't help turning around. He barely managed to say, "You know where to find me," before she shut the door in his face.

The next evening, Vic was mucking Titan's stall when Morgan came trotting up to the stable on a chest-nut mare.

"I didn't know you were here," he said in greeting. He'd been in his own head a lot lately, which was the reason he was out here laboring. The busier his hands, the quieter his mind.

"It's a beautiful night. I couldn't resist a ride. Why are you still working?" His sister climbed off the horse.

He shrugged, not wanting to share, well, anything. She didn't let him off the hook.

"You forget, Vic, I know you. Your sad expression says it all."

"I'm not sad," he snapped. Which wasn't true. He was so sad, he might as well be wearing the emotion like a fluorescent-pink bunny costume.

He took the wheelbarrow by the handles, intending to put distance between himself and Morgan, and any talk of what was festering inside him, but his overly involved sister moved to block his path. "Hey, talk to me."

Resigned, because Morgan could and would dig in if he didn't tell her something, he set the wheelbarrow down. It was hot this evening. He pulled off his gloves and swiped the sweat from his brow. "You have nothing to worry about. I'm not interested in talking with any more women this week, given the way my last conversation went."

Morgan cocked her head. "You went to see her, didn't you?"

"Went to see her, told her the truth. Confessed that I never stopped loving her and left the engagement ring on her kitchen counter." He shrugged, but he felt nowhere near that casual. He felt like a pile of glass shards. In a word, *broken*. And he had no one to blame but himself. "She kicked me out."

"Oh, Vic." Morgan slung both arms around his neck, and those glass shards splintered into smaller pieces and cut deeper. She gave him a squeeze. "Are you going to be okay?"

He gave her a light squeeze in return and cleared his suspiciously full throat. "Of course."

"It's a lot," she continued. "What you're going through. With the ranch drama and reuniting with Aubrey. We knew her finding out the truth was an inevitability, but I'd hoped she'd see you had the best intentions."

"Me, too," he croaked. It hadn't worked out that way, though.

"You know I'm here for you. I love you, big brother."

"I love you, too." Morgan was the best. It hurt to smile, if that's what he was doing. He might be grimacing for all he knew.

"Is that Alexa?" Morgan gestured to the driveway. Vic looked over his shoulder at the car he hadn't noticed as Chelsea and Layla exited the front door of the ranch house.

Jayden's sister—slash—attorney-at-law climbed from her vehicle to greet the other two women, and then the three of them headed in Vic and Morgan's direction.

"Do you think it's good news?" Morgan asked him.

"The way my week's going?" he mumbled. "I doubt it."

"I told you she was a good girl, didn't I, Morg?" Layla called out as she approached. She took the mare's reins in hand as soon as she was close enough.

"You never miss a chance to smell like a horse," Alexa teased Layla as she pulled the sunglasses off her nose.

"Never," Layla agreed with her best friend before planting a smacking kiss on the horse's muzzle.

"You look awful," Chelsea told Vic.

"He's fine," Morgan snapped before turning to Alexa and complimenting her outfit. Ever the city girl at heart, Alexa's jeans and shirt were crisp and pressed.

"So?" Chelsea prompted their visitor.

Alexa got right to the point. "There's been a new development."

Vic didn't have to look at his siblings to know he wasn't the only one whose ears had perked.

Alexa recapped what they'd learned about the surveyor Vic had seen on the property. Her name was Ruby. She'd been hired by Heath—nothing new there.

Vic braced for bad news to follow. That seemed par for the course. Bad news on top of bad news, and then to the left of that, oh, look…more bad news.

Alexa leveled him with a sharp look. "I spoke with Jonas Shaw and asked for an update. He finally touched base with Sylvia."

"Sylvia, as in your grandfather's retired secretary," Layla said, her eyebrows lifting meaningfully.

"One and the same. She wrapped up her wilderness trek and reached out to the investigator. She had plenty to say. It won't come as a surprise to you all to hear she confirmed that my grandfather Augustus and your grandfather Victor Senior were as thick as thieves."

"Tell us something we don't know," Chelsea said.

"Okay, I will." Alexa tucked a lock of hair behind her ear. "Sylvia also mentioned an oil survey done the year before our grandfathers signed over the rights to Cynthia."

Cynthia, as in Heath and Nolan Thurston's mother. After Cynthia and her daughter, Ashley, had subsequently died, Heath had taken it upon himself to stir up trouble. Vic could understand acting out of grief to avenge his family, but the damage he was causing was unforgivable. The ranch was more to the Lattimores and Grandins than a chunk of land to fight over in court.

"There's no proof of oil on this land," Chelsea said.

"Which I'm sure is why the surveyor was poking around your property and ours," Alexa said. "Sylvia swears there was an oil survey done in the past. According to her, the results were clear. There was never oil on this land."

"That's great," Vic said, not trusting the relief in his voice.

"Not so fast." Alexa held up a hand. "Sylvia can't confirm it without paperwork. She went so far as to suggest the purported oil rights were given to Cynthia to keep her quiet."

"Like hush money?" Morgan asked.

"What better way to keep the pregnancy quiet?" Alexa said.

Layla snorted. "It's beginning to sound like Ashley Thurston was Uncle Daniel's daughter after all."

"The timing works," Alexa admitted, "but without DNA, we can't know for sure. The PI told me he was getting in touch with the surveyor Sylvia told him about, in the hopes of uncovering the original paperwork. We know his name's Harry Lawrence and that he lives outside Houston. If he's the stickler for record-keeping Sylvia swears he is, it's only a matter of time before we know the truth."

"What a mess," Vic grumbled, eyes on the pile of shit he'd mucked from Titan's stall. What an apt metaphor for his life right now. If that survey existed, it would prove whether or not there was oil on the land. If there was oil, hell…

Vic didn't want to think about what might happen next.

Eighteen

Aubrey had angry-cleaned her apartment so many times, a speck of dust wouldn't dare settle onto a surface without her express permission.

She'd scheduled a visit with her doctor this afternoon. To her credit, Dr. Mitchell had apologized for any consequential turmoil that had come as a result of Aubrey's treatment plan. She'd explained her reasoning, which had involved another patient having a massive lapse and requiring further hospitalization after well-meaning family members and friends told her everything about her past.

Aubrey didn't wholly agree with her doctor's choices, but she understood why her parents had tried to protect her. They'd been frightened and worried. Involving Vic had gone too far, though, and she hadn't quite forgiven them for it yet.

The bottom line was that Aubrey's memory was

back. Dr. Mitchell assured Aubrey that she could continue living her life as she had before her fall, as long as she introduced each piece gradually. She'd informed her well-meaning doctor that the Vic piece would not be introduced again.

She drove—herself, thank you very much—to lunch for a Reuben sandwich with french fries. She'd called her principal on the way to ask how soon she could return to work. Thankfully the answer was "Monday," and her principal assured her she'd be welcomed back with open arms. It was the good news she'd needed to hear.

She was excited to return to her classroom and to the students she'd missed so much. She was also looking forward to having a schedule she created herself, without parameters.

At an outdoor table at the restaurant, she was scribbling her work schedule into her pocket calendar when a familiar voice said her name. She looked up to find Chelsea Grandin, wearing slim-fitting jeans, a flannel and a pair of dark sunglasses, standing over her.

"Chelsea. Hi." She resisted tacking on *How odd to see you here.*

"May I?" The other woman's smile was friendly as she gestured to the empty chair.

"Sure." Just when Aubrey had convinced herself running into Vic's oldest sister was a coincidence, Chelsea laid waste to that idea.

"You're a hard woman to find." She pushed her sunglasses into her dark hair and ordered an iced tea from the waiter. "It's a hot one today. I figured you were either at home or with your parents, but you weren't at your apartment when I stopped by, and a phone call confirmed you weren't speaking to your mom and dad any longer."

Aubrey's heart crushed as she pictured her mother disclosing that fact. Even so, she managed, "That's hardly any of your business, Chelsea."

"I know. I'm meddling." She waved a hand. "I was ready to give up, but then I saw your red hair gleaming from this very patio."

The waiter approached and asked if they were ready to order. Aubrey ordered her Reuben, and Chelsea ordered the same.

"Why are you searching for me? Did you want to congratulate me on my wise decision to never speak to your brother again?"

Chelsea's features softened. "No. The opposite."

The hurt in her expression reminded Aubrey of the day Vic had come over and said the most beautiful words he'd ever said to her. Words that, unfortunately, had come too late. Words she'd tried to convince herself meant nothing. Words that had taken hold of a tiny part of her, but she refused to give them access to the rest of her.

"He's different from the boy you remember, Aubrey."

Voice hard, Aubrey replied, "I remember everything."

"Yes, but you broke up with a different guy than you've been dating. Vic is…" His sister lifted her hand and dropped it on the table. "My God, he used to be my nemesis. He has been a burr in my ass for as long as I can remember. Cocky. Headstrong. Entitled. I never knew what you saw in him back then. You were, and still are, a strong woman with your own ideas. From where I was standing, it seemed like he was trying to cram you into his mold."

Aubrey agreed with every word of that, so she sat straighter, feeling seen for the first time.

"But when you came back—" Chelsea's wide smile reappeared. "He was different with you. He was different with *me*. With Layla. With everyone. You unlocked a part of his heart no one could reach. A part that never would have been accessible if you didn't break up with him in the first place. Don't you see, Aubrey? Even if you never take him back, he's better for having had you in his life. That change will last forever."

Aubrey wasn't sure what to do with that information.

"I hear he gave you a ring."

"He left it on my kitchen counter." She'd stashed it in her dresser drawer. "I intend on returning it. If you want to follow me back to my apartment, I can give it to you and—"

"No way." Chelsea held up both hands. "I don't blame you for being upset with him. You feel betrayed. And probably overwhelmed. But if you think back on the days you spent with Vic recently, and the feelings you've had for him for years, you might realize you still love him. If that's the case, then, well, you two might have a shot at making this work."

"Did he tell you about the house?" Aubrey asked, anxious to move this conversation along and not dwell on the *L* word Chelsea had brought up.

"What house?"

Aubrey detailed the neighborhood they used to drive through when they'd been teenagers, dreaming of the house they'd move into when they were married. Then she dropped the bombshell. "He bought it. For us. He's kept it up for ten years."

"Seriously?" His sister appeared shell-shocked. "I

always assumed he had an apartment in town, but he's been staying in a house?"

"No. It's empty." Aubrey's voice cracked. Telling Chelsea about the house was supposed to serve as proof of the ultimate betrayal: Vic attempting to gift her a house to cover for his lies. But as she described him bringing her there, and how he'd shared that he'd let it sit unoccupied for a decade, it didn't sound like a betrayal. It sounded almost…romantic.

"I can only imagine what you must be thinking right now," Chelsea said, "but that is Vic saying *I love you* in big bold letters. Ten years he's been hiding this? I have given him so much hell about moving out and being the man of his own house. How did he keep this from everyone for so long?"

"He brought me there to break the worst news of my life to me," Aubrey continued, stubbornly not wanting to give him the benefit of the doubt. Her heart was raw, and her recently returned memory was smarting like a fresh cut. "Who knows how many other women he's brought there?"

But she knew. *None.* It wasn't his style. Vic had been heartbroken when he'd shown Aubrey the house—more so by the time she'd walked out of it.

"He brought you there, to the home you'd always wanted, to break your fall, sweetheart. You might not want to see it that way, but I know my brother. I know he loved you more than anything in the world when we were kids, and I know he's lost without you now. I don't want you to feel sorry for him, or make a rash decision because I'm taking his side. I want you to evaluate your own feelings and trust them."

"How can I trust them when I couldn't trust myself for the last six weeks?" And that was the real issue, wasn't it? Aubrey had been her own guiding light for a good ten years, and then suddenly she hadn't been able to count on herself for anything. What she'd felt while with Vic had *seemed* real. But was it? Should she trust the way she'd felt then or the way she was feeling now?

"You're going to have to learn." Chelsea put her hand over Aubrey's and in a stern, oldest-sister-knows-best tone added, "You are strong. You always have been. You know what you want out of life, and you aren't afraid to say what it is. I'm asking you to entertain the idea that Vic could be part of your future. What if you miss the opportunity for a second chance?"

"You sound like him. I was injured, and he took advantage of my weakness." How come no one understood that?

"Then why did you wake up after your accident asking for my brother? Why did him showing up to your hospital room change everything for you? What was the last memory you had of him? The Vic who you fought with and left years ago, or the Vic who went out of his way to show you how much he cares about you?"

Chelsea let the question hang. Their sandwiches were delivered. Aubrey didn't answer as she picked at her food. She didn't want to admit that the last memory she'd had of Vic when she woke up after her accident was the incredible night she'd spent with him.

"Why don't you let me buy you a drink? You can eat your cannoli here. I promise I'll be nice."

"Nice *is not a description of Vic Grandin one hears very often.*"

He'd persisted that night and had talked her into sleeping with him. It should have been a ludicrous idea—one she never should have considered.

Why did *you consider it?*

An excellent question.

The answer was as complicated and as simple as the fact that she'd simply wanted to experience him again. Experience his smile, his dark eyes on hers. Taste his mouth and feel safe and protected by his strength. Relax knowing the man in her bed would deliver a beautiful night to remember.

Only she'd forgotten the most important part. She'd forgotten his promise to go away after the sex. A promise he'd broken...

But you broke it first.

She stared at her plate, her thoughts dipping and swirling. Not because she'd forgotten why she'd said yes, but because she *remembered*. She remembered the intensity of being in bed with Vic. He'd consumed her that night. He'd been so present and real and perfect. She'd done her level best to keep her walls up, but if she were being honest, she'd been sad when he'd left the following morning. Sad about them not having another night in their future. When she'd seen him at the TCC pool party that afternoon, it'd been Vic who'd offered a smile and a polite nod hello. He hadn't approached her, instead giving her ample room to kick the crack in the door wider. In spite of wanting him again—very badly—she'd reached for the handle and pulled it closed instead.

She'd been protecting herself. Then, and now.

When she'd woken up in the hospital asking for Vic, part of her must have wanted the strength and security he offered. So much so that she'd pushed away any memories that hadn't fed that narrative. Her subconscious had lied to her. A coconspirator to Vic, unbeknownst to her.

"Aubrey? Are you okay?" Chelsea asked.

"So much has happened since the day Vic and I broke up. I moved on. I dated other people. He dated other people."

Chelsea's lips flattened before she said, "I don't see either of you with other people now."

"A lot has happened since I was twenty," Aubrey whispered, hanging on to her weak argument with both hands.

"Even more has happened since Vic showed up. As *you* requested." Rather than try and convince Aubrey of her part in this drama, Chelsea raised her hand to signal the waiter. "How about dessert? I want dessert."

Aubrey nodded automatically, but she didn't care if she ate dessert or not. What she cared about was her heart, her future. Her *life*.

She'd decided when she'd been in college to honor her dreams and build a life she deserved, no matter what.

Which left one nagging question: What kind of life did she want now?

Nineteen

On her way to her classroom, Aubrey was stopped no fewer than seven times by friends and coworkers.

She received hugs, well-wishes and handshakes. Everyone was welcoming and happy to see her. It felt good to be back.

"Aubrey!" Elise approached from the long, empty hallway, ever the picture of sophistication in a navy blue pencil skirt, white silk shirt and red high heels.

"You look gorgeous."

Elise gave her a quick hug. "I'd talk. Your legs are incredible."

Aubrey wore a green-and-white-striped skirt that flared at the knee, paired with a fitted white T-shirt. Her sandals were wedges with cork heels. "I was going for professional."

"You overshot the mark, my friend."

"I hope I remember how to do this." Aubrey made a face as she unlocked her classroom door.

"You were *born* to do this. One doesn't forget something that's been baked into them since birth." Elise followed her into the classroom. She chewed her lip and studied her shoes. Normally outspoken, it was odd behavior for her. "I'm sorry for not telling you the truth about Vic."

"You don't have to apologize."

"I do. As your friend, I should have taken your side. I will hate that man until the end of time out of loyalty to you." Elise cocked her head, a somewhat hopeful expression on her face. "Unless…you've forgiven him?"

"Not exactly."

She shrugged. "My vow stands."

"I appreciate your loyalty, but I'm not sure if it's that easy."

"Was that Aubrey I saw sneak in here?" Primrose walked into the classroom next and swept Aubrey into a warm hug. "We heard about Vic. That rat."

"How?" Aubrey hadn't talked to anyone about what'd happened between them except for Chelsea.

"He came here!" Primrose exclaimed. "He pulled each of us aside and apologized."

"And then he said he was in love with you." Brooke strolled in next, her lips pursed. "These two want me to hate him, but out of principle, I can't hate a man that beautiful. Even though I love you so very much."

"Thanks, Brooke." Aubrey's smile felt forced as she pictured Vic apologizing to her friends and declaring his love for her. "I don't hate him, so that seems fair."

"Really?" Primrose wrinkled her nose.

"Really." Aubrey lowered into her chair, weighed down by everything. "His sister Chelsea told me he is lost without me. She claims his behavior was because he's still in love with me."

"He should have told you he loved you," Elise stated.

"Oh, he did. He told me and gave me my engagement ring back."

Brooke gasped.

"As much as I'd love to share more, I have to refamiliarize myself with how to do my job before I have thirty sixteen-year-olds in my class."

"Good call." Primrose hustled for the door, grabbing Brooke on the way. "They are brutally honest, so mind yourself."

"Do you want some Mace?" Elise whispered. "Bear spray?"

"I'm good," Aubrey answered with a laugh. "I appreciate you all thinking of me. By the way, I don't blame any of you for playing along. I would have done the same for you, unless I believed you were in some sort of danger." Once Primrose and Brooke were gone, Aubrey met Elise's eyes. "You know Vic. If you believed he was taking advantage of me, you'd have told me."

Elise gave a reluctant nod. "I suppose you're right."

Halfway through her day, Aubrey readied herself for the next class to pour through her doors. She knew she wasn't supposed to have favorites, but this group of students had quickly risen to the top within the first three weeks of the new school year.

As the students filed in, a few left behind cards or small mementos to welcome their teacher back. Her heart lifted. She was infinitely grateful to be here and focusing her attention on something other than her eroding personal life.

"Thank you for the gifts. It's good to be back." Cheers erupted, and she held her hands out to quiet her class. "I haven't done this with every class, but you're special. I know you have questions. So ask them."

"Anything?" Brennon McCreedy asked, his thick eyebrows lifting impishly.

"Anything you would ask your mom," she retorted to much of the class's approval.

"I have a question," Jamaica Barnard, one of her star students, said.

"I'm all ears."

"Did you miss us?" She grinned.

"More than any of my other students," Aubrey mock-whispered. "Come on. I know you are curious about my amnesia."

"Is it true? Is that really why you were gone?" asked Anderson Phillips. "Sounds like bullshit."

"I agree," Aubrey said. "Amnesia happens more often than you think, but it's not common. And it wasn't something I fully understood before going through it. In my case, there were gaps in my memory, while I remembered other parts of my life vividly."

"Did your memory return all at once?" Jamaica asked.

"It was a bit of a trickle until a friend intervened. He shared the parts that had been missing. With my doctor's permission, of course."

"He?" Madison Black waggled her eyebrows, and Aubrey's hormone-riddled class made *oooh* sounds, hinting that they thought this "he" might be romantically linked to Aubrey. "Ms. Collins, we were not aware you had a boyfriend."

"He's an old boyfriend," Aubrey admitted in spite of herself.

"Old as in geriatric?"

"No, Jacob. Old as in from my past."

"You know, like you and Ava," Madison put in.

"Burn!" Anderson pointed at Jacob, who turned a bright shade of pink.

"Did it work out?" The blunt question came from quiet, polite Mia Stoker.

"No. We see life differently. Then and now."

"Isn't that what you always tell us makes our writing strong?" Mia pressed. "Remember to—"

"'See the scene from the other person's eyes,'" the rest of the class quoted in unison.

Aubrey was both peeved and proud. "You're using my words against me."

"Have you seen things through his eyes?" Jamaica asked. "Or is he a lowly dog, like Caleb?"

"Hey!" Caleb, arguably the sweetest guy in their grade, protested. Aubrey noticed Jamaica sending him a flirty smile. Ah, teenagers.

"A story for another day, perhaps. We're running out of time, and I know you're anxious to discuss your reading assignment, yes?"

"We don't get a pass because you were gone?" Jacob asked.

"Sorry. Your substitute teacher told me that she kept you on course while I was away."

A few groans rippled through the classroom.

"But," she interjected, "I might grant you an extension if you participate in the lesson today. Raise your hand, attempt to answer, read aloud. You know, that sort of thing."

The groans this time around sounded more light-hearted than before.

"Now, open your texts to page…"

After Jayden helped Vic untangle a cow that'd wrapped its leg in barbed wire, Vic invited him over for sandwiches. They'd been hard at work all morning, and he was half-starved.

In the Grandin family kitchen, Vic thanked the kitchen staff for setting out the sandwich ingredients on the counter before dismissing them. Privacy was a hard thing to come by in this house, and something he had been craving since Aubrey had kicked him out of her apartment.

"Slumming it today, I see," Jayden joked as he grabbed a plate for himself.

"It's good to get your hands dirty every once in a while."

After a minute of them silently putting together their sandwiches, Jayden asked, "So, did you buy her something to hammer home your apology? New car? Another piece of jewelry?"

Vic didn't pretend not to know whom his friend was referring to. He took a breath and confessed, "I bought her a house."

Jayden stared at Vic in frozen disbelief. "A house."

"Well, the same house."

"The house you bought when you were dating her? Tell me you sold that."

Vic shook his head. He probably should have sold it.

Jayden whistled long and low before taking a seat at the counter to eat his lunch. "You need therapy."

"It didn't seem right to live there without her. I couldn't bring myself to sell it, either."

"Because?"

Vic shrugged, but he knew why. "Selling it would be admitting I knew she'd never take me back."

"Damn. I cannot believe you've been this gone for this girl for this long and never told me."

"I was trying to get over her."

"Well, it didn't work," Jayden added unhelpfully before he bit into his sandwich. After he chewed and swallowed, he regarded Vic with a modicum of sincerity. "What now? Is she done with you?"

Vic winced. "I don't want to accept it, but she might be. She has the engagement ring. She hasn't given it back yet, but I'm afraid to hope." He dropped his sandwich on his plate without tasting it. "I love her, and I want to spend the rest of my life with her. I tried to prove to her that I've changed, but I fucked everything up."

"Don't be so hard on yourself, baby brother. Hey, Jayden," Chelsea greeted as she strode into the kitchen. She pulled off her work gloves and set them on the counter, surveying the spread in front of her. "Are we fending for ourselves today?"

"Apparently," Jayden grumbled.

She began building her own sandwich. "I spoke to Aubrey the other day. It didn't seem to me like she hated you."

Vic, his sandwich halfway to his mouth, dropped it on his plate again. "Tell me you're kidding."

"Not kidding. We had lunch at that cute café downtown with the—"

"Chels, this isn't any of your business."

"Like Nolan and me weren't any of yours?"

Jayden chuckled. Vic sent him a death glare.

"I care about you, okay?" His sister moved to where Vic was standing, elbowing Jayden as she passed by. "We all care about you."

"Yeah, I care, too," Jayden said around another bite.

"Are you going to the fall festival at the Texas Cattleman's Club?"

"Of course," Jayden answered at the same time Vic said, "No way."

"You have to go," Chelsea informed Vic.

"Yes, you do." Jayden polished off his sandwich and took a swig from his soda can. "You cannot leave me to my own devices. God knows what I'll do."

"You'll survive. You can bob for apples or carve pumpkins or whatever they plan on doing this year."

"What if you-know-who is there?" Chelsea asked.

"All the more reason not to go." Vic finally took a bite of his sandwich, but it sat like wet cement on his tongue, flavorless and heavy.

He *wanted* to see Aubrey. If only to figure out if she still hated him as much as she had the other day. He was too afraid to hope she didn't. If she had decided she felt nothing for him, he'd have a funeral to plan— his own. This time around, a broken heart would kill him. He was sure of it.

He'd held on to the house to keep hope alive, and he needed to know if Aubrey had held on to the engagement ring for the same reason. As long as she had it in her possession, that meant she was still possibly, *maybe* considering marrying him. If not…well, she wasn't.

He didn't know what else he could do to convince her he loved her and wanted her in his life until his dying day. Time apart hadn't helped them the first time around.

"Just go and see what happens. If she shows, she might be glad to see you." Chelsea said.

"That's very naive of you, sis. I'm surprised."

"Love can change a person. It changed you. I barely recognize you anymore."

"Hear, hear." Jayden held up his soda can and toasted

Chelsea's glass of water. "He used to be a beast. Now he's a puppy."

"I'm eating in my room," Vic grumbled, tired of everyone's input on what had happened between him and Aubrey.

Once he'd closed himself in his suite, he pulled out his cell phone to check his texts. Nothing. The last five he'd sent to Aubrey had gone unanswered.

He sent one more anyway.

Twenty

Another text appeared on Aubrey's phone screen, beneath the previous five she hadn't answered. Not that Vic had asked a question. He hadn't said, "I miss you" or "I love you" or trotted out multiple apologies. Each of his five texts was as random as they came, the tone casual, like when he and Aubrey were dating, talking to and seeing each other every day.

The latest entry into the diary of Vic's day read, These tomatoes are damn good. I know you don't typically eat them, but they're stripey and sort of sweet. Jayden is being a prick. Why are we best friends, again? Chelsea, meanwhile, is being sweet. It's weird.

Aubrey read it twice, tempted to respond. She could tell him how, stripey or not, she wasn't interested in *any* tomato. Or she could explain that he was best friends with Jayden because no other male understood Vic better. On the Chelsea front, she longed to encourage him to embrace his oldest sister's doting.

Aubrey understood why Chelsea had crashed the lunch she'd intended to have by herself. Chelsea loved her family, loved the ranch and cared about Aubrey a great deal. As an only child, Aubrey saw the value of having an interfering sibling.

But responding would give Vic false hope, and she didn't want to hurt him further. She didn't want him to believe all was forgiven because he'd sent several texts as if nothing was wrong.

Everything was wrong.

She parked in her parents' driveway and stepped onto the porch. Normally she'd let herself in, but she hesitated at the front door. After she'd drawn a hard line with them, she wasn't sure how welcome she'd be here.

Mary Collins answered the door, her red hair pulled off her face and tied into a short ponytail. Her freckles were out in droves. She appeared tired, if a little fragile. Aubrey's heart hurt.

"Hi, Mom."

"Aubrey. It's good to see you." Mary held up the dish towel in her hand. "I was cleaning the kitchen and swearing because I couldn't reach the cabinet above the refrigerator. How are you?"

"I'm…" Aubrey wanted to say "fine" or "okay" but decided to tell the truth instead. A truth that caused her chin to wobble and her eyes to heat. "I'm overflowing with regret."

"Oh, honey, come in here." Mary tugged her daughter into the house and sat her down at the kitchen table. "Coffee will fix it."

Aubrey let out a watery laugh. She wasn't sure coffee would fix it, but she was willing to try.

Five minutes later, two mugs of coffee on the table in front of them, Aubrey apologized to her mother. "I was harsh and unreasonable."

"You've been through a lot."

"I love you and Dad so much. I never should have said the awful things I said before I left. And not speaking to you…what if something terrible had happened to you or him, and the last thing I said to you was—" She hiccupped and covered her mouth, not willing to finish that sentence.

"Nothing has happened. Your father's at the home improvement store. He's perfectly fine. I know, because he's called me twice and asked me to measure the shelves in the garage. He's on a mission to completely reorganize." Her mother rolled her eyes. "We figured you didn't mean it, Aub. Your father knows you. He was the one who told Vic to give you time. You needed to be alone, and we respected that."

"Vic was here?"

"The day he dropped you off and you went to your room to pack. He came to the door."

Of course he did.

"He's come to see me since then, too."

"Did he?"

"He says he loves me. He wants a second chance. I guess if I say yes, it would be a *third* chance. I'm not willing to do that. Or I wasn't, anyway. Until my students reminded me how I taught them the most successful storytellers see life from the other characters' points of view as well as their own. Then I started thinking about how Vic must have felt for the last ten years. And about how he felt when he was asked to pretend to date me because being with him was one of the last things I remembered." Hands around her coffee mug, she spoke to her mother more earnestly than she'd intended. "We slept together the night before the chili cook-off."

Mary's cheeks went pink, but she didn't try and stop Aubrey from sharing.

"It was supposed to be one night. I saw him at the bar at the Silver Saddle, and he was so familiar. Like the boy I dated. Except he was a man, and there were only good parts left. He seemed so grown-up. So different from before. And I had an escape hatch—one night to be with the Vic I used to love, and then I could return to my regularly scheduled life." She shook her head at her own naivete. As if one night with Vic wouldn't be burned into her memory forever—hell, that single memory had survived while countless others had temporarily perished.

"That night was so…intense," she continued. "The emotions I thought were long gone returned and made themselves at home. Nothing but positive feelings for him remained after I lost my memory. It's like I forgot everything bad that happened in the four years we dated."

"There wasn't much bad, Aub. You two had a lot of wonderful years together. At the end, you had a disagreement."

"A disagreement? We had totally different life plans." Aubrey nested her fingers into her hair.

"Honey." Mary touched Aubrey's arm. "You did the right thing then, and I'll never not back you on that. You wanted to focus on school and attain your degrees. You wanted to live your life untethered. Who could blame you? So, now that you've been untethered for ten years, what do you want? Do you want to reclaim the life you had before with Vic, or do you want to move forward and chalk up the days you spent with him as a learning experience? It sounds like both options are on the table. All you have to do is choose one."

Aubrey gave her mother a beseeching look. "Choose one. As if it's that simple?"

Her mother patted Aubrey's arm. "It's not simple. But your father and I will back you no matter which one you choose."

"You look like dog shit." Vic's youngest sister, Morgan, entered his office and plopped onto the sofa. She crossed her legs, tugging at the skirt of a stylish dress, no doubt from her shop.

"Won't you come in." He shut his laptop and rubbed his eyes. It was noon, and he'd been at it for six hours already.

"I brought you something to cheer you up," Morgan said, ignoring his sarcasm. She hopped off the sofa and ran into the hallway, returning with her fingers looped around the handle of a paper bag half the size of his desk.

"I already ate."

"Open it, smart-ass."

He unearthed the contents: a shirt, suit jacket, dark-wash jeans and a new belt. Holding up the silver buckle with the Grandin family ranch's logo on it, he sent Morgan a questioning look. "It's October. Too early for Christmas."

"It's not a Christmas gift. It's for you to wear to the fall festival at the TCC."

He piled the clothing back into the bag. "I'm not going."

"You have to go. I bought you all this stuff!"

"First off, you have a million connections in the

clothing industry who would gift you anything you asked for."

She blushed, hinting that while she might have spent time selecting the pieces, she certainly hadn't spent money.

"Second, I don't need it, because I'm not going. Thirdly, Chelsea and Jayden have already been bothering me about going, and I told them no, too."

"It's tomorrow. You *have* to go. Actually, we all have to go. Daddy's orders."

"What's he going to do, fire me?"

"Working all hours of the day and night isn't going to speed up the process of finding out if there's oil under our property. And it's also not going to heal your heart."

"If you don't mind—" he reopened his laptop "—I have some invoices to finalize."

Morgan slapped his laptop shut and regarded him with redheaded ire. "I remember what you were like back when you and Aubrey broke up."

"I was a jackass. That's what I was like."

"That's what everyone thought. But I saw the truth. You were heartbroken. You were sad and you cried and told no one. Then you were withdrawn. Then you were angry and short-tempered. When you and Jayden went out to pick up women, you were gross. You pretended like being a playboy was your favorite pastime, but that's not you, Vic."

He'd had no idea she'd been paying such close attention, or he might've behaved better. The idea that his youngest sister, who had always looked up to him, had found him "gross" and seen through his actions made him feel slightly sick.

"Whenever you were out all night, you never came home the next morning looking happy. I saw you at a TCC event with another girl more times than I can count, and your smile was fake. Admit it. You are not complete without Aubrey Collins."

"I tried, okay?" he snapped, because the truth fucking hurt.

"*Not* okay. What's your plan? To sit around and wait for another ten years?"

"She's not interested in what I have to say, Morgan!" His voice lifted out of frustration. Every one of his previous attempts to reach Aubrey had been futile. She was icing him. It was over.

"So you're going to be like this again." His sister gestured to his slumped posture. "You're going to be sad and withdrawn. Or angry and short-tempered. You're going to date miscellaneous women and be unhappy."

"I'm not dating anyone."

"So you're going to be single and unhappy."

"You're single, and you're not unhappy."

"I'm not in love with my ex." She cocked her head and hoisted an eyebrow. "Go to the festival. You need a night away, to feel something other than regret. Plus, you're wrong. I special-ordered the belt buckle and paid for it with my own money. It's not returnable."

She turned on her boot heel and clomped out of his office.

Vic sighed as he moved the paper bag from desktop to floor. What difference a fall festival was going to make, he had no idea. He'd figured out at least one benefit to going, however—it'd get his siblings and his friend off his back.

"Knock, knock." Layla entered his office next.

"I'm going to the fall festival," he announced before she started in on him. "I'm going to bob for apples and pin the tail on the scarecrow or whatever shit they do there. I'll take first prize for whatever contest they hold. Are you happy?"

Layla's eyebrows climbed her forehead. "The contest they're having is for the best needlepoint. I've seen your clumsy fingers, brother. I doubt you could create anything that would final."

A reluctant smile crept across his lips. He scratched his cheek. "Sorry. It's been a morning."

"I don't care if you go to the fall festival or not." Layla knelt to dig through the bag on the floor. She held up the suit jacket. "This is nice."

"Morgan."

"I saw her. She's on a mission."

"Everyone is. It's Operation Help Vic Because He's a Pathetic Bastard."

"You're not a pathetic bastard." She patted his head. "You're lovesick and giving up. Which, I guess, is another way to say you're a pathetic bastard. So, in a way, you're right."

"I didn't give up."

"No?"

"I know you think I should skywrite Aubrey's name over her apartment complex, or buy her a horse and tie it to her car, but she deserves to have the space I didn't give her after her accident. She's the woman she grew into without me. She's incredible. And she broke up with me to become that woman. I can't demand she take me back. I tried demanding when we split up the first time around. All I managed to do was create a rift between us that was irreparable."

"I doubt that." Layla cocked her blond head. "You two were behaving like you loved each other from what I could see. She's not the same Aubrey who dumped you, true. She's an adult who knows her heart and mind.

She is intelligent and thoughtful. Even if she was missing a memory or two while you were sleeping together and making out in the stable—"

He sent her a warning look that didn't slow her down in the least.

"—she knew in her heart that you were meant for her, and she was meant for you."

"I want to believe that, Lay, I do. But—"

"Then believe it. Lose this hangdog thing you have going on." She tossed the suit jacket on his lap. "Walk into the fall festival with your head held high. You're the sole male Grandin of your generation, Vic. You're a catch. Aubrey would be a lucky woman to have a man like you loving her for the rest of her life."

He narrowed his eyes at his sister. "There something else you want? It would explain the abject flattery."

"You to be happy, baby bro. That's enough." She offered a sincere smile, blew him a kiss and stepped out of his office.

Twenty-One

The Texas Cattleman's Club used to be an old-school men's club, through and through. Built around 1910, the large, rambling, single-story building had been ground zero for too many parties to count. From the dark wood floors to the leather-upholstered furniture and the high, regal ceilings, the TCC made for a lush backdrop for any festivity.

After the club began admitting female members over a decade ago, things started to change for the better. Helping lure in a younger demographic were parents demanding their children's attendance, as well as a recent renovation. Newly added windows brought much-needed light to the space, and there were splashes of color where there'd been earth tones before.

Tonight the decor was autumn leaves, pumpkins and tall cornstalks adorned with fancy ribbons. Vic didn't see apple bobbing or pumpkin carving, but he'd bet they were doing that in the on-site day care.

His sister Morgan had kept a close eye on him tonight. She had stopped by the house to fuss over his wardrobe and then demanded he drive her to the event. He suspected that was so she could further ensure he showed up, but he hadn't protested.

Being here wasn't as bad as he'd thought. He'd spent a long, frustrating week at his desk poring over spreadsheets or on the phone with countless suppliers. While the Grandin family home was as large as five decent-size homes, the walls had begun to feel as if they were closing in on him.

The bartender handed over his glass of whiskey. Vic turned and knocked his glass against Jayden's. "Go hunt," he teased his best friend before taking a sip. "No sense in wasting your evening hanging around with me."

"True story. You're a downer." Jayden caught the eye of a woman across the room, her smile as dazzling as her short, sparkling dress. "Looks like I'm up."

"Have fun." One of them should.

Vic wandered through the well-dressed crowd, pretending not to look for the only woman who could turn his head nowadays. Then, on his second pass, he spotted her.

Aubrey was wearing a floor-length, autumnal red-orange dress, gold bangle bracelets stacked on one wrist. From her auburn hair to her strappy gold shoes, she was fall personified, like the burnished leaves on an oak tree at the height of the season. Her lips were painted reddish-brown, her smile, while not beaming, polite for anyone who approached. From the looks of it, she hadn't made it far past the entrance—and wouldn't anytime soon, given the crowd surrounding her.

No doubt the men and women forming a semicircle around her were curious about Aubrey's accident and her subsequent miraculous recovery. She'd arrived alone, from the looks of it. Being new to the club, with her honorary membership, she had yet to learn how to politely disentangle herself from the crowd.

He paced back to the bar and ordered a glass of chardonnay and then, wineglass in hand, he inserted himself directly between the regular club members and Aubrey. Her expressive green eyes widened in surprise when he offered her the drink.

"If you'll excuse us." He didn't offer further explanation, but he did offer Aubrey his arm. After a reluctant beat, she laid her hand on his forearm. In what felt like the most natural move ever, he led her to the other side of the room, his heart pounding fiercely with each step he took.

He stopped in a quiet corner near a sizable modern painting. "I thought you might need to catch your breath, or at least have a drink before answering a zillion medical and personal questions from every busybody in the county."

"Thanks. I was trapped." Her laugh caused his chest to tighten. He hadn't been sure she'd appreciate his intervening, but it seemed she had.

She sipped her wine as music drifted through the room. It reminded him of the night at the botanical gardens, when he'd held her and she'd shared what she remembered from prom night. That felt like an eternity ago already.

"Any word about the issues with the ranch?" she asked.

He shook his head. "Alexa updated us on where the PI is with the investigation. There's been a new development, but no one knows anything for sure. Except that Heath believes his mother was bribed with oil rights. The PI is searching for paperwork."

"That must be hard for you. Knowing your future could change on a dime, and work like nothing has changed."

Her sincere gaze was the least surprising thing about her. She'd always thought of him, of his well-being, first. How he'd ever accused her of being selfish was beyond him.

"It's not as hard as losing you a second time," he told her. There was no going back now. Ever since his sisters and Jayden had given him hell about being a miserable sack, Vic had done a lot of thinking. He'd decided that as long as he was drawing air, he'd remind Aubrey how much she meant to him. He wouldn't stop unless she told him she didn't love him anymore. Until then, she was going to have to endure him.

She pressed her lips together, and he couldn't tell if her expression was embarrassment or sadness or something else entirely.

He smiled at the floor. "I'm thinking of moving out of the ranch. Know any good neighborhoods?"

"Just one," she said. "It's a beautiful neighborhood. Ideal, really."

He shut his eyes against the flood of memories. It was his turn to be pummeled by everything he'd rather not recall. In his case, every *I love you* she had offered during their second chance. Every soft moan and pleasured sigh that had escaped her mouth when they'd made love. Every hand-holding moment or beaming smile she'd given him before he'd forced himself to tell her the truth.

When he lifted his head, she was watching him. *Not* like she hated him. Her expression was soft and open, the darkness behind her eyes missing. She'd come to a conclusion. He knew it in his gut.

His rotten, sinking gut.

She set her wineglass on the small table next to them. From the small clutch she carried, she pulled out a familiar velvet box. "I, um, I brought the engagement ring."

Fuck, I knew it.

His heart stopped, sputtered and restarted its clumsy rhythm. He had instinctively known coming here tonight would result in a conclusion. He could deal with Aubrey's rejection one of two ways—he could beg her to change her mind, or he could accept that she'd made the decision that was best for her. He'd given her time. He'd given her his best reasons to say yes to him.

"I respect your decision, Aub."

"You do?" Her eyebrows lifted into her wavy hair. Auburn surrounding a face he would have liked to look into for the rest of his days.

"I do. That might surprise you, given how I tried to talk you into doing things my way when we were kids, but believe it or not, I've changed. I respect you. I love you. Still. But I won't stand in your way when your mind's made up. Just promise me—" he offered a wan smile "—if I hit my head and lose my memory, you'll tell me the truth at the start about us being a couple."

"Of course I will." Her tone was mild as she offered the box. A box that might as well weigh a metric ton for the strength it took out of his arm when he accepted it. "I love you, too, Vic."

"I understand," he said automatically. "I never should have expected you to..." He blinked at the box in his hand and then at the woman in front of him. "What did you say?"

This smile was his favorite Aubrey smile. The beaming one. "Of course I'll tell everyone we're a couple if you forget. Because we will be."

He was hardly able to believe his ears.

She adjusted the collar of his jacket, smoothing the lapels with both hands. His field of vision was filled with her: red, red and more red. From her dress to her hair to the lips he wanted to kiss more than anything.

"I thought about everything you said," she told him. "And everything Chelsea said. And everything my mom said." She rolled her eyes playfully. "We aren't the same people who split up ten years ago. I'm not the headstrong woman who wanted to do everything by myself. You're not the man with world domination in mind. I've learned that family is everything and that my life is so, so much better with you in it. Whenever I picture my future, I see two things—me, teaching until I'm old and gray and as sassy as ever."

He had to grin. She had enough sass to last her two lifetimes.

"And coming home to you and our house, with the curved hallway and the rich wood floors, after a day of teaching."

He closed his eyes, unwilling to wake up from the hallucination he was surely having. That's when he felt it. Her lips on his. Soft and plush, and pressing into him with an insistence he'd been praying for every night since he'd told her what she'd so inconveniently forgotten.

He lost her lips too soon.

"I brought you this." She took the box from his hand and held it between them. "To ask if you wanted to put it on my finger."

He narrowed one eye. "You didn't fall and hit your head again, did you?"

"No. I remember everything, Vic. You coming to my apartment to say some of the sweetest words I've ever heard. You taking me to our dream home, which you held on to for ten years in the hopes I'd come back. The loft. The stable. The shower. Your bed..."

"Okay, okay." He gripped her waist and pulled her close to him, inhaling her light, familiar scent. His Aubrey. For real, this time. For good. "If you don't want me to limp out of here, you're going to have to stop talking dirty."

He opened the velvet box of the ring that used to sit at home on Aubrey's hand. A ring that, like the dream house he'd bought her, had sat untouched for ten years. A ring that, until this very moment, he'd believed she was returning with an apology instead of an *I love you*.

"I don't have anything fancy to say." He dropped to one knee and looked up at the only woman he'd ever loved. Around them, the room hushed, conversations trailing off into muted whispers. He ignored them and focused on Aubrey. "Will you be my wife, and move into our dream home, and teach until you're old and gray, and let me love you for the rest of my life?"

Tears welled in her eyes as she nodded. He slid the diamond onto her ring finger and then stood. Applause rippled through the room. With the thumb of the hand cradling her cheek, he swiped away a lone tear. "I love you, Aubrey."

"I love you, Vic."

He kissed her as cheers joined the applause around

them. But he wasn't thinking about the crowd or the questions that would follow. He wasn't even thinking about what would happen after they left the party and he could finally be alone with his future bride.

He touched the ring on her left hand, thinking of one word: *home*.

He'd finally found where he belonged. He loved his family ranch, but his home wasn't on the Grandin estate. Not any longer. His home was in the arms of the woman who'd given him more chances than he'd deserved. The woman who'd returned to him against all odds.

He'd happily spend the rest of his life reminding her of the reasons he loved her so that she never forgot a single one again.

* * * * *

COMING SOON!

We really hope you enjoyed reading this book. If you're looking for more romance, be sure to head to the shops when new books are available on

Thursday 13ᵗʰ October

To see which titles are coming soon, please visit

millsandboon.co.uk/nextmonth

MILLS & BOON

THE HEART OF ROMANCE

A ROMANCE FOR EVERY READER

MODERN

Prepare to be swept off your feet by sophisticated, sexy and seductive heroes, in some of the world's most glamourous and romantic locations, where power and passion collide.

HISTORICAL

Escape with historical heroes from time gone by. Whether your passion is for wicked Regency Rakes, muscled Vikings or rugged Highlanders, awaken the romance of the past.

MEDICAL

Set your pulse racing with dedicated, delectable doctors in the high-pressure world of medicine, where emotions run high and passion, comfort and love are the best medicine.

True Love

Celebrate true love with tender stories of heartfelt romance, from the rush of falling in love to the joy a new baby can bring, and a focus on the emotional heart of a relationship.

Desire

Indulge in secrets and scandal, intense drama and plenty of sizzling hot action with powerful and passionate heroes who have it all: wealth, status, good looks…everything but the right woman.

HEROES

Experience all the excitement of a gripping thriller, with an intense romance at its heart. Resourceful, true-to-life women and strong, fearless men face danger and desire - a killer combination!

To see which titles are coming soon, please visit

millsandboon.co.uk/nextmonth

LET'S TALK

Romance

For exclusive extracts, competitions
and special offers, find us online:

 facebook.com/millsandboon

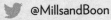 @MillsandBoon

@MillsandBoonUK

Get in touch on 01413 063232

For all the latest titles coming soon, visit
millsandboon.co.uk/nextmonth

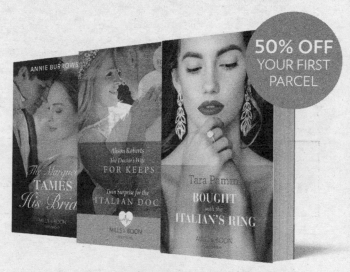